THE VALLEY OF THE MOON

BY

JACK LONDON

INTRODUCTION BY
RUSS KINGMAN

PUBLISHED BY

DAVID REJL   CALIFORNIA

Cover design by Robert Herstek

Library of Congress Catalog Card Number: 87-092222

ISBN: 0-9614181-1-7   (previously ISBN 0-87905-052-7)

Manufactured in the United States of America.

PUBLISHER'S NOTE

I was fiften years old when I first read the novel *"Valley of the Moon"* in the Czechoslovakian translation. The year was 1972. It was the first publication of this novel in our country since the second world war; since Czechoslovakia had become a socialist state and part of the Eastern Block. I was behind an Iron Curtain, but like Jack London I was unwilling to become a victim of circumstance because of the place I was born. In my childhood I became a voracious reader. It was not unusual for me to devour fifteen to twenty books a month. Reading allowed me to escape in dreams, away from the ordinary, everyday life, to unknown exotic places; to new countries full of exciting adventures. I had no idea that my most challenging adventure would be my childhood spent in socialist Czechoslovakia.

It was the novel *"The Valley of the Moon"* that changed the course of my life. The main character of this novel, Saxon, is faced with the reality of her unsatisfying existence in Oakland and she knows that this city is not a place where she can be happy. It was the character and vitality of the twelve year old fisherman John, that inspired me and I discovered like Saxon that this place doesn't have to be a final destination, but a place to start from. (This story was later added by Jack to book version.)

As a young boy I heard many times the question: "What do you want to be?" But nobody ever answered this question for me so accurately as John:

"What do I want?" he repeated after her.

Turning his head slowly, he followed the sky-line, pausing especially when his eyes rested landward on the brown Contra Mesa hills, and seaward, past Alcatraz, on the Golden Gate. The wistfulness in his eyes was overwelming and went to her heart.

"That," he said, sweeping the circle of the word with a wave of his arm.

"That?" she queried.

Publisher's Note

He looked at her, perplexed in that he had not made his meaning clear.

"Don't you ever feel that way?" he asked, bidding for sympathy with his dream. "Don't you sometimes feel you'd die if you didn't know what's beyond them hills an' what's beyond the other hills behind them hills? An' the Golden Gate! There's the Pacific Ocean beyond, and China, an' Japan, an' India. an' ... an' all the coral islands. You can go anywhere out through the Golden Gate - to Australia, to Africa, to the seal islands, to the North Pole, to Cape Horn. Why, all them places are just waitin' for me to come an' see 'em. I've lived in Oakland all my life, but I'm not going to live in Oakland the rest of my life, not by a long shot. I'm goin' to get away... away..."

It was these words which began the plan in my mind as a fifteen year old boy, which five years later actualized in a masterful escape from behind the Iron Curtain. But that is another book...

This edition of *"Valley of the Moon,"* in its original version is as it appeared in Cosmopolitain Magazine in 1913. This book is my personal thanks to master writer Jack London for his incredible contribution to my life... a gift of freedom and self realization.

It is my deepest wish that this really remarkable novel will become an inspiration for you my dear reader, so that you will know from now on, that life is the most beautiful gift and your dreams are only as far as the reach of your hand. If you have the courage to dream it, you have the potential and the power to have it.

TO IVA, MY DEAR FRIEND AND WIFE.

David Rejl
Middletown, California
1992

INTRODUCTION

The Valley of the Moon has been out of print in the United States for several years. This republication makes a truly unique book available again. The story carries on the American literary tradition advocating a life style based on a closeness to the soil, a rejection of urban values and problems, and an appreciation for the pleasures of "the road" - the theme which has appealed to American writers from Walt Whitman to Jack Kerouac. The story is set in Northern California, and the reader is treated to vivid descriptions of a California less crowded where the natural environment still makes the predominant impact on human senses.

The Valley of the Moon is a proletarian novel portraying the point of view of the working class - a viewpoint seldom elucidated in American letters.

Fiction at the turn of century expressed primarily the genteel side of life. Stephen Crane, Frank Norris, and others had made great contributions to the school of realism, but it was Jack London's vigor and strength of narrative style that made realism a vital part of American literature. His writings are alive with virility, and his characters are exceedingly true to the lives of the people he used for models. The introduction to *Tales of Adventure* describes it perfectly:

The world was still knee-deep in Victorian, morals, traditions, and ideals when Jack London burst upon the literary scene. To the generations exposed to the sentimental pap of the popular writers of the day, his stories of savage realism and heroic conflict had the effect of a tidal wave, sweeping before them the false, romantic idealism that was the vogue... He bridged the gap between the nineteenth and twentieth centuries and blazed the trail for a new, more realistic school of writing.

This is especially true of *The Valley of the Moon* which came right out of London's heart and his own experience. Saxon Brown and Billy Roberts, the central characters, are a composite drawn largely from Jack and Charmian London.

Introduction

The story is a California romance based on London's youth in Oakland, his experiences with Bohemian artists in Carmel, his four-horse trip to Oregon in 1911, his many adventures on the delta waters off the Sacramento and San Joaquin Rivers, and his ranch in the actual Valley of the Moon, just sixty miles north of San Francisco. These experiences are mirrored in the lives of Billy and Saxon, who, living behind a miserable working class existence in Oakland, embark on an epic walking journey in search of prosperity, fulfillment, and a dream ranch they thought could only exist in " a valley on the moon."

Jack London arrived in Oakland in 1886 during an era when East Bay culture was just beginning to develop. Oakland's population mushroomed from 48,682 in 1890 to over 150,000 in 1910, with most of the growth due to the influx of people from San Francisco following the earthquake and fire of 1906. The rapid growth resulted in economic and social disorganization to which was added severe industrial turmoil as, nationwide, the old capitalistic system was wracked by the early struggles of the fledgling labor movement during the early twentieth century. To help support his impoverished family during those years, Jack worked at a prodigious number of odd jobs. But his real introduction to the system which he was later to term the "economic trap," came in 1890 when, like Billy and Saxon, he graduated from grammar school right into a job working ten or more hours a day, six days a week, for wages averaging ten cents an hour.

I was barely turned fifteen, and working long hours in a cannery. Month in and month out, the shortest day I ever worked was ten hours. When to ten hours of actual work at a machine is added the noon hour, the walking to work and walking home from work; the getting up in the morning, dressing, and eating; the eating at night, undressing, and going to bed, there remains no more than the nine hours out of the twenty-four required by a healthy youngster for sleep... Many a night I did not knock off work until midnight. On occasion I worked at my machine for thirty-six consecutive hours. And there were weeks on end when I never knocked off work earlier than eleven o'clock, got home and in bed at half after midnight, and was called at half-past five to dress, eat, walk to work, and be at my machine at seven o-clock whistle blow.

From this experience, Jack London developed a feeling of love and kinship for the exploited workers of the world and contempt of gigantic proportions for those who willingly exploited them. Strong seeds of rebellion were born and flourished in this work-beast environment. It was a world controlled by capitalism-

Introduction

rich versus poor, and the educated versus the ignorant. His feelings of kinship appear in *The Valley of the Moon* in his powerful description of Billy and Saxon's Oakland experiences.

But Jack yearned for something better, and the books he read awakened him to possibilities. In the novel, this awakening comes to Saxon through a young fisherman on the Bay, whose advice, "Oakland is just a place to start from," becomes her strength in leaving behind her miserable life there. The Bay fisherman is surely a personification of the obsession that fired Jack London to brief stints as an oyster pirate, fish patrolman, and able-bodied seaman. These periodic escapes from the city made apparent to him the folly of remaining caught in its urban industrial bondage.

Billy and Saxon express the same realization when Saxon comments, "All I do know is that poor people can't be happy in the city where they have labor troubles all the time. If they can't be happy in the country, then there's no happiness anywhere, and that doesn't seem fair, does it?"

With their bindles on their backs, Billy and Saxon begin a walking trip through Northern California - a journey which serves as their educational awakening and eventually leads them to their dream ranch in Sonoma Valley - The Valley of the Moon.

They first meet Mrs. Mortimer, a thriving gentlewoman farmer, formerly a head librarian, who has learned her skills from books. From her they learn that with a limited amount of land, money, and labor, it is possible to live comfortably and with style in the country. The characterization of Mrs. Mortimer is almost certainly drawn in part from Jack's mentor, Oakland city librarian Ina Coolbrith.

The walking journey continues south to Carmel, where the former teamster and fancy starch laundress encounter the playful Bohemian artists' colony. Prior to 1906, many of Jack London's artist friends had congregated in a Bohemian-like subculture which revolved around the famous Coppa's Restaurant in San Francisco. George Sterling, Xavier Martinez, Jimmy Hopper, Herman Whitaker, Edwin Emerson, Gelett Burgess, Porter Garnett, Will and Wallace Irwin, Bobby Aitken, Perry and "Buttsky" Newberry, Harry A. Lafler, Maynard Dixon, Arnold Genthe and others were among the group. After the earthquake and fire, many of the Coppa's group fled to Carmel and formed the nucleus of the Carmel art colony. They were joined there by Harry Leon Wilson, Ferdinand Burgdorff, Sinclair Lewis, Mary Austin, and others.

As Billy and Saxon join the tribe of abalone eaters at Bierce's Cove, London gives the reader an inside look at the Lotus-land antics of these famous personalities. Jimmy Hopper is met as Jim Hazard, George Sterling as Mark Hall,

IX

Introduction

Herbert Bashford as the drama critic, and probably Harry Lafler, the poet, as Hafler. Jack and Charmian London appear later as Jack and Clara Hastings.

From the Bohemians, Billy and Saxon learn a principle very important to Jack London - that grownups, like children, can successfully mix work with play and be lightspirited. This ideal becomes an essential ingredient of the life they are seeking.

After wintering in Carmel, the adventurers return to the road in the spring. Their wandering takes them north to the river lands of the Sacramento and San Joaquin deltas where they meet Jack and Charmian London as Jack and Clara Hastings on their yawl *Roamer*. Jack and Clara suggest that the sought-after dream ranch might be found in the Sonoma Valley.

But Billy and Saxon first turn north, in order to explore the country up to the Oregon border. On their return trip, they meet Jack and Clara again, on the 1350 mile four-horse wagon trip to Oregon upon which the Londons embarked in 1911.

And finally, Billy and Saxon turn their steps toward the valley where they will end their journey. Jack London loved adventure, but the adventure he loved most was "making two blades of grass grow where only one grew before." He had fallen in love with the Sonoma Valley at first sight in 1903, and in 1905 bought his first valley land. More and more acreage was added as opportunity arose until he owned over 1400 acres from the valley floor to the top of Sonoma Mountain. The ranch was near Wake Robin Lodge which becomes Trillium Covert to Billy and Saxon. In real life, Edmund and Annette Hale were Edward Biron Payne and Ninetta Payne. Ninetta was Charmian London's aunt who had raised her from the age of six. One day as Jack looked out over the ranch, he reportedly turned to Charmian and said, "When I look out over it all it kind of makes me ache in the throat with things in my heart I can't find words to say."

Billy and Saxon upon entering the valley, find all the conditions and requirements to be right at last. Their education nearly complete, the wanderers are ready to settle and begin building in reality the life they have been building so long in their imaginations. As they enter the valley, Billy affirms, "I guess we won't winter in Carmel. This place was specially manufactured for us." and Saxon: "There isn't the slightest doubt. This is our place, I know it."

Russ Kingman
Glen Ellen, California
1988

THE VALLEY OF THE MOON

Saxon took off her hat, then suddenly sat down on the bed. She sobbed softly, with considered repression, but the weak-latched door swung noiselessly open, and she was startled by her sister-in-law's voice: "*Now* what s the matter with you? If you didn't like them beans—" "No, no," Saxon explained hurriedly. "I'm just tired, that's all, and my feet hurt. I wasn't hungry, Sarah. I'm just beat out"

The Valley of the Moon

THE STORY OF A FIGHT AGAINST ODDS FOR LOVE AND A HOME

By Jack London

Author of "Martin Eden," "Burning Daylight," "Smoke Bellew," etc.

Illustrated by Howard Chandler Christy

"YOU hear me, Saxon. Come on along. What if it is the Bricklayers? I'll have gentlemen friends there, and so'll you. The Al Vista band'll be along, an' you know it plays heavenly. An' you just love dancin'—"

Twenty feet away, a stout elderly woman interrupted the girl's persuasions. The elderly woman's back was turned, and the back—loose, bulging, and misshapen—began a convulsive heaving. "Gawd!" she cried out. "O Gawd!"

She flung wild glances, like those of an entrapped animal, up and down the big whitewashed room that panted with heat and that was thickly humid with the steam that sizzled from the damp cloths under the irons of the many ironers. From the girls and women near her, all swinging irons steadily but at high pace, came quick glances, and labor efficiency suffered to the extent of a score of suspended or inadequate movements. The elderly woman's cry had caused a tremor of money-loss to pass among the piece-work ironers of fancy starch.

The girl gripped herself and her iron with a visible effort, and dabbed futilely at the frail, frilled garment on the board under her hand. "I thought she'd got 'em again, didn't you?" she said.

"It's a shame, a woman of her age," Saxon answered, as she frilled a lace ruffle with a hot fluting-iron. Her movements were delicate, safe, and swift, and though her face was wan with fatigue and exhausting heat, there was no slackening in her pace.

"An' her with seven, an' two of 'em in reform school," the girl at the next board sniffed sympathetic agreement. "But you just got to come to Weasel Park to-morrow, Saxon. The Bricklayers is always lively—tugs-of-war, fat-man races, real Irish jiggin',"

an'—an' everything. An' the floor of the pavilion's swell."

But the elderly woman brought another interruption. She dropped her iron on the shirt-waist, clutched at the board, fumbled it, caved in at the knees and hips, and like a half-empty sack collapsed on the floor, her long shriek rising in the pent room to the acrid smell of scorching cloth. The women at the boards near to her scrambled, first to the hot iron to save the cloth, and then to her, while the forewoman hurried belligerently down the aisle. The women farther away continued unsteadily at their work, losing movements to the extent of a minute's set-back to the totality of the efficiency of the fancy-starch room.

"Enough to kill a dog," the girl muttered, thumping her iron down on its rest with reckless determination. "Workin' girls' life ain't what it's cracked up. Me to quit—that's what I'm comin' to."

"Mary!" Saxon uttered the other's name with a reproach so profound that she was compelled to rest her own iron for emphasis and so lose a dozen movements.

Mary flashed a half-frightened look across, at the same time piteous and defiant. "I didn't mean it, Saxon," she whimpered. "Honest to God, I didn't. I wouldn't never go that way. But I leave it to you if a day like this don't get on anybody's nerves. Listen to that!"

The stricken woman, on her back, drumming her heels on the floor, was shrieking persistently and monotonously, like a mechanical siren. Two women, clutching her under the arms, were dragging her down the aisle. She drummed and shrieked the length of it. The door opened, and a vast muffled roar of machinery burst in; and in the roar of it the drumming and the shrieking were drowned ere the door swung shut. Remained of the episode only

3

the scorch of cloth drifting ominously through the air.

"It's sickenin'," said Mary.

And thereafter, for a long time, the many irons rose and fell, the pace of the room in no wise diminished; while the forewoman strode the aisles with a threatening eye for incipient breakdown and hysteria. Occasionally an ironer lost the stride for an instant, gasped or sighed, then caught it up again with weary determination. The long summer day waned, but not the heat, and under the raw flare of electric light the work went on.

By nine o'clock the first women began to go home. The mountain of fancy starch had been demolished—all save the few remnants, here and there, on the boards, where the ironers still labored.

Saxon finished ahead of Mary, at whose board she paused on the way out.

"Saturday night, an' another week gone," Mary said mournfully, her young cheeks pallid and hollowed, her black eyes blue shadowed and tired. "What d'you think you've made, Saxon?"

"Twelve and a quarter," was the answer, just touched with pride. "And I'd a-made more if it wasn't for that fake bunch of starchers."

"My! I got to pass it to you," Mary congratulated. "You're a sure fierce hustler— just eat it up. Me—I've only ten an' a half, an' for a hard week. See you on the nine-forty. Sure now. We can just fool around until the dancin' begins. A lot of my gentlemen friends 'll be there in the afternoon."

Two blocks from the laundry, where an arc-light showed a gang of toughs on the corner, Saxon quickened her pace. Unconsciously her face set and hardened as she passed. She did not catch the words of the muttered comment, but the rough laughter it raised made her guess and warmed her cheeks with resentful blood. Three blocks more, turning once to left and once to right, she walked on through the night that was already growing cool. On either side were workingmen's houses, of weathered wood, rented, the ancient paint grimed with the dust of years, conspicuous only for cheapness and ugliness.

Dark it was, but she made no mistake, the familiar sag and screeching reproach of the front gate welcome under her hand. She went along the narrow walk to the rear, avoided the missing step without thinking about it, and entered the kitchen, where a solitary gas-jet flickered. She turned it up to the best of its flame. It was a small room, not disorderly because of lack of furnishings to disorder it. The plaster, discolored by the steam of many wash-days, was crisscrossed with cracks from the big earthquake of the previous spring. The floor was ridged, wide cracked, and uneven, and in front of the stove it was worn through and repaired with a five-gallon oil-can hammered flat and double. A sink, a dirty roller-towel, several chairs, and a wooden table completed the picture.

An apple-core crunched under her foot as she drew a chair to the table. On the frayed oilcloth, a supper waited. She attempted the cold beans, thick with grease, but gave them up, and buttered a slice of bread.

The rickety house shook to a heavy, prideless tread, and through the inner door came Sarah, middle-aged, lop-breasted, hair tousled, her face lined with care and fat petulance.

"Huh, it's you," she grunted a greeting. "I just couldn't keep things warm. Such a day! I near died of the heat. An' little Henry cut his lip awful. The doctor had to put four stitches in it."

Sarah came over and stood mountainously by the table.

"What's the matter with them beans?" she challenged.

"Nothing, only"— Saxon caught her breath and avoided the threatened outburst—"only I'm not hungry. It's been so hot all day. It was terrible in the laundry."

Recklessly she took a mouthful of the cold tea that had been steeped so long that it was like acid in her mouth, and recklessly, under the eye of her sister-in-law, she swallowed it and the rest of the cupful. She wiped her mouth on her handkerchief and got up.

"I guess I'll go to bed."

"Wonder you ain't out to a dance," Sarah sniffed. "Funny, ain't it, you come home so dead tired every night, an' yet any night in the week you can get out an' dance unearthly hours."

Saxon started to speak, suppressed herself with tightened lips, then lost control and blazed out, "Wasn't you ever young?"

Without waiting for reply, she turned to her bedroom, which opened directly off the kitchen. It was a small room, eight by twelve, and the earthquake had left its marks upon the plaster. A bed and chair of cheap pine and a very ancient chest of drawers constituted the furniture. Saxon had known this chest of drawers all her life. The vision of it was woven into her earliest recollections. She knew it had crossed the plains with her people in a prairie-schooner. It was of solid mahogany. One end was cracked and dented from the capsize of the wagon in Rock Canyon. A bullet-hole, plugged, in the face of the top drawer, told of the fight with the Indians at Little Meadow. Of these happenings her mother had told her; also, had she told that the chest had come with the family originally from England in a day even earlier than the day on which George Washington was born.

Above the chest of drawers, on the wall, hung a small looking-glass. Thrust under the molding were photographs of young men and women, and of picnic groups wherein the young men, with hats rakishly on the backs of their heads, encircled the girls with their arms. Farther along on the wall were a colored calendar and numerous colored advertisements and sketches torn out of magazines. Most of these sketches were of horses. From the gas-fixture hung a tangled bunch of well-scribbled dance-programs.

Saxon took off her hat, then suddenly sat down on the bed. She sobbed softly, with considered repression, but the weak-latched door swung noiselessly open, and she was startled by her sister-in-law's voice.

"*Now* what's the matter with you? If you didn't like them beans—"

"No, no," Saxon explained hurriedly. "I'm just tired, that's all, and my feet hurt. I wasn't hungry, Sarah. I'm just beat out."

"If you took care of this house," came the retort, "an' cooked an' baked, an' washed, an' put up with what I put up, you'd have something to be beat out about. You've got a snap, you have. But just wait." Sarah broke off to cackle gloatingly. "Just wait, that's all, an' you'll be fool enough to get married some day, like me, an' then you'll get yours—an' it'll be brats, an' brats, an' brats, an' no more dancin', an' silk stockin's, an' three pairs of shoes at one time. You've got a cinch—nobody to think of but your own precious self—an' a lot of young hoodlums makin' eyes at you an' tellin' you how beautiful your eyes are. Huh! Some fine day you'll tie up to one of 'em, an' then, mebbe, on occasion, you'll wear black eyes for a change."

"Don't say that, Sarah," Saxon protested. "My brother never laid hands on you. You know that."

"No more he didn't. He never had the gumption. Just the same he's better stock than that tough crowd you run with, if he can't make a livin' an' keep his wife in three pairs of shoes. Just the same he's oodles better'n your bunch of hoodlums that no decent woman'd wipe her one pair of shoes on. How you've missed trouble this long is beyond me. Mebbe the younger generation is wiser in such things—I don't know. But I do know that a young woman that has three pairs of shoes ain't thinkin' of anything but her own enjoyment, an' she's goin' to get hers, I can tell her that much. When I was a girl there wasn't such doin's. My mother'd taken the hide off me if I done the things you do. An' she was right, just as everything in the world is wrong now. Look at your brother, a-runnin' around to socialist meetin's, an' chewin' hot air, an' diggin' up extra strike dues to the union, that means so much bread out of the mouths of his children, instead of makin' good with his bosses. Why, the dues he pays would keep me in seventeen pairs of shoes if I was nannygoat enough to want 'em. Some day, mark my words, he'll get his time, an' then what'll we do? What'll I do, with five mouths to feed an' nothin' comin' in?" She stopped, out of breath, but seething with the tirade yet to come.

"Oh, Sarah, please won't you shut the door?" Saxon pleaded.

The door slammed violently, and Saxon, ere she fell to crying again, could hear her sister-in-law lumbering about the kitchen and talking loudly to herself.

II

EACH bought her own ticket at the entrance to Weasel Park. And each, as she laid her half-dollar down, automatically reckoned how many pieces of fancy starch were represented by the coin. It was too early for the crowd, but bricklayers and their families, laden with huge lunch-baskets and armfuls of babies, were already going in—a healthy, husky race of workmen, well paid and robustly fed. And with them, here and there, undisguised by their decent American clothing, smaller in bulk and stature, wizened not alone by age but by the pinch of lean years and early

DRAWN BY HOWARD CHANDLER CHRISTY

On a grassy slope, tree surrounded, they spread a newspaper and sat down on the short grass already tawny-
six days of insistent motion, half in conservation for the hours of dancing to come. "Bert Wanhope'll
all the fellows call him. He's just a big boy, but he's awfully tough. He's a prize-fighter, an' all
he just slides and glides around. You wanta have a dance with'm anyway.

dry under the California sun. Half were they minded to do this because of the grateful indolence after be sure to come," Mary chattered. "An' he said he was going to bring Billy Roberts — ' Big Bill,' the girls run after him. You won't like him, but he's a swell dancer. He's heavy, you know, an' He's a good spender, too. Never pinches. But my!—he's got one temper"

hardship, were grandfathers and mothers who had patently first seen the light of day on old Irish soil. Their faces showed content and·pride as they limped along with this lusty progeny of theirs that had fed on better food.

Not with these did Mary and Saxon belong. They knew them not, had no acquaintance among them. It did not matter whether the festival were Irish, German, or Slavonian; whether the picnic was the Bricklayers', the Brewers', or the Butchers'. They, the girls, were of the dancing crowd that swelled by a certain constant percentage the gate receipts of all the picnics.

They strolled about among the booths where peanuts were grinding and popcorn was roasting in preparation for the day, and went on and inspected the dance-floor of the pavilion. Saxon, clinging to an imaginary partner, essayed a few steps of the dip-waltz. Mary clapped her hands.

"My!" she cried. "You're just swell! An' them stockin's is peaches."

Saxon smiled with appreciation, pointed out her foot, velvet slippered with high Cuban heels, and slightly lifted the tight black skirt, exposing a trim ankle and delicate swell of calf, the white flesh gleaming through the thinnest and flimsiest of fifty-cent black silk stockings. She was slender, not tall, yet the due round lines of womanhood were hers. On her white shirt-waist was a pleated jabot of cheap lace, caught with a large novelty pin of imitation coral. Over the shirt-waist was a natty jacket, elbow sleeved, and to the elbows she wore gloves of imitation suède. The one essentially natural touch about her appearance were the few curls, strangers to curling-irons, that escaped from under the little naughty hat of black velvet pulled low over the eyes.

Mary's dark eyes flashed with joy at the sight, and with a swift little run she caught the other girl in her arms and kissed her in a breast-crushing embrace. She released her, blushing at her own extravagance. "You look good to me," she cried, in extenuation. "If I was a man I couldn't keep my hands off you. I'd eat you, I sure would."

They went out of the pavilion hand in hand, and on through the sunshine they strolled, swinging hands gaily, reacting exuberantly from the week of deadening toil. They hung over the railing of the bear-pit, shivering at the huge and lonely denizen, and

passed quickly on to ten minutes of laughter at the monkey-cage. Crossing the grounds, they looked down into the little race-track on the bed of a natural amphitheater where the early afternoon games were to take place. After that they explored the woods, threaded by countless paths, ever opening out in new surprises of green-painted rustic tables and benches in leafy nooks, many of which were already preempted by family parties. On a grassy slope, tree surrounded, they spread a newspaper and sat down on the short grass already tawny-dry under the California sun. Half were they minded to do this because of the grateful indolence after six days of insistent motion, half in conservation for the hours of dancing to come.

"Bert Wanhope'll be sure to come," Mary chattered. "An' he said he was going to bring Billy Roberts—'Big Bill,' all the fellows call him. He's just a big boy, but he's awfully tough. He's a prize-fighter, an' all the girls run after him. I'm afraid of him. He ain't quick in talkin'. He's more like that big bear we saw. Brr-rf! Brr-rf!—bite your head off, just like that. He ain't really a prize-fighter. He's a teamster—belongs to the union. Drives for Corberly and Morrison. But sometimes he fights in the clubs. Most of the fellows are scared of him. He's got a bad temper, an' he'd just as soon hit a fellow as eat, just like that. You won't like him, but he's a swell dancer. He's heavy, you know, an' he just slides and glides around. You wanta have a dance with 'm anyway. He's a good spender, too. Never pinches. But my! he's got one temper."

The talk wandered on, a monologue on Mary's part, that centered always on Bert Wanhope.

"You and he are pretty thick," Saxon ventured tentatively.

"I'd marry 'm to-morrow," Mary flashed out impulsively. Then her face went bleakly forlorn, hard almost, in its helpless pathos. "Only, he never asks me. He's—" Her pause was broken by sudden passion. "You watch out for him, Saxon, if he ever comes foolin' around you. He's no good. Just the same, I'd marry him to-morrow. He'll never get me any other way." Her mouth opened, but instead of speaking she drew a long sigh. "It's a funny world, ain't it?" She added: "More like a scream. And all the stars are worlds, too. I wonder where God hides. Bert Wanhope says there ain't no God. But he's just terrible. He says the most terrible things. I believe in God. Don't you? What do you think about God, Saxon?"

Saxon shrugged her shoulders and laughed.

"But if we do wrong we get ours, don't we?" Mary persisted. "That's what they all say, except Bert. He says he don't care what he does, he'll never get his, because when he dies he's dead, an' when he's dead he'd like to see anyone put anything across on him that'd wake him up. Ain't he terrible, though? But it's all so funny. Sometimes I get scared when I think God's keepin' an eye on me all the time. Do you think he knows what I'm sayin' now? What do you think he looks like, anyway?"

"I don't know," Saxon answered. "He's just a funny proposition."

"Oh!" the other gasped.

"He *is* just the same, from what all people say of him," Saxon went on stoutly. "My brother thinks he looks like Abraham Lincoln. Sarah thinks he has whiskers."

A strain of music from the dancing-pavilion brought both girls scrambling to their feet.

"We can get a couple of dances in before we eat," Mary proposed. "An' then it'll be afternoon an' all the fellows'll be here. Most of them are pinchers—that's why they don't come early, so as to get out of taking the girls to dinner. But Bert's free with his money, an' so is Billy. If we can beat the other girls to it, they'll take us to the restaurant. Come on, hurry, Saxon."

There were few couples on the floor when they arrived at the pavilion, and the two girls essayed the first waltz together.

"There's Bert now," Saxon whispered, as they came around the second time.

"Don't take any notice of them," Mary whispered back. "We'll just keep on goin.' They needn't think we're chasin' after them."

But Saxon noted the heightened color in the other's cheek, and felt her quicker breathing.

"Did you see that other one?" Mary asked, as she backed Saxon in a long slide across the far end of the pavilion. "That was Billy Roberts. Bert said he'd come. He'll take you to dinner, and Bert'll take me. It's goin' to be a swell day, you'll see. My! I only wish the music'll hold out till we can get back to the other end."

Down the long floor they danced, on man-trapping and dinner-getting intent, two fresh young things that undeniably danced well and that were delightfully surprised when the music stranded them perilously near to their desire.

Bert and Mary addressed each other with their given names, but to Saxon Bert was "Mr. Wanhope," though he called her by her first name. The only introduction was of Saxon and Billy Roberts. Mary carried it off with a flurry of nervous carelessness.

"Mr. Roberts—Miss Brown. She's my best friend. Her first name's Saxon. Ain't it a scream of a name?"

"Sounds good to me," Billy retorted, hat off and hand extended. "Pleased to meet you, Miss Brown."

As their hands clasped and she felt the teamster callous spots on his palm, her quick eyes saw a score of things. About all that he saw was her eyes, and then it was with a vague impression that they were blue. Not till later in the day did he realize that they were gray. She, on the contrary, saw his eyes as they really were—deep blue, wide, and handsome in a sullen, boyish way. She saw that they were straight looking, and she liked them, as she had liked the glimpse she had caught of his hand, and as she liked the contact of his hand itself. Then, too, but not sharply, she had perceived the short, square-set nose, the rosiness of cheek, and the firm, short upper lip, ere delight centered her flash of gaze on the well-modeled, large clean mouth where red lips smiled clear of the white, enviable teeth. *A boy, a great big man-boy*, was her thought; and, as they smiled at each other and their hands slipped apart, she was startled by a glimpse of his hair—short and crisp and sandy, hinting almost of palest gold, save that it was too flaxen to hint of gold at all.

So blond was he that she was reminded of stage-types she had seen, such as Ole Oleson and Yon Yonson; but there resemblance ceased. It was a matter of color only, for the eyes were dark lashed and dark browed, and were cloudy with temperament rather than staring a child-gaze of wonder, and the suit of smooth brown cloth had been made by a tailor. Saxon appraised the suit on the instant, and her secret judgment was, *not a cent less than fifty dollars*. Further, he had none of the awkwardness of the Scandinavian immigrant. On the contrary, he was one of those rare individuals that radiate muscular grace through the ungraceful man-garments of civilization. Every movement was supple, slow, and apparently automatically considered. This she did not see nor analyze. She saw only a clothed man with grace of carriage and movement. She felt, rather than perceived, the calm and certitude of all the muscular play of him, and she felt, too, the promise of easement and rest that was especially grateful and craved for by one who had incessantly, for six days and at top speed, ironed fancy starch. As the touch of his hand had been good, so, to her, this subtler feel of all of him, body and mind, was good.

As he took her program and skirmished and joked after the way of young men, she realized the immediacy of delight she had taken in him. Never in her life had she been so affected by any man. She wondered to herself, *Is this the man?*

He danced beautifully. The joy was hers that good dancers take when they have found a good dancer for a partner. The grace of those slow-moving certain muscles of his accorded perfectly with the rhythm of the music. There was never doubt, never a betrayal of indecision. She glanced at Bert, dancing "tough" with Mary, caroming down the long floor with more than one collision with the increasing couples. Graceful himself in his slender, tall, lean-stomached way, Bert was accounted a good dancer; yet Saxon did not remember ever having danced with him with keen pleasure. Just a bit of a jerk spoiled his dancing—a jerk that did not occur, usually, but that always impended. There was something spasmodic in his mind. He was too quick, or he continually threatened to be too quick. He always seemed just on the verge of over-running the time. It was disquieting. He made for unrest.

"You're a dream of a dancer," Billy Roberts was saying to her. "I've heard lots of the fellows talk about your dancing."

"I love it," she answered.

But from the way she said it he sensed her reluctance to speak, and danced on in silence, while she warmed with the appreciation of a woman for gentle consideration. Gentle consideration was a thing rarely encountered in the life she lived. *Is this the man?* She remembered Mary's "I'd marry him to-morrow," and caught herself speculating on marrying Billy Roberts by the next day—if he asked her.

With eyes that dreamily desired to close, she moved on in the arms of this masterful, guiding pressure. A *prize-fighter!* She experienced a thrill of wickedness as she thought of what Sarah would say could she see her now. Only he wasn't a prize-fighter, but a teamster.

Came an abrupt lengthening of step, the guiding pressure grew more compelling, and she was caught up and carried along, though her velvet-shod feet never left the floor. Then came the sudden control down to the shorter step again, and she felt herself being held slightly from him so that he might look into her face and laugh with her in joy at the exploit. At the end, as the band slowed in the last bars, they, too, slowed, their dance fading with the music in a lengthening glide that ceased with the last lingering tone.

"We're sure cut out for each other when it comes to dancin'," he said, as they made their way to rejoin the other couple.

"It was a dream," she replied.

So low was her voice that he bent to hear, and saw the flush in her cheeks that seemed communicated to her eyes, which were softly warm and sensuous. He took the program from her and gravely and gigantically wrote his name across all the length of it.

"An' now it's no good," he dared. " Ain't no need for it."

He tore it across and tossed it aside.

"Me for you, Saxon, for the next," was Bert's greeting, as they came up. "You take Mary for the next whirl, Bill."

"Nothin' doin', Bo," was the retort. "Me an' Saxon's framed up to last the day."

"Watch out for him, Saxon," Mary warned facetiously. "He's liable to get a crush on you."

"I guess I know a good thing when I see it," Billy responded gallantly.

"And so do I," Saxon aided and abetted.

"I'd 'a' known you if I'd seen you in the dark," Billy added.

Mary regarded them with mock alarm, and Bert said good-naturedly:

"All I got to say is you ain't wastin' any time gettin' together. Just the same, if you can spare a few minutes from each other after a couple more whirls, Mary an' me'd be complimented to have your presence at dinner."

"Just like that," chimed Mary.

"Quit your kiddin'," Billy laughed back, turning his head to look into Saxon's eyes.

"Don't listen to 'em. They're grouched because they got to dance together. Bert's a rotten dancer, and Mary ain't so much. Come on, there she goes. See you after two more dances."

III

THEY had dinner in the open-air, tree-walled dining-room, and Saxon noted that it was Billy who paid the reckoning for the four. They knew many of the young men and women at the other tables, and greetings and fun flew back and forth. Bert was very possessive with Mary, almost roughly so, resting his hand on hers, catching and holding it, and, once, forcibly slipping off her two rings and refusing to return them for a long while. At times, when he put his arm around her waist, Mary promptly disengaged it; and at other times, with elaborate obliviousness that deceived no one, she allowed it to remain.

And Saxon, talking little but studying Billy Roberts very intently, was satisfied that there would be an utter difference in the way he would do such things—if ever he would do them. Anyway, he'd never paw a girl as Bert and lots of the other fellows did. She measured the breadth of Billy's heavy shoulders.

"Why do they call you 'Big Bill'?" she asked. "You're not so very tall."

"Nope," he agreed. "I'm only five feet eight an' three-quarters. I guess it must be my weight."

"He fights at a hundred an' eighty," Bert interjected.

"Oh, cut it," Billy said quickly, a cloud-rift of displeasure showing in his eyes. "I ain't a fighter. I ain't fought in six months. I've quit it. It don't pay."

"You got two hundred the night you put the Frisco Slasher to the bad," Bert urged proudly.

"Cut it. Cut it now. . . . Say, Saxon, you ain't so big yourself, are you? But you're built just right if anybody should ask you. You're round an' slender at the same time. I bet I can guess your weight."

"Everybody guesses over it," she warned, while inwardly she was puzzled that she should at the same time be glad and regretful that he did not fight any more.

"Not me," he was saying. "I'm a wooz at weight-guessin'. Just you watch me." He regarded her critically, and it was patent

that warm approval played its little rivalry with the judgment of his gaze. "Wait a minute."

He reached over to her and felt her arm at the biceps. The pressure of the encircling fingers was firm and honest, and Saxon thrilled to it. There was magic in this man-boy. She would have known only irritation had Bert or any other man felt her arm. But this man! *Is he the man?* she was questioning, when he voiced his conclusion.

"Your clothes don't weigh more'n seven pounds. And seven from—hum—say one hundred an' twenty-three—one hundred an' sixteen is your stripped weight."

But at the penultimate word, Mary cried out with sharp reproof,

"Why, Billy Roberts, people don't talk about such things."

He looked at her with slow-growing, uncomprehending surprise. "What things?" he demanded finally.

"There you go again! You ought to be ashamed of yourself. Look! You've got Saxon blushing!"

"I am not," Saxon denied indignantly.

"An' if you keep on, Mary, you'll have me blushing," Billy growled. "I guess I know what's right an' what ain't. It ain't what a guy says, but what he thinks. An' I'm thinkin' right, an' Saxon knows it. How near did I come to it, Saxon?"

"One hundred and twenty-two," she answered, looking deliberately at Mary. "One twenty-two—with my clothes."

Billy burst into hearty laughter, in which Bert joined.

"I don't care," Mary protested. "You're terrible, both of you—an' you, too, Saxon. I'd never a-thought it of you."

"Listen to me, kid," Bert began soothingly, as his arm slipped around her waist.

Billy discreetly began to make conversation with Saxon. "Say, you know, your name *is* a funny one. I never heard it tagged on anybody before. But it's all right. I like it."

"My mother gave it to me. She was educated, and knew all kinds of words. She was always reading books, almost until she died. And she wrote lots and lots. I've got some of her poetry, published in a San Jose newspaper long ago. The Saxons were a race of people—she told me all about them when I was a little girl. They were wild, like Indians, only they were white. And they had blue eyes, and yellow hair, and they were awful fighters."

Billy discreetly began to make conversation with Saxon. "Say, you know, your name *is* a funny one. I Saxon. "She was educated, and knew all kinds of words. She was always reading books, almost until she ago. The Saxons were a race of people — she told me all about them when I was a little girl. They were awful fighters." As she talked, Billy followed her solemnly, his eyes steadily turned

never heard it tagged on anybody before. But it's all right. I like it." "My mother gave it to me," said
died. And she wrote lots and lots. I've got some of her poetry, published in a San Jose newspaper long
were wild, like Indians, only they were white. And they had blue eyes, and yellow hair, and they
on hers. "Never heard of them," he confessed. "Did they live anywhere around here?"

As she talked, Billy followed her solemnly, his eyes steadily turned on hers. "Never heard of them," he confessed. "Did they live anywhere around here?"

She laughed. "No. They lived in England. They were the first English, and you know the Americans came from the English. We're Saxons, you an' me, an' Mary, an' Bert, and all the Americans that are real Americans, you know, and not Dagoes and Japs and such."

"My folks lived in America a long time," Billy said slowly, digesting the information she had given and relating himself to it. "Anyway, my mother's folks did. They crossed to Maine hundreds of years ago."

"My father was state of Maine," she broke in, with a little gurgle of joy. "And my mother was born in Ohio, or where Ohio is now. She used to call it the 'Great Western Reserve.' What was your father?"

"Don't know." Billy shrugged his shoulders. "He didn't know himself. Nobody ever knew, though he was American, all right all right."

"His name's regular old American," Saxon suggested. "There's a big English general right now whose name is Roberts. I've read it in the papers."

"But Roberts wasn't my father's name. He never knew what his name was. Roberts was the name of a gold-miner who adopted him. You see, it was this way. When they was Indian-fightin' up there with the Modoc Indians, a lot of the miners an' settlers took a hand. Roberts was captain of one outfit, and once, after a fight, they took a lot of prisoners—squaws an' kids an' babies. An' one of the kids was my father. They figured he was about five years old. He didn't know nothin' but Indian."

Saxon clapped her hands, and her eyes sparkled, as she cried, "He'd been captured on an Indian raid!"

"That's the way they figured it," Billy nodded. "They recollected a wagon-train of Oregon settlers that'd been killed by the Modocs four years before. Roberts adopted him, and that's why I don't know his real name. But you can bank on it he crossed the plains just the same."

"So did my father," Saxon said proudly.

"An' my mother, too," Billy added, pride touching his own voice. "Anyway, she came pretty close to crossin' the plains, because she was born in a wagon on the River Platte on the way out."

"My mother, too," said Saxon. "She was eight years old, an' she walked most of the way after the oxen began to give out."

Billy thrust out his hand. "Put her there, kid," he said. "We're just like old friends, what with the same kind of folks behind us."

With shining eyes, Saxon extended her hand to his, and gravely they shook. "Isn't it wonderful?" she murmured. "We're both old American stock. And if you ain't a Saxon there never was one—your hair, your eyes, your skin, everything. And you're a fighter, too."

"I guess all our old folks was fighters when it comes to that. It come natural to 'em, an' dog-gone it they just had to fight or they'd never come through."

"What are you two talkin' about so seriously?" Mary broke in upon them.

"They're thicker'n mush in no time," Bert girded. "You'd think they'd known each other a week already."

"Oh, we knew each other longer than that," Saxon returned. "Before ever we were born our folks were walkin' across the plains together."

"When your folks was waitin' for the railroad to be built an' all the Indians killed off before they dasted to start for California," was Billy's way of proclaiming the new alliance. "We're the real goods, Saxon an' me, if anybody should ride up on a buzz-wagon an' ask you."

"Oh, I don't know," Mary boasted with quick petulance. "My father stayed behind to fight in the Civil War. He was a drummer-boy. That's why he didn't come to California until afterward."

"And my father went back to fight in the Civil War," Saxon said.

"And mine, too," said Billy.

They looked at each other gleefully. Again they had found a new contact.

"Well, they're all dead, ain't they?" was Bert's saturnine comment. "There ain't no difference dyin' in battle or in the poorhouse. The thing is they're dead. I wouldn't care a rap if my father'd been hanged. It's all the same in a thousand years. This braggin' about folks makes me tired. Besides, my father couldn't 'a' fought. He wasn't born till two years after the war. Just the same, two of my uncles were killed at Gettysburg. Guess we done our share."

"Just like that," Mary applauded.

Bert's arm went around her waist again. "We're here, ain't we?" he said. "An' that's what counts. The dead are dead, an' you can bet your sweet life they just keep on stayin' dead."

Mary put her hand over his mouth and began to chide him for his awfulness, whereupon he kissed the palm of her hand and put his head closer to hers.

The merry noise and clatter of dishes was increasing as the dining-room filled up. Here and there voices were raised in snatches of song. There were shrill squeals and screams and bursts of heavier male laughter as the everlasting skirmishing between the young men and girls played on. Among some of the men the signs of drink were already manifest. At a near table girls were calling out to Billy. And Saxon, the sense of temporary possession already strong on her, noted with jealous eyes that he was a favorite and desired object to them.

"Ain't they awful!" Mary voiced her disapproval. "They got a nerve. I know who they are. No respectable girl'd have a thing to do with them. Listen to that!"

"Oh, you, Bill, you!" one of them was calling. "Hope you ain't forgotten me, Bill."

"Oh, you chicken!" he called back gallantly.

Saxon flattered herself that he showed vexation, and she conceived an immense dislike for the other girl.

"Goin' to dance?" the latter called.

"Mebbe," he answered, and turned abruptly to Saxon. "Say, we old Americans oughta stick together, don't you think? They ain't many of us left. The country's fillin' up with all kinds of foreigners."

He talked on steadily, in a low, confidential voice, head close to hers, as advertisement to the other girl that he was occupied.

From the next table on the opposite side, a young man had singled out Saxon. His dress was tough. His companions, male and female, were tough. His face was inflamed, his eyes touched with wildness. "Hey, you," he called—"you with the velvet slippers. Me for you."

The girl beside him put her arm around his neck and tried to hush him, and through the mufflement of her embrace they could hear him gurgling:

"I tell you she's some goods. Watch me go across an' win her from them cheap skates."

"Butchertown hoodlums," Mary sniffed.

Saxon's eyes encountered the eyes of the girl, who glared hatred across at her. And in Billy's eyes she saw moody anger smoldering. The eyes were more sullen, more handsome, than ever, and clouds and veils and lights and shadows shifted and deepened in the blue of them until they gave her a sense of unfathomable depth. He had stopped talking, and he made no effort to talk.

"Don't start a rough-house, Bill," Bert cautioned. "They're from across the bay, an' they don't know you, that's all."

Bert stood up suddenly, stepped over to the other table, whispered briefly, and came back. Every face at the table was turned on Billy. The offender arose brokenly, shook off the detaining hand of his girl, and came over. He was a large man, with a hard, malignant face and bitter eyes. Also, he was a subdued man.

"You're Big Bill Roberts," he said thickly, clinging to the table as he reeled. "I take my hat off to you. I apologize. I admire your taste in skirts, an' take it from me, that's a compliment; but I didn't know who you was. If I'd knowed you was Bill Roberts there wouldn't been a peep from my fly-trap. D'ye get me? I apologize. Will you shake hands?"

Gruffly, Billy said, "It's all right, forget it, sport"; and sullenly he shook hands and with a slow, massive movement thrust the other back toward his own table.

Saxon was glowing. Here was a man, a protector, something to lean against, of whom even the Butchertown toughs were afraid as soon as his name was mentioned.

IV

At eight o'clock the Al Vista band played "Home, Sweet Home," and, following the hurried rush through the twilight to the picnic train, the four managed to get double seats facing each other. When the aisles and platforms were packed by the hilarious crowd, the train pulled out for the short run from the suburbs into Oakland. All the car was singing a score of songs at once, and Bert, his head pillowed on Mary's breast with her arms around him, started "On the Banks of the Wabash." And he sang the song through, undeterred by the bedlam of two general fights, one on the adjacent platform, the other at the opposite end of the car, both of which were finally subdued by special policemen to the screams of women and the crash of glass.

Billy sang a lugubrious song of many stanzas about a cowboy, the refrain of which was, "Bury me out on the lone pr-rairie."

"That's one you never heard before; my father used to sing it," he told Saxon, who was glad that it was ended.

She had discovered the first flaw in him. He was tone-deaf. Not once had he been on the key.

"I don't sing often," he added.

"You bet your sweet life he don't," Bert explained. "His friends'd kill him if he did."

"They all make fun of my singin'," he complained to Saxon. "Honest, now, do you find it as rotten as all that?"

"It's—it's maybe flat a bit," she admitted reluctantly.

"It don't sound flat to me," he protested. "It's a regular josh on me. I'll bet Bert put you up to it. You sing something, now, Saxon. I bet you sing good. I can tell it from lookin' at you."

She began "When the Harvest Days are Over." Bert and Mary joined in; but when Billy attempted to add his voice he was dissuaded by a shin-kick from Bert. Saxon sang in a clear, true soprano, thin but sweet, and she was aware that she was singing to Billy.

"Now *that is* singing what is," he proclaimed, when she had finished. "Sing it again. Aw, go on. You do it just right. It's great."

His hand slipped to hers and gathered it in, and as she sang again she felt the tide of his strength flood warmingly through her.

"Look at 'm holdin' hands!" Bert jeered. "Just a-holdin' hands like they was afraid. Look at Mary an' me. Come on an' kick in, you cold-feets. Get together."

"Get onto yourself, Bert," Billy reproved.

"Shut up!" Mary added the weight of her indignation. "You're awfully raw, Bert Wanhope, an' I won't have anything more to do with you—there!" She withdrew her arms and shoved him away, only to receive him forgivingly half a dozen seconds afterward.

"Come on, the four of us," Bert went on irrepressibly. "The night's young. Let's make a time of it—Pabst's Café first, and then some. What you say, Bill? What you say, Saxon? Mary's game."

Saxon waited and wondered, half sick with apprehension of this man beside her whom she had known so short a time.

"Nope," he said slowly. "I got to get up to a hard day's work to-morrow, and I guess the girls have got to, too."

Saxon forgave him his tone-deafness in her gratitude. Here was the kind of man she always had known existed. It was for some such man that she had waited. She was twenty-two, and her first marriage offer had come when she was sixteen. The last had occurred only the month before, from the foreman of the washing-room, and he had been good and kind, but not young. But this one beside her—he was strong and kind and good and *young*. She was too young herself not to desire youth. There would have been rest from fancy starch with the foreman, but there would have been no warmth. But this man beside her— She caught herself on the verge involuntarily of pressing his hand that held hers.

"No, Bert, don't tease; he's right," Mary was saying. "We've got to get some sleep. It's fancy starch to-morrow, and all day on our feet."

It came to Saxon with a chill pang that she was surely older than Billy. She stole glances at the smoothness of his face, and the essential boyishness of him, so much desired, shocked her. Of course, he would marry some girl years younger than himself, than herself. How old was he? Could it be that he was too young for her? As he seemed to grow inaccessible, she was drawn toward him more compellingly. He was so strong, so gentle. She lived over the events of the day. There was no flaw there. He had considered her, and Mary, always. And he had torn the program up and danced only with her. Surely he had liked her, or he would not have done it.

She slightly moved her hand in his and felt the harsh contact of his callous palm. The sensation was exquisite. He, too, moved his hand, to accommodate the shift of hers, and she waited fearfully. She did not want him to prove like other men, and she could have hated him had he dared to take advantage of that slight movement of her fingers and put his arm around her. He did not, and she flamed toward him. There was fineness in him. He was neither rattle brained, like Bert, nor coarse like other men she had encountered. For she had had experiences, not nice, and she had been made to suffer by the lack of what was termed chivalry, though she, in turn, lacked that word to describe what she divined and desired.

And he was a prize-fighter. The thought of it almost made her gasp. Yet he answered not at all to her conception of a prize-fighter. But then, he wasn't a prize-fighter. He had said he was not. She resolved to ask him about it some time if— if he took her out again. Yet there was little doubt of that, for when a man danced with one girl a whole day he did not drop her immediately. Almost she hoped that he was a prize-fighter. There was a delicious tickle of wickedness about it. Prize-fighters were such terrible and mysterious men. In so far as they were out of.the ordinary and were not mere common workingmen such as carpenters and laundrymen, they represented romance. Power, also, they represented. They did not work for bosses, but spectacularly and magnificently, with their own might, grappled with the great world and wrung a splendid living from its reluctant hands. Some of them even owned automobiles and traveled with a retinue of trainers and servants. Perhaps it had been only Billy's modesty that made him say he had quit fighting. And yet, there were the callous spots on his hands. That showed he had quit.

V

THEY said good-by at the gate. Billy betrayed awkwardness that was sweet to Saxon. He was not one of the take-it-for-granted young men. There was a pause, while she feigned desire to go into the house, yet waited in secret eagerness for the words she wanted him to say.

"When am I goin' to see you again?" he asked, holding her hand in his.

She laughed consentingly.

"I live 'way up in East Oakland," he explained. "You know there's where the stable is, an' most of our teaming is done in that section, so I don't knock around down this way much. But, say," his hand tightened on hers, "we just got to dance together some more. I'll tell you, the Orindore Club has its dance Wednesday. If you haven't a date—have you?"

"No," she said.

"Then Wednesday. What time'll I come for you?"

And when they had arranged the details, and he had agreed she should dance some of the dances with the other fellows, and said good night again, his hand closed more tightly on hers and drew her toward him. She resisted slightly, but honestly. It was the custom, but she felt she ought not for fear he might misunderstand. And yet she wanted to kiss him as she had never wanted to kiss a man. When it came, her face upturned to his, she realized that on his part it was an honest kiss. There hinted nothing behind it. Rugged and kind as himself, it was virginal, almost, and betrayed not for long practice in the art of saying good-by. All men were not brutes, after all, was her thought.

"Good-night," she murmured, the gate screeched under her hand, and she hurried along the narrow walk that led around to the corner of the house.

"Wednesday," he called.

"Wednesday," she answered.

But in the shadow of the narrow alley between the two houses she stood still and pleasured in the ring of his footfalls down the cement sidewalk. Not until they had quite died away did she go on. She crept up the back stairs and across the kitchen to her room, registering her thanksgiving that Sarah was asleep.

She lighted the gas, and, as she removed the little velvet hat, she felt her lips still tingling with the kiss. Yet it had meant nothing. It was the way of the young men. They all did it. Yet their good-night kisses had never tingled, while this one tingled in her brain as well as on her lips. What was it? What did it mean? With a sudden impulse she looked at herself in the glass. The eyes were happy and bright. The color that tinted her cheeks so easily was in them and glowing. It was a pretty reflection, and she smiled, partly in joy, partly in appreciation, and the smile grew at sight of the even rows of strong white teeth. Why shouldn't Billy like that face? was her unvoiced query. Other men had liked it. Other men did like it. Even the other girls admitted she was a good-looker. Charley Long certainly liked it from the way he made life miserable for her.

She glanced aside to the rim of the looking-glass where his photograph was wedged, shuddered, and made a *moue* of distaste. There was cruelty in those eyes, and brutishness. He was a brute. For a year, now, he had bullied her. Other fellows were afraid to go with her. He warned them off. She had been forced into almost slavery to his attentions. She remembered the young bookkeeper at the laundry—not a working-man, but a soft-handed, soft-voiced gentle-man—whom Charley had beaten up at the corner because he had been bold enough to come to take her to the theater. And she had been helpless. For his own sake she had never dared accept another invitation to go out with him.

And now, Wednesday night, she was go-ing with Billy. Billy! Her heart leaped. There would be trouble, but Billy would save her from him. She'd like to see him try to beat Billy up.

With a quick movement, she jerked the photograph from its niche and threw it face downward upon the chest of drawers. It fell beside a small square case of dark and tarnished leather. With a feeling as of prof-anation, she again seized the offending photograph and flung it across the room into a corner. At the same time she picked up the leather case. Springing it open, she gazed at the daguerreotype of a worn little woman with steady gray eyes and a hopeful, pathetic mouth. Opposite, on the velvet lining, done in gold lettering, was, CARL-TON: FROM DAISY. She read it rever-ently, for it represented the father she had never known, and the mother she had so little known, though she could never forget that those wise sad eyes were gray.

Despite lack of conventional religion, Saxon's nature was deeply religious. Her thoughts of God were vague and nebulous, and there she was frankly puzzled. She could not vision God. Here, in the da-guerreotype, was the concrete; much she had grasped from it, and always there seemed an infinite more to grasp. She did not go to church. This was her high altar and holy of holies. She came to it in trouble, in loneliness, for counsel, divina-tion, and comfort. In so far as she found herself different from the girls of her ac-quaintance, she quested here to try to iden-tify her characteristics in the pictured face. Her mother had been different from other women, too. This, forsooth, meant to her what God meant to others. To this she strove to be true, and not to hurt nor vex. And how little she really knew of her mother, and of how much was conjecture and surmise, she was unaware; for it was

through many years she had erected this mother-myth.

With dewy eyes Saxon kissed the da-guerreotype passionately, and closed the case, abandoning 'the mystery and godhead of mother and all the strange enigma of living.

In bed, she projected against her closed eyelids the few rich scenes of her mother that her child-memory retained. It was her favorite way of wooing sleep. She had done it all her life—sunk into the death-blackness of sleep with her mother limned to the last on her fading consciousness. But this mother was not the Daisy of the plains nor of the daguerreotype. They had been before Saxon's time. This that she saw nightly was an older mother, broken with insomnia and brave with sorrow, who crept, always crept, a pale, frail creature, gentle and unfaltering, dying from lack of sleep, living by will, and by will refraining from going mad, who, nevertheless, could not will sleep, and whom not even the whole tribe of doctors could make sleep. Crept, always she crept, about the house, from weary bed to weary chair and back again, through long days and weeks of torment, never com-plaining, though her unfailing smile was twisted with pain, and the wise gray eyes, still wise and gray, were grown unutterably large and profoundly deep.

But on this night, Saxon did not win to sleep quickly; the little creeping mother came and went; and in the intervals the face of Billy, with the cloud-drifted sullen-handsome eyes, burned against her eyelids. And once again, as sleep welled up to smother her, she put to herself the question: *Is this the man?*

VI

THE work in the ironing-room slipped off, but the three days until Wednesday night were very long. She hummed over the fancy starch that flew under the iron at an astounding clip.

"I can't see how you do it," Mary ad-mired. "You'll make thirteen or fourteen this week at that rate."

Saxon laughed, and in the steam from the iron she saw dancing golden letters that spelled *Wednesday*.

"What do you think of Billy?" Mary asked.

"I like him," was the frank answer.

DRAWN BY HOWARD CHANDLER CHRISTY

In the shadow of the narrow alley between the two houses she stood still and pleasured in the ring of
Billy's footfalls down the cement sidewalk. Not until they had quite died away did she go on

"Well, don't let it go farther than that."

"I will if I want to," Saxon retorted gaily.

"Better not," came the warning. "You'll only make trouble for yourself. He ain't marryin'. Many a girl's found that out. They just throw themselves at his head, too."

"I'm not going to throw myself at him, or any other man."

"Just thought I'd tell you," Mary concluded. "A word to the wise."

Saxon had become grave. "He's not—not—?" she began, then looked the significance of the question she could not complete.

"Oh, nothin' like that—though there's nothin' to stop him. He's straight, all right. But he just won't fall for anything in skirts. He dances, an' runs around, an' has a good time, an' beyond that—nitsky. A lot of 'em's got fooled on him. I bet you there's a dozen girls in love with him right now. An' he just goes on turnin' 'em down. There was Lily Sanderson, you know her. You seen her at that picnic last summer at Shellmound—that tall, nice-lookin' blonde that was with Butch Willows?"

"Yes, I remember her," Saxon said. "What about her?"

"Well, she'd been runnin' with Butch Willows pretty steady, an', just because she could dance, Billy dances a lot with her. Butch ain't afraid of nothin'. He wades right in for a show-down, an' nails Billy outside, before everybody, an' reads the riot act. An' Billy listens in that slow, sleepy way of his, an' Butch gets hotter an' hotter, an' everybody expects a scrap. An' then Billy says to Butch, 'Are you done?' 'Yes,' Butch says; 'I've said my say, an' what are you goin' to do about it?' An' Billy says—an' what d'ye think he said, with everybody lookin' on an' Butch with blood in his eye? Well, he said, 'I guess nothin', Butch.' Just like that. Butch was that surprised you could 'a' knocked him over with a feather. 'An' never dance with her no more?' he says. 'Not if you say I can't, Butch,' Billy says. Just like that.

"Well, you know any other man to take water the way he did from Butch—why, everybody'd despise him. But not Billy. You see, he can afford to. He's got a rep as a fighter, an' when he just stood back an' let Butch have his way, everybody knew he wasn't scared, or backin' down, or anything. He didn't care a rap for Lily Sanderson, that

was all, an' anybody could see she was just crazy after him."

The telling of this episode caused Saxon no little worry. Hers was the average woman's pride, but in the matter of man-conquering prowess she was not unduly conceited. Billy had enjoyed her dancing, and she wondered if that was all. If Charley Long bullied up to him would he let her go as he had let Lily Sanderson go? He was not a marrying man; nor could Saxon blind her eyes to the fact that he was eminently marriageable. No wonder the girls ran after him. And he was a man-subduer as well as a woman-subduer. Men liked him. Bert Wanhope seemed actually to love him. She remembered the Butchertown tough in the dining-room at Weasel Park who had come over to the table to apologize, the moment he learned his identity.

A very much spoiled young man, was a thought that flitted frequently through Saxon's mind, and each time she condemned it as ungenerous. He was gentle in that tantalizing slow way of his. Despite his strength, he did not walk rough-shod over others. There was the affair with Lily Sanderson. Saxon analyzed it over and again. He had not cared for the girl, and he had immediately stepped from between her and Butch. It was just the thing that Bert, out of sheer wickedness and love of trouble, would not have done. There would have been a fight, hard feelings, Butch turned into an enemy, and nothing profited to Lily. But Billy had done the right thing—done it slowly and imperturbably and with the least hurt to everybody. All of which made him more desirable to Saxon and less possible.

She bought another pair of silk stockings that she had hesitated at for weeks, and on Tuesday night sewed and drowsed wearily over a new shirt-waist, and earned complaint from Sarah concerning her extravagant use of gas.

Wednesday night, at the Orindore dance, all was not undiluted pleasure. It was shameless the way the girls made up to Billy, and, at times, she found his easy consideration for them almost irritating. Yet she was compelled to acknowledge to herself that he hurt none of the other fellows' feelings in the way the girls hurt hers. They all but asked him outright to dance with them, and little of their open pursuit of him escaped her eyes. She resolved that she would not be guilty of throwing herself at him, and withheld dance after dance, and yet was secretly and thrillingly aware that she was pursuing the right tactics. She deliberately demonstrated that she was desirable to other men, as he involuntarily demonstrated his own desirableness to the women.

Her happiness came when he coolly overrode her objections and insisted on two dances more than she had allotted him. And she was pleased, as well as angered, when she chanced to overhear two of the strapping young cannery girls. "The way that little sawed-off is monopolizin' him," said one. And the other, "You'd think she might have the good taste to run after somebody of her own age." "Cradle-snatcher," was the final sting that sent the angry blood into Saxon's cheeks as the two girls moved away, unaware that they had been overheard.

Billy saw her home, kissed her at the gate, and got her consent to go with him to the dance at Germania Hall on Friday night. "I wasn't thinkin' of goin'," he said. "But if you'll say the word—Bert's goin' to be there."

Next day, at the ironing-boards, Mary told her that she and Bert were dated for Germania Hall. "Are you goin'?" Mary asked.

Saxon nodded.

"Billy Roberts?"

The nod was repeated, and Mary, with suspended iron, gave her a long and curious look.

"Say, an' what if Charley Long butts in?"

Saxon shrugged her shoulders. They ironed swiftly and silently for a quarter of an hour.

"Well," Mary decided, "if he does butt in maybe he'll get his. I'd like to see him get it—the big stiff! It all depends how Billy feels—about you, I mean."

"I'm no Lily Sanderson," Saxon answered indignantly. "I'll never give Billy Roberts a chance to turn me down."

"You will, if Charley Long butts in. Take it from me, Saxon, he ain't no gentleman. Look what he done to Mr. Moody. That was a awful beatin.' An' Mr. Moody only a quiet little man that wouldn't harm a fly. Well, he won't find Billy Roberts a sissy by a long shot."

That night, outside the laundry entrance, Saxon found Charley Long waiting. As he stepped forward to greet her and walk alongside, she felt the sickening palpitation that he had so thoroughly taught her to know. The blood ebbed from her face with the apprehension and fear his appearance caused. She was afraid of the rough bulk of the man; of the heavy brown eyes, dominant and confident; of the big blacksmith-hands and the thick, strong fingers with the hairpads on the backs to every first joint. He was unlovely to the eye, and he was unlovely to all her finer sensibilities. It was not his strength itself, but the quality of it and the misuse of it, that affronted her. The beating he had given the gentle Mr. Moody had meant half-hours of horror to her afterward. Always did the memory of it come to her accompanied by a shudder.

"You're lookin' white an' all beat to a frazzle," he was saying. "Why don't you cut the work? You got to some time anyway. You can't lose me, kid."

"I wish I could," she replied.

He laughed with harsh joviality. "Nothin' to it, Saxon. You're just cut out to be Mrs. Long, an' you're sure goin' to be."

"I wish I was as certain about all things as you are," she said with mild sarcasm that missed.

"Take it from me," he went on, "there's just one thing you can be certain of—an' that is that I am certain." He was pleased with the cleverness of his idea and laughed approvingly. "When I go after anything, I get it, an' if anything gets in between it gets hurt. D'ye get that? It's me for you, an' that's all there is to it, so you might as well make up your mind and go to workin' in my home instead of the laundry. Why, it's a snap. There wouldn't be much to do. I make good money, an' you wouldn't want for anything. You know, I just washed up from work an' skinned over here to tell it to you once more so you wouldn't forget. I ain't 'te 'ate yet, an' that shows how much I think of you."

"You'd better go and eat then," she advised, though she knew the futility of attempting to get rid of him.

She scarcely heard what he said. It had come upon her suddenly that she was very tired and very small and very weak alongside this Colossus of a man. Would he dog her always? she asked despairingly, and seemed to glimpse a vision of all her future life stretched out before her, with always the form and face of the burly blacksmith pursuing her.

"Come on, kid, an' kick in," he continued. "It's the good old summer time, an' that's the time to get married."

"But I'm not going to marry you," she protested. "I've told you a thousand times already."

"Aw, forget it. You want to get them ideas out of your think-box. Of course you're goin' to marry me. It's a pipe. An' I'll tell you another pipe. You an' me's goin' acrost to Frisco Friday night. There's goin' to be big doin's with the Horse-shoers."

"Only I'm not," she contradicted.

"Oh, yes, you are," he asserted with absolute assurance. "We'll catch the last boat back, an' you'll have one fine time. An' I'll put you next to some of the good dancers. Oh, I ain't a pincher, an' I know you like dancin'."

"But I tell you I can't," she reiterated.

He shot a glance of suspicion at her from under the black thatch of brows that met above his nose and were as one brow. "Why can't you?"

"A date," she said.

"Who's the bloke?"

"None of your business, Charley Long. I've got a date, that's all."

"I'll make it my business. Remember that lah-de-dah bookkeeper rummy? Well, just keep on rememberin' him an' what he got."

"I wish you'd leave me alone," she pleaded resentfully. "Can't you be kind just for once?"

The blacksmith laughed unpleasantly. "If any rummy thinks he can butt in on you an' me he'll learn different, an' I'm the little boy that'll learn 'm. Friday night, eh?"

"I won't tell you."

"Where?" he repeated.

Her lips were drawn in tight silence, and in her cheeks were little angry spots of blood.

"Huh! As if I couldn't guess! Germania Hall. Well, I'll be there, an' I'll take you home afterward. D'ye get that? An' you'd better tell the rummy to beat it unless you want to see 'm get his face hurt."

Saxon, hurt as a prideful woman can be hurt by cavalier treatment, was tempted to cry out the name and prowess of her new-found protector. And then came fear. This was a big man, and Billy was only a boy. That was the way he affected her.

She remembered her first impression of his hands and glanced quickly at the hands of the man beside her. They seemed twice as large as Billy's, and the mats of hair seemed to advertise a terrible strength. No; Billy could not fight this big brute. He must not. And then to Saxon came a wicked little hope that by the mysterious and unthinkable ability that prize-fighters possessed, Billy might be able to whip this bully and rid her of him. With the next glance doubt came again, for her eye dwelt on the blacksmith's broad shoulders, the cloth of the coat muscle wrinkled and the sleeves bulging above the biceps.

"If you lay a hand on anybody I'm going with again—" she began.

"Why, they'll get hurt, of course," Long grinned. "And they'll deserve it, too. Any rummy that comes between a fellow an' his girl ought to get hurt."

"But I'm not your girl, and all your saying so doesn't make it so."

"That's right, get mad," he approved. "I like you for that, too. You've got spunk an' fight. I like to see it. It's what a man needs in his wife."

She stopped before the house and put her hand on the gate. "Good-by," she said. "I'm going in."

"Come on out afterward for a run to Idora Park," he suggested.

"No, I'm not feeling good, and I'm going straight to bed as soon as I eat supper."

"Huh!" he sneered. "Gettin' in shape for the fling to-morrow night, eh?"

With an impatient movement she opened the gate and stepped inside.

"I've given it to you straight," he went on. "If you don't go with me to-morrow night somebody'll get hurt."

"I hope it will be you," she cried vindictively.

He laughed as he threw his head back, stretched his big chest, and half-lifted his heavy arms. The action reminded her disgustingly of a big lion she had once seen in a circus.

"Well, good-by," he said. "See you to-morrow night at Germania Hall."

"I haven't told you it was Germania Hall."

"And you haven't told me it wasn't. All the same, I'll be there. And I'll take you home, too. Be sure an' keep plenty of round dances open for me. That's right. Get mad. It makes you look fine."

The Valley of the Moon

THE STORY OF A FIGHT AGAINST ODDS FOR LOVE AND A HOME

By Jack London

Author of "Martin Eden," "Burning Daylight," "Smoke Bellew," etc.

Illustrated by Howard Chandler Christy

SYNOPSIS: Is this the man? So Saxon questioned of herself when she had met "Big Bill" Roberts, one-time prize-fighter, on the dancing-floor at Weasel Park, whither she and Mary, ironers of fancy starch, had gone for a Sunday outing. Never had she come so near to losing her heart as Billy, blue eyed, boyish, gentlemanly, had come to winning it after a few hours' acquaintance. Planned by Mary and Bert Wanhope, the meeting had taken a happy turn, for both Saxon and Billy had seized the future in the present and grasped at its chance for happiness. Billy was a teamster and knew what hard work meant, so they went home early, Saxon glorying in his refusal to "make a time of it," as Bert suggested. He kissed her good night at the gate, with Wednesday night's dance as their next meeting. Friday's dance was next arranged for, but on Thursday night Charley Long, a rebuffed suitor, met her outside the laundry and warned her that if she did not go with him "somebody'll get hurt." But Saxon bore the notion that Billy, at least, could take care of himself.

THE music stopped at the end of the waltz, leaving Billy and Saxon at the big entrance doorway of the ballroom. Her hand rested lightly on his arm, and they were promenading on to find seats when Charley Long, evidently just arrived, thrust his way in front of them.

"So you're the buttinsky, eh?" he demanded, his face malignant with passion and menace.

"Who? Me?" Billy queried gently. "Some mistake, sport. I never butt in."

"You're goin' to get your head beaten off if you don't make yourself scarce pretty lively."

"I wouldn't want that to happen for the world," Billy drawled. "Come on, Saxon. This neighborhood's unhealthy for us."

He started to go on with her, but Long thrust in front again.

"You're too fresh to keep, young fellow," he snarled. "You need saltin' down. D'ye get me?"

Billy scratched his head, on his face exaggerated puzzlement. "No, I don't get you," he said. "Now just what was it you said?"

But the big blacksmith turned contemptuously away from him to Saxon. "Come here, you. Let's see your program."

"Do you want to dance with him?" Billy asked.

She shook her head.

"Sorry, sport, nothin' doin'," Billy said, again making to start on.

For the third time the blacksmith blocked the way.

"Get off your foot," said Billy. "You're standin' on it."

Long all but sprang upon him, his hands clenched, one arm just starting back for the punch, while at the same instant shoulders and chest were coming forward. But he restrained himself at sight of Billy's unstartled body and cold and cloudy eyes. He had made no move of mind or muscle. It was as if he were unaware of the threatened attack. All of which constituted a new thing in Long's experience.

"Maybe you don't know who I am," he bullied.

"Yep, I do," Billy answered airily. "You're a record-breaker at rough-housin'." Here Long's face showed pleasure. "You ought to have the diamond belt for rough-housin' baby-buggies. I guess there ain't a one you're afraid to tackle."

"Leave 'm alone, Charley," advised one of the young men who had crowded about them. "He's Bill Roberts, the fighter. You know 'm—Big Bill."

"I don't care if he's Jim Jeffries. He can't butt in on me this way."

Nevertheless it was noticeable, even to Saxon, that the fire had gone out of his fierceness. Billy's name seemed to have a quieting effect on obstreperous males.

"Do you know him?" Billy asked her.

She signified yes with her eyes, though it seemed she must cry out a thousand things against this man who so steadfastly persecuted her. Billy turned to the blacksmith.

"Look here, sport, you don't want trouble with me. I've got your number. Besides,

23

Billy shook his head slowly. "No; you're in wrong. I think she has a say in the matter." "Well, say it then,"
Long snarled at Saxon. "Who're you goin' to go with—me or him? Let's get it settled." For reply, Saxon
reached her free hand over to the hand that rested on Billy's arm. "Nuff said," was Billy's remark

24

what do we want to fight for? Hasn't she got a say-so in the matter?"

"No, she hasn't. This is my affair an' yourn."

Billy shook his head slowly. "No; you're in wrong. I think she has a say in the matter."

"Well, say it then," Long snarled at Saxon. "Who're you goin' to go with—me or him? Let's get it settled."

For reply, Saxon reached her free hand over to the hand that rested on Billy's arm.

"Nuff said," was Billy's remark.

Long glared at Saxon, then transferred the glare to her protector. "I've a good mind to mix it with you anyway," Long gritted through his teeth.

Saxon was elated as they started to move away. Lily Sanderson's fate had not been hers, and her wonderful man-boy, without the threat of a blow, had conquered the big blacksmith.

"He's forced himself upon me all the time," she whispered to Billy. "He's tried to run me, and beaten up every man that came near me. I never want to see him again."

Billy halted immediately. Long, who was reluctantly moving to get out of the way, also halted.

"She says she don't want anything more to do with you," Billy said to him. "An' what she says goes. If I get a whisper any time, that you've been botherin' her, I'll attend to your case. D'ye get that?"

Long glowered and remained silent.

"D'ye get that?" Billy repeated, more imperatively.

A growl of assent came from the blacksmith.

"All right, then. See you remember it. An' now get outa the way or I'll walk over you."

Long slunk back, muttering inarticulate threats, and Saxon moved on as in a dream. Charley Long had taken water. He had been afraid of this smooth-skinned, blue-eyed boy. She was quit of him—something no other man had dared attempt for her.

Twice Saxon tried to tell Billy the details of her acquaintance with Long, but each time was put off.

"I don't care a rap about it," Billy said the second time. "You're here, ain't you?"

But she insisted, and when, worked up and angry by the recital, she had finished, he patted her hand soothingly.

"It's all right, Saxon," he said. "He's

just a big stiff. I took his measure as soon as I looked at him. He won't bother you again. I know his kind. He's a dog. Rough-house? He couldn't rough-house a milk-wagon."

"But how do you do it?" she asked breathlessly. "Why are men so afraid of you? You're just wonderful."

He smiled in an embarrassed way and changed the subject. "Say," he said, "I like your teeth. They're so white an' regular, an' not big, an' not dinky little baby's teeth either. They're—they're just right, an' they fit you. I never seen such fine teeth on a girl yet. D'ye know, honest, they kind of make me hungry when I look at 'em. They're good enough to eat."

At midnight, leaving the insatiable Bert and Mary still dancing, Billy and Saxon started for home. It was on his suggestion that they left early, and he felt called upon to explain.

"It's one thing the fightin' game's taught me," he said—"to take care of myself. A fellow can't work all day and dance all night and keep in condition. It's the same way with drinkin'—an' not that I'm a little tin angel. I know what it is. I've been soused to the guards an' all the rest of it. I like my beer—big schooners of it; but I don't drink all I want of it. I've tried, but it don't pay. Take that big stiff to-night that butted in on us. He ought to had my number. He's a dog, anyway, but besides he had beer bloat. I sized that up the first rattle, an' that's the difference about who takes the other fellow's number. Condition, that's what it is."

"But he is so big," Saxon protested. "Why, his fists are twice as big as yours."

"That don't mean anything. What counts is what's behind the fists. He'd turn loose like a buckin' bronco. If I couldn't drop him at the start, all I'd do is keep away, smother up, an' wait. An' all of a sudden he'd blow up—go all to pieces, you know, wind, heart, everything, and then I'd have him where I wanted him. And the point is he knows it, too."

"You're the first prize-fighter I ever knew," Saxon said, after a pause.

"I'm not any more," he disclaimed hastily. "That's one thing the fightin' game taught me—to leave it alone. It don't pay. A fellow trains as fine as silk—till he's all silk, his skin, everything, and he's fit to live for a hundred years; an' then he climbs through the ropes for a hard twenty-rounds with some tough customer that's just as good as he is, and in those twenty rounds he frazzles out all his silk an' blows in a year of his life. Yes, sometimes he blows in five years of it, or cuts it in half, or uses up all of it. I've watched 'em. I've seen fellows strong as bulls fight a hard battle and die inside the year of consumption, or kidney disease, or anything else. Now what's the good of it? Money can't buy what they throw away. That's why I quit the game and went back to drivin' team. I got my silk, an' I'm goin' to keep it, that's all."

"It must make you feel proud to know you are the master of other men," she said softly, aware herself of pride in the strength and skill of him.

"It does," he admitted, frankly. "I'm glad I went into the game—just as glad as I am that I pulled out of it. Yep, it's taught me a lot—to keep my eyes open an' my head cool. Oh, I've got a temper, a peach of a temper. I get scared of myself sometimes. I used to be always breaking loose. But the fightin' taught me to keep down the steam an' not do things I'd be sorry for afterward."

"Why, you're the sweetest, easiest-tempered man I know," she interjected.

"Don't you believe it. Just watch me, and sometime you'll see me break out that bad that I won't know what I'm doin' myself. Oh, I'm a holy terror when I get started."

This tacit promise of continued acquaintance gave Saxon a little joy-thrill.

"Say," he said, as they neared her neighborhood, "what are you doin' next Sunday?"

"Nothing. No plans at all."

"Well, suppose you an' me go buggy-riding all day out in the hills?"

She did not answer immediately, and for the moment she was seeing the nightmare vision of her last buggy-ride; of her fear and her leap from the buggy, and of the long miles and the stumbling through the darkness in thin-soled shoes that bruised her feet on every rock. And then it came to her with a great swell of joy that this man beside her was not such a man.

"I love horses," she said. "I almost love them better than I do dancing, only I don't know anything about them. My father rode a great roan war-horse. He was a captain of cavalry, you know. I never saw him, but somehow I always can see him on that big

horse, with a sash around his waist and his sword at his side. My brother has the sword now, but he says it is mine because it wasn't his father's. You see, he's only my half-brother. I was the only child by my mother's second marriage. That was her real marriage—her love-marriage, I mean."

Saxon ceased abruptly, embarrassed by her own garrulity; and yet the impulse was strong to tell this young man all about herself, and it seemed to her that these far memories were a large part of her.

"Go on an' tell me about it," Billy urged. "I like to hear about the old people of the old days. My people were along in there, too, an' somehow I think it was a better world to live in than now. Things were more sensible and natural. I don't exactly say what I mean. But it's like this: I don't understand life to-day. There are the labor unions an' employers' associations, an' strikes, an' hard times, an' huntin' for jobs, an' all the rest. Things wasn't like that in the old days. Everybody farmed, an' shot their meat, an' got enough to eat, an' took care of their old folks. But now it's all a mix-up that I can't understand. Mebbe I'm a fool, I don't know. But anyway, go ahead an' tell us about your mother."

"Well, you see, when she was only a young woman she and Captain Brown fell in love. He was a soldier then, before the war. And he was ordered East for the war when she was away nursing her sister Laura. And then came the news that he was killed at Shiloh. And she married a man who had loved her for years and years. He was a boy in the same wagon-train coming across the plains. She liked him, but she didn't love him. And afterward came the news that my father wasn't killed after all. So it made her very sad, but it did not spoil her life. She was a good mother and a good wife and all that, but she was always sad, and sweet, and gentle, and I think her voice was the most beautiful in the world."

"She was game, all right," Billy approved.

"And my father never married. He loved her all the time. I've got a lovely poem home that she wrote to him. It's just wonderful, and it sings like music. Well, long, long afterward her husband died, and then she and my father made their love-marriage. They didn't get married until 1882, and she was forty-two years old."

More she told him, as they stood by the

gate, and Saxon tried to think that the good-by kiss was a trifle longer than just ordinary.

"How about nine o'clock?" he queried across the gate. "Don't trouble about lunch or anything. I'll fix all that up. You just be ready at nine."

VIII

SUNDAY morning Saxon was beforehand in getting ready, and on her return to the kitchen from her second journey to peep through the front windows, Sarah began her customary attack.

"It's a shame an' a disgrace the way some people can afford silk stockings," she began. "Look at me, a-toilin' and a-stewin' day an' night, and I never get silk stockings—nor shoes, three pairs of them all at one time. But there's a just God in heaven, and there'll be some mighty big surprises for some when the end comes and folks get passed out what's comin' to them."

Tom, smoking his pipe and cuddling his youngest born, dropped an eyelid surreptitiously in token that Sarah was in a tantrum. Saxon devoted herself to tying a ribbon in the hair of one of the little girls. Sarah lumbered heavily about the kitchen, washing and putting away the breakfast dishes. She straightened her back from the sink with a groan and glared at Saxon with fresh hostility.

"You ain't sayin' anything, eh? An' why don't you? Because I guess you still got some natural shame in you—a-runnin' with a prize-fighter. Oh, I've heard about your going-ons with Bill Roberts. A nice specimen he is. But just you wait till Charley Long gets his hands on him, that's all."

"Oh, I don't know," Tom intervened. "Bill Roberts is a pretty good boy, from what I hear."

Saxon smiled with superior knowledge, and Sarah, catching her in the act, was infuriated.

"Why don't you marry Charley Long? He's crazy for you, and he ain't a drinkin' man."

"I guess he gets outside his share of beer," Saxon retorted.

"That's right," her brother supplemented. "An' I know for a fact that he keeps a keg in the house all the time, too."

"Maybe you've been guzzling from it," Sarah snapped.

"Maybe I have," Tom said.

"Well, he can afford to keep a keg in the house if he wants to," she returned to the attack, which now was directed at her husband as well. "He pays his bills, and he certainly makes good money—better than most men, anyway."

"An' he hasn't a wife an' children to watch out for," Tom said.

"Nor everlastin' dues to unions that don't do him no good."

"Oh, yes, he has," Tom urged genially. "Blamed little he'd work in that shop, or any other shop in Oakland, if he didn't keep in good standing with the Blacksmiths. You don't understand labor conditions, Sarah. The unions have got to stick, if the men aren't to starve to death."

"Oh, of course not," Sarah sniffed. "I don't understand anything. I ain't got a mind. I'm a fool, an' you tell me so right before the children."

Saxon, for the moment, lost control of herself. "Oh, for Heaven's sake, can't we be together five minutes without quarreling?" she blazed.

Sarah turned upon her sister-in-law. "Who's quarreling? Can't I open my head without bein' jumped on by the two of you?"

Saxon shrugged her shoulders despairingly, and Sarah swung about on her husband.

"Seein' you love your sister so much better than your wife, why did you want to marry me, that's borne your children for you, an' slaved for you, an' toiled for you, an' worked her finger-nails off for you? An' what have you ever did for me? That's what I want to know. Look at that!"

She thrust out a shapeless, swollen foot, encased in a monstrous, untended shoe, the dry, raw leather of which showed white on the edges of bulging cracks.

"Look at that! That's what I say. Look at that!" Her voice was persistently rising and at the same time growing throaty. "The only shoes I got. Me. Your wife. Ain't you ashamed? Where are my three pairs? Look at that stockin'."

Speech failed her, and she sat down suddenly on a chair at the table, glaring unutterable malevolence and misery. She arose with the abrupt stiffness of an automaton, poured herself a cup of cold coffee, and in the same jerky way sat down again. As if too hot for her lips, she filled her saucer with the greasy-looking nondescript fluid, and continued her set glare, her breast rising and falling with staccato, mechanical movement.

"Now·Sarah, be ca'm, be ca'm," Tom pleaded anxiously.

In response, slowly, with utmost deliberation, as if the destiny of empires rested on the certitude of her act, she turned the saucer of coffee upside down on the table. She lifted her right hand, slowly, hugely, and in the same slow, huge way landed the open palm with a sounding slap on Tom's astounded cheek. Immediately thereafter she raised her voice in the shrill, hoarse, monotonous madness of hysteria, sat down on the floor, and rocked back and forth in the throes of an abysmal and non-understandable grief.

Tom's face was drawn and white, though the smitten cheek still blazed, and Saxon wanted to put her arms comfortingly around him, yet dared not. He bent over his wife. "Sarah, you ain't feelin' well. Let me put you to bed, and I'll finish tidying up."

"Don't touch me! Don't touch me!" she screamed, jerking away from him.

"Take the children out in the yard, Tom, for a walk, anything—get them away," Saxon said. She was sick, and white, and trembling. "Go, Tom, please, please. There's your hat. I'll take care of her. I know just how."

Left to herself, Saxon worked with frantic haste, assuming the calm she did not possess, but which she must impart to the screaming bedlamite upon the floor. The light frame house leaked the noise hideously, like a sieve, and Saxon knew that the houses on either side were hearing, and the street itself and the houses across the street. Her fear was that Billy would arrive in the midst of it. Further, she was incensed, violated. Every fiber rebelled, almost in a nausea; yet she maintained cool control and stroked Sarah's forehead and hair with slow, soothing movements. Soon, with one arm around her, she managed to win the first diminution in the strident, atrocious, unceasing scream. A few minutes later, sobbing heavily, the older woman lay in bed, across her forehead and eyes a wet-pack of towel for easement of the headache she and Saxon tacitly accepted as substitute for the brain-storm.

When a clatter of hoofs came down the street and stopped, Saxon was able to slip to the front door and wave her hand to Billy. In the kitchen she found Tom waiting in sad anxiousness.

"It's all right," she said. "Billy Roberts has come, and I've got to go. You go in and sit beside her for a while, and maybe she'll go to sleep. But don't rush her. Let her have her own way. If she'll let you take her hand, why do it. Try it anyway. But first of all, as an opener and just as a matter of course, start wetting the towel over her eyes."

He was a kindly, easy-going man; but, after the way of a large percentage of the Western stock, he was undemonstrative. He nodded, turned toward the door to obey, and paused irresolutely. The look he gave back to Saxon was almost dog-like in gratitude and all brotherly in love. She felt it, and in spirit leaped toward it.

"It's all right—everything's all right," she cried hastily.

Tom shook his head. "No, it ain't. It's a shame, a blamed shame, that's what it is." He shrugged his shoulders. "Oh, I don't care for myself. But it's for you. You got your life before you yet, little kid sister. You'll get old, and all that means, fast enough. But it's a bad start for a day off. The thing for you to do is to forget all this, and skin out with your fellow, an' have a good time." In the open door, he halted a second time. A spasm contracted his brow. "Hell! Think of it! Sarah and I used to go buggy-riding once on a time. And I guess she had her three pairs of shoes, too. Can you beat it?"

In her bedroom Saxon completed her dressing, for an instant stepping upon a chair so as to glimpse critically in the small wall-mirror the hang of her ready-made linen skirt. This, and the jacket, she had altered to fit, and she had doubled-stitched the seams to achieve the coveted tailored effect. Down from the chair, she pinned on a firm sailor-hat of white straw with a brown ribbon around the crown that matched her ribbon belt. She rubbed her cheeks quickly and fiercely to bring back the color Sarah had driven out of them, and delayed a moment longer to put on her tan lisle-thread gloves. Once, in the fashion-page of a Sunday supplement, she had read that no lady ever put on her gloves after she left the door.

With a resolute self-grip, as she crossed the parlor and passed the door to Sarah's bedroom, through the thin wood of which came elephantine moanings and low slubberings, she steeled herself to keep the color in her cheeks and the brightness in her eyes. And

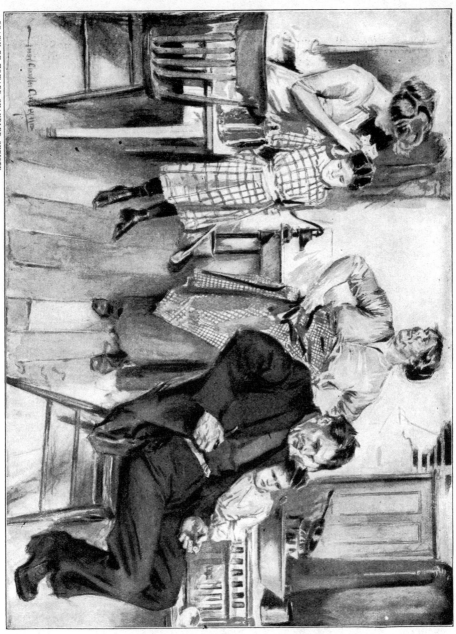

DRAWN BY HOWARD CHANDLER CHRISTY

Sarah straightened her back from the sink with a groan and glared at Saxon with fresh hostility. "You ain't sayin' anything, eh? An' why don't you? Because I guess you still got some natural shame in you —a-runnin' with a prize-fighter. Oh, I've heard about your going-ons with Bill Roberts. A nice specimen he is. But just you wait till Charley Long gets his hands on him, that's all."

so well did she succeed that Billy never dreamed that the radiant, live young thing, tripping lightly down the steps to him, had just come from a bout with soul-sickening hysteria and madness.

To her, in the bright sun, Billy's blondness was startling. His cheeks, smooth as a girl's, were touched with color. The blue eyes seemed more cloudily blue than usual, and the crisp sandy hair hinted more than ever of the pale straw-gold that was not there. Never had she seen him quite so royally young. As he smiled to greet her, with a slow white flash of teeth from between red lips, she caught again the promise of easement and rest. Fresh from the shattering chaos of her sister-in-law's mind, Billy's tremendous imperturbable calm was especially satisfying, and Saxon mentally laughed to scorn the terrible temper he had charged to himself.

She had been buggy-riding before, but always behind one horse, jaded and livery, in a top-buggy, heavy and dingy, such as livery-stables rent because of sturdy unbreakableness. But here stood two horses, head-tossing and restless, shouting in every high-light glint of their satin, golden-sorrel coats that they had never been rented out in all their glorious young lives. Between them was a pole inconceivably slender, on them were harnesses preposterously string-like and fragile. And Billy belonged here, by elemental right, a part of them and of it, a master-part and a component, along with the spidery delicate, narrowed-boxed, wide and yellow-wheeled, rubber-tired rig, efficient and capable, as different as he was different from the other men who had taken her out behind stolid, lumbering horses. He held the reins in one hand, yet, with low steady voice, confident and assuring, held the nervous young animals more by the will and the spirit of him.

It was no time for lingering. With the quick glance and foreknowledge of a woman, Saxon saw, not merely the curious children clustering about, but the peering of adult faces from open doors and windows and past window-shades lifted up or held aside. With his free hand, Billy drew back the linen robe and helped her to a place beside him. The high-backed, luxuriously upholstered seat of brown leather gave her a sense of great comfort; yet even greater, it seemed to her, were the nearness and comfort of the man himself and of his body.

"How d'ye like 'em?" he asked, changing the reins to both hands and chirruping to the horses, which went out with a jerk in an immediacy of action that was new to her. "They're the boss's, you know. Couldn't rent animals like them. He lets me take them out for exercise sometimes. If they ain't exercised regular they're a handful. Look at King, there, prancin'. Some style, eh? Some style! The other one's the real goods, though. Prince is his name. Got to have some bit on him to hold 'm. . . . Would you? Did you see 'm, Saxon? Some horse! Some horse!"

From behind came the admiring cheer of the neighborhood children, and Saxon, with a sigh of content, knew that the happy day had at last begun.

IX

"I don't know horses," Saxon said. "I've never been on one's back, and the only ones I've tried to drive were single, and lame, or almost falling down, or something. But I'm not afraid of horses. I just love them. I was born loving them, I guess."

Billy threw an admiring glance at her. "That's the stuff. That's what I like in a woman—grit. Some of the girls I've had out—well, take it from me, they made me sick. Oh, I'm hep to 'em. Nervous, an' trembly, an' screechy, an' wabbly. I reckon they come out on my account an' not for the ponies. But me for the brave kid that likes the ponies. You're the real goods, Saxon, honest to God you are. Why, I can talk like a streak with you. The rest of 'em make me sick. I'm like a clam. They don't know nothin', an' they're that scared all the time—well, I guess you get me."

"You have to be born to love horses, maybe," she answered. "Maybe it's because I always think of my father on his roan war-horse that makes me love horses. But, anyway, I do. When I was a little girl, I was drawing horses all the time. My mother always encouraged me. I've a scrapbook mostly filled with horses I drew when I was little. Do you know, Billy, sometimes I dream I actually own a horse, all my own. And lots of times I dream I'm on a horse's back, or driving him."

"I'll let you drive 'em, after a while, when they've worked their edge off. They're pullin' now. There, put your hands in front of mine—take hold tight. Feel that?

Sure you feel it. An' you ain't feelin' it all by a long shot. I don't dast slack, you bein' such a lightweight."

Her eyes sparkled as she felt the apportioned pull of the mouths of the beautiful, live things; and he, looking at her, sparkled with her in her delight.

"What's the good of a woman if she can't keep up with a man?" he broke out enthusiastically.

"People that like the same things always get along best together," she answered with a triteness that concealed the joy that was hers at being so spontaneously in touch with him.

"Why, Saxon, I've fought battles, good ones, frazzlin' my silk away to beat the band before whiskey-soaked, smokin' audiences of rotten fight-fans that just made me sick clean through. An' them, that couldn't take just one stiff jolt or hook to jaw or stomach, a-cheerin' me an' yellin' for blood. Blood, mind you! An' them without the blood of a shrimp in their bodies. Why, honest, now, I'd sooner fight before a audience of one—you, for instance, or anybody I liked. It'd do me proud. But them sickenin', sapheaded stiffs, with the grit of rabbits and the silk of mangy ki-yi's, a-cheerin' me —me! Can you blame me for quittin' the dirty game? Why, I'd sooner fight before broke-down old plugs of workhorses that's candidates for chicken-meat than before them rotten bunches of stiffs with nothin' thicker 'n water in their veins, an' Contra Costa water at that when the rains is heavy on the hills."

"I—I didn't know prize-fighting was like that," she faltered, as she released her hold on the lines and sank back again beside him.

"It ain't the fightin', it's the fight-crowds," he defended with instant jealousy. "Of course, fightin' hurts a young fellow because it frazzles the silk outa him an' all that. But it's the low-lifers in the audience that gets me. Why, the good things they say to me, the praise an' that, is insulting. Do you get me? It makes me cheap. Think of it!—booze-guzzlin' stiffs that'd be afraid to mix it with a sick cat, not fit to hold the coat of any decent man, think of them a-standin' up on their hind legs an' yellin' an' cheerin' me—me!

"Honest to God, Saxon, there's times when I've hated them, when I wanted to jump over the ropes and wade into them,

knock-down and drag out, an' show 'm what fightin' was. Take that night with Billy Murphy. Billy Murphy!—if you only knew him. My friend. As clean an' game a boy as ever jumped inside the ropes to take the decision. Him! We went to the Durant School together. We grew up chums. His fight was my fight. My trouble was his trouble. We both took to the fightin' game. They matched us. Not the first time. Twice we'd fought draws. Once the decision was his; once it was mine. The fifth fight of the two lovin' men that just loved each other. He's three years older'n me. He's a wife and two or three kids, an' I know them, too. And he's my friend. Get it?

"I'm ten pounds heavier, but with heavyweights that's all right. He can't time an' distance as good as me, an' I can keep set better, too. But he's cleverer an' quicker. I never was quick like him. We both can take punishment, an' we're both two-handed, a wallop in all our fists. I know the kick of his, an' he knows my kick, an' we're both real respectful. And we're even matched. Two draws and a decision to each. Honest, I ain't any kind of a hunch who's goin' to win, we're that even. Now, the fight. You ain't squeamish, are you?"

"No, no," she cried. "I'd just love to hear—you are so wonderful."

He took the praise with a clear unwavering look and without hint of acknowledgment. "We go along—six rounds, seven rounds, eight rounds; an' honors even. I've been timin' his rushes an' straight-leftin' him, an' meetin' his duck with a wicked little right upper-cut, an' he's shaken me on the jaw an' walloped my ears till my head's all singin' an' buzzin'. An' everything lovely with both of us, with a noise like a draw decision in sight. Twenty rounds is the distance, you know.

"An' then his bad luck comes. We're just mixin' into a clinch that ain't arrived yet, when he shoots a short hook to my head—his left, an' a real hay-maker if it reaches my jaw. I make a forward duck, not quick enough, an' he lands bingo on the side of my head. Honest to, Saxon, it's that heavy I see some stars. But it don't hurt an' ain't serious, that high up where the bone's thick. An' right there he finishes himself, for his bad thumb, which I've known since he first got it as a kid fightin'

DRAWN BY HOWARD CHANDLER CHRISTY

In her bedroom Saxon completed her dressing, for an instant stepping upon a chair so as to glimpse critically in the small wall-mirror the hang of her ready-made linen skirt

32

in the sand-lot at Watts Tract—he smashes that thumb right there, on my hard head, back into the socket with an out-twist, an' all the old cords that'd never got strong gets theirs again. I didn't mean it. A dirty trick, fair in the game, though, to make a guy smash his hand on your head. But not between friends. I couldn't 'a' done that to Billy Murphy for a million dollars. It was a accident, just because I was slow, because I was born slow.

"The hurt of it! Honest, Saxon, you don't know what hurt is till you've got a old hurt like that hurt again. What can Billy Murphy do but slow down? He's got to. He ain't fightin' two handed any more. He knows it; I know it; the referee knows it; but nobody else. He goes on a-moving that left of his like it's all right. But it ain't. It's hurtin' him like a knife dug into him. He don't dast strike a real blow with that left of his. But it hurts, anyway. Just to move it or not to move it, it hurts, an' every little dab-feint that I'm too wise to guard, knowin' there's no weight behind —why, them little dab-touches on that poor thumb goes right to the heart of him, an' hurts worse than a thousand boils or a thousand knockouts—just hurts all over again, an' worse, each time an' touch.

"He has to go easy now, an' I ain't a-forc-in' him none. I'm all shot to pieces. I don't know what to do. So I slow down, an' the fans get hep to it. 'Why don't you fight?' they begin to yell. 'Fake! Fake!' 'Why don't you kiss 'm?' 'Lovin'-cup for yours, Bill Roberts!' An' that sort of bunk.

"'Fight!' says the referee to me, low an' savage. 'Fight, or I'll disqualify you— you, Bill, I mean you.' An' this to me, with a touch on the shoulder so there's no mistakin'.

"'Quit,' I says to Billy Murphy in a clinch; 'for the love of God, Bill, quit.' An' he says back, in a whisper, 'I can't, Bill— you know that.'

"An' then the referee drags us apart. an' a lot of the fans begins to hoot an' boo.

"'Now kick in, Bill Roberts, an' finish 'm,' the referee says to me, an' I tell 'm to go to hell as Bill an' me flop into the next clinch, not hittin', an' Bill touches his thumb again, an' I see the pain, like a spasm, shoot across his face. Game? That good boy's the limit. An' to look into the eyes of a brave man that's sick with pain, an' love 'm, an' see love in them eyes of his, an'

then have to go on givin' 'm pain—call that sport? I can't see it. But the crowd's got its money on us. We don't count. We've sold ourselves, for a hundred bucks, an' we got to deliver the goods.

"Let me tell you, Saxon, honest to God, that was one of the times I wanted to go through the ropes an' drop them fans a-yell-in' for blood an' show 'em what blood is.

"'For God's sake finish me, Bill,' Bill says to me in that clinch; 'put her over an' I'll fall for it, but I can't lay down.'

"D'ye want to know? I cry there, right in the ring, in that clinch. The weeps for me. 'I can't do it, Bill,' I whisper back, hangin' onto 'm like a brother an' the ref-eree ragin' an' draggin' at us to get us apart, an' all the wolves in the house snarlin'.

"'You got 'm!' the audience is yellin'. 'Go in an' finish 'm!' 'The hay for him, Bill; put her across to the jaw an' see 'm fall!'

"'You got to, Bill, or you're a dog,' Bill says, lookin' love at me in his eyes as the referee's grip untangles us clear.

"An' them wolves of fans yellin': 'Fake! Fake! Fake!' like that, an' keepin' it up.

"Well, I done it. There's only that way out. I done it. I had to. I feint for 'm, draw his left, duck to the right past it, takin' it across my shoulder, an' come up with my right to his jaw. An' he knows the trick. He's hep. He's beaten me to it an' blocked it with his shoulder a thousand times. But this time he don't. He keeps himself wide open on purpose. Blim! It lands. He's dead in the air, an' he goes down sideways, strikin' his face first on the rosin canvas an' then layin' dead, his head twisted under 'm till you'd a-thought his neck was broke. *Me*—I did that for a hundred bucks an' a bunch of stiffs I'd be ashamed to wipe my feet on. An' then I pick Bill up in my arms an' carry 'm to his corner, an' help bring 'm around. Well, there ain't no kick comin'. They pay their money an' they get their blood, an' a knockout. An' a better man than them, that I love, layin' there dead to the world with a skinned face, on the mat."

For a moment Billy was still, gazing straight before him at the horses, his face hard and angry. He sighed, looked at Saxon, and smiled.

"An' I quit the game right there. An' Billy Murphy's laughed at me for it. He still follows it—a side-line, you know, be-cause he works at a good trade. But once in a while, when the house needs paintin' or the doctor-bills are up, or his oldest kid wants a bicycle, he jumps out an' makes fifty or a hundred bucks before some of the clubs. I want you to meet him when it comes handy. He's some boy, I'm tellin' you. But it did make me sick that night."

Again the harshness and anger were in his face, and Saxon amazed herself by doing unconsciously what women higher in the social scale have done with deliberate sincerity. Her hand went out impulsively to his holding the lines, resting on top of it for a moment with quick firm pressure. Her reward was a smile from lips and eyes, as his face turned toward her.

"Gee!" he exclaimed. "I never talk a streak like this to anybody. I just hold my hush an' keep my thinks to myself. But somehow, I guess it's funny, I kind of have a feelin' I want to make good with you. An' that's why I'm tellin' you my thinks. Anybody can dance."

The way led up-town, past the City Hall and the Fourteenth Street skyscrapers, and out Broadway to Mountain View. Turning to the right at the cemetery, they climbed the Piedmont Heights to Blair Park and plunged into the green coolness of Jack Hays Canyon. Saxon could not suppress her surprise and joy at the quickness with which they covered the ground.

"They are beautiful," she said. "I never dreamed I'd ever ride behind horses like them. I'm afraid I'll wake up now and find it's a dream. You know, I dream horses all the time. I'd give anything to own one some time."

"It's funny, ain't it?" Billy answered. "I like horses that way. The boss says I'm a wooz at horses. An' I know he's a dub. He don't know the first thing. An' yet he owns two hundred big heavy drafts, besides this light drivin' pair, an' I don't own one."

Saxon laughed appreciatively. "I just love fancy shirt-waists, an' I spend my life ironing some of the beautifulest I've ever seen. It's funny, an' it isn't fair."

Billy gritted his teeth in another of his rages. "An' the way some of them women gets their shirt-waists. It makes me sick, thinkin' of you ironin' 'em. You know what I mean, Saxon. They ain't no use wastin' words over it. You know. I know. Everybody knows. An' it's a queer world if men an' women sometimes can't talk

to each other about such things." His manner was almost apologetic, yet it was defiantly and assertively right. "I never talk this way to other girls. They'd think I'm workin' up to designs on 'em. They make me sick the way they're always lookin' for them designs. But you're different. I can talk to you that way. I know I've got to. It's the square thing. You're like Billy Murphy, or any other man a man can talk to."

She sighed with a great happiness, and looked at him with unconscious, love-shining eyes. "It's the same way with me," she said. "The fellows I've run with I've never dared let talk about such things, because I knew they'd take advantage of it. Why, all the time, with them, I've a feeling that we're cheating and lying to each other, playing a game like a masquerade ball." She paused for a moment, hesitant and debating, then went on in a queer low brave voice: "I haven't been asleep. I've seen— and heard. I've had my chances, when I was that tired of the laundry I'd have done almost anything. I could have got those fancy shirt-waists—an' all the rest—and maybe a horse to ride. There was a bank-cashier—married, too, if you please. He talked to me straight out. I didn't count, you know. I wasn't a girl, with a girl's feelings, or anything. I was nobody. It was just like a business talk. I learned about men from him. He told me what he'd do. He—" Her voice died away in voiceless sadness, and in the silence she could hear Billy grit his teeth.

"You can't tell me," he cried. "I know. It's a dirty world. I can't make it out. They's no squareness in it. Women, with the best that's in 'em, bought an' sold like horses. I don't understand women that way. I don't understand men that way. I can't see how a man gets anything but cheated when he buys such things. It's funny, ain't it? Take my boss an' his horses. He owns, women, too. Why should he own two hundred horses, an' women, an' the rest, an' you an' me own nothin'?"

"You own your silk, Billy," she said.

"An' you yours. Yet we sell it to 'm like it was cloth across the counter at so much a yard. I guess you're hep to what a few more years in the laundry'll do to you. Take me; I'm sellin' my silk slow every day I work. See that little finger?" He shifted the reins to one hand for a moment and held up the free hand for inspection. "I can't straighten it like the others, an' it's a-growin'. I never put it out fightin'. The teamin's done it. That's silk gone across the counter, that's all. Ever see a old four-horse teamster's hands? They look like claws, they're that crippled an' twisted."

"Things weren't like that in the old days when our folks crossed the plains," she answered. "They might 'a' got their fingers twisted, but they owned the best goin' in the way of horses and such."

"Sure. They worked for themselves. They twisted their fingers for themselves. But I'm twistin' my fingers for my boss. Why, d'ye know, Saxon, his hands is soft as a woman's that's never done any work. Yet he owns the horses an' the stables, an' never does a tap of work, an' I manage to scratch my meal-ticket an' my clothes. It's got my goat the way things is run. An' who runs 'em that way? That's what I want to know. Times has changed. Who changed 'em?"

"God didn't."

"You bet your life he didn't. An' that's another thing that gets me. Who's God, anyway? If he's runnin' things—an' what good is he if he ain't?—then why does he let my boss, an' men like that cashier you mentioned—why does he let them own the horses, an' buy the women, the nice little girls that ought to be lovin' their own husbands, an' havin' children they're not ashamed of, an' just bein' happy accordin' to their nature?"

X

THE horses, resting frequently and lathered by the work, had climbed the steep grade of the old road to Moraga Valley, and on the divide of the Contra Costa hills the way descended sharply through the green and sunny stillness of Redwood Canyon.

"Say, ain't it swell?" Billy queried, with a wave of his hand indicating the circled tree-groups, the trickle of unseen water, and the summer hum of bees.

"I love it," Saxon affirmed. "It makes me want to live in the country, and I never have."

"Me, too, Saxon. I've never lived in the country in my life—an' all my folks was country folks."

"No cities then. Everybody lived in the country."

"I guess you're right," he nodded. "They just had to live in the country."

There was no brake on the light carriage, and Billy became absorbed in managing his team down the steep, winding road. Saxon leaned back, eyes closed, with a feeling of ineffable rest. Time and again he shot glances at her closed eyes.

"What's the matter?" he asked finally, in mild alarm. "You ain't sick?"

"It's so beautiful I'm afraid to look," she answered. "It's so brave it hurts."

"Brave? Now that's funny."

"Isn't it? But it just makes me feel that way. It's brave. Now the houses and streets and things in the city aren't brave. But this is. I don't know why. It just is."

"By golly, I think you're right," he acclaimed. "It strikes me that way, now you speak of it. They ain't no games or tricks here, no cheatin' an' no lyin'. Them trees just stand up natural an' strong an' clean like young boys their first time in the ring before they've learned its rottenness an' how to double-cross an' lay down to the bettin' odds an' the fight-fans. Yep; it is brave. Say, Saxon, you see things, don't you?" His pause was almost wistful, and he looked at her and studied her with a caressing softness that ran through her in resurgent thrills.

A little later, swinging along the flat of the valley, through the little clearings of the farmers and the ripe grain-stretches golden in the sunshine, Billy turned to Saxon again. "Say, you've been in love with fellows, lots of times. Tell me about it. What's it like?"

She shook her head slowly. "I only thought I was in love—and not many times, either."

"Many times!" he cried.

"Not really ever," she assured him, secretly exultant at his unconscious jealousy. "I never was really in love. If I had been I'd be married now. You see, I couldn't see anything else to it but to marry a man if I loved him."

"But suppose he didn't love you?"

"Oh, I don't know," she smiled, half with facetiousness and half with certainty and pride. "I think I could make him love me."

"I guess you sure could," Billy proclaimed enthusiastically.

"The trouble is," she went on, "the men that loved me I never cared for that way. Oh, look!"

A cottontail rabbit had scuttled across the road, and a tiny dust-cloud lingered like smoke, marking the way of his flight. At the next turn a dozen quail exploded into the air from under the noses of the horses. Billy and Saxon exclaimed in mutual delight.

"Gee!" he muttered, "I almost wisht I'd been born a farmer. Folks wasn't made to live in cities."

"Not our kind, at least," she agreed. Followed a pause and a long sigh. "It's all so beautiful. It would be a dream just to live all your life in it. I'd like to be an Indian squaw sometimes."

Several times Billy checked himself on the verge of speech. "About those fellows you thought you was in love with," he said finally. "You ain't told me, yet."

"You want to know?" she asked. "They didn't amount to anything."

"Of course I want to know. Go ahead. Fire away."

"Well, first there was Al Stanley."

"What did he do for a livin'?" Billy demanded, almost as with authority.

"He was a gambler."

Billy's face abruptly stiffened, and she could see his eyes cloudy with doubt in the quick glance he flung at her.

"Oh, it was all right," she laughed. "I was only eight years old. You see, I'm beginning at the beginning. It was after my mother died and when I was adopted by Cady. He kept a hotel and saloon. It was down in Los Angeles. Just a small hotel. Workingmen, just common laborers, mostly, and some railroad men, stopped at it, and I guess Al Stanley got his share of their wages. He was so handsome and so quiet and soft-spoken. And he had the nicest eyes and the softest, cleanest hands. I can see them now. He played with me sometimes, in the afternoon, and gave me candy and little presents. He used to sleep most of the day. I didn't know why, then. I thought he was a fairy prince in disguise. And then he got killed, right in the barroom, but first he killed the man that killed him. So that was the end of that love affair.

"Next was after the asylum, when I was thirteen and living with my brother—I've lived with him ever since. He was a boy that drove a bakery-wagon. Almost every morning, on the way to school, I used to pass him. He would come driving down Wood Street and turn in on Twelfth. Maybe it was because he drove a horse that attracted me. Anyway, I must have loved

him for a couple of months. Then he lost his job, or something, for another boy drove the wagon. And we'd never even spoken to each other.

"Then there was a bookkeeper when I was sixteen. I seem to run to bookkeepers. It was a bookkeeper at the laundry that Charley Long beat up. This other one was when I was working in Hickmeyer's cannery. He had soft hands, too. But I quickly got all I wanted of him. He was—well, anyway, he had ideas like your boss. And I never really did love him, truly and honest, Billy. I felt from the first that he wasn't just right. And when I was working in the paper-box factory I thought I loved a clerk in Kahn's shoe-store—you know, on Eleventh and Washington. He was all right. That was the trouble with him. He was too much all right. He didn't have any life in him, any go. He wanted to marry me, though. But somehow I couldn't see it. That shows I didn't love him.

"And after that—well, there isn't any after that. I must have got particular, I guess, but I didn't see anybody I could love. It seemed more like a game with the men I met, or a fight. And we never fought fair on either side. Seemed as if we always had cards up our sleeves. We weren't honest or outspoken, but instead it seemed as if we were trying to take advantage of each other. Charley Long was honest, though. And so was that bank cashier. And even they made me have the fight feeling harder than ever. All of them always made me feel I had to take care of myself. They wouldn't. That was sure."

She stopped and looked with interest at the clean profile of Billy's face as he watched and guided the horses. He looked at her inquiringly, and her eyes laughed lazily into his as she stretched her arms.

"That's all," she concluded. "I've told you everything, which I've never done before to anyone. And it's your turn now."

"Not much of a turn, Saxon. I've never cared for girls—that is, not enough to want to marry 'em. I always liked men better—fellows like Billy Murphy. Besides, I guess I was too interested in trainin' an' fightin' to bother with women much. Why, Saxon, honest, while I ain't been altogether good—you understand what I mean—just the same I ain't never talked love to a girl in my life. They was no call to."

"The girls have loved you just the same,"

she teased, while in her heart was a curious elation at his virginal confession.

He devoted himself to the horses.

"Lots of them," she urged.

Still he did not reply.

"Now, haven't they?"

"Well, it wasn't my fault," he said slowly. "If they wanted to look sideways at me it was up to them. And it was up to me to sidestep if I wanted to, wasn't it? You've no idea, Saxon, how a prize-fighter is run after. Why, sometimes it's seemed to me that girls an' women ain't got an ounce of natural shame in their make-up. Oh, I was never afraid of them, believe muh, but I didn't hanker after 'em. A man's a fool that'd let them kind get his goat."

"Maybe you haven't got love in you," she challenged.

"Maybe I haven't," was his discouraging reply. "Anyway, I don't see myself lovin' a girl that runs after me. It's all right for Charley-boys, but a man that is a man don't like bein' chased by women."

At one o'clock Billy turned off the road and drove into an open space among the trees. "Here's where we eat," he announced. "I thought it'd be better to have a lunch by ourselves than to stop at one of these roadside dinner-counters. An' now, just to make everything safe an' comfortable, I'm goin' to unharness the horses. We got lots of time. You can get the lunch-basket out an' spread it on the lap-robe."

As Saxon unpacked the basket she was appalled at his extravagance. It had the appearance of a reckless attempt to buy out a whole delicatessen-shop.

"You oughtn't to blow yourself that way," she reproved him as he sat down beside her. "Why, it's enough for half a dozen bricklayers."

"It's all right, isn't it?"

"Yes," she acknowledged. "But that's the trouble. It's too much so."

"Then it's all right," he concluded. "I always believe in havin' plenty.

Later, the meal finished, he lay on his back, smoking a cigarette, and questioned her about her earlier history. She had been telling him of her life in her brother's house, where she paid four dollars and a half a week board. At fifteen she had graduated from grammar school and gone to work in the jute-mills for four dollars a week, three of which she had paid to Sarah.

"How about that saloon-keeper?" Billy asked. "How came it he adopted you?"

She shrugged her shoulders. "I don't know, except that all my relatives were hard up. It seemed they just couldn't get on. They managed to scratch a lean living for themselves, and that was all. Cady— he was the saloon-keeper—had been a soldier in my father's company, and he always swore by Captain Kit, which was their nickname for him. My father had kept the surgeons from amputating his leg in the war, and he never forgot it. He was making money in the hotel and saloon, and I found out afterward he helped out a lot to pay the doctors and to bury my mother alongside of father. I was to go to Uncle Will—that was my mother's wish; but there had been fighting up in the Ventura Mountains where his ranch was, and men had been killed. It was about fences and cattlemen or something, and anyway he was in jail a long time, and when he got his freedom the lawyers had got his ranch. He was an old man, then, and broken, and his wife took sick, and he got a job as night watchman for forty dollars a month. So he couldn't do anything for me, and Cady adopted me.

"Cady was a good man, if he did run a saloon. His wife was a big, handsome-looking woman. I don't think she was all right—and I've heard so since. But she was good to me. I don't care what they say about her, or what she was. She was awful good to me. After he died, she went altogether bad, and so I went into the orphan-asylum. It wasn't any too good there, and I had three years of it. And then Tom had married and settled down to steady work, and he took me out to live with him. And— well, I've been working pretty steady ever since."

She gazed sadly away across the fields until her eyes came to rest on a fence bright splashed with poppies at its base. Billy, who from his supine position had been looking up at her, studying and pleasuring in the pointed oval of her woman's face, reached his hand out slowly as he murmured,

"You poor little kid." ·

His hand closed sympathetically on her bare forearm, and as she looked down to greet his eyes she saw in them surprise and delight.

"Say, ain't your skin cool though," he said. "Now me, I'm always warm. Feel my hand."

DRAWN BY HOWARD CHANDLER CHRISTY

As Saxon unpacked the basket she was appalled at Billy's extravagance. It had the appearance of a reckless
"Why, it's enough for half a dozen bricklayers." "It's all right, isn't it?" "Yes," she acknowledged. "But

attempt to buy out a whole delicatessen-shop. "You oughtn't to blow yourself that way," she reproved him. "that's the trouble. It's too much so." "Then it's all right," he concluded. "I always believe in havin' plenty"

It was warmly moist, and she noted microscopic beads of sweat on his forehead and clean-shaven upper lip.

"My, but you are sweaty."

She bent to him and with her handkerchief dabbed his lip and forehead dry, then dried his palms.

"I breathe through my skin, I guess," he explained. "The wise guys in the trainin'-camps and gyms say it's a good sign for health. But somehow I'm sweatin' more than usual now. Funny, ain't it?"

She had been forced to unclasp his hand from her arm in order to dry it, and, when she finished, it returned to its old position.

"But say, ain't your skin cool!" he repeated with renewed wonder. "Soft as velvet, too, an' smooth as silk. It feels great."

Gently explorative he slid his hand from wrist to elbow and came to rest half-way back. Tired and languid from the morning in the sun, she found herself thrilling to his touch and half-dreamily deciding that here was a man she could love, hands and all.

"Now I've taken the cool all out of that spot." He did not look up to her, but she could see the roguish smile that curled on his lips. "So I guess I'll try another."

He shifted his hand along her arm with soft sensuousness, and she, looking down at his lips, remembered the long tingling they had given hers the first time they had met.

"Go on and talk," he urged, after a delicious five minutes of silence. "I like to watch your lips talking. It's funny, but every move they make looks like a tickly kiss."

Greatly she wanted to stay where she was. Instead, she said,

"If I talk, you won't like what I say."

"Go on," he insisted. "You can't say anything I won't like."

"Well, there's some poppies over there by the fence I want to pick. And then it's time for us to be going."

"I lose," he laughed. "But you made twenty-five tickly kisses just the same. I counted 'em. I'll tell you what: you sing, 'When the Harvest Days are Over,' and let me have your other cool arm while you're doin' it, and then we'll go."

She sang looking down into his eyes, which were centered, not on hers, but on her lips. When she finished, she slipped his hands from her arms and got up. He was about to start for the horses, when she held her jacket out to him. Despite the independence natural to a girl who earned her own living, she had an innate love of the little services and finenesses; and, also, she remembered from her childhood the talk by the pioneer women of the courtesy and attendance of the caballeros of the Spanish-California days.

Sunset greeted them when, after a wide circle to the east and south, they cleared the divide of the Contra Costa hills and began dropping down the long grade that led past Redwood Peak to Fruitvale. Beneath them stretched the flatlands to the bay, checker-boarded into fields and broken by the towns of Elmhurst, San Leandro, and Haywards. The smoke of Oakland filled the western sky with haze and murk, while beyond, across the bay, they could see the first winking lights of San Francisco.

Darkness was on them, and Billy had become curiously silent. For half an hour he had given no recognition of her existence save once, when the chill evening wind caused him to tuck the robe tightly about her and himself. Half a dozen times Saxon found herself on the verge of the remark, "What's on your mind?" but each time let it remain unuttered. She sat very close to him, aware of a great restfulness and content.

"Say, Saxon," he began abruptly. "It's no use my holdin' it in any longer. It's been in my mouth all day, ever since lunch. What's the matter with you an' me gettin' married?"

She knew, very quietly and very gladly, that he meant it. Instinctively she was impelled to hold off, to make him woo her, to make herself more desirably valuable ere she yielded. Further, her woman's sensitiveness and pride were offended. She had never dreamed of so forthright and bald a proposal from the man to whom she would give herself. The simplicity and directness of Billy's proposal constituted almost a hurt. On the other hand, she wanted him so much—how much she had not realized until now, when he had so unexpectedly made himself accessible.

"Well, you gotta say something, Saxon. Hand it to me, good or bad; but anyway hand it to me. An' just take into consideration that I love you. Why, I love you like the very devil, Saxon. I must, because I'm askin' you to marry me, an' I never asked any girl that before."

Another silence fell, then "How old are you, Billy?" she questioned, with a suddenness and irrelevance as disconcerting as his first words had been.

"Twenty-two," he answered.

"I am twenty-four."

"As if I didn't know. When you left the orphan asylum and how old you were, how long you worked in the jute-mills, the cannery, the paper-box factory, the laundry—maybe you think I can't do addition. I knew how old you was, even to your birthday."

"That doesn't change the fact that I'm two years older."

"What of it? If it counted for anything, I wouldn't be lovin' you, would I? Love's what counts. Don't you see? I just love you, an' I gotta have you. It's natural, I guess; and I've always found with horses, dogs, and other folks, that what's natural is right. There's no gettin' away from it, Saxon; I gotta have you, an' I'm just hopin' hard you gotta have me. Maybe my hands ain't soft like bookkeepers' an' clerks', but they can work for you, an' fight like Sam Hill for you, and, Saxon, they can love you."

The old sex antagonism which she had always experienced with men seemed to have vanished. She had no sense of being on the defensive. This was no game. It was what she had been looking for and dreaming about. Before Billy she was defenseless, and there was an all-satisfaction in the knowledge. She could deny him nothing. Not even if he proved to be like the others. And out of the greatness of the thought arose a greater thought—he would not so prove himself.

She did not speak. Instead, in a glow of spirit and flesh, she reached out to his left hand and gently tried to remove it from the rein. He did not understand; but when she persisted he shifted the rein to his right and let her have her will with the other hand. Her head bent over it, and she kissed the teamster callouses.

For the moment he was stunned. "You mean it?" he stammered.

For reply, she kissed the hand again and murmured: "I love your hands, Billy. To me they are the most beautiful hands in the world, and it would take hours of talking to tell you all they mean to me."

"Whoa!" he called to the horses.

He pulled them in to a standstill, soothed them with his voice, and made the reins fast around the whip. Then he turned to her with arms around her and lips to lips.

"Oh, Billy, I'll make you a good wife," she sobbed, when the kiss was broken.

He kissed her wet eyes and found her lips again. "Now you know what I was thinkin' and why I was sweatin' when we was eatin' lunch. Just seemed I couldn't hold in much longer from tellin' you. Why, you know, you looked good to me from the first moment I spotted you."

"And I think I loved you from that first day, too, Billy. And I was so proud of you all that day, you were so kind and gentle, and so strong, and the way the men all respected you and the girls all wanted you. I couldn't love or marry a man I wasn't proud of, and I'm proud of you, so proud."

"Not half as much as I am right now of myself," he answered, "for having won you. It's too good to be true. Maybe the alarm-clock'll go off and wake me up in a couple of minutes. Well, anyway, if it does, I'm goin' to make the best of them two minutes first. Watch out I don't eat you, I'm that hungry for you."

He smothered her in an embrace, holding her so tightly to him that it almost hurt. After what was to her an age-long period of bliss, his arms relaxed and he seemed to make an effort to draw himself together.

"An' the clock ain't gone off yet," he whispered against her cheek. "and it's a dark night, an' there's Fruitvale right ahead, an' if there ain't King and Prince standin' still in the middle of the road. I never thought the time'd come when I wouldn't want to take the ribbons on a fine pair of horses. But this is that time. I just can't let go of you, and I've gotta some time to-night. It hurts worse 'n poison, but here goes."

He restored her to herself, tucked the disarranged robe about her, and chirruped to the impatient team.

Half an hour later he called: "Whoa! I know I'm awake now, but I don't know but maybe I dreamed all the rest, and I just want to make sure."

And again he made the reins fast and took her in his arms.

<h1 style="text-align:center">XI</h1>

THE days flew by for Saxon. She worked on steadily at the laundry, even doing more overtime than usual, and all her free waking hours were devoted to preparations for the great change and to Billy. He had proved himself God's own impetuous lover by insisting on getting married the next day after the proposal, and then by resolutely refusing to compromise on more than a week's delay.

"Why wait?" he demanded. "We're not gettin' any younger so far as I can notice, an' think of all we lose every day we wait."

In the end, he gave in to a month, which was well, for in two weeks he was transferred, with half a dozen other drivers, to work from the big stables of Corberly and Morrison in West Oakland. House-hunting in the other end of town ceased, and on Pine Street, between Fifth and Fourth, and in immediate proximity to the great Southern Pacific railroad yards, Billy and Saxon rented a neat cottage of four small rooms for ten dollars a month.

"Dog-cheap is what I call it, when I think of the small rooms I've been soaked for," was Billy's judgment. "Look at the one I got now, not as big as the smallest here, an' me payin' six dollars a month for it."

"But it's furnished," Saxon reminded him. "You see, that makes a difference."

But Billy didn't see. "I ain't much of a scholar, Saxon, but I know simple arithmetic; I've soaked my watch when I was hard up, and I can calculate interest. How much do you figure it will cost to furnish the house, carpets on the floor, linoleum in the kitchen, and all?"

"We can do it nicely for three hundred dollars," she answered. "I've been thinking it over, and I'm sure we can do it for that."

"Three hundred," he muttered, wrinkling his brows with concentration. "Three hundred, say at six per cent.—that'd be six cents on the dollar, sixty cents on ten dollars, six dollars on the hundred, on three hundred eighteen dollars. Say, I'm a bear at multiplyin' by ten. Now divide eighteen by twelve, that'd be a dollar an' a half a month interest." He stopped, satisfied that he had proved his contention. Then his face quickened with a fresh thought. "Hold on! That ain't all. That'd be the interest on the furniture for four rooms. Divide by four. What's a dollar an' a half divided by four?"

"Four into fifteen, three times and three to carry," Saxon recited glibly. "Four into thirty is seven, twenty-eight, two to carry;

and two-fourths is one-half. There you are."

"Gee! You're the real bear at figures." He hesitated. "I didn't follow you. How much did you say it was?"

"Thirty-seven and a half cents."

"Ah, ha! Now we'll see how much I've been gouged for my one room. Ten dollars a month for four rooms is two an' a half for one. Add thirty-seven an' a half cents interest on furniture, an' that makes two dollars an' eighty-seven.an' a half cents. Subtract from six dollars—"

"Three dollars and twelve and a half cents," Saxon supplied quickly.

"There we are! Three dollars an' twelve an' a half cents I'm jiggered out of on the room I'm rentin'. Say! Bein' married is like savin' money, ain't it, eh?"

"But furniture wears out, Billy."

"By golly, I never thought of that. It ought to be figured, too. Anyway, we've got a snap here, and next Saturday afternoon you've gotta get off from the laundry so's we can go an' buy our furniture. I saw Salinger's last night. I give 'm fifty down, and the rest instalment plan, ten dollars a month. In twenty-five months the furniture's ourn. An' remember, Saxon, you wanta buy everything you want, no matter how much it costs. No scrimpin' on what's for you an' me. Get me?"

She nodded, with no betrayal on her face of the myriad secret economies that filled her mind. A hint of moisture glistened in her eyes. "You're so good to me, Billy," she murmured as she came to him and was met inside his arms.

"So you've gone an' done it," Mary commented, one morning in the laundry. They had not been at work ten minutes ere her eye had glimpsed the topaz ring on the third finger of Saxon's left hand. "Who's the lucky one? Charley Long or Billy Roberts?"

"Billy," was the answer.

"Huh! Takin' a young boy to raise, eh?"

Saxon showed that the stab had gone home, and Mary was all contrition.

"Can't you take a josh? I'm glad 'to death at the news. Billy's a awful good man, and I'm glad to see you get him. There ain't many like him knockin' 'round, an' they ain't to be had for the askin'. An' you're both lucky. You was just made for each other, an' you'll make him a better wife than any girl I know. When is it to be?"

The Valley of the Moon

THE STORY OF A FIGHT AGAINST ODDS FOR LOVE AND A HOME

By Jack London

Author of "Martin Eden," "Burning Daylight," "Smoke Bellew," etc.

Illustrated by Howard Chandler Christy

SYNOPSIS: Is this the man? So Saxon questioned of herself when she had met "Big Bill" Roberts, one-time prize-fighter, on the dancing-floor at Weasel Park, whither she and Mary, ironers of fancy starch, had gone for a Sunday outing. Never had she come so near to losing her heart as Billy, blue eyed, boyish, gentlemanly, had come to winning it after a few hours' acquaintance. Planned by Mary and Bert Wanhope, the meeting had taken a happy turn, for both Saxon and Billy had seized the future in the present and grasped at its chance for happiness. Billy was a teamster and knew what hard work meant, so they went home early, Saxon glorying in his refusal to "make a time of it," as Bert suggested. He kissed her good night at the gate, with Wednesday night's dance as their next meeting. Friday's dance was next arranged for, but on Thursday night Charley Long, a rebuffed suitor, met her outside the laundry and warned her that if she did not go with him "somebody'll get hurt." But Saxon bore the notion that Billy, at least, could take care of himself.

Billy did, and Saxon experienced the delightful sensation of knowing that this big boy cared enough for her to risk a fight—which wasn't needed. Billy next proposed a Sunday buggy-ride. They drove out of the city behind a spirited team, Saxon glad to get away from the abuse which Sarah, her sister-in-law, had heaped upon her because she preferred Billy, a prize-fighter, to Charley Long, an honest laboring man. Home cares were soon forgotten as they drove into the hills, each happy in the first true comradeship ever experienced with one of the opposite sex. In the hills they ate a luncheon provided by Billy, and then lingered until warnings of dusk urged them homeward. Darkness overtook them—and silence. Then out of it came Billy's frank proposal, and Saxon, countering only with the objection that she was the older—an objection overruled by Billy's statement that "Love's what counts"—accepted him. Billy wanted to be married the next day, but Saxon put him off for a month—a month that, crowded with preparations, flew by on wings of happiness.

SARAH was conservative. Worse, she had crystallized at the end of her love-time with the coming of her first child. After that she was as set in her ways as plaster in a mold. Her mold was the prejudices and notions of her girlhood and the house she lived in. So habitual was she that any change in the customary round assumed the proportions of a revolution. Tom had gone through many of these revolutions, three of them when he moved house. Then his stamina broke, and he never moved house again.

So it was that Saxon had held back the announcement of her approaching marriage until it was unavoidable. She expected a scene, and she got it.

"A prize-fighter, a hoodlum, a plug-ugly," Sarah sneered, after she had exhausted herself of all calamitous forecasts of her own future and the future of her children in the absence of Saxon's weekly four dollars and a half. "I don't know what your mother'd thought if she'd lived to see the day when you took up with a tough like Bill Roberts. Bill! Why, your mother was too refined to associate with a man that was called Bill. And all I can say is you can say good-by to silk stockings and your three pairs of shoes. It won't be long before you'll think yourself lucky to go sloppin' around in Congress gaiters and cotton stockin's two pair for a quarter."

"Oh, I'm not afraid of Billy not being able to keep me in all kinds of shoes," Saxon retorted with a proud toss of her head.

"You don't know what you're talkin' about." Sarah paused to laugh in mirthless discordance. "Watch for the babies to come. They come faster than wages raise these days."

"But we're not going to have any babies —that is, at first. Not until after the furniture is all paid for, anyway."

"Wise in your generation, eh? In my days girls were more modest than to know anything about disgraceful subjects."

"As babies?" Saxon queried, with a touch of gentle malice.

"Yes, as babies."

"The first I knew that babies were disgraceful. Why, Sarah, you, with your five, how disgraceful you have been. Billy and I have decided not to be half as disgraceful. We're only going to have two—a boy and a girl."

Tom chuckled, but held the peace by hiding his face in his coffee-cup. Sarah, though checked by this flank attack, was an old hand in the art. So temporary was the setback that she scarcely paused ere hurling her assault from a new angle.

"An' marryin' so quick, all of a sudden, eh? If that ain't suspicious, nothin' is. I don't know what young women's comin' to. They ain't decent, I tell you. They ain't

43

decent. That's what comes of Sunday dancin' an' all the rest."

Saxon was white with anger, but while Sarah wandered on in her diatribe, Tom managed to wink privily and prodigiously at his sister and to implore her to help in keeping the peace.

"It's all right, kid sister," he comforted Saxon when they were alone. "There's no use talkin' to Sarah. Bill Roberts is a good boy. I know a lot about him. It does you proud to get him for a husband. You're bound to be happy with him." His voice sank, and his face seemed suddenly to be very old and tired as he went on anxiously: "Take warning from Sarah. Don't nag. Whatever you do, don't nag. Don't give him a perpetual-motion line of chin. Kind of let him talk once in a while. Men have some horse-sense, though Sarah don't know it. Why, Sarah actually loves me, though she don't make a noise like it. The thing for you is to love your husband, and, by thunder, to make a noise of lovin' him, too. And then you can kid him into doing 'most anything you want. Let him have his way once in a while, and he'll let you have yourn. But you just go on lovin' him, and leanin' on his judgment—he's no fool—and you'll be all hunky-dory. I'm scared from goin' wrong, what of Sarah. But I'd sooner be loved into not going wrong."

"Oh, I'll do it, Tom," Saxon nodded, smiling through the tears his sympathy had brought into her eyes. "And on top of it I'm going to do something else. I'm going to make Billy love me and just keep on loving me. And then I won't have to kid him into doing some of the things I want. He'll do them because he loves me, you see."

"You got the right idea, Saxon. Stick with it, an' you'll win out."

Later, when she had put on her hat to start for the laundry, she found Tom waiting for her at the corner.

"An' Saxon," he said, hastily and haltingly, "you won't take anything I've said—you know—about Sarah—as bein' in any way disloyal to her? She's a good woman, an' faithful. An' her life ain't so easy by a long shot. I'd bite out my tongue before I'd say anything against her. I guess all folks have their troubles. It's hell to be poor, ain't it?"

"You've been awful good to me, Tom. I can never forget it. And I know Sarah means right. She does her best."

"I won't be able to give you a wedding present," her brother ventured apologetically. "Sarah won't hear of it. Says we didn't get none from my folks when we got married. But I got something for you, just the same. A surprise. You'd never guess it."

Saxon waited.

"When you told me you was goin' to get married, I just happened to think of it, an' I wrote to brother George, askin' him for it for you. An' by thunder he sent it by express. I didn't tell you because I didn't know but maybe he'd sold it. He did sell the silver spurs. He needed the money, I guess. But the other, I had it sent to the shop so as not to bother Sarah, an' I sneaked it in last night an' hid it in the woodshed."

"Oh, it is something of my father's! What is it? Oh, what is it?"

"His army sword."

"The one he wore on his roan war-horse! Oh, Tom, you couldn't give me a better present. Let's go back now. I want to see it. We can slip in the back way. Sarah's washing in the kitchen, and she won't begin hanging out for an hour."

In the woodshed Tom resurrected the hidden treasure and took off the wrapping-paper. Appeared a rusty, steel-scabbarded saber of the heavy type carried by cavalry officers in Civil War days. It was attached to a moth-eaten sash of thick-woven crimson silk from which hung heavy silk tassels. Saxon almost seized it from her brother in her eagerness—then she drew forth the blade and pressed her lips to the steel.

XIII

"WHY, Bert! you're squiffed!" Mary cried reproachfully.

The four were at the table in the private room at Barnum's. The wedding supper had been eaten. Bert, in his hand a glass of California red wine, was on his feet endeavoring a speech. His face was flushed; his black eyes were feverishly bright.

"You've been drinkin' before you met me," Mary continued. "I can see it stickin' out all over you."

"Consult an oculist, my dear," he replied. "Bertram is himself to-night. An' he is here, a-risin' to his feet to give the glad hand to his old pal. Bill, old man, here's to you. It's how-de-do an' good-by, I guess. You're a married man now, Bill, an' you got to keep regular hours. No more runnin' around with the boys."

His glittering eyes rested for a moment in bantering triumph on Mary.

"Who says I'm squiffed? Me? Not on your life. I'm seein' all things in a clear white light. An I see Bill there, my old friend Bill. An' I don't see two Bills. I see only one. Bill was never two-faced in his life. Bill, old man, when I look at you there in the married harness, I'm sorry." He ceased abruptly and turned on Mary. "Now don't go up in the air, old girl. I'm onto my job My grandfather was a state senator, and he could spiel graceful an' pleasin' till the cows come home. So can I. Bill, when I look at you, I'm sorry. I repeat, I'm sorry"—he glared challengingly at Mary—"for myself when I look at you an' know all the happiness you got a hammerlock on. Take it from me, you're a wise guy, bless the women. You've started well. Keep it up. Marry 'em all, bless 'em. Bill, here's to you. You're a Mohican with a scalp-lock. An' you got a squaw that is some squaw, take it from me. Minnehaha, here's to you—to the two of you—an' to the papooses, too!"

He drained the glass suddenly and collapsed in his chair, blinking his eyes across at the wedded couple. "Kick in, Bill," he cried. "It's your turn now."

"I'm no hot-air artist," Billy grumbled. "What'll I say, Saxon? They ain't no use tellin' 'em how happy we are. They know that."

"Tell them we're always going to be happy," she said. "And thank them for all their good wishes, and we both wish them the same. And

Saxon held the treasure for a moment before she drew forth the blade and pressed her lips to the steel

we're always going to be together, like old times, the four of us. And tell them they're invited down to 507 Pine Street next Sunday for dinner. And, Mary, if you want to come Saturday night you can sleep in the spare bedroon."

"You've told 'm yourself, better'n I could." Billy clapped his hands. "You did yourself proud, an' I guess they ain't much to add to it, but just the same I'm goin' to pass them a hot one."

He stood up, his hand on his glass. His clear blue eyes, under the dark brows and framed by the dark lashes, seemed a deeper blue, and accentuated the blondness of hair and skin. The smooth cheeks were rosy— not with wine, for it was only his second glass—but with health and joy. Saxon, looking up at him, thrilled with pride in him, he was so well dressed, so strong, so handsome, so clean looking—her man-boy. And she was aware of pride in herself, in her woman's desirableness that had won for her so wonderful a lover.

"Well, Bert an' Mary, here you are at Saxon's and my wedding supper. We're just goin' to take all your good wishes to heart; we wish you the same back, and when we say it we mean more than you think we mean. Saxon an' I believe in tit for tat. So we're wishin' for the day when the table is turned clear around an' we're sittin' as guests at your wedding supper. And then, when you come to Sunday dinner, you can both stop Saturday night in the spare bedroom. I guess I was wised up when I furnished it, eh?"

"I never thought it of you, Billy!" Mary exclaimed. "You're every bit as raw as Bert. But just the same—" There was a rush of moisture to her eyes. Her voice faltered and broke. She smiled through her tears at them, then turned to look at Bert, who put his arm around her and gathered her onto his knees.

When they left the restaurant, the four walked to Eighth and Broadway, where they stopped beside the electric car. Bert and Billy were awkward and silent, oppressed by a strange aloofness. But Mary embraced Saxon with fond anxiousness.

"It's all right, dear," Mary whispered. "Don't be scared. It's all right. Think of all the other women in the world."

The conductor clanged the gong, and the two couples separated in a sudden hubbub of farewell.

"Oh, you Mohican!" Bert called after, as the car got under way. "Oh, you Minnehaha!"

"Remember what I said," was Mary's parting to Saxon.

The car stopped at Seventh and Pine, the terminus of the line. It was only a little over two blocks to the cottage. At the front door Billy took the key from his pocket.

"Funny, isn't it?" he said, as the key turned in the lock. "You an' me. Just you an' me."

While he lighted the lamp in the parlor, Saxon was taking off her hat. He went into the bedroom and lighted the lamp there, then turned back and stood in the doorway. Saxon, still unaccountably fumbling with her hatpins, stole a glance at him. He held out his arms.

"Now," he said.

She came to him, and in his arms he could feel her trembling.

XIV

THE first evening after the marriage night, Saxon met Billy at the door as he came up the front steps. After their embrace, and as they crossed the parlor hand in hand toward the kitchen, he filled his lungs through his nostrils with audible satisfaction.

"My, but this house smells good, Saxon! It ain't the coffee—I can smell that, too. It's the whole house. It smells—well, it just smells good to me, that's all."

He washed himself at the kitchen sink, while she heated the frying-pan on the front hole of the stove with the lid off. As he wiped his hands he watched her keenly, and cried out with approbation as she dropped the steak in the frying-pan.

"Where'd you learn to cook steak on a dry, hot pan? It's the only way, but darn few women seem to know about it."

As she took the cover off a second frying-pan and stirred the savory contents, he came behind her, passed his arms under her arm-pits, and bent his head over her shoulder till cheek touched cheek.

"Um — um — um-m-m! Fried potatoes with onions like mother used to make. Me for them. Don't they smell good, though! Um—um—m-m-m!"

The pressure of his hands relaxed, and his cheek slid caressingly past hers as he started to release her. Then his hands closed down again. She felt his lips on her hair and heard his advertised inhalation of delight.

"Um—um—m-m! Don't you smell good yourself though! I never understood what they meant when they said a girl was sweet. I know, now. And you're the sweetest I ever knew."

His joy was boundless. When he returned from combing his hair in the bedroom and sat down at the small table opposite her, he paused with knife and fork in hand.

"Say, bein' married is a whole lot more than it's cracked up to be by most married folks. Honest to God, Saxon, we can show 'em a few. We can give 'em cards and spades an' little casino, an' win out on big casino and the aces. I've got but one kick comin'."

The instant apprehension in her eyes provoked a chuckle from him.

"An' that is that we didn't get married quick enough. Just think, I've lost a whole week of this."

Her eyes shone with gratitude and happiness, and in her heart she solemnly pledged herself that never in all their married life would it be otherwise.

Supper finished, she cleared the table and began washing the dishes at the sink. When he evinced the intention of wiping them, she caught him by the lapels of the coat and backed him into a chair.

"You'll sit right there, if you know what's good for you. Now be good and mind what I say. No, you're not going to watch me. There's the morning paper beside you. And if you don't hurry to read it, I'll be through with these dishes before you've started."

As he read at the paper, she continually glanced across at him from her work. One thing more, she thought—slippers; and then the picture of comfort and content would be complete.

When the dishes were put away, Saxon led Billy into the parlor, where, by the open window, they succeeded in occupying the same Morris chair. It was the most expensive comfort in the house. It had cost seven dollars and a half, and, though it was grander than anything she had dreamed of possessing, the extravagance of it had worried her in a half-guilty way all day.

The salt chill of the air that is the blessing of all the bay cities after the sun goes down crept in about them. They heard the switch-engines puffing in the railroad yards, and the rumbling thunder of the Seventh Street local slowing down in its run from the Mole to stop at West Oakland station. From the street came the noise of children playing in the summer night, and from the steps of the house next door the low voices of gossiping housewives.

"Can you beat it?" Billy murmured. "When I think of that six-dollar furnished room of mine, it makes me sick to think what I was missin' all the time. But there's one satisfaction. If I'd changed it sooner I wouldn't 'a' had you."

His hand crept along her bare forearm and up and partly under the elbow-sleeve. "Your skin's so cool," he said. "It ain't cold; it's cool. It feels good to the hand."

"Pretty soon you'll be calling me your cold-storage baby," she laughed.

"And your voice is cool," he went on. "It gives me the feeling just as your hand does when you rest it on my forehead. It's funny. I can't explain it. But your voice just goes all through me, cool and fine. It's like a wind of coolness—just right. It's like the first of the sea-breeze settin' in in the afternoon after a scorchin' hot morning. An' sometimes, when you talk low, it sounds round and sweet like a 'cello. And it never goes high up, or sharp, or squeaky, or scratchy, like some women's voices when they're mad, or fresh, or excited, till they remind me of a bum phonograph record. Why, your voice, it just goes through me till I'm all trembling-like with the everlastin' cool of it. It's—it's straight delicious. I guess angels in heaven, if they is any, must have voices like that."

After a few minutes, in which, so inexpressible was her happiness that she could only pass her hand through his hair and cling to him, he broke out again.

"Say, Saxon, I got a new name for you. You're my Tonic Kid. That's what you are, the Tonic Kid."

"And you'll never get tired of me?" she queried.

"Tired? Why, we was made for each other."

"Isn't it wonderful—our meeting, Billy? We might never have met. It was just by accident that we did."

"We was born lucky," he proclaimed. "That's a cinch."

"Maybe it was more than luck," she ventured.

"Sure. It just had to be. It was fate. Nothing could 'a' kept us apart."

XV

SAXON had been clear eyed all her days, though her field of vision had been restricted. Clear eyed, from her childhood days with the saloonkeeper Cady and Cady's good-natured but unmoral spouse, she had observed, and, later, generalized much upon sex. She knew the post-nuptial problem of retaining a husband's love as few wives of any class knew it, just as she knew the pre-nuptial problem of selecting a husband as few girls of the working class knew it.

She had of herself developed an eminently rational philosophy of love. Instinctively, and consciously, too, she had made toward delicacy, and shunned the perils of the habitual and commonplace. Thoroughly aware she was that as she cheapened herself so did she cheapen love. Never, in the weeks of their married life, had Billy found her dowdy, or harshly irritable, or lethargic. And she had deliberately permeated her house with her personal atmosphere of coolness, and freshness, and equableness. Nor had she been ignorant of such assets as surprise and charm. Her imagination had not been asleep, and she had been born with wisdom. In Billy she had won a prize, and she knew it. She appreciated his lover's ardor and was proud. His open-handed liberality, his desire for everything of the best, his own personal cleanliness and care of himself, she placed as far beyond the average. He was never coarse. He met delicacy with delicacy, though it was obvious to her that the initiative in all such matters lay with her and must lie with her always. He was largely unconscious of what he did and why. But she knew in all full clarity of judgment that he was a prize among men.

With ardor Saxon now devoted herself to her household, to her pretty clothes, and to her charms. She marketed with a keen desire for the best, though never ignoring the need for economy. She made for herself simple house-slips of pretty ginghams, with neat low collars turned back from her fresh round throat. She crocheted yards of laces, and made Battenburg in abundance for her table and for the bureau. As the happy months went by, she was never idle. Nor was Billy forgotten. When the cold weather came on, she knitted him wristlets, which he always religiously wore from the house and pocketed immediately thereafter.

The two sweaters she made for him, however, received a better fate, as did the slippers which she insisted on his slipping into on the evenings they remained at home.

Invariably, on Saturday night, Billy poured his total wages into her lap. He never asked for an accounting of what she did with it, though he continually reiterated that he had never fed so well in his life. And always, the wages still untouched in her lap, she had him take out what he estimated he would need for spending-money for the week to come. Not only did she bid him take plenty, but she insisted on his taking any amount extra that he might desire at any time through the week. And, further, she insisted he should not tell her what it was for.

"You've always had money in your pocket," she reminded him, "and there's no reason why marriage should change that. If it did, I'd wish I'd never married you. Oh, I know about men when they get together. First one treats and then another, and it takes money. Now if you can't treat just as freely as the rest of them—why, I know you so well that I know you'd stay away from them. And that wouldn't be right—to you, I mean. I want you to be together with men. It's good for a man."

And Billy buried her in his arms and swore she was the greatest little bit of a woman that ever came down the pike. "Why," he jubilated, "not only do I feed better, and live more comfortable, and hold up my end with the fellows; but I'm actually saving money—or you are for me. Here I am, with furniture being paid for regular every month, and a little woman I'm mad over, and on top of it money in the bank. How much is it now?"

"Sixty-two dollars," she told him. "Not so bad for a rainy day. You might get sick, or hurt, or something happen."

It was in mid-winter, when Billy, with quite a deal of obvious reluctance, broached a money matter to Saxon. His old friend, Billy Murphy, was laid up with the grippe, and one of his children, playing in the street, had been seriously injured by a passing wagon. Billy Murphy, still feeble after two weeks in bed, had asked Billy for the loan of fifty dollars.

"It's perfectly safe," Billy concluded to Saxon. "I've known him since we was kids at the Durant School together. He's straight as a die."

"That's got nothing to do with it," Saxon chided. "If you were single you'd have lent it to him immediately, wouldn't you?"

Billy nodded.

"Then it's no different because you're married. It's your money, Billy."

"Not by a long shot," he cried. "It ain't mine. It's ourn. And I wouldn't think of lettin' anybody have it without seein' you first."

"I hope you didn't tell him that," she said with quick concern.

"Nope," Billy laughed. "I knew, if I did, you'd be madder 'n a hatter. I just told him I'd try an' figure it out. After all, I was pretty sure you'd stand for it if you had it."

"Oh, Billy," she murmured, her voice rich and low with love, "maybe you don't know it, but that's one of the sweetest things you've said since we got married."

XVI

THREE eventful things happened in the course of the winter. Mary and Bert married and rented a cottage in the neighborhood three blocks away. Billy's wages were cut, along with the wages of all the teamsters in Oakland. And, finally, Saxon was proved a false prophet and Sarah a true one.

Saxon made up her mind, beyond any doubt, ere she confided the news to Billy. At first, while still suspecting, she had felt a frightened sinking of the heart and a fear of the unknown and unexperienced. Then had come economic fear, as she contemplated the increased expense entailed. But by the time she had made surety doubly sure, all was swept away before a wave of passionate gladness. *Hers and Billy's!* The phrase was continually in her mind, and each recurrent thought of it brought an actual physical pleasure-pang to her heart.

The night she told the news to Billy he withheld his own news of the wage-cut, and joined with her in welcoming the little one.

"What'll we do—go to the theater to celebrate?" he asked, relaxing the pressure of his embrace so that she might speak. "Or suppose we stay in, just you and me, and—and the three of us?"

"Stay in," was her verdict. "I just want you to hold me, and hold me, and hold me."

"That's what I wanted, too; only I wasn't sure, after bein' in the house all day, but maybe you'd want to go out."

There was frost in the air, and Billy brought the Morris chair in by the kitchen stove. She lay cuddled in his arms, her head on his shoulder, his cheek against her hair.

"We didn't make no mistake in our lightning marriage with only a month's courtin'," he reflected aloud. "Why, Saxon, we've been courtin' ever since just the same. And now—my God, Saxon, it's too wonderful to be true. Think of it! Ourn! The three of us! The little rascal! I bet he's goin' to be a boy. An' won't I learn 'm to put up his fists an' take care of himself! An' swimmin', too. If he don't know how to swim by the time he's six—"

"And if *he's* a girl?"

"*She's* goin' to be a boy," Billy retorted.

And both laughed and kissed, and sighed with content.

"I'm goin' to turn pincher, now," he announced, after quite an interval of meditation. "No more drinks with the boys. It's me for the water-wagon. And I'm goin' to ease down on smokes. Huh! Don't see why I can't roll my own cigarettes. They're ten times cheaper'n tailor-mades. An' I can grow a beard. The amount of money the barbers get out of a fellow in a year would keep any baby."

"Just you let your beard grow, Mister Roberts, and I'll get a divorce," Saxon threatened. "You're just too handsome and strong with a smooth face. I love your face too much to have it covered up. Oh, you dear! you dear! Billy, I never knew what happiness was until I came to live with you."

"Nor me neither."

"And it's always going to be so?"

"You can just bet," he assured her.

"I thought I was going to be happy married," she went on; "but I never dreamed it would be like this." She turned her head on his shoulder and kissed his cheek. "Billy, it isn't happiness; it's heaven."

Billy resolutely kept undivulged the cut in wages. Not until two weeks later, when it went into effect, and he poured the diminished sum into her lap, did he break it to her. The next day, Bert and Mary, already a month married, had Sunday dinner with them, and the matter came up for discussion. Bert was particularly pessimistic, and muttered dark hints of an impending strike in the railroad shops.

"If you'd all shut your traps, it'd be all right," Mary criticized. "These union

The wedding supper had been eaten. Bert, in his hand a glass of California red wine, was on his fee
before you met me," Mary declared. "I can see it stickin' out all over you."
An' he is here, a-risin' to his feet to give the gla

50

endeavoring a speech. His face was flushed; his black eyes were feverishly bright. "You've been drinkin'
"Consult an oculist, my dear," he replied. "Bertram is himself to-night.
hand to his old pal. Bill, old man, here's to you "

agitators get the railroad sore. They give
me the cramp, the way they butt in an'
stir up trouble. If I was boss I'd cut the
wages of any man that listened to them."
"Yet you belonged to the laundry workers' union," Saxon rebuked gently.
"Because I had to or I wouldn't 'a' got
work. An' much good it ever done me."
"But look at Billy," Bert argued. "The
teamsters ain't been sayin' a word, not a
peep, an' everything lovely, and then, bang,
right in the neck, a ten per cent. cut. What
chance have we got? We lose. There's
nothin' left for us in this country we've
made and our fathers an' mothers before us.
We're all shot to pieces. We can see our
finish—we, the old stock, the children of the
white people that broke away from England
an' licked the tar outa her, that freed the
slaves, an' fought the Indians, an' made
the West. Any gink with half an eye can
see it comin'."
"But what are we going to do about it?"
Saxon questioned anxiously.
"Fight. That's all. The country's in the
hands of a gang of robbers. Look at the
Southern Pacific. It runs California."
"Aw, rats, Bert," Billy interrupted.
"You're talkin' through your lid. No railroad can run California."
"You're a bonehead," Bert sneered.
"And some day, when it's too late, you an'
all the other boneheads'll realize the fact.
Rotten? I tell you it stinks. Why, there
ain't a man who wants to go to state Legis-
lature but has to make a trip to San Francisco,
an' go into the S. P. offices, an' take his hat
off, an' humbly ask permission. Why, the
governors of California has been railroad
governors since before you an' I was born.
Huh! You can't tell me. We're finished.
We're licked to a frazzle. But it'd do my
heart good to help string up some of the
dirty thieves before I passed out. D'ye
know what we are?—we old white stock that
fought in the wars, an' broke the land, an'
made all this? I'll tell you. We're the last
of the Mohicans."

Saxon was happy and busy every waking
moment, nor was preparation for the little
one neglected. The only ready-made garments she bought were three fine little knit
shirts. As for the rest, every bit was made
by her own hands—feather-stitched pin-
ning-blankets, a crocheted jacket and cap,
knitted mittens, embroidered bonnets; slim

little princess slips of sensible length; under-
skirts on absurd Lilliputian yokes; silk-em-
broidered white flannel petticoats; stockings
and crocheted boots, seeming to burgeon
before her eyes with wriggly pink toes and
plump little calves; and, last, many deliciously soft squares of bird's-eye linen.
A little later, as a crowning masterpiece,
she was guilty of a dress coat of white silk,
embroidered. And into all the tiny garments, with every stitch, she sewed love.
Yet this love, so unceasingly sewn, she
knew, when she came to consider and marvel,
was more of Billy than of the nebulous,
ungraspable new bit of life that eluded her
fondest attempts at visioning.
"Huh," was Billy's comment, as he went
over the mite's wardrobe and came back to
center on the little knit shirts, "they look
more like a real kid than the whole kit an'
caboodle. Why, I can see him in them
regular man-shirts."
Saxon, with a sudden rush of happy,
unshed tears, held one of the little shirts
up to his lips. He kissed it solemnly, his
eyes resting on Saxon's.
"That's some for the boy," he said, "but
a whole lot for you."
Saxon now broached a subject which she
had been debating in her mind for days.
"Billy," she said, "I could sell some of my
pretties and get money for material to make
lots more—for me and the boy. You don't
know how much some women pay for things
no nicer than I can make. Let me try,
Billy," she unconsciously pleaded.
"Nope. That's one thing I won't stand
for, Saxon," said Billy. "Not that I don't
like fancy work. I do. I like every bit you
make, but I like it on you. Go ahead and
make all you want of it, for yourself, an'
I'll put up for the goods. Why, I'm just
whistlin' an' happy all day long, thinkin'
of the boy an' seein' you at home here workin' away on all them nice things. Because
I know how happy you are a-doin' it. But
honest to God, Saxon, it'd all be spoiled if
I knew you was doin' it to sell. You see,
Bill Roberts's wife don't have to work.
That's my brag—to myself, mind you. An'
besides, it ain't right."
"You're a dear," she whispered, happy
despite her disappointment.
"I want you to have all you want," he
continued. "An' you're goin' to get it as
long as I got two hands stickin' on the ends
of my arms. I guess I know how good the

things are you wear—good to me, I mean, too. Maybe I learned a few things I oughtn't to before I knew you, but I know what I'm talkin' about, and I want to say that outside the clothes down underneath, an' the clothes down underneath the outside ones, I never saw a woman like you. Oh—"

He threw up his hands as if despairing of ability to express what he thought and felt, then essayed a further attempt.

"It's not a matter of bein' only clean, though that's a whole lot. Lots of women are clean. It ain't that. It's something more, an' different. It's—well, it's the look of it, so white, an' pretty, an' tasty. It gets on the imagination. It's something I can't get out of my thoughts of you. You're a wonder, that's all, and you can't get too many of them nice things to suit me, and you can't get them too nice.

"For that matter, Saxon, you can just blow yourself. There's lots of easy money layin' around. I'm in great condition. Billy Murphy pulled down seventy-five round iron dollars only last week for puttin' away the Pride of North Beach. That's what he paid us the fifty back out of."

But this time it was Saxon who rebelled. "There's Carl Hansen," Billy urged. "The second Sharkey, the alfalfa sportin' writers are callin' him. An' he calls himself champion of the United States navy. Well, I got his number. He's just a big stiff. I've seen 'm fight, an' I can pass him the sleep medicine just as easy. The secretary of the Sportin' Life Club offered to match me. An' a hundred iron dollars in it for the winner. And it'll all be yours to blow in any way you want. What d'ye say?"

"If I can't work for money, you can't fight," was Saxon's ultimatum, immediately withdrawn. "But you and I don't drive bargains. Even if you'd let me work for money, I wouldn't let you fight. I've never forgotten what you told me about how prize-fighters lose their silk. Well, you're not going to lose yours. It's half my silk, you know. And if you won't fight, I won't work—there. And more, I'll never do anything you don't want me to, Billy."

"Same here," Billy agreed. "Though just the same I'd like 'most to death to have just one go at that squarehead Hansen." He smiled with pleasure at the thought. "Say, let's forget it all now, an' you sing me 'Harvest Days.'"

When she had complied, she suggested his weird "Cowboy's Lament." In some inexplicable way of love, she had come to like her husband's one song. Because he sang it, she liked its inanity and monotonousness; and most of all, it seemed to her, she loved his hopeless and adorable flatting of every note. She could even sing with him, flatting as accurately and deliciously as he. Nor did she undeceive him in his sublime faith.

"I guess Bert an' the rest have joshed me all the time," he said.

"You and I get along together with it fine," she equivocated; for in such matters she did not deem the untruth a wrong.

XVII

Spring was on when the strike came in the railroad shops. The Sunday before it was called, Saxon and Billy had dinner at Bert's house. Saxon's brother came. Bert was blackly pessimistic, and they found him singing with sardonic glee:

"Nobody loves a mil-yun-aire.
    Nobody likes his looks.
Nobody'll share his slightest care,
    He classes with thugs and crooks.
Thriftiness has become a crime,
    So spend everything you earn;
We're living now in a funny time,
    When money is made to burn."

Mary went about the dinner preparations, flaunting unmistakable signals of rebellion; and Saxon, rolling up her sleeves and tying on an apron, washed the breakfast dishes. The three men smoked and talked about the coming strike.

"It oughta come years ago," was Bert's dictum. "It can't come any too quick now to suit me, but it's too late. We're beaten thumbs down. Here's where the last of the Mohicans get theirs, in the neck, ker-whop!"

"Oh, I don't know," Tom, who had been smoking his pipe gravely, began to counsel. "Organized labor's gettin' stronger every day. Why, I can remember when there wasn't any unions in California. Look at us now—wages, an' hours, an' everything."

"You talk like an organizer," Bert sneered, "shovin' the bull con on the bone-heads. But we know different. Organized wages won't buy as much now as unorganized wages used to buy. They've got us whipsawed. Look at Frisco, the labor leaders doin' dirtier politics than the old parties, pawin' an' squabblin' over graft, an' goin' to San Quentin, while—what are the Frisco carpenters doin'? Let me tell you one thing, Tom Brown, if you listen to all you hear you'll hear that every Frisco carpenter is union an' gettin' full union wages. Do you believe it? It's a lie. There ain't a carpenter that don't rebate his wages Saturday night to the contractor. An' that's your buildin' trades in San Francisco, while the leaders are makin' trips to Europe on the earnings of the tenderloin— when they ain't coughing it up to lawyers to get out of wearin' stripes."

"That's all right," Tom concurred. "Nobody's denyin' it. The trouble is labor ain't quite got its eyes open. It ought to play politics, but the politics ought to be the right kind."

"Socialism, eh?" Bert caught him up with scorn. "Wouldn't they sell us out just as the Ruefs and Schmidts have?"

"Get men that are honest," Billy said. "That's the whole trouble. Not that I stand for socialism. I don't. All our folks was a long time in America, an' I for one won't stand for a lot of foreigners tellin' me how to run my country when they can't speak English yet."

"*Your* country!" Bert cried. "Why, you bonehead, you ain't got a country. That's a fairy story the grafters shove at you every time they want to rob you some more."

"But don't vote for the grafters," Billy contended. "If we selected honest men we'd get honest treatment."

"I wish you'd come to some of our meetings, Billy," Tom said wistfully. "If you would, you'd get your eyes open an' vote the Socialist ticket next election."

"Not on your life," Billy declined. "When you catch me in a Socialist meeting 'll be when they can talk like white men."

Mary was too angry with her husband because of the impending strike and his incendiary utterances, to hold conversation with Saxon, and the latter, bepuzzled, listened to the conflicting opinions of the men.

"Where are we at?" she asked them, with a merriness that concealed her anxiety at heart.

"We ain't at," Bert snarled. "We're gone."

"But meat and oil have gone up again," she chafed. "And Billy's wages have been cut, and the shop men's were cut last year. Something must be done."

"The only thing to do is fight," Bert answered. "Fight, an' go down fightin'. That's all. We're licked anyhow, but we can have a last run for our money."

"That's no way to talk," Tom rebuked.

"The time for talkin' 's past, old rock. The time for fightin' 's come."

"A fine chance you'd have against regular troops and machine guns," Billy retorted.

"Oh, not that way. There's such things as greasy sticks that go up with a loud noise and leave holes. There's such things as emery powder—"

"Oh, ho!" Mary burst out upon him, arms akimbo. "So that's what it means. That's what the emery in your vest pocket meant."

Her husband ignored her. Tom smoked with a troubled air. Billy was hurt. It showed plainly in his face.

"You ain't been doin' that, Bert?" he asked, his manner showing his expectancy of his friend's denial.

"Sure thing, if you want to know."

"He's a bloody-minded anarchist," Mary complained. "He'll be hung. You'll see. Mark my words."

"It's hot air," Billy comforted her.

"He's just teasing you," Saxon soothed. "He always was a josher."

But Mary shook her head. "I know. I hear him talkin' in his sleep. He swears and curses something awful, an' grits his teeth. Listen to him now."

Bert, his handsome face bitter and devil-may-care, had tilted his chair back against the wall and was singing:

"Nobody loves a mil-yun-aire,
    Nobody likes his looks,
Nobody'll share his slightest care,
    He classes with thugs and crooks."

Tom was saying something about reasonableness and justice, and Bert ceased from singing to catch him up.

"Justice, eh? Another pipe-dream. I'll show you where the working class gets justice. You remember Forbes—J. Alliston Forbes—wrecked the Alta California Trust Company an' salted down two cold millions. I saw him yesterday, in a big hell-bent automobile. What'd he get? Eight years' sentence. How long did he serve? Less 'n two years. Pardoned out on account of ill health. We'll be dead an' rotten before he kicks the bucket. Here. Look out this window. You see the back of that house with the broken porch rail. Mrs. Danaker

"Funny, isn't it?" said Billy, as the key turned in the lock. "You an me. Just you an me

55

lives there. She takes in washin'. Her old man was killed on the railroad. Nitsky on damages—contributory negligence, or fellow-servant-something-or-other flimflam. That's what the courts handed her. Her boy, Archie, was sixteen. He was on the road, a regular road-kid. He blew into Fresno an' rolled a drunk. Do you want to know how much he got? Two dollars and eighty cents. Get that? Two-eighty. And what did the alfalfa judge hand 'm? Fifty years. He's served eight of it already in San Quentin. And he'll go on serving it till he croaks. Mrs. Danaker says he's bad with consumption—caught it inside, but she ain't got the pull to get 'm pardoned. Archie the Kid steals two dollars an' eighty cents from a drunk and gets fifty years. J. Alliston Forbes sticks up the Alta Trust for two million an' gets less 'n two years. Who's country is this, anyway? Yourn an' Archie the Kid's? Guess again. It's J. Alliston Forbes's."

Mary, at the sink, where Saxon was just finishing the last dish, untied Saxon's apron and kissed her with the sympathy that women alone feel for each other under the shadow of maternity. "Now you sit down, dear. You mustn't tire yourself, and it's a long way to go yet. I'll get your sewing for you, and you can listen to the men talk. But don't listen to Bert. He's crazy."

Saxon sewed and listened, and Bert's face grew bleak and bitter as he contemplated the baby clothes in her lap.

"There you go," he blurted out; "bringin' kids into the world when you ain't got any guarantee you can feed 'em."

"You must 'a' had a souse last night," Tom grinned.

Bert shook his head.

"Aw, what's the use of gettin' grouched?" Billy cheered. "It's a pretty good country."

"It *was* a pretty good country," Bert replied, "when we was all Mohicans. But not now. We're jiggerooed. We're hornswoggled. We're backed to a standstill. We're double-crossed to a fare-you-well. My folks fought for this country. So did yourn, all of you. We freed the niggers, killed the Indians, an' starved, an' froze, an' sweat, an' fought. This land looked good to us. We cleared it, an' broke it, an' made the roads, an' built the cities. And there was plenty for everybody. And we went on fightin' for it. I had two uncles

killed at Gettysburg. All of us was mixed up in that war. Listen to Saxon talk any time what her folks went through to get out here an' get ranches, an' horses, an' cattle, an' everything. And they got 'em. All our folks got 'em, Mary's too—"

"And if they'd been smart they'd 'a' held on to them," she interpolated.

"Sure thing," Bert continued. "That's the very point. We're the losers. We've been robbed. We couldn't mark cards, deal from the bottom, an' ring in cold decks like the others. We're the white folks that failed. You see, times changed, and there was two kinds of us, the lions and the plugs. The plugs only worked, the lions only gobbled. They gobbled the farms, the mines, the factories, an' now they've gobbled the government. We're the white folks an' the children of white folks that was too busy being good to be smart. We're the white folks that lost out. We're the ones that's been skinned. D'ye get me?"

"You'd make a good soap-boxer," Tom commended, "if only you'd get the kinks straightened out in your reasoning."

"It sounds all right, Bert," Billy said, "only it ain't. Any man can get rich to-day—"

"Or be President of the United States," Bert snapped. "Sure thing—if he's got it in him. Just the same, I ain't heard you makin' a noise like a millionaire or a President. Why? You ain't got it in you. You're a bonehead, a plug. That's why. Skiddoo for you. Skiddoo for all of us."

At the table, while they ate, Tom talked of the joys of farm life he had known as a boy and as a young man, and confided that it was his dream to go and take up government land somewhere as his people had done before him. Unfortunately, as he explained, Sarah was set, so that the dream must remain a dream.

"It's all in the game," Billy sighed. "It's played to rules. Some one has to get knocked out, I suppose."

A little later, while Bert was off on a fresh diatribe, Billy became aware that he was making comparisons. This house was not like his house. Here was no satisfying atmosphere. Things seemed to run with a jar. He recollected that when they arrived, the breakfast dishes had not yet been washed. With a man's general obliviousness of household affairs, he had not noted details; yet it had been borne in on him, all

Jack London   57

morning, in a myriad ways, that Mary was
not the housekeeper Saxon was. He glanced
proudly across at her, and felt the spur of
an impulse to leave his seat, go around, and
embrace her. She *was* a wife. He remembered her dainty undergarmenting, and on
the instant, into his brain, leaped the image
of her so appareled, only to be shattered by
Bert.

"Hey, Bill, you seem to think I've got a
grouch. Sure thing. I have. You ain't
had my experiences. You've always done
teamin' an' pulled down easy money prize-
fightin'. You ain't known hard times.
You ain't been through strikes. You ain't
had to take care of an old mother an' swal-
low dirt on her account. It wasn't until
after she died that I could rip loose an' take
or leave as I felt like it.

"Take that time I tackled the Niles
Electric an' see what a work-plug gets
handed out to him. The Head Cheese sizes
me up, pumps me a lot of questions, an'
gives me an application-blank. I make it
out, payin' a dollar to a doctor they sent
me to for a health certificate. Then I got
to go to a picture-garage an' get my mug
taken—for the Niles Electric rogues' gallery.
And I cough up another dollar for the mug.
The Head Squirt takes the blank, the health
certificate, and the mug, an' fires more questions. *Did I belong to a labor union. Me?*
Of course I told 'm the truth I guess nit.
I needed the job. The grocery wouldn't
give me any more tick, and there was my
mother.

"Huh, thinks I, here's where I'm a real
carman. Back platform for me, where I
can pick up the fancy skirts. Nitsky. Two
dollars, please. Me—my two dollars. All
for a pewter badge. Then there was the
uniform—nineteen fifty, and get it anywhere else for fifteen. Only that was to
be paid out of my first month. And then,
five dollars in change in my pocket, my own
money. That was the rule. I borrowed
that five from Tom Donovan, the policeman. Then what? They worked me for
two weeks without pay, breakin' me in."

"Did you pick up any fancy skirts?"
Saxon queried teasingly.

Bert shook his head glumly. "I only
worked a month. Then we organized, and
they busted our union higher 'n a kite."

"And you boobs in the shops will be
busted the same way if you go out on
strike," Mary informed him.

"That's what I've been tellin' you all
along," Bert replied. "We ain't got a
chance to win."

"Then why go out?" was Saxon's question.

He looked at her with lack-luster eyes for
a moment, then answered, "Why did my
two uncles get killed at Gettysburg?"

XVIII

SAXON went about her housework greatly
troubled. She no longer devoted herself to
the making of pretties. The materials cost
money, and she did not dare. Bert's thrust
had sunk home. It remained in her quivering consciousness like a shaft of steel that
ever turned and rankled. She and Billy were
responsible for this coming young life.
Could they be sure, after all, that they
could adequately feed and clothe it and
prepare it for its way in the world? Where
was the guaranty? She remembered, dimly,
the blight of hard times in the past, and the
plaints of fathers and mothers in those days
returned to her with a new significance.
Almost could she understand Sarah's
chronic complaining.

Hard times was already in the neighborhood where lived the families of the shopmen who had gone out on strike. Among
the small storekeepers, Saxon, in the course
of the daily marketing, could sense the air
of despondency. Light and geniality seemed
to have vanished. Gloom pervaded everywhere. The mothers of the children that
played in the streets showed the gloom
plainly in their faces. When they gossiped
in the evenings, over front gates and on
door-stoops, their voices were subdued, and
less of laughter rang out.

Mary Donahue, who had taken three
pints from the milkman, now took one pint.
There were no more family trips to the
moving-picture shows. Scrap-meat was
harder to get from the butcher. Nora De-
laney, in the third house, no longer bought
fresh fish for Friday. Salted codfish, not of
the best quality, was now on her table.
The sturdy children that ran out upon the
street between meals with huge slices of
bread and butter and sugar, now came out
with no sugar and with thinner slices spread
more thinly with butter. The very custom
was dying out, and some children already
had desisted from piecing between meals.
Everywhere was manifest a pinching and

Supper finished, she cleared the table and began washing the dishes at the sink. When he evinced the intentio
if you know what's good for you. Now be good and mind what I say. No, you ar
to read it, I'll be through with these dishes before you've started." As h

58   One thing more, she thought—slippers; and then th

f wiping them, she caught him by the lapels of the coat and backed him into a chair. " You'll sit right there,
ot going to watch me. There's the morning paper beside you. And if you don't hurry
ead at the paper, she continually glanced across at him from her work.
icture of comfort and content would be complete

scraping, a cutting down of expenditure. And everywhere was more irritation. Women became angered with one another, and with the children, more quickly than of yore; and Saxon knew that Bert and Mary bickered incessantly.

"If she'd only realize I've got troubles of my own," Bert complained to Saxon.

She looked at him closely, and felt fear of him in a vague, numb way. His black eyes seemed to burn with a continuous madness. The brown face was leaner, the skin drawn tightly across the cheek-bones. A slight twist had come to the mouth, which seemed frozen into bitterness. The very carriage of his body and the way he wore his hat advertised a recklessness more intense than had been his in the past.

Sometimes, in the long afternoons, sitting by the window with idle hands, she caught herself reconstructing in her vision that folk-migration of her people across the plains and mountains and deserts to the sunset land by the Western sea. And often she found herself dreaming of the arcadian days of her people, when they did not live in cities and were not vexed with labor unions and employers' associations. She would remember the old people's tales of self-sufficingness, when they shot or raised their own meat, grew their own vegetables, were their own blacksmiths and carpenters, made their own shoes—yes, and spun the cloth of the clothes they wore. And something of the wistfulness in Tom's face she could see as she recollected it when he talked of his dream of taking up government land.

A farmer's life must be fine, she thought. Why was it that people had to live in cities? Why had times changed? If there had been enough in the old days, why was there not enough now? Why was it necessary for men to quarrel and jangle, and strike and fight, all about the matter of getting work? Why wasn't there work for all? Only that morning, and she shuddered with the recollection, she had seen two scabs, on their way to work, beaten up by the strikers, by men she knew by sight, and some by name, who lived in the neighborhood. It had happened directly across the street. It had been cruel, terrible—a dozen men on two. The children had begun it by throwing rocks at the scabs and cursing them in ways children should not know. Policemen had run upon the scene with drawn revolvers,

and the strikers had retreated into the houses and through the narrow alleys between the houses. One of the scabs, unconscious, had been carried away in an ambulance; the other, assisted by special railroad police, had been taken away to the shops. At him, Mary Donahue, standing on her front stoop, her child in her arms, had hurled such vile abuse that it had brought the blush of shame to Saxon's cheeks. On the stoop of the house on the other side, Saxon had noted Mercedes Higgins, an elderly neighbor, in the height of the beating up, looking on with a queer smile. She had seemed very eager to witness it, her nostrils dilated and swelling like the beat of pulses as she watched. It had struck Saxon at the time that the old woman was quite unexcited and only curious to see.

"I was frightened to death," Saxon declared to her later. "I was made sick by it. And yet you—I saw you—you looked on as cool as you please, as if it was a show."

"It was a show, my dear."

"Oh, how could you?"

"La, la, I have seen men killed. It is nothing strange. All men die. The stupid ones die like oxen, they know not why. It is quite funny to see. They strike each other with fists and clubs, and break each other's heads. It is gross. They are like a lot of animals. They are like dogs wrangling over bones. Jobs are bones, you know. Now, if they fought for women, or ideas, or bars of gold, or fabulous diamonds, it would be splendid. But no; they are only hungry, and fight over scraps for their stomach."

"Oh, if I could only understand!" Saxon murmured, her hands tightly clasped in anguish of incomprehension and vital need to know.

As the weeks passed, the strike in the railroad shops grew bitter and deadly. Billy shook his head and confessed his inability to make head or tail of the troubles that were looming on the labor horizon.

"I don't get the hang of it," he told Saxon. "It's a mix-up. It's like a roughhouse with the lights out. Look at us teamsters. Here we are, the talk just starting of going out on sympathetic strike for the mill-workers. They've been out a week, most of their places is filled, an' if us teamsters keep on haulin' the mill-work the strike's lost."

Jack London

"Yet you didn't consider striking for yourselves when your wages were cut," Saxon said with a frown.

"Oh, we wasn't in position then. But now the Frisco teamsters and the whole Frisco Water Front Confederation is liable to back us up. Anyway, we're just talkin' about it, that's all. But if we do go out, we'll try to get back that ten per cent. cut."

"It's rotten politics," he said another time. "Everybody's rotten. If we'd only wise up and agree to pick out honest men—"

"But if you, and Bert, and Tom can't agree, how do you expect all the rest to agree?" Saxon asked.

"It gets me," he admitted. "It's enough to give a guy the willies thinkin' about it. And yet it's plain as the nose on your face. Get honest men for politics, an' the whole thing's straightened out. Honest men'd make honest laws, an' then honest men'd get their dues."

The next evening when Billy came home from work, Saxon caused him to know and undertake more of the responsibilities of fatherhood. "I've been thinking it over, Billy," she began, "and I'm such a healthy, strong woman that it won't have to be very expensive. There's Martha Skelton—she's a good mid-wife."

But Billy shook his head. "Nothin' doin' in that line, Saxon. You're goin' to have Doc Hentley. He's Bill Murphy's doc, an' Bill swears by him. He's an old cuss, but he's a wooz."

"She confined Mary Donahue," Saxon argued; "and look at her, and her baby."

"Well, she won't confine you—not so as you can notice it."

"But the doctor will charge twenty dollars," Saxon pursued, "and make me get a nurse because I haven't any womenfolk to come in. But Martha Skelton would do everything, and it would be so much cheaper."

But Billy gathered her tenderly in his arms and laid down the law. "Listen to me, little wife. The Roberts family ain't on the cheap. Never forget that. You've gotta have the baby. That's your business, an' it's enough for you. My business is to get the money an' take care of you. An' the best ain't none too good for you. Why, I wouldn't run the chance of the teeniest accident happenin' to you for a million dollars. It's you that counts. An' dollars is dirt. Maybe you think I like that kid

some. I do. Why, I can't get him outa my head. I'm thinkin' about 'm all day long. If I get fired, it'll be his fault. I'm clean dotty over him. But just the same, Saxon, honest to God, before I'd have anything happen to you, break your little finger, even, I'd see him dead an' buried first. That'll give you something of an idea what you mean to me.

"Why, Saxon, I had the idea that when folks got married they just settled down and after a while their business was to get along with each other. Maybe it's the way it is with other people; but it ain't that way with you an' me. I love you more 'n' more every day. Right now I love you more 'n when I began talkin' to you five minutes ago. An' you won't have to get a nurse. Doc Hentley'll come every day, an' Mary'll come in an' do the housework, an' take care of you an' all that, just as you'll do for her if she ever needs it."

As the days and weeks passed, Saxon was possessed by a conscious feeling of proud motherhood in her swelling breasts. So essentially a normal woman was she that motherhood was a satisfying and passionate happiness. It was true that she had her moments of apprehension, but they were so momentary and faint that they tended, if anything, to give zest to her happiness.

Only one thing troubled her, and that was the puzzling and perilous situation of labor which no one seemed to understand, herself least of all.

"They're always talking about how much more is made by machinery than by the old ways," she said to her brother Tom. "Then, with all the machinery we've got now, why don't we get more?"

"Now you're talkin'," he answered. "It wouldn't take you long to understand socialism."

But Saxon had a mind to the immediate need of things. "Tom, how long have you been a Socialist?"

"Eight years."

"And you haven't got anything by it?"

"But we will—in time."

"At that rate you'll be dead first," she challenged.

Tom sighed. "I'm afraid so. Things move so slow."

Again he sighed. She noted the weary, patient look in his face, the bent shoulders, the labor-gnarled hands, and it all seemed to symbolize the futility of his social creed.

The Valley of the Moon

THE STORY OF A FIGHT AGAINST ODDS FOR LOVE AND A HOME

By Jack London

Author of "Martin Eden," "Burning Daylight," "Smoke Bellew," etc.

Illustrated by Howard Chandler Christy

SYNOPSIS: Is this the man? So Saxon questioned of herself when she had met "Big Bill" Roberts, one-time prize-fighter, on the dancing-floor at Weasel Park, whither she and Mary, ironers of fancy starch, had gone for a Sunday outing. Never had she come so near to losing her heart as Billy, blue eyed, boyish, gentlemanly, had come to winning it after a few hours' acquaintance. Planned by Mary and Bert Wanhope, the meeting had taken a happy turn, for both Saxon and Billy had seized the future in the present and grasped at its chance for happiness. Billy was a teamster and knew what hard work meant, so they went home early, Saxon glorying in his refusal to "make a time of it," as Bert suggested. He kissed her good night at the gate, with Wednesday night's dance as their next meeting. Friday's dance was next arranged for, but on Thursday night Charley Long, a rebuffed suitor, met her outside the laundry and warned her that if she did not go with him "somebody 'll get hurt." But Saxon bore the notion that Billy, at least, could take care of himself. Billy did, and Saxon experienced the delightful sensation of knowing that this big boy cared enough for her to risk a fight—which wasn't needed. Billy next proposed a Sunday buggy-ride. They drove out of the city behind a spirited team, Saxon glad to get away from the abuse which Sarah, her sister-in-law, had heaped upon her because she preferred Billy, a prize-fighter, to Charley Long, an honest laboring man. Home cares were soon forgotten as they drove into the hills, each happy in the first true comradeship ever experienced with one of the opposite sex. In the hills they ate a lunch-eon provided by Billy, and then lingered until warnings of dusk urged them homeward. Darkness overtook them—and silence. Then out of it came Billy's frank proposal, and Saxon, countering only with the objection that she was the older—an objection overruled by Billy's statement that "Love's what counts"—accepted him. Billy wanted to be married the next day, but Saxon put him off for a month—a month that, crowded with preparations, flew by on wings of happiness. In spite of her sister-in-law's objections, Saxon completed her preparations and married Billy at the promised time. They and Mary and Bert ate the wedding supper at Barnum's, and then Saxon and Billy went to their Pine Street cottage alone. Later Mary and Bert married and became their neighbors. The winter passed without an event to mar their happiness, though Billy's wages were cut. But in the spring came a strike in the railroad shops, a strike that soon grew bitter and deadly, and threw a pall over their whole neighborhood. To Saxon, approaching motherhood, the passing days bore a menace, for Bert was in the strike and Billy saw the time approaching when he would have to join it.

IT began quietly, as the fateful unex-pected so often begins. Children, of all ages and sizes, were playing in the street, and Saxon, by the open front window, was watching them and dream-ing day-dreams of her child soon to be. The sunshine mellowed peacefully down, and a light wind from the bay cooled the air and gave to it a tang of salt. One of the children pointed up Pine Street toward Seventh. All the children ceased playing, and stared and pointed. They formed into groups, the larger boys, of from ten to twelve, by themselves, the older girls anxiously clutching the small children by the hands or gathering them into their arms.

Saxon could not see the cause of all this, but she could guess when she saw the larger boys rush to the gutter, pick up stones, and sneak into the alleys between the houses. Smaller boys tried to imitate them. The girls, dragging the tots by the arms, banged gates and clattered up the front steps of the small houses. The doors slammed behind them, and the street was deserted, though here and there front shades were drawn aside so that anxious-faced women might peer forth. Saxon heard the up-town train puff-ing and snorting as it pulled out from Center Street. Then, from the direction of Seventh, came a hoarse, throaty man-roar. Still she could see nothing, and she remembered the words of Mercedes Higgins: *"They are like dogs wrangling over bones. Jobs are bones, you know."*

The roar came closer, and Saxon, leaning out, saw a dozen "scabs," convoyed by as many special police and Pinkertons, coming down the sidewalk on her side of the street. They came compactly, as if with discipline, while behind, disorderly, yelling confusedly, stooping to pick up rocks, were seventy-five or a hundred of the striking shopmen. Saxon discovered herself trembling with apprehen-sion, knew that she must not, and controlled herself. She was helped in this by the con-duct of Mercedes Higgins. The old woman came out of her front door, dragging a chair, on which she coolly seated herself on the tiny stoop at the top of the steps.

In the hands of the special police were clubs. The Pinkertons carried no visible weapons. The strikers, urging on from be-hind, seemed content with yelling their rage and threats, and it remained for the chil-dren to precipitate the conflict. From

63

across the street, between the Olsen and Isham houses, came a shower of stones. Most of these fell short, though one struck a scab on the head. The man was no more than twenty feet away from Saxon. He reeled toward her front picket-fence, drawing a revolver. With one hand he brushed the blood from his eyes, and with the other he discharged the revolver into the Isham house. A Pinkerton seized his arm to prevent a second shot, and dragged him along. At the same instant a wilder roar went up from the strikers, while a volley of stones came from between Saxon's house and Mrs. Donahue's. The scabs and their protectors made a stand, drawing revolvers. From their hard, determined faces—fighting men by profession—Saxon could augur nothing but bloodshed and death. An elderly man, evidently the leader, lifted a soft felt hat and mopped the perspiration from the bald top of his head. He was a large man, very rotund of belly and helpless looking. His gray beard was stained with streaks of tobacco-juice, and he was smoking a cigar. He was stoop-shouldered, and Saxon noted the dandruff on the collar of his coat.

One of the men pointed into the street, and several of his companions laughed. The cause of it was the little Olsen boy, barely four years old, escaped somehow from his mother and toddling toward his economic enemies. In his right hand he bore a rock so heavy that he could scarcely lift it. With this he feebly threatened them. His rosy little face was convulsed with rage, and he was screaming over and over: "Damn scabs! Damn scabs! Damn scabs!" The laughter with which they greeted him only increased his fury. He toddled closer, and with a mighty exertion threw the rock. It fell a scant six feet beyond his hand.

This much Saxon saw, and also Mrs. Olsen rushing into the street for her child. A rattling of revolver shots from the strikers drew Saxon's attention to the men beneath her. One of them cursed sharply and examined the biceps of his left arm, which hung limply by his side. Down the hand she saw the blood beginning to drip. She knew she ought not remain and watch, but the memory of her fighting forefathers was with her, making her feel no more than normal human fear—if anything, less. She forgot her child in the eruption of battle that had broken upon her quiet street. And

she forgot the strikers, and everything else, in amazement at what had happened to the round-bellied, cigar-smoking leader. In some strange way, she knew not how, his head had become wedged at the neck between the tops of the pickets of her fence. His body hung down outside, the knees not quite touching the ground. His hat had fallen off, and the sun was making an astounding high light on his bald spot. The cigar, too, was gone. She saw he was looking at her. One hand, between the pickets, seemed waving at her, and almost he seemed to wink at her jocosely, though she knew it to be the contortion of deadly pain.

Possibly a second, or, at most, two seconds, she gazed at this, when she was aroused by Bert's voice. He was running along the sidewalk, in front of her house, and behind him charged several more strikers, while he shouted: "Come on, you Mohicans! We got 'em nailed to the cross!"

In his left hand he carried a pick-handle, in his right a revolver, already empty, for he clicked the cylinder vainly around as he ran. With an abrupt stop, dropping the pick-handle, he whirled half about, facing Saxon's gate. He was sinking down, when he straightened himself to throw the revolver into the face of a scab who was jumping toward him. Then he began swaying, at the same time sagging at the knees and waist. Slowly, with infinite effort, he caught a gate-picket in his right hand, and, still slowly, as if lowering himself, sank down, while past him leaped the crowd of strikers he had led.

It was battle without quarter—a massacre. The scabs and their protectors, surrounded, backed against Saxon's fence, fought like cornered rats, but could not withstand the rush of a hundred men. Clubs and pick-handles were swinging, revolvers were exploding, and cobblestones were being flung with crushing effect at arm's distance. Saxon saw young Frank Davis, a friend of Bert's and a father of several months' standing, press the muzzle of his revolver against a scab's stomach and fire. There were curses and snarls of rage, wild cries of terror and pain. Mercedes was right. These things were not men. They were beasts, fighting over bones, destroying one another for bones.

Jobs are bones; jobs are bones. The phrase was an incessant iteration in Saxon's brain. Much as she might have wished it, she was powerless now to withdraw from the window. It was as if she were paralyzed. Her brain no longer worked. She sat numb, staring, incapable of anything save seeing the rapid horror before her eyes that flashed along like a moving-picture film gone mad. She saw Pinkertons, special police, and strikers go down. One scab, terribly wounded, on his knees and begging for mercy, was kicked in the face. As he sprawled backward, another striker, standing over him, fired a revolver into his chest, quickly and deliberately, again and again, until the weapon was empty. Another scab, backed over the pickets by a hand clutching his throat, had his face pulped by a revolver butt. Again and again, continually, the revolver rose and fell, and Saxon knew the man who wielded it—Chester Johnson. She had met him at dances and danced with him in the days before she was married. He had always been kind and good natured. It was impossible that this could be the same Chester Johnson. And as she looked, she saw the round-bellied leader, still wedged by the neck between the pickets, draw a revolver with his free hand, and, squinting horribly sidewise, press the muzzle against Chester's side. She tried to scream a warning. She did scream, and Chester looked up and saw her. At that moment the revolver went off, and he collapsed prone upon the body of the scab. And the bodies of three men hung on her picket fence.

Anything could happen now. Quite without surprise, she saw the strikers leaping the fence, trampling her few little geraniums and pansies into the earth as they fled between Mercedes's house and hers. Up Pine Street, from the railroad yards, was coming a rush of railroad police and Pinkertons, firing as they ran; while down Pine Street, gongs clanging, horses at a gallop, came three patrol-wagons packed with police. The strikers were in a trap. The only way out was between the houses and over the back-yard fences. The jam in the narrow alley prevented them all from escaping. A dozen were cornered in the angle between the front of her house and the steps. And as the strikers had done, so were they done by. No effort was made to arrest. They were clubbed down and shot down to the last man by the guardians of the peace, who were infuriated by what had been wreaked on their brethren.

It was all over, and Saxon, moving as in a dream, clutching the bannister tightly, came down the front steps. The gate was off its hinges, which seemed strange, for she had been watching all the time and had not seen it happen.

Bert's eyes were closed. His lips were blood-flecked, and there was a gurgling in his throat as if he were trying to say something. As she stooped above him, with her handkerchief brushing the blood from his cheek where some one had stepped on him, his eyes opened. The old defiant light was in them. He did not know her. The lips moved, and faintly, almost reminiscently, he murmured, "The last of the Mohicans, the last of the Mohicans." Then he groaned, and the eyelids drooped down again. He was not dead. She knew that. The chest still rose and fell, and the gurgling still continued in his throat.

She looked up. Mercedes stood beside her. The old woman's eyes were very bright, her withered cheeks flushed.

"Will you help me carry him to the house?" Saxon asked.

Mercedes nodded, turned to a sergeant of police, and made the request to him. The sergeant gave a swift glance at Bert, and his eyes were bitter and ferocious as he refused.

"To hell with 'm. We'll care for our own."

"Maybe you and I can do it," Saxon said.

"Don't be a fool." Mercedes was beckoning to Mrs. Olsen across the street. "You go into the house, little mother that is to be. This is bad for you. We'll carry him in. Mrs. Olsen is coming, and we'll get Mrs. Donahue."

Saxon led the way into the back bedroom. As she opened the door, the carpet seemed to fly up into her face as with the force of a blow, for she remembered Bert had laid that carpet. And as the women placed him on the bed she recalled that it was Bert and she, between them, who had set the bed up one Sunday morning.

And then she felt very queer, and was surprised to see Mercedes regarding her with questioning, searching eyes. After that her queerness came on very fast, and she descended into the hell of pain that is given to women alone to know. She was supported, half carried, to the front bedroom. Many faces were about her—Mercedes, Mrs. Olsen, Mrs. Donahue. It seemed she must ask Mrs. Olsen if she had saved little Emil

Saxon was aroused by Bert's voice. He was running along the sidewalk in front of her house, and behind cross!" In his left hand he carried a pick-handle, in his right a revolver,

him charged several more strikers, while he shouted: "Come on, you Mohicans. We got em nailed to the
already empty, for he clicked the cylinder vainly around as he ran

from the street, but Mercedes cleared Mrs. Olsen out to look after Bert, and Mrs. Donahue went to answer a knock at the front door. From the street came a loud hum of voices, punctuated by shouts and commands, and from time to time there was a clanging of the gongs of ambulances and patrol-wagons. Then appeared the fat, comfortable face of Martha Skelton, and, later, Doctor Hentley came. Once, in a clear interval, through the thin wall Saxon heard the high opening notes of Mary's hysteria. And, another time, she heard Mary repeating over and over: "I'll never go back to the laundry. Never. Never."

XX

BILLY could never get over the shock, during that period, of Saxon's appearance. Morning after morning, and evening after evening when he came home from work, he would enter the room where she lay and fight a royal battle to hide his feelings and make a show of cheerfulness and geniality. She looked so small lying there, so small and shrunken and weary, and yet so child-like in her smallness. Tenderly, as he sat beside her, he would take up her pale hand and stroke the slim, transparent arm, marveling at the smallness and delicacy of the bones.

One of her first questions, puzzling alike to Billy and Mary, was, "Did you save little Emil Olsen?"

And when she told them how he had attacked, single handed, the whole twenty-four fighting men, Billy's face glowed with appreciation.

"The little cuss!" he said. "That's the kind of a kid to be proud of."

He halted awkwardly, and his very evident fear that he had hurt her touched Saxon. She put her hand out to his.

"Billy," she began; then waited till Mary had left the room. "I never asked before—not that it matters now—but I waited for you to tell me. Was it—?"

He shook his head. "No; it was a girl, a perfect little girl."

She pressed his hand, and almost it was she that sympathized with him in his affliction. "I never told you, Billy—you were so set on a boy; but I planned, just the same, if it *was* a girl, to call her Daisy. You remember, that was my mother's name."

He nodded his approbation. "Say, Saxon, you know I did want a boy like the

very dickens. Well, I don't care now. I think I'm set just as hard on a girl, an', well, here's hopin' the next will be called —you wouldn't mind, would you?"

"What?"

"If we call it the same name, Daisy?"

"Oh, Billy! I was thinking the very same thing."

Then his face grew stern, as he went on. "Only there ain't goin' to be a next. I didn't know what havin' children was like before. You can't run any more risks like that."

"Hear the big, strong, afraid-man talk!" she jeered, with a wan smile. "You don't know anything about it. How can a man? I am a healthy, natural woman. Everything would have been all right this time if—if all that fighting hadn't happened." Her lips trembled, and she began to cry weakly, clinging to Billy's hand with both of hers. "I—I can't help it," she sobbed. "I'll be all right in a minute. Our little girl, Billy. Think of it! And I never saw her!"

As Saxon's strength came back to her she herself took up the matter of the industrial tragedy that had taken place before her door. The militia had been called out immediately, Billy informed her, and was encamped then at the foot of Pine Street on the waste ground next the railroad yards. As for the strikers, fifteen of them were in jail. A house-to-house search had been made in the neighborhood by the police, and in this way nearly the whole fifteen, all wounded, had been captured. It would go hard with them, Billy foreboded gloomily. The newspapers were demanding blood for blood, and all the ministers in Oakland had preached fierce sermons against the strikers. The railroad had filled every place, and it was well known that the striking shopmen not only would never get their old jobs back, but were blacklisted by every railroad in the United States. Already they were beginning to scatter. A number had gone to Panama, and four were talking of going to Ecuador to work in the shops of the railroad that ran over the Andes to Quito.

With anxiety keenly concealed, she tried to feel out Billy's opinion on what had happened. "That shows what Bert's violent methods come to," she said.

He shook his head slowly and gravely. "They'll hang Chester Johnson anyway," he answered indirectly. "You know him.

Jack London 69

You told me you used to dance with him. He was caught red handed, lyin' on the body of a scab he beat to death. Old Jelly Belly's got three bullet-holes in him, but he ain't goin' to die, and he's got Chester's number. They'll hang 'm on Jelly Belly's evidence. It was all in the papers. Jelly Belly shot him, too, a hangin' by the neck on our pickets."

Vainly Saxon waited for Billy to say something that would show he did not countenance the killing of the scabs.

"It was wrong," she ventured finally.

"They killed Bert," he countered. "An' a lot of others. An' Frank Davis. Did you know he was dead? Had his whole lower jaw shot away—died in the ambulance before they could get him to the receiving hospital. There was never so much killin' at one time in Oakland before."

"But it was their fault," she contended. "They began it. It was murder."

"What of it?" Billy laughed harshly, as if in answer to her unuttered questions. "It's dog eat dog, I guess, and it's always been that way. Take that scrap outside there. They killed each other just like the North an' South did in the Civil War."

"But workingmen can't win that way, Billy. You say yourself that it spoiled their chance of winning."

"I suppose not," he admitted reluctantly. "But what other chance they've got to win I don't see. Look at us. We'll be up against it next."

"Not the teamsters?" she cried.

He nodded gloomily. "The bosses are cuttin' loose all along the line for a high old time. Say they're goin' to beat us to our knees till we come crawlin' back a-beggin' for our jobs. They've bucked up real high an' mighty, what of all that killin' the other day. Havin' the troops out is half the fight, along with havin' the preachers an' the papers an' the public behind 'em. They're shootin' off their mouths already about what they're goin' to do. They're sure gunning for trouble. First, they're goin' to hang Chester Johnson an' as many more of the fifteen as they can. They say that flat. They're all union-bustin' to beat the band. No more closed shop. Fine, eh? You bet it's fine.

"Look at us. It ain't a case any more of a sympathetic strike for the mill-workers. We got our own troubles. They've fired our four best men—the ones that was always on the conference committees. Did it without cause. They're lookin' for trouble, as I told you, an' they'll get it, too, if they don't watch out. We got our tip from the Frisco Water Front Confederation. With them backin' us we'll go some."

"You mean you'll—strike?" Saxon asked. He bent his head.

"But isn't that what they want you to do?—from the way they're acting?"

"What's the difference?" Billy shrugged his shoulders, then continued: "It's better to strike than to get fired. We beat 'em to it, that's all, an' we catch 'em before they're ready. Don't we know what they're doin'? They're collectin' gradin'-camp drivers an' mule-skinners all up an' down the state. They got forty of 'em, feedin' 'em in a hotel in Stockton right now, an' ready to rush 'em in on us, an' hundreds more like them. So this Saturday's the last wages I'll likely bring home for some time."

Saxon closed her eyes and thought quietly for five minutes. It was not her way to take things excitedly. The coolness of poise that Billy so admired never deserted her in time of emergency. She realized that she herself was no more than a mote caught up in this tangled, nonunderstandable conflict of many motes.

"We'll have to draw from our savings to pay for this month's rent," she said brightly.

Billy's face fell. "We ain't got as much in the bank as you think," he confessed. "Bert had to be buried, you know, an' I coughed up what the others couldn't raise."

"How much was it?"

"Forty dollars. I was goin' to stand off the butcher an' the rest for a while. They knew I was good pay. But they put it to me straight. They'd been carryin' the shopmen right along an' was up against it themselves. An' now, with that strike smashed, they're pretty much smashed themselves. So I paid them, too. I knew you wouldn't mind. You don't, do you?"

She smiled bravely, and bravely overcame the sinking feeling at her heart. "It was the only right thing to do, Billy. I would have done it if you were lying sick, and Bert would have done it for you an' me if it had been the other way around."

His face was glowing. "Gee, Saxon, a fellow can always count on you. You're like my right hand. That's why I say no more babies. If I lose you I'm crippled for life."

"We've got to economize," she mused, nodding her appreciation. "And you must watch out for yourself, Billy. I don't want to lose you either."

"Aw, that's all right. I can take care of myself. An' besides, it ain't as though we was licked. We got a good chance."

"But you'll lose if there's any killing."

"Yep; we gotta keep an eye out against that."

"No violence."

"No gun-fightin' or dynamite," he assented. "But a heap of scabs'll get their heads broke. That has to be."

"But you won't do any of that, Billy."

"Not so as any slob can testify before a court to havin' seen me."

XXI

WITH Billy on strike and away doing picket duty, Saxon was left much to herself in a loneliness that even to one as healthy minded as she, could not fail to produce morbidness. Mary, too, had left, having spoken vaguely of taking a job at housework in Piedmont.

Billy could help Saxon little in her trouble. He dimly sensed her suffering, without comprehending the scope and intensity of it. He was too man-practical, and, by his very sex, too remote from the intimate tragedy that was hers. He was an outsider at the best, a friendly onlooker who saw little. To her the baby had been quick and real. It was still quick and real. That was her trouble. By no deliberate effort of will could she fill the aching void of its absence. Its reality became, at times, an hallucination. Somewhere it still was, and she must find it. She would catch herself, on occasion, listening with strained ears for the cry she had never heard, yet which, in fancy, she had heard a thousand times in the happy months before the end. Twice she left her bed in her sleep and went searching—each time coming to herself beside her mother's chest of drawers in which were the tiny garments. To herself, at such moments, she would say, "I had a baby once." And she would say it, aloud, as she watched the children playing in the street.

One day, on the Eighth Street cars, a young mother sat beside her, a crowing infant in her arms. And Saxon said to her: "I had a baby once. It died."

The mother looked at her, startled, half drew the baby tighter in her arms, jealously, or as if in fear; then she softened as she said, "You poor thing."

"Yes," Saxon nodded. "It died."

Tears welled into her eyes, and the telling of her grief seemed to have brought relief. But all the day she suffered from almost overwhelming desire to recite her sorrow to the world—to the paying teller at the bank, to the elderly floor-walker in Salinger's, to the blind woman, guided by a little boy, who played on the concertina—to everyone save the policeman. The police were new and terrible creatures to her now. She had seen them kill the strikers as mercilessly as the strikers had killed the scabs. And, unlike the strikers, the police were professional killers. They were not fighting for jobs. They did it as a business. They could have taken prisoners that day, in the angle of her front steps and the house. But they had not. Unconsciously, whenever approaching one, she edged across the sidewalk so as to get as far as possible away from him. She did not reason it out, but deeper than consciousness was the feeling that they were typical of something inimical to her and hers.

As the summer months dragged along, the industrial situation grew steadily worse. Capital everywhere seemed to have selected this city for the battle with organized labor. So many men in Oakland were out on strike, or were locked out, or were unable to work because of the dependence of their trades on the other tied-up trades, that odd jobs at common labor were hard to obtain. Billy occasionally got a day's work to do, but did not earn enough to make both ends meet, despite the small strike wages received at first, and despite the rigid economy he and Saxon practised.

The table she set had scarcely anything in common with that of their first married year. Not alone was every item of cheaper quality, but many items had disappeared. Meat, even the poorest, was very seldom on the table. Cow's milk had given place to condensed milk, and even the sparing use of the latter had ceased. A roll of butter, when they had it, lasted half a dozen times as long as formerly. Where Billy had been used to drinking three cups of coffee for breakfast, he now drank one. Saxon boiled this coffee an atrocious length of time, and she paid twenty cents a pound for it.

The blight of hard times was on all the neighborhood. The families not involved in one strike were touched by some other strike or by the cessation of work in some dependent trade. Many single young men who were lodgers had drifted away, thus increasing the house rent of the families which had sheltered them.

"Gott!" said the butcher to Saxon. "We working class all suffer together. My wife she cannot get her teeth fixed now. Pretty soon I go smash broke maybe."

Once, when Billy was preparing to pawn his watch, Saxon suggested his borrowing the money from Billy Murphy.

"I was plannin' that," Billy answered, "only I can't now. I didn't tell you what happened Tuesday night at the Sporting Life Club. You remember that square-head champion of the United States navy? Bill was matched with him, an' it was sure easy money. Bill had 'm goin' south by the end of the sixth round, an' at the seventh went in to finish 'm. And then —just his luck, for his trade's idle now—he snaps his right forearm. Of course the squarehead comes back at 'm on the jump, an' it's good night for Bill. Gee! Us Mohicans are gettin' our bad luck handed to us in chunks these days."

"Don't!" Saxon cried, shuddering involuntarily.

"What?" Billy asked with open mouth of surprise.

"Don't say that word again. Bert was always saying it."

"Oh, Mohicans. All right, I won't. You ain't superstitious, are you?"

"No; but just the same there's too much truth in the word for me to like it. Sometimes it seems as though he was right. Times have changed. They've changed even since I was a little girl. We crossed the plains and opened up this country, and now we're losing even the chance to work for a living in it. And it's not my fault, it's not your fault. We've got to live well or bad just by luck, it seems. There's no other way to explain it."

"It beats me," Billy concurred. "Look at the way I worked last year. Never missed a day. I wanted to never miss a day this year, an' here I haven't done a tap for weeks an' weeks an' weeks. Say! Who runs this country anyway?"

Saxon had stopped the morning paper, but frequently Mrs. Donahue's boy, who served a *Tribune* route, tossed an "extra" on her steps. From its editorials Saxon gleaned that organized labor was trying to run the country, and that it was making a mess of it. It was all the fault of domineering labor—so ran the editorials, column after column, day by day; and Saxon was convinced, yet remained unconvinced. The social puzzle of living was too intricate.

The teamsters' strike, backed financially by the teamsters of San Francisco and by the allied unions of the San Francisco Water Front Confederation, promised to be long-drawn, whether or not it was successful. The Oakland harness-washers and stablemen, with few exceptions, had gone out with the teamsters. The teaming firms were not half-filling their contracts, but the employers' association was helping them. In fact, half the employers' associations of the Pacific Coast were helping the Oakland Employers' Association.

Saxon was behind a month's rent, which, when it is considered that rent was paid in advance, was equivalent to two months. Likewise, she was two months behind in the instalments on the furniture. Yet she was not pressed very hard by Salingers, the furniture-dealers.

"We're givin' you all the rope we can," said their collector. "My orders is to make you dig up every cent I can and at the same time not be too hard. Salingers are trying to do the right thing, but they're up against it, too. You've no idea how many accounts like yours they're carrying along. Sooner or later they'll have to call a halt or get it in the neck themselves. And in the meantime just see if you can't scrape up five dollars by next week—just to cheer them along, you know."

One of the stablemen who had not gone out, Henderson by name, worked at Billy's stables. Despite the urging of the bosses to eat and sleep in the stable like the other men, Henderson had persisted in coming home each morning to his little house around the corner from Saxon's on Fifth Street. Several times she had seen him swinging along defiantly, his dinner-pail in his hand, while the neighborhood boys dogged his heels at a safe distance and informed him in yapping chorus that he was a scab and no good. But one evening, on his way from work, in a spirit of bravado he went into the Pile-Driver's Home, the saloon at Seventh and Pine. There it was his mortal mischance to encounter Otto Frank, a striker who drove from the same stable. Not many minutes later an ambulance was hurrying Henderson to the receiving hospital with a fractured skull, while a patrol wagon was no less swiftly carrying Otto Frank to the city prison.

Mrs. Donahue it was, eyes shining with gladness, who told Saxon of the happening. "Served him right, too, the dirty scab," she concluded.

"But his poor wife!" was Saxon's cry. "She's not strong. And then the children. She'll never be able to take care of them if her husband dies."

"An' serves her right. 'Tis all she or anny woman deserves that'll put up an' live with a scab. What about her children? Let 'm starve, an' her man a-takin' the food out of other children's mouths."

Mrs. Olsen's attitude was different. Beyond passive sentimental pity for Henderson's children and wife, she gave them no thought, her chief concern being for Otto Frank and Otto Frank's wife and children— herself and Mrs. Frank being full sisters.

"If he dies, they will hang Otto," she said. "And then what will poor Hilda do? She has varicose veins in both legs, and she never can stand on her feet all day an' work for wages. And me, I cannot help. Ain't Carl out of work, too?"

Billy had still another point of view. "It will give the strike a black eye, especially if Henderson croaks," he worried, when he came home. "They'll hang Frank in record time. Besides, we'll have to put up a defense, an' lawyers charge like Sam Hill. They'll eat a hole in our treasury you could drive every team in Oakland through. An' if Frank hadn't been screwed up with whiskey he'd never a-done it. He's the mildest, good-naturedest man sober you ever seen."

Twice that evening Billy left the house to find out if Henderson was dead yet. In the morning the papers gave little hope, and the evening papers published his death. Otto Frank lay in jail without bail. The *Tribune* demanded a quick trial and summary execution, calling on the prospective jury manfully to do its duty and dwelling at length on the moral effect that would be so produced upon the lawless working class. It went further, emphasizing the salutary effect machine guns would have on the mob that had taken the fair city of Oakland by the throat.

And all such occurrences struck at Saxon personally. Practically alone in the world, save for Billy, it was her life, and his, and their mutual love-life, that was menaced. From the moment he left the house to the moment of his return, she knew no peace of mind. Rough work was afoot, of which he told her nothing, and she knew he was playing his part in it. On more than one occasion she had noticed fresh-broken skin on his knuckles. At such times he was remarkably taciturn, and would sit in brooding silence or go almost immediately to bed. She was afraid to have this habit of reticence grow on him, and bravely she bid for his confidence. She climbed into his lap and inside his arms, one of her arms around his neck, and with the free hand she caressed his hair back from the forehead and smoothed out the moody brows.

"Now listen to me, Billy Boy," she began lightly. "You haven't been playing fair, and I won't have it. No!" She pressed his lips shut with her fingers. "I'm doing the talking now, and because you haven't been doing your share of the talking for some time. You remember we agreed at the start to always talk things over. You're not talking things over with me. You are doing things you don't tell me about.

"Billy, you're dearer to me than anything else in the world. You know that. We're sharing each other's lives; only, just now, there's something you're not sharing. Every time your knuckles are sore, there's something you don't share. If you can't trust me, you can't trust anybody. And, besides, I love you so that no matter what you do I'll go on loving you just the same."

Billy gazed at her with fond incredulity. "Don't be a pincher," she teased. "Remember, I stand for whatever you do."

"And you won't buck against me?" he queried.

"How can I? I'm not your boss, Billy. I wouldn't boss you for anything in the world. And if you'd let me boss you I wouldn't love you half as much."

He digested this slowly, and finally nodded. "An' you won't be mad?"

"With you? You've never seen me mad yet. Now come on and be generous and tell me how you hurt your knuckles. It's fresh to-day. Anybody can see that."

"All right. I'll tell you how it happened." He stopped and giggled with genuine boyish glee at some recollection. "It's like this.

It was all over, and Saxon, moving as in a dream, came down the front steps. Bert's eyes were closed.
His lips moved, and faintly, almost reminiscently, he murmured, "The last
of the Mohicans, the last of the Mohicans!"

73

You won't be mad, now? We gotta do these sort of things to hold our own. Well, here's the show, a regular movin' picture except for the talkin'. Here's a big rube comin' along, hayseed stickin' out all over, hands like hams an' feet like Mississippi gunboats. He'd make half as much again as me in size, an' he's young, too. Only he ain't lookin' for trouble, an' he's as innocent as— well, he's the innocentest scab that ever come down the pike an' bumped into a couple of pickets. Not a regular strike-breaker, you see, just a big rube that's read the bosses' ads an' come a-humpin' to town for the big wages.

"An' here's Bud Strothers an' me comin' along. We always go in pairs that way, an' sometimes bigger bunches. I flag the rube. 'Hello,' says, I, 'lookin' for a job?' 'You bet,' says he. 'Can you drive?' 'Yep.' 'Four horses?' 'Show me to 'em,' says he. 'No josh, now,' says I; 'you're sure wantin' to drive?' 'That's what I come to town for,' he says. 'You're the man we're lookin' for,' says I. 'Come along, an' we'll have you busy in no time.'

"You see, Saxon, we can't pull it off there, because there's a cop only a couple of blocks away an' pipin' us off, though not recognizin' us. So away we go, the three of us, Bud an' me leadin' that boob to take our jobs away from us, I guess nit. We turn into the alley back of Campwell's grocery. Nobody in sight. Bud stops short, and the rube an' me stop.

"'I don't think he wants to drive,' Bud says, considerin'. An' the rube says quick, 'You betcher life I do.' 'You're dead sure you want that job?' I says. Yes, he's dead sure. Nothin' 's goin' to keep him away from that job. Why, that job's what he come to town for, an' we can't lead him to it too quick.

"'Well, my friend,' says I, 'it's my sad duty to inform you that you've made a mistake.' 'How's that?' says he. 'Go on,' I says; 'you're standin' on your foot.' An' honest to God, Saxon, that gink looks down at his feet to see. 'I don't understand,' says he. 'We're goin' to show you,' says I.

"An' then—Biff! Bang! Bingo! Swat! Zooie! Ker-slam-bango-blam! Fireworks, Fourth of July, Kingdom Come, blue lights, sky-rockets, an' hell fire—just like that. It don't take long when you're scientific an' trained to tandem work. Of course it's hard on the knuckles. But say, Saxon, if you'd seen that rube before an' after you'd thought he was a lightnin'-change artist. You'd 'a' busted."

Billy halted to give vent to his own mirth. Saxon forced herself to join with him, but down in her heart was horror. Mercedes was right. The stupid workers wrangled and snarled over jobs. The clever masters rode in automobiles and did not wrangle and snarl. They hired other stupid ones to do the wrangling and snarling for them. It was men like Bert and Frank Davis, like Chester Johnson and Otto Frank, like Henderson and all the rest of the scabs who were beaten up, shot, clubbed, or hanged. Ah, the clever ones were very clever. Nothing happened to them. They only rode in their automobiles.

"'You big stiffs,' the rube snivels as he crawls to his feet at the end," Billy was continuing. "'You think you want still that job?' I ask. He shakes his head. Then I read 'm the riot act: 'They's only one thing for you to do, old hoss, an' that's beat it. D'ye get me? Beat it. Back to the farm for *you*. An' if you come monkeyin' around town again, we'll be real mad at you. We was only foolin' this time. But next time we catch you your own mother won't know you when we get done with you.'

"An' say! you oughta seen 'm beat it. I bet he's goin' yet. An' when he gets back to Milpitas, or Sleepy Hollow, or wherever he hangs out, an' tells how the boys does things in Oakland, it's dollars to doughnuts they won't be a rube in his district that'd come to town to drive if they offered ten dollars an hour."

"It was awful," Saxon said, then laughed well-simulated appreciation.

"But that was nothin'," Billy went on. "A bunch of the boys caught another one this morning. They didn't do a thing to him. My goodness gracious, no. In less 'n two minutes he was the worst wreck they ever hauled to the receivin' hospital. The evenin' papers gave the score: nose broken, three bad scalp wounds, front teeth out, a broken collarbone, an' two broken ribs. Gee! He certainly got all that was comin' to him. But that's nothin'. D'ye want to know what the Frisco teamsters did in the big strike before the Earthquake? They took every scab they caught 'an' broke both his arms with a crowbar. That was so he couldn't drive, you see. Say, the hospitals was filled with 'em. An' the teamsters won that strike, too."

"But is it necessary, Billy, to be so terrible? I know they're scabs, and that they're taking the bread out of the strikers' children's mouths to put in their own children's mouths, and that it isn't fair and all that; but just the same is it necessary to be so terrible?"

"Sure thing," Billy answered confidently. "We just gotta throw the fear of God into them—when we can do it without bein' caught."

"And if you're caught?"

"Then the unions hires the lawyers to defend us, though that ain't much good now, for the judges are pretty hostyle, an' the papers keep hammerin' away at them to give stiffer an' stiffer sentences. Just the same, before this strike's over there'll be a whole lot of guys a'wishin' they'd never gone scabbin'.'"

Very cautiously, in the next half-hour, Saxon tried to feel out her husband's attitude, to find if he doubted the rightness of the violence he and his brother teamsters committed. But Billy's ethical sanction was rock-bedded and profound. It never entered his head that he was not absolutely right. It was the game. Caught in its tangled meshes, he could see no other way to play it than the way all men played it. He did not stand for dynamite and murder, however. But then the unions did not stand for such. Quite naive was his explanation that dynamite and murder did not pay; that such actions always brought down the condemnation of the public and broke the strikes. But the healthy beating up of a scab, he contended—the "throwing of the fear of God into a scab," as he expressed it—was the only right and proper thing to do.

"Our folks never had to do such things," Saxon said finally. "They never had strikes nor scabs in those times."

"You bet they didn't," Billy agreed. "Them was the good old days. I'd like to a-lived then." He drew a long breath and sighed. "But them times will never come again."

"Would you have liked living in the country?" Saxon asked.

"Sure thing."

"There's lots of men living in the country now," she suggested.

"Just the same I notice them a-hikin' to town to get our jobs," was his reply.

A gleam of light came when Billy got a job driving a grading team for the contractors of the big bridge then building at Niles. Before he went he made certain that it was a union job. And a union job it was for two days, when the concrete-workers threw down their tools. The contractors, evidently prepared for such a happening, immediately filled the places of the concrete-men with non-union Italians. Whereupon the carpenters, structural ironworkers, and teamsters walked out; and Billy, lacking train fare, spent the rest of the day in walking home. "I couldn't work as a scab," he concluded his tale.

"No," Saxon said; "you couldn't work as a scab."

But she wondered why it was that when men wanted to work, and there was work to do, they were yet unable to work because their unions said no. Why were these unions? And if unions had to be, why were not all workingmen in them? Then there would be no scabs, and Billy could work every day. Also, she wondered where she was to get the next sack of flour, for she had long since ceased the extravagance of baker's bread. And so many other of the neighborhood women had done this that the little Welsh baker had closed up shop and gone away, taking his wife and two little daughters with him. Look where she would, everybody was being hurt by the industrial strife.

XXII

One afternoon came a caller at her door, and that evening came Billy with dubious news. He had been approached that day. All he had to do, he told Saxon, was say the word, and he could go into the stable as foreman at one hundred dollars a month.

The nearness of such a sum, the possibility of it, was almost stunning to Saxon, sitting at a supper which consisted of boiled potatoes, warmed-over beans, and a small dry onion which they were eating raw. There was neither bread, coffee, nor butter. The onion Billy had pulled from his pocket, having picked it up in the street. *One hundred dollars a month!* She moistened her lips and fought for control.

"What made them offer it to you?" she questioned.

"That's easy," was his answer. "They got a dozen reasons. The guy the boss has had exercisin' Prince and King is a dub. King has gone lame in the shoulders. Then they're guessin' pretty strong that I'm the party that's put a lot of their scabs outa commission. Macklin's been their foreman for years an' years—why, I was in knee pants when he was foreman. Well, he's sick an' all in. They gotta have somebody to take his place. Then, too, I've been with 'em a long time. An' on top of that, I'm the man for the job. They know I know horses from the ground up."

"Think of it, Billy!" she breathed. "A hundred dollars a month!"

"An' throw the fellows down," he said.

It was not a question. Nor was it a statement. It was anything Saxon chose to make of it. They looked at each other. She waited for him to speak; but he continued merely to look. It came to her that she was facing one of the decisive moments of her life, and she gripped herself to face it in all coolness. Nor would Billy proffer the slightest help. Whatever his own judgment might be, he masked it with an expressionless face. His eyes betrayed nothing. He looked and waited.

"You, you can't do that, Billy," she said finally. "You can't throw the fellows down."

His hand shot out to hers, and his face was a sudden, radiant dawn. "Put her there!" he cried. "You're the truest true-blue wife a man ever had. If all the other fellows' wives was like you, we could win any strike we tackled."

"What would you have done if you weren't married, Billy?"

"Seen 'em in hell first."

"Then it doesn't make any difference being married. I've got to stand by you in everything you stand by. I'd be a nice wife if I didn't."

She remembered her caller of the afternoon, and knew the moment was too propitious to let pass. "There was a man here this afternoon, Billy. He wanted a room. I told him I'd speak to you. He said he would pay six dollars a month for the back bedroom. That would pay half a month's instalment on the furniture and buy a sack of flour, and we're all out of flour."

Billy's old hostility to the idea was instantly uppermost, and Saxon watched him anxiously. "Some scab in the shops, I suppose?"

"No; he's firing on the freight run to San Jose. Harmon, he said his name was,

James Harmon. They've just transferred him from the Truckee division. He'll sleep days mostly, he said; and that's why he wanted a quiet house without children in it."

In the end, with much misgiving, and only after Saxon had insistently pointed out how little work it entailed on her, Billy consented, though he continued to protest, as an afterthought: "But I don't want you makin' beds for any man. It ain't right, Saxon. I oughta take care of you."

"And you would," she flashed back at him, "if you'd take the foremanship. Only you can't. It wouldn't be right. And if I'm to stand by you it's only fair to let me do what I can."

James Harmon proved even less a bother than Saxon had anticipated. For a fireman he was scrupulously clean, always washing up in the roundhouse before he came home. He used the key to the kitchen door, coming and going by the back steps. To Saxon he barely said how-do-you-do or good day; and, sleeping in the daytime and working at night, he was in the house a week before Billy laid eyes on him.

Billy had taken to coming home later and later, and to going out after supper by himself. He did not offer to tell Saxon where he went. Nor did she ask. For that matter, it required little shrewdness on her part to guess. The fumes of whiskey were on his lips at such times. His slow, deliberate ways were even slower, even more deliberate. Liquor did not affect his legs. He walked as soberly as any man. There was no hesitancy, no faltering, in his muscular movements. The whiskey went to his brain, making his eyes heavy lidded and the cloudiness of them more cloudy. Not that he was flighty, nor quick, nor irritable. On the contrary, the liquor imparted to his mental processes a deep gravity and brooding solemnity. He talked little, but that little was ominous and oracular. At such times there was no appeal from his judgment, no discussion. He knew, as God knew. And when he chose to speak a harsh thought, it was tenfold harsher than ordinarily, because it seemed to proceed out of such profundity of cogitation, because it was as prodigiously deliberate in its incubation as it was in its enunciation.

It was not a nice side he was showing to Saxon. It was almost as if a stranger had come to live with her. Despite herself,

"Saxon, won't you strike a light?" asked Billy. "My fingers is all thumbs." Saxon hastened to
light the lamp. . . . When she turned to look at him, though she had heard his
voice and knew him to be Billy, for the instant she did not recognize him

77

she found herself beginning to shrink from him. And little could she comfort herself with the thought that it was not his real self, for she remembered his gentleness and considerateness, all his finenesses of the past. Then, he had made a continual effort to avoid trouble and fighting. Now he enjoyed it, exulted in it, went looking for it. All this showed in his face. No longer was he the smiling, pleasant-faced boy. He smiled infrequently now. His face was a man's face. The lips, the eyes, the lines, were harsh as his thoughts were harsh.

He was rarely unkind to Saxon; but, on the other hand, he was rarely kind. His attitude toward her was growing negative. He was disinterested. Despite the fight for the union she was enduring with him, putting up with him shoulder to shoulder, she occupied but little space in his mind. When he acted toward her gently, she could see that it was merely mechanical, just as she was well aware that the endearing terms he used, the endearing caresses he gave, were only habitual. The spontaneity and warmth had gone out. Often, when he was not in liquor, flashes of the old Billy came back, but even such flashes dwindled in frequency. He was growing preoccupied, moody. Hard times and the bitter stresses of industrial conflict strained him.

One thing, however, Saxon saw clearly. By no deliberate act of Billy's was he becoming this other and unlovely Billy. Were there no strike, no snarling and wrangling over jobs, there would be only the old Billy she had loved in all absoluteness. This sleeping terror in him would have lain asleep. It was something that was being awakened in him, an image incarnate of outward conditions, as cruel, as ugly, as maleficent as were those outward conditions, But if the strike continued, then she feared, with reason, would this other and grisly self of Billy strengthen to fuller and more forbidding stature. And this, she knew, would mean the wreck of their love-life. Such a Billy she could not love; in its nature such a Billy was not lovable nor capable of love. And then, at the thought of offspring, she shuddered. It was too terrible. And at such moments of contemplation, from her soul the inevitable plaint of the human went up: *Why? Why? Why?*

Billy, too, had his unanswerable queries.

"Why won't the building trades come out?" he demanded wrathfully of the obscurity that veiled the ways of living and the world. "But no; O'Brien won't stand for a strike, and he has the Building Trades Council under his thumb. But why don't they chuck him and come out anyway? We'd win hands down all along the line. If all the railroad boys had come out, wouldn't the shop-men have won instead of bein' licked to a frazzle? Lord, I ain't had a smoke of decent tobacco or a cup of decent coffee in a coon's age. I've forgotten what a square meal tastes like. I weighed myself yesterday. Fifteen pounds lighter than when the strike begun. If it keeps on much more I can fight middleweight. An' this is what I get after payin' dues into the union for years and years. I can't get a square meal, an' my wife has to make other men's beds. It makes my tired ache. Some day I'll get real huffy an' chuck that lodger out."

"But it's not his fault, Billy," Saxon protested.

"Who said it was?" Billy snapped roughly. "Can't I kick in general if I want to? Just the same it makes me sick. What's the good of organized labor if it don't stand together? What's the good of supportin' a union that can't win a strike? What's the good of knockin' the blocks off of scabs when they keep a-comin' thick as ever? The whole thing's bughouse, an' I guess I am, too."

Such an outburst on Billy's part was so unusual that it was the only time Saxon knew it to occur. Always he was sullen, and dogged, and unwhipped; while whiskey only served to set the maggots of certitude crawling in his brain.

XXIII

FROM now on, to Saxon, life seemed bereft of its last reason and rhyme. It had become senseless, nightmarish. Anything irrational was possible. There was nothing stable in the anarchic flux of affairs that swept Saxon she knew not to what catastrophic end. Had Billy been dependable, all would still have been well. With him to cling to she would have faced everything fearlessly. But he had been whirled away from her in the prevailing madness. So radical was the change in him that he seemed almost an intruder in the house. Spiritually he was such an intruder. Another man looked out of his eyes—a man whose thoughts were of violence and hatred; a man to whom there was no good in anything, and who had become an ardent protagonist of the evil that was rampant and universal. This man no longer condemned Bert, himself muttering vaguely of dynamite, and sabotage, and revolution.

Saxon strove to maintain that sweetness and coolness of flesh and spirit that Billy had praised in the old days. Once, only, she lost control. He had been in a particularly ugly mood, and a final harshness and unfairness cut her to the quick.

"Who are you speaking to?" she flamed out at him.

He was speechless and abashed, and could only stare at her face, which was white with anger.

"Don't you ever speak to me like that again, Billy," she commanded imperatively.

"Aw, can't you put up with a piece of bad temper?" he muttered, half apologetically yet half defiantly. "God knows I got enough to make me cranky."

After he left the house she flung herself on the bed and cried heart-brokenly. For she, who knew so thoroughly the humility of love, was a proud woman. Only the proud can be truly humble, as only the strong may know the fullness of gentleness. But what was the use, she demanded, of being proud and game, when the only being in the world who mattered to her lost his own pride and gameness and fairness and gave her the worse share of their mutual trouble?

And now, as she had faced alone the deeper, organic hurt of the loss of her baby, she faced alone another, and, in a way, an even greater personal trouble. Perhaps she loved Billy none the less, but her love was changing into something less proud, less confident, less trusting; it was becoming shot through with pity—with the pity that is parent to contempt. Her own loyalty was threatening to weaken, and she shuddered and shrank from the contempt she could see creeping in.

She struggled to steel herself to face the situation. Forgiveness stole into her heart, and she knew relief until the thought came that in the truest, highest love forgiveness should have no place. And again she cried, and continued her battle. After all, one thing was incontestable: *This Billy was not the Billy she had loved.* This Billy was another man, a sick man, and no more to be held responsible than a fever-patient in the ravings of delirium. She must be Billy's nurse, without pride, without contempt, with nothing to forgive. Besides, he was really bearing the brunt of the fight, was in the thick of it, dizzy with the striking of blows and the blows he received. If fault there was, it lay elsewhere—somewhere in the tangled scheme of things that made men snarl over jobs like dogs over bones.

So Saxon arose and buckled on her armor again for the hardest fight of all in the world's arena—the woman's fight. She ejected from her thought all doubting and distrust. She forgave nothing, for there was nothing requiring forgiveness. She pledged herself to an absoluteness of belief that her love and Billy's was unsullied, unperturbed—serene as it had always been, as it would be when it came back again after the world settled down once more to rational ways.

That night, when he came home, she proposed, as an emergency measure, that she should sell some of her needlework and help keep the pot boiling until the strike was over. But Billy would hear nothing of it.

"It's all right," he assured her repeatedly. "They ain't no call for you to work. I'm goin' to get some money before the week is out. An' I'll turn it over to you. An' Saturday night we'll go to the show—a real show, no movin' pictures. Harvey's nigger minstrels is comin' to town. We'll go Saturday night. I'll have the money before that, as sure as beans is beans."

Friday evening he did not come home to supper, which Saxon regretted, for Mrs. Donahue had returned a pan of potatoes and two quarts of flour (borrowed the week before), and it was a hearty meal that awaited him. Saxon kept the stove going till nine o'clock, when, despite her reluctance, she went to bed. Her preference would have been to wait up, but she did not dare, knowing full well what the effect would be on him did he come home in liquor.

The clock had just struck one when she heard the click of the gate. Slowly, heavily, ominously, she heard him come up the steps and fumble with his key at the door. He entered the bedroom, and she heard him sigh as he sat down. She remained quiet, for she had learned the hypersensitiveness induced by drink, and was fastidiously careful not to

"'You can't win,' Bill says. 'Watch me,' says I. An' with that I make a rush for the Terror, catchin'
him unexpected. I'm that groggy I can't stand, but I just keep a-goin', wallopin'
the Terror clean across the ring to his corner'"

80

hurt him even with the knowledge that she had lain awake for him. It was not easy. Her hands were clenched till the nails dented the palms, and her body was rigid in her passionate effort for control. Never had he come home as bad as this.

"Saxon?" he called thickly. "Saxon?" She stirred and yawned. "What is it?" she asked.

"Won't you strike a light? My fingers is all thumbs."

She hastened to light the lamp, but so violent was the nervous trembling of her hands that the glass chimney tinkled against the globe, and the match went out.

"I ain't drunk, Saxon," he said in the darkness, a hint of amusement in his thick voice. "I've only had two or three jolts—of that sort."

On her second attempt with the lamp she succeeded. When she turned to look at him, though she had heard his voice and knew him to be Billy, for the instant she did not recognize him. His face was a face she had never known. Swollen, bruised, discolored, every feature had been beaten out of all semblance of familiarity. One eye was entirely closed, the other showed through a narrow slit of blood-congested flesh. One ear seemed to have lost most of its skin. The whole face was a swollen pulp. His right jaw, in particular, was twice the size of the left. No wonder his speech had been thick, was her thought, as she regarded the fearfully cut and swollen lips that still bled. She was sickened by the sight, and her heart went out to him in a great wave of tenderness. She wanted to put her arms around him, and cuddle and soothe him; but her practical judgment bade otherwise.

"You poor, poor boy," she cried. "Tell me what you want me to do first. I don't know about such things."

"If you could help me get my clothes off," he suggested meekly and thickly. "I got 'em on before I stiffened up."

"And then hot water—that will be good," she said, as she began gently drawing his coat sleeve over a puffed and helpless hand.

"I told you they was all thumbs," he grimaced, holding up his hand and squinting at it with the fraction of sight remaining to him.

"You sit and wait," she said, "till I start the fire and get the hot water going. I won't be a minute. Then I'll finish getting your clothes off."

From the kitchen she could hear him mumbling to himself, and when she returned he was repeating over and over:

"We needed the money, Saxon. We needed the money."

Drunken he was not, she could see that, and from his babbling she knew he was partly delirious.

"He was a surprise box," he wandered on, while she proceeded to undress him; and bit by bit she was able to piece together what had happened. "He was an unknown from Chicago. They sprang him on me. The secretary of the Acme Club warned me I'd have my hands full. An' I'd 'a' won if I'd been in condition. But I'd been drinkin' pretty regular, an' I didn't have my wind."

But Saxon, stripping his undershirt, no longer heard him. As with his face, she could not recognize his splendidly muscled back. The white sheath of silken skin was torn and bloody. The lacerations occurred oftenest in horizontal lines, though there were perpendicular lines as well.

"How did you get all that?" she asked.

"The ropes. I was up against 'em more times than I like to remember. Gee! He certainly gave me mine. But I fooled 'm. He couldn't put me out. I lasted the twenty rounds, an' I wanta tell you he's got some marks to remember me by. If he ain't got a couple of knuckles broke in the left hand I'm a geezer. Here, feel my head here. Swollen, eh? Sure thing. He hit that more times than he's wishin' he had right now. But, oh, what a lacin'! What a lacin'! I never had anything like it before. The Chicago Terror, they call 'm. I take my hat off to 'm. He's some bear. But I could 'a' made 'm take the count if I'd been in condition an' had my wind. Oh! Ouch! Watch out! It's like a boil!"

Fumbling at his waistband, Saxon's hand had come in contact with a brightly inflamed surface larger than a soup-plate.

"That's from the kidney blows," Billy explained. "He was a regular devil at it. Most every clinch, like clockwork, down he'd chop one on me. It got so sore I was wincin' until I got groggy an' didn't know much of anything. It ain't a knockout blow, you know, but it's awful wearin' in a long fight. It takes the starch out of you."

When his knees were bared, Saxon could see the skin across the knee-caps was broken and gone.

"The skin ain't made to stand a heavy fellow like me on the knees," he volunteered. "An' the rosin in the canvas cuts like Sam Hill."

The tears were in Saxon's eyes, and she could have cried over the manhandled body of her beautiful sick boy. As she carried his pants across the room to hang them up, a jingle of money came from them. He called her back, and from the pocket drew forth a handful of silver.

"We needed the money, we needed the money," he kept muttering, as he vainly tried to count the coins; and Saxon knew that his mind was wandering again.

It cut her to the heart, for she could not but remember the harsh thoughts that had threatened her loyalty during the week past. After all, Billy, the splendid physical man, was only a boy, her boy. And he had faced and endured all this terrible punishment for her, for the house and the furniture that were their house and furniture. He said so, now, when he scarcely knew what he said. He said, "We needed the money." She was not so absent from his thoughts as she had fancied. Here, down to the naked tie-ribs of his soul, when he was half unconscious, the thought of her persisted, was uppermost. We needed the money. We!

The tears were trickling down her cheeks as she bent over him, and it seemed she had never loved him so much as now.

"Here; you count," he said, abandoning the effort and handing the money to her. "How much do you make it?"

"Nineteen dollars and thirty-five cents," said Saxon.

"That's right—the loser's end—twenty dollars. I had some drinks, an' treated a couple of the boys, an' then there was carfare. If I'd 'a' won, I'd 'a' got a hundred. That's what I fought for. It 'd 'a' put us on Easy Street for a while. You take it an' keep it. It's better 'n nothin'."

In bed, he could not sleep because of his pain, and hour by hour she worked over him, renewing the hot compresses over his bruises, soothing the lacerations with witch hazel and cold cream and the tenderest of finger-tips. And all the while, with broken intervals of groaning, he babbled on, living over the fight, seeking relief in telling her his trouble, voicing regret at loss of the money, and crying out the hurt to his pride. Far worse than the sum of his physical hurts was his hurt pride.

"He couldn't put me out, anyway. He had full swing at me in the times when I was too much in to get my hands up. The crowd was crazy. I showed 'em some stamina. They was times when he only rocked me, for I'd evaporated plenty of his steam for him in the openin' rounds. I don't know how many times he dropped me. Things was gettin' too dreamy. . . . Sometimes, toward the end, I could see three of him in the ring at once, an' I wouldn't know which to hit an' which to duck.

"But I fooled 'm. When I couldn't see, or feel, an' when my knees was shakin' an' my head goin' like a merry-go-round, I'd fall safe into clinches just the same. I bet the referee's arms is tired from draggin' us apart.

"But what a lacin'! What a lacin'! Say, Saxon, where are you? Oh, there, eh? I guess I was dreamin'. But, say, let this be a lesson to you. I broke my word an' went fightin', an' see what I got. Look at me, an' take warnin' so you won't make the same mistake an' go to makin' an' sellin' fancy work.

"But I fooled 'em—everybody. At the beginnin' the bettin' was even. By the sixth round the wise gazabas was offerin' two to one against me. I was licked from the first drop outa the box—anybody could see that; but he couldn't put me down for the count. By the tenth round they was offerin' even that I wouldn't last the round. At the eleventh they was offerin' I wouldn't last the fifteenth. An' I lasted the whole twenty. But some punishment, I want to tell you, some punishment.

"Why, they was four rounds I was in dreamland all the time—only I kept on my feet an' fought, or took the count to eight an' got up, an' stalled an' covered an' whanged away. I don't know what I done, except I must 'a' done like that, because I wasn't there. I don't know a thing from the thirteenth, when he sent me to the mat on my head, till the eighteenth. . . .

"Where was I? Oh, yes. I opened my eyes, or one eye, because I had only one that would open. An' there I was, in my corner, with the towels goin' an ammonia in my nose an' Bill Murphy with a chunk of ice at the back of my neck. An' there, across the ring, I could see the Chicago Terror, an' I had to do some thinkin' to remember I was fightin' him. It was like I'd been away somewhere an' just got back.

'What round's this comin'?' I ask Bill. 'The eighteenth,' says he. 'The hell,' I says. 'What's come of all the other rounds? The last I was fightin' in was the thirteenth.' 'You're a wonder,' says Bill. 'You've been out four rounds, only nobody knows it except me. I've been tryin' to get you to quit all the time.' Just then the gong sounds, an' I can see the Terror startin' for me. 'Quit,' says Bill, makin' a move to throw in the towel. 'Not on your life,' I says. 'Drop it, Bill.' But he went on wantin' me to quit. By that time the Terror had come across to my corner an' was standin' with his hands down, lookin' at me. The referee was lookin', too, an' the house was that quiet, lookin', you could hear a pin drop. An' my head was gettin' some clearer, but not much.

"'You can't win,' Bill says.

"'Watch me,' says I, An' with that I make a rush for the Terror, catchin' him unexpected. I'm that groggy I can't stand, but I just keep a-goin', wallopin' the Terror clear across the ring to his corner, where he slips an' falls, an' I fall on top of 'm. Say, that crowd goes crazy. . . .

"Where was I? My head's still goin' around, I guess. It's buzzin' like a swarm of bees."

"You'd just fallen on top of him in his corner," Saxon prompted.

"Oh, yes. Well, no sooner are we on our feet—an' I can't stand—I rush 'm the same way back across to my corner an' fall on 'm. That was luck. We got up, an I'd 'a' fallen, only I clinched an' held myself up by him.

"'I got your goat,' I says to him. 'An' now I'm goin' to eat you up.'

"I hadn't his goat, but I was playin' to get a piece of it, an' I got it, rushin' 'm as soon as the referee drags us apart an' fetchin' 'm a lucky wallop in the stomach that steadied 'm an' made 'm almighty careful. Too almighty careful. He was afraid to chance a mix with me. He thought I had more fight left in me than I had. So, you see, I got that much of his goat anyway.

"An' he couldn't get me. He didn't get me. An' in the twentieth we stood in the middle of the ring an' exchanged wallops even. Of course I'd made a fine showin' for a licked man, but he got the decision, which was right. But I fooled 'm. He couldn't get me. An' I fooled the gazabas

that was bettin' he would put me out on short order."

At last, as dawn came on, Billy slept. He groaned and moaned, his face twisting with pain, his body vainly moving and tossing in quest of easement.

So this was prize-fighting, Saxon thought. It was much worse than she had dreamed. She had had no idea that such damage could be wrought with padded gloves. He must never fight again. Street rioting was preferable. She was wondering how much of his silk had been lost, when he mumbled and opened his eyes.

"What is it?" she asked, ere it came to her that his eyes were unseeing and that he was in delirium.

"Saxon! Saxon!" he called.

"Yes, Billy. What is it?"

His hand fumbled over the bed where ordinarily it would have encountered her. Again he called her, and she cried her presence loudly in his ear. He sighed with relief and muttered brokenly:

"I had to do it, Saxon. We needed the money."

His eyes closed, and he slept more soundly, though his muttering continued. She had heard of congestion of the brain, and was frightened. Then she remembered his telling her of the ice Billy Murphy had held against his head.

Throwing a shawl over her head, she ran to the Pile-Drivers' Home on Seventh Street. The barkeeper had just opened, and was sweeping out. From the refrigerator he gave her all the ice she wished to carry, breaking it into convenient pieces for her. Back in the house, she applied a compress of the ice to the base of Billy's brain, placed hot irons to his feet, and bathed his head with witch hazel made cold by resting on the ice.

He slept in the darkened room until late afternoon, when, to Saxon's dismay, he insisted on getting up.

"Gotta make a showin'," he explained defiantly. "They ain't goin' to have the laugh on me."

In torment he was helped by her to dress, and in torment he went forth from the house so that his world should have ocular evidence that the beating he had received did not keep him in bed.

It was another kind of pride, different from a woman's, and Saxon wondered if it were the less admirable for that.

Ocean steamships passed up and down the estuary, and lofty-masted ships towed by red-stacked tugs.
She gazed at the sailors on the ships, wondered on what far voyages and to what
far lands they went, wondered what freedoms were theirs

The Valley of the Moon

THE STORY OF A FIGHT AGAINST ODDS FOR LOVE AND A HOME

By Jack London

Author of "Martin Eden," "Burning Daylight," "Smoke Bellew," etc.

Illustrated by Howard Chandler Christy

SYNOPSIS:—Is this the man? So Saxon questioned of herself when she had met "Big Bill" Roberts, one-time prize-fighter, on the dancing-floor at Weasel Park, whither she and Mary, ironers of fancy starch, had gone for a Sunday outing. Never had she come so near to losing her heart as Billy, blue eyed, boyish, gentlemanly, had come to winning it after a few hours' acquaintance. Planned by Mary and Bert Wanhope, the meeting had taken a happy turn, for both Saxon and Billy had seized the future in the present and grasped at its chance for happiness. Billy was a teamster and knew what hard work meant, so they went home early, Saxon glorying in his refusal to "make a time of it," as Bert suggested. He kissed her good-night at the gate, with Wednesday night's dance as their next meeting. Friday's dance was next arranged for, but on Thursday night Charley Long, a rebuffed suitor, met her outside the laundry and warned her that if she did not go with him "somebody'll get hurt." But Saxon bore the notion that Billy, at least, could take care of himself.
Billy did, and Saxon experienced the delightful sensation of knowing that this big boy cared enough for her to risk a fight—which wasn't needed. Billy next proposed a Sunday buggy-ride. They drove out of the city behind a spirited team, Saxon glad to get away from the abuse which Sarah, her sister-in-law, had heaped upon her because she preferred Billy, a prize-fighter, to Charley Long, an honest laboring man. Home cares were soon forgotten as they drove into the hills, each happy in the first true comradeship ever experienced with one of the opposite sex. In the hills they ate a lunch-eon provided by Billy, and then lingered until warnings of dusk urged them homeward. Darkness overtook them—and silence. Then out of it came Billy's frank proposal, and Saxon's countering only with the objection that she was the older—an objection overruled by Billy's statement that "Love's what counts"—accepted him.
In spite of her sister-in-law's objections, Saxon completed her preparations and married Billy at the promised time. They and Mary and Bert ate the wedding supper at Barnum's, and then Saxon and Billy went to their Pine Street cottage alone. Later Mary and Bert married and became their neighbors. The winter passed without an event to mar their happiness, though Billy's wages were cut. But in the spring came a strike in the railroad shops, a strike that soon grew bitter and deadly, and threw a pall over their whole neighborhood. To Saxon, approaching motherhood, the passing days bore a menace.
The strike proved to be very serious. The neighborhood was full of rioting. In one encounter Bert was killed, and several of Billy's friends are at length responsible for the death of scabs. In the midst of the excitement, Saxon's baby—a girl—is born and dies. Billy was compelled to go on strike, and this brought much hardship to the Pine Street cottage; funds and provisions gave out. Harmon, a railroad fireman, was taken as a lodger. Saxon stood stoutly by her husband and refused to let him take any job that would "throw the other fellows down." Billy began to drink. One night he came home terribly bruised, after a boxing bout with the "Chicago Terror." But he brought twenty dollars, the loser's end.

I N the days that followed, Billy's swellings went down and the bruises passed away with surprising rapidity. Only remained the black eyes, unduly conspicuous on a face as blond as his. The discoloration was stubborn, persisting half a month, in which time happened divers events of importance.

Otto Frank's trial had been expeditious. Found guilty by a jury notable for the business and professional men on it, the death sentence was passed on him, and he was removed to San Quentin.

The cases of Chester Johnson and the fourteen others had taken longer, but within the same week they, too, were finished. Chester Johnson was sentenced to be hanged. Two got life; three, twenty years. Only two were acquitted. The remaining seven received terms of from two to ten years.

The effect on Saxon was to throw her into deep depression. Billy was made gloomy, but his fighting spirit was not subdued.

"Always some men killed in battle," he said. "That's to be expected. But the way of sentencin' 'em gets me. All found guilty was responsible for the killin'; or none was responsible. If all was, then they should all get the same sentence. They oughta hang like Chester Johnson, or else he oughtn't to hang. I'd just like to know how the judge makes up his mind. It must be like markin' China lottery-tickets. He plays hunches. He looks at a guy an' waits for a spot or a number to come into his head. How else could he give Johnny Black four years an' Cal Hutchins twenty years? He played the hunches as they came into his head, an' it might just as easy been the other way around an' Cal Hutchins got four years an' Johnny Black twenty.

"I know both them boys. They hung out with the Tenth an' Kirkham gang mostly, though sometimes they ran with my gang. We used to go swimmin' after school down to Sandy Beach on the marsh, an' in the Transit Slip. An' once, on a Thursday, we dug a lot of clams together, an' played hookey Friday to peddle them. An' we used to go out on the Rock Wall an' catch

85

pogies an' rock cod. One day—the day of the eclipse—Cal caught a perch half as big as a door. I never seen such a fish. An' now he's got to wear the stripes for twenty years. Lucky he wasn't married. If he don't get the consumption he'll be an old man when he comes out."

"I used to dance with Chester Johnson," Saxon said. "And I knew his wife, Kitty Brady, long and long ago. She had next place at the table to me in the paper-box factory. She's gone to San Francisco to her married sister's. She's going to have a baby, too. She was awfully pretty, and there was always a string of fellows after her."

The effect of the convictions and severe sentences was a bad one on the union men. Instead of being disheartening, it intensified the bitterness. Billy's repentance for having fought, and the sweetness and affection which had flashed up in the days of Saxon's nursing of him were blotted out. At home he scowled and brooded, while his talk took on the tone of Bert's in the last days ere that Mohican died. Also, Billy stayed away from home longer hours, and was again steadily drinking.

Saxon well-nigh abandoned hope. Almost was she steeled to the inevitable tragedy which her morbid fancy painted in a thousand guises. Oftenest, it was of Billy being brought home on a stretcher. Sometimes it was a call to the telephone in the corner grocery and the curt information by a strange voice that her husband was lying in the receiving hospital or the morgue. And when the mysterious horse-poisoning cases occurred, and when the residence of one of the teaming magnates was half destroyed by dynamite, she saw Billy in prison, or wearing stripes, or mounting to the scaffold at San Quentin; while at the same time she could see the little cottage on Pine Street besieged by newspaper reporters and photographers.

Yet her lively imagination failed altogether to anticipate the real catastrophe. Harmon, the fireman lodger, passing through the kitchen on his way out to work, had paused to tell Saxon about the previous day's train-wreck in the Alviso marshes, and of how the engineer, imprisoned under the overturned engine and unhurt, being drowned by the rising tide, had begged to be shot. Billy came in at the end of the narrative, and from the somber light in his

heavy-lidded eyes Saxon knew he had been drinking. He glowered at Harmon, and, without greeting to him or Saxon, leaned his shoulder against the wall.

Harmon felt the awkwardness of the situation, and did his best to appear oblivious. "I was just telling your wife—" he began, but was savagely interrupted.

"I don't care what you was tellin' her. But I got something to tell you, Mister Man. My wife's made up your bed too many times to suit me."

"Billy!" Saxon cried, her face scarlet with resentment and hurt and shame.

Billy ignored her. Harmon was saying, "I don't understand—"

"Well, I don't like your mug," Billy informed him. "You're standin' on your foot. Get off of it. Get out. Beat it. D'ye understand that?"

"I. don't know what's got into him," Saxon gasped hurriedly to the fireman. "He's not himself. Oh, I am so ashamed, so ashamed."

Billy turned on her. "You shut your mouth an' keep outa this."

"But, Billy," she remonstrated.

"An' get outa here. You go into the other room."

"Here, now," Harmon broke in. "This is a fine way to treat a fellow."

"I've given you too much rope as it is," was Billy's answer.

"I've paid my rent regularly, haven't I?"

"An' I oughta knock your block off for you. Don't see any reason I shouldn't, for that matter."

"If you do anything like that, Billy—" Saxon began.

"You here still? Well, if you won't go into the other room, I'll see that you do."

His hand clutched her arm. For an instant she resisted his strength; and in that instant, when the flesh crushed under his fingers, she realized the fullness of his strength.

In the front room she could only lie back in the Morris chair sobbing, and listen to what occurred in the kitchen.

"I'll stay to the end of the week," the fireman was saying. "I've paid in advance."

"Don't make no mistake," came Billy's voice, so slow that it was almost a drawl, yet quivering with rage. "You can't get out too quick if you wanta stay healthy—you an' your traps with you. I'm likely to start something any moment."

"Oh, I know you're a slugger—" the fireman's voice began.

Then came the unmistakable impact of a blow; the crash of glass; a scuffle on the back porch, and, finally, the heavy bumps of a body down the steps. She heard Billy re-enter the kitchen, move about, and knew he was sweeping up the broken glass of the kitchen door. Then he washed himself at the sink, whistling while he dried his face and hands, and walked into the front room. She did not look at him. She was too sick and sad. He paused irresolutely, seeming to make up his mind.

"I'm goin' up town," he stated. "There's a meetin' of the union. If I don't come back it'll be because that geezer's sworn out a warrant."

He opened the front door and paused. She knew he was looking at her. Then the door closed, and she heard him go down the steps.

Saxon was stunned. She did not think. She did not know what to think. The whole thing was incomprehensible, incredible. She lay back in the chair, her eyes closed, her mind almost a blank, crushed by a leaden feeling that the end had come to everything.

The voices of children playing in the street aroused her. Night had fallen. She groped her way to a lamp and lighted it. In the kitchen she stared, lips trembling, at the pitiful, half-prepared meal. The fire had gone out. The water had boiled away from the potatoes. When she lifted the lid, a burnt smell arose. Methodically she scraped and cleaned the pot, put things in order, and peeled and sliced the potatoes for next day's frying. And just as methodically she went to bed. Her lack of nervousness, her placidity, was abnormal, so abnormal that she closed her eyes and was almost immediately asleep. Nor did she awaken till the sunshine was streaming into the room.

It was the first night she and Billy had spent apart. She was amazed that she had not lain awake worrying about him. She lay with eyes wide open, scarcely thinking, until pain in her arm attracted her attention. It was where Billy had gripped her. On examination she found the bruised flesh fearfully black and blue. She was astonished, not by the spiritual fact that such bruise had been administered by the one she loved most in the world, but by the sheer physical fact that an instant's pressure had inflicted so much damage. The strength of a man was a terrible thing. Quite impersonally, she found herself wondering if Charley Long was as strong as Billy.

It was not until she dressed and built the fire that she began to think about more immediate things. Billy had not returned. Then he was arrested. What was she to do: leave him in jail, go away, and start life afresh? Of course it was impossible to go on living with a man who had behaved as he had. But then came another thought. *Was* it impossible? After all, he was her husband. *For better or worse*—the phrase reiterated itself, a monotonous accompaniment to her thoughts. To leave him was to surrender. She carried the matter before the tribunal of her mother's memory. No; Daisy would never have surrendered. Daisy was a fighter. Then, she, Saxon, must fight. Besides—and she acknowledged it readily, though in a cold, dead way—besides, Billy was better than most husbands. Better than any other husband she had heard of, she concluded, as she remembered many of his earlier nicenesses and finenesses, and especially his eternal chant, "Nothing is too good for us. The Robertses ain't on the cheap."

At eleven o'clock she had a caller. It was Bud Strothers, Billy's mate on strike-duty. Billy, he told her, had refused bail, refused a lawyer, had asked to be tried by the court, had pleaded guilty, and had received a sentence of sixty dollars or thirty days. Also, he had refused to let the boys pay his fine.

"He's clean looney," Strothers summed up. "Won't listen to reason. Say's he'll serve the time out. He's been tankin' up too regular, I guess. His wheels are buzzin'. Here, he give me this note for you. Any time you want anything, send for me. The boys'll all stand by Bill's wife. You belong to us, you know. How are you off for money?"

Proudly she disclaimed any need for money, and not until her visitor departed did she read Billy's note:

DEAR SAXON: Bud Strothers is going to give you this. Don't worry about me. I am going to take my medicine. I deserve it, you know that. I guess I am gone bughouse. Just the same I am sorry for what I done. Don't come to see me. I don't want you to. If you need money the union will give you some. The business agent is all right. I will be out in a month. Now, Saxon, you know

"Billy!" Saxon cried, her face scarlet with resentment and hurt and shame. Billy ignored her. Harmo

on your foot. Get off of it. Get out

was saying, "I don't understand—" "Well, I don't like your mug," Billy informed him. "You're standin'
Beat it. D'ye understand that?"

I love you and just say to yourself that you forgive me this time and you won't never have to do it again.

BILLY.

Bud Strothers was followed by Maggie Donahue and Mrs. Olsen, who paid neighborly calls of cheer and were tactful in their offers of help and in studiously avoiding more reference than was necessary to Billy's predicament.

In the afternoon, James Harmon arrived. He limped slightly, and Saxon divined that he was doing his best to minimize that evidence of hurt. She tried to apologize to him, but he would not listen.

"I don't blame you, Mrs. Roberts," he said. "I know it wasn't your doing. But your husband wasn't just himself, I guess. He was fightin' mad on general principles, and it was just my luck to get in the way, that was all."

"But just the same—"

The fireman shook his head. "I know all about it. I used to punish the drink myself, and I done some funny things in them days. And I'm sorry I swore that warrant out and testified. But I was hot in the collar. I'm cooled down now, an' I'm sorry I done it."

"You're awfully good and kind," she said, and then began hesitantly on what was worrying her. "You—you can't stay now with him—away, you know."

"Yes; that wouldn't do, would it? I'll tell you: I'll pack up right now and skin out, and then, before six o'clock, I'll send a wagon for my things. Here's the key to the kitchen door."

Much as he demurred, she compelled him to receive back the rent for the rest of his week. He shook her hand heartily at leaving, and tried to get her to promise to call upon him for a loan any time she might be in need.

"It's all right," he assured her. "I'm married and got two boys. One of them's got his lungs touched, and she's with 'em down in Arizona campin' out."

And as he went down the steps she wondered that so kind a man should be in so madly cruel a world.

The Donahue boy threw in a spare evening paper, and Saxon found half a column devoted to Billy. It was not nice. The fact that he had stood up in the police court with his eyes blacked from some other fray was noted. He was described as a bully, a hoodlum, a rough-neck, a professional slugger whose presence in the ranks was a disgrace to organized labor. The assault he had pleaded guilty of was atrocious and unprovoked, and if he was a fair sample of a striking teamster, the only wise thing for Oakland to do was to break up the union and drive every member from the city. And, finally, the paper complained at the mildness of the sentence. It should have been six months at least. The judge was quoted as expressing regret that he had been unable to impose a six months' sentence, this inability being due to the condition of the jails, already crowded beyond capacity by the many cases of assault committed in the course of the various strikes.

That night Saxon experienced her first loneliness. Her brain seemed in a whirl, and her sleep was broken by vain gropings for the form of Billy she imagined at her side.

In the morning she received a visit from Sarah—the second in all the period of her marriage; and she could easily guess her sister-in-law's ghoulish errand. No exertion was required for the assertion of all of Saxon's pride. She refused to be in the slightest on the defensive. There was nothing to defend, nothing to explain. Everything was all right, and it was nobody's business anyway. This attitude but served to vex Sarah.

"I warned you, and you can't say I didn't," her diatribe ran. "I always knew he was no good, a jailbird, a hoodlum, a slugger. My heart sunk into my boots when I heard you was runnin' with a prizefighter. I told you so at the time. But no; you wouldn't listen, you with your highfalutin' notions an' more pairs of shoes than any decent woman should have. You knew better'n me. An' I said then, to Tom, I said, 'It's all up with Saxon now.' Them was my very words. Them that touches pitch is defiled. If you'd only a-married Charley Long! Then the family wouldn't 'a' been disgraced. An' this is only the beginnin', mark me, only the beginnin'. Where it'll end, God knows. He'll kill somebody yet, that plug-ugly of yourn, an' be hanged for it. You wait an' see, that's all, an' then you'll remember my words. As you make your bed, so you will lay in it."

"Best bed I ever had," Saxon commented.

"So you can say; so you can say," Sarah snorted.

"I wouldn't trade it for a queen's bed," Saxon added.

"A jailbird's bed," Sarah rejoined witheringly.

"Oh, it's the style," Saxon retorted airily. "Everybody's getting a taste of jail. Wasn't Tom arrested at some street meeting of the socialists? Everybody goes to jail these days."

The barb had struck home.

"But Tom was acquitted," Sarah hastened to proclaim.

"Just the same he lay in jail all night without bail."

This was unanswerable, and Sarah executed her favorite tactic of attack in flank.

"A nice come-down for you, I must say, that was raised straight an' right, a-cuttin' up didoes with a lodger."

"Who says so?" Saxon blazed with an indignation quickly mastered.

"Oh, a blind man can read between the lines. A lodger, a young married woman with no self-respect, an' a prize-fighter for a husband—what else would they fight about?"

"Just like any family quarrel, wasn't it?" Saxon smiled placidly.

Sarah was shocked into momentary speechlessness.

"And I want you to understand it," Saxon continued. "It makes a woman proud to have men fight over her. I am proud. Do you hear? I am proud. I want you to tell them so. I want you to tell all your neighbors. Tell everybody. I am no cow. Men like me. Men fight for me. Men go to jail for me. What is a woman in the world for, if it isn't to have men like her? Now, go, Sarah; go at once, and tell everybody what you've read between the lines. Tell them Billy is a jailbird and that I am a bad woman whom all men desire. Shout it out, and good luck to you. And get out of my house. And never put your feet in it again. You are too decent a woman to come here. You might lose your reputation. And think of your children. Now get out. Go!"

Not until Sarah had taken an amazed and horrified departure did Saxon fling herself on the bed in a convulsion of tears. She had been ashamed, before, merely of Billy's inhospitality and surliness and unfairness. But she could see, now, the light in which others looked on the affair. It had not entered Saxon's head. She was confi-

dent that it had not entered Billy's. She knew his attitude from the first. Always he had opposed taking a lodger because of his proud faith that his wife should not work. Only hard times had compelled his consent, and, now that she looked back, almost had she inveigled him into consenting.

But all this did not alter the viewpoint the neighborhood must hold, that everyone who had ever known her must hold. And for this, too, Billy was responsible. It was more terrible, more horrible, than all the other things he had been guilty of put together. She could never look anyone in the face again. Mrs. Donahue and Mrs. Olsen had been very kind, but of what must they have been thinking all the time they talked with her? And what must they have said to each other? What was everybody saying?

Later, exhausted by her grief, when the tears no longer fell, she grew more impersonal, and dwelt on the disasters that had befallen so many women since the strike troubles began—Otto Frank's wife, Henderson's widow, pretty Kitty Brady, Mary, all the womenfolk of the other workmen who were now wearing the stripes in San Quentin. Her world was crashing about her ears. No one was exempt. Not only had she not escaped, but hers was the worst disgrace of all. Desperately she tried to hug the delusion that she was asleep, that it was all a nightmare, and that soon the alarm would go off and she would get up and cook Billy's breakfast so that he could go to work.

XXV

ALL that night Saxon lay, unsleeping, without taking off her clothes; and when she arose in the morning and washed her face and dressed her hair, she was aware of a strange numbness, of a feeling of constriction about her head as if it were bound by a heavy band of iron. It seemed like a dull pressure upon her brain. It was the beginning of an illness that she did not know as illness. All she knew was that she felt queer. It was not fever. It was not cold. Her bodily health was as it should be, and, when she thought about it, she put her condition down to nerves—nerves, according to her ideas and the ideas of her class, being unconnected with disease.

She had a strange feeling of loss of self, of being a stranger to herself, and the world in which she moved seemed a vague and shrouded world. It lacked sharpness of definition. Its customary vividness was gone. She had lapses of memory, and was continually finding herself doing unplanned things. Thus, to her astonishment, she came to in the back yard, hanging up the week's wash. She had no recollection of having done it, yet it had been done precisely as it should have been done. She had boiled the sheets and pillow-slips and the table linen. Billy's woollens had been washed in warm water only, with the home-made soap the recipe of which Mercedes had given her. On investigation, she found she had eaten a mutton-chop for breakfast. This meant that she had been to the butcher shop, yet she had no memory of having gone. Curiously, she went into the bedroom. The bed was made up, and everything was in order.

At twilight she came upon herself in the front room, seated by the window, crying in an ecstasy of joy. At first she did not know what this joy was; then it came to her that it was because she had lost her baby. "A blessing, a blessing," she was chanting aloud, wringing her hands, but with joy. She knew it was with joy that she wrung her hands.

The days came and went. She had little notion of time. Sometimes, centuries ago it seemed to her it was since Billy had gone to jail. At other times it was no more than the night before. But through it all two ideas persisted: she must not go to see Billy in jail; it was a blessing she had lost her baby.

Once Bud Strothers came to see her. She sat in the front room and talked with him, noting with fascination that there were fringes to the heels of his trousers. Another day, the business agent of the union called. She told him, as she had told Bud Strothers, that everything was all right, that she needed nothing, that she could get along comfortably until Billy came out.

At times the silent cottage became un-endurable, and Saxon would throw a shawl about her head and walk out the Oakland Mole, or cross the railroad yards and the marshes to Sandy Beach, where Billy had said he used to swim. Also, by going out the Transit Slip, by climbing down the piles on a precarious ladder of iron spikes, and by crossing a boom of logs, she won access to the Rock Wall that extended far out into the bay and that served as a barrier between the mud flats and the tide-scoured channel of Oakland Estuary. Ocean steamships passed up and down the estuary, and lofty-masted ships towed by red-stacked tugs. She gazed at the sailors on the ships, wondered on what far voyages and to what far lands they went, wondered what free-doms were theirs.

Especially she liked the Rock Wall. There was a freedom about it, a wide spa-ciousness that she found herself instinc-tively trying to breathe, holding her arms out to embrace and make part of herself. It was a natural world, a more rational world. She could understand it—under-stand the green crabs with white-bleached claws that scuttled before her and which she could see pasturing on green-weeded rocks when the tide was low. Here, hope-lessly man-made as the great wall was, nothing seemed artificial. There were no men there, no laws or conflicts of men. The tide flowed and ebbed; the sun rose and set; regularly each afternoon the brave west wind came romping in through the Golden Gate, darkening the water, cresting tiny wavelets, making the sailboats fly. Everything ran with frictionless order. Everything was free. Firewood lay about for the taking. No man sold it by the sack. Small boys fished with poles from the rocks, with no one to drive them away for trespass, catching fish as Billy had caught fish, as Cal Hutchins had caught fish. Billy had told her of the great perch Cal Hutchins caught on the day of the eclipse, when he had little dreamed the heart of his manhood would be spent in convict's garb.

And here was food, food that was free. She watched the small boys on a day when she had eaten nothing, and emulated them, gathering mussels from the rocks at low water, cooking them by placing them among the coals of a fire she built on top of the wall. They tasted particularly good. She learned to knock the small oysters from the rocks, and once she found a string of fresh-caught fish some small boy had forgotten to take home with him.

Here drifted evidences of man's sinister handiwork—from a distance, from the cities. One flood tide she found the water cov-ered with muskmelons. They bobbed and bumped along up the estuary in countless thousands. Where they stranded against the rocks she was able to get them. But

"And I want you to understand it." Saxon continued. "It makes a woman proud to have men fight over her. I am proud. Do you hear? I am proud"

each and every melon—and she patiently tried scores of them—had been spoiled by a sharp gash that let in the salt water. She could not understand. She asked an old Portuguese woman gathering driftwood.

"They do it, the people who have too much," the old woman explained, straightening her labor-stiffened back with such an effort that Saxon could almost hear it creak. The old woman's black eyes flashed angrily, and her wrinkled lips, drawn tightly across toothless gums, wry with bitterness. "The people that have too much. It is to keep up the price. They throw them overboard in San Francisco."

"But why don't they give them away to the poor people?" Saxon asked.

"They must keep up the price."

"But the poor people cannot buy them anyway," Saxon objected. "It would not hurt the price."

The old woman shrugged her shoulders. "I do not know. It is their way. They chop each melon so that the poor people cannot fish them out and eat anyway. They do the same with the oranges, with the apples. Ah, the fisherman! There is a trust. When the boats catch too much fish, the trust throws them overboard from Fisherman Wharf, boat-loads and boat-loads and boat-loads of the beautiful fish. And the beautiful good fish sink and are gone. And no one gets them. Yet they are dead and only good to eat. Fish are very good to eat."

And Saxon could not understand a world that did such things—a world in which some men possessed so much food that they threw it away, paying men for their labor of spoiling it before they threw it away; and in the same world so many people who did not have enough food, whose babies died because their mothers' milk was not nourishing, whose young men fought and killed each other for the chance to work, whose old men and women went to the poorhouse because there was no food for them in the little shacks they wept at leaving. She wondered if all the world were that way—the poorhouse for the stupid, jewels and automobiles for the clever ones. She must be.

She was one of the stupid. She must be.

93

The evidence all pointed that way. Yet Saxon refused to accept it. She was not stupid. Her mother had not been stupid, nor had the pioneer stock before her. Still it must be so. Here she sat, nothing to eat at home, her love-husband changed to a brute beast and lying in jail, her arms and heart empty of the babe that would have been there if only the stupid ones had not made a shambles of her front yard in their wrangling over jobs.

She sat there, racking her brain, the smudge of Oakland at her back, staring across the bay at the smudge of San Francisco. Yet the sun was good; the wind was good, as was the keen salt air in her nostrils; the blue sky, flecked with clouds, was good. All the natural world was right, and sensible, and beneficent. It was the man-world that was wrong, and mad, and horrible. Why were the stupid stupid? Was it a law of God? No; it could not be. God had made the wind and air and sun. The man-world was made by man, and a rotten job it was. Yet, and she remembered it well, the teaching in the orphan asylum was that God had made everything. Her mother, too, had believed this, had believed in this God. Things could not be different. It was ordained.

For a time Saxon sat crushed, helpless. Then smoldered protest, revolt. Vainly she asked why God had it in for her. What had she done to deserve such fate? She briefly reviewed her life in quest of deadly sins committed, and found them not.

No; God was not responsible. She could have made a better world herself—a finer, squarer world. This being so, then there was no God. God could not make a botch. The matron had been wrong; her mother had been wrong. Then there was no immortality, and Bert, wild and crazy Bert, falling at her front gate with his foolish death-cry, was right. One was a long time dead.

Looking thus at life, shorn of its super-rational sanction, Saxon floundered into the morass of pessimism. There was no justification for right conduct in the universe, no square deal for her who had earned reward, for the millions who worked like animals, died like animals, and were a long time and forever dead. Like the hosts of more learned thinkers before her, she concluded that the universe was unmoral and without concern for man.

And now she sat crushed in greater help-lessness than when she had included God

in the scheme of injustice. As long as God was, there was always chance for a miracle, for some supernatural intervention, some rewarding with ineffable bliss. With God missing, the world was a trap. Life was a trap. She was like a linnet, caught by small boys and imprisoned in a cage. That was because the linnet was stupid. But she rebelled. She fluttered and beat her soul against the hard face of things as did the linnet against the bars of wire. She was not stupid. She did not belong in the trap. She would fight her way out of the trap. There must be such a way out. When canal-boys and rail-splitters, the lowliest of the stupid lowly, as she had read in her school history, could find their way out and become presidents of the nation and rule over even the clever ones in their automobiles, then could she find her way out and win to the tiny reward she craved—Billy, a little love, a little happiness. She would not mind that the universe was unmoral, that there was no God, no immortality. She was willing to go into the black grave and remain in its blackness forever, if only she could get her small meed of happiness first.

How she would work for that happiness! How she would appreciate it, make the most of each least particle of it! But how was she to do it? Where was the path? She could not vision it.

XXVI

Her vague, unreal existence continued. It seemed in some previous lifetime that Billy had gone away, that another lifetime would have to come before he returned. She still suffered from insomnia. Long nights passed in succession, during which she never closed her eyes. At other times she slept through long stupors, waking stunned and numbed, scarcely able to open her heavy eyes, to move her weary limbs. The pressure of the iron band on her head never relaxed. She was poorly nourished. Nor had she a cent of money. She often went a whole day without eating. Once, seventy-two hours elapsed without food passing her lips. She dug clams in the marsh, knocked the tiny oysters from the rocks, and gathered mussels.

And yet, when Bud Strothers came to see how she was getting along, she convinced him that all was well. One evening after work Tom came, and forced two dollars upon her. He was terribly worried. He would like to help more, but Sarah was expecting another baby. There had been slack times in his trade because of the strikes in the other trades. He did not know what the country was coming to. And it was all so simple. All they had to do was see things in his way and vote the way he voted. Then everybody would get a square deal. Christ was a socialist, he told her.

"Christ died two thousand years ago," Saxon said.

"Well?" Tom queried, not catching her implication.

"Think," she said, "think of all the men and women who died in those two thousand years, and socialism has not come yet. And in two thousand years more it may be as far away as ever. Tom, your socialism never did you any good. It is a dream."

"It wouldn't be if—" he began with a flash of resentment.

"If they believed as you do. Only they don't. You don't succeed in making them."

"But we are increasing every year," he argued.

"Two thousand years is an awfully long time," she said quietly.

Her brother's tired face saddened as he nodded. Then he sighed. "Well, Saxon, if it's a dream, it is a good dream."

"I don't want to dream," was her reply. "I want things real. I want them now."

And before her fancy passed the countless generations of the stupid lowly, the Billys and Saxons, the Berts and Marys, the Toms and Sarahs. And to what end? The stupid must always be under the heels of the clever ones. Only she, Saxon, daughter of Daisy who had written wonderful poems, and of a soldier-father who had ridden a roan warhorse, daughter of the strong generations who had won half a world from wild nature and the savage Indian—no, she was not stupid. It was as if she suffered false imprisonment. There was some mistake. She would find the way out.

With the two dollars she bought a sack of flour and half a sack of potatoes. This relieved the monotony of her clams and mussels. Like the Italian and Portuguese women, she gathered driftwood and carried it home, though always she did it with shamed pride, timing her arrival so that it would be after dark.

On the day that Otto Frank was hanged she remained indoors. The evening papers published the account. There had been no reprieve. In Sacramento was a railroad governor who might reprieve or even pardon bank-wreckers and grafters, but who dared not lift his finger for a workingman. All this was the talk of the neighborhood. It had been Billy's talk. It had been Bert's talk.

The next day Saxon started out for the Rock Wall, and the specter of Otto Frank walked by her side. And with him was a dimmer, mistier specter that she recognized as Billy. Was he, too, destined to tread his way to Otto Frank's dark end? Surely so, if the blood and strife continued. He was a fighter. He felt he was right in fighting. It was easy to kill a man. Even if he did not intend it, some time, when he was slugging a scab, the scab would fracture his skull on a stone curbing or a cement sidewalk. And then Billy would hang. That was why Otto Frank hanged. He had not intended to kill Henderson. It was only by accident that Henderson's skull was fractured. Yet Otto Frank had been hanged for it just the same.

XXVII

THE day before Billy's release, Saxon completed her meager preparations to receive him. She was without money, and, except for her resolve not to offend Billy in that way again, she would have borrowed ferry fare from Mrs. Donahue and journeyed to San Francisco to sell some of her personal pretties. As it was, with bread and potatoes and salted sardines in the house, she went out at the afternoon low tide and dug clams for a chowder. Also, she gathered a load of driftwood, and it was nine in the evening when she emerged from the marsh, on her shoulder a bundle of wood and a short-handled spade, in her free hand the pail of clams. She sought the darker side of the street at the corner and hurried across the zone of electric light to avoid detection by the neighbors. But a woman came toward her, looked sharply, and stopped in front of her. It was Mary.

"My God, Saxon!" she exclaimed. "Is it as bad as this?"

Saxon looked at her old friend curiously, with a swift glance that sketched all the tragedy. Mary was thinner, though there was more color in her cheeks—color of which

Saxon had her doubts. Mary's bright eyes were handsomer, larger—too large, too feverish bright, too restless. She was well-dressed—too well dressed; and she was suffering from nerves. She turned her head apprehensively to glance into the darkness behind her.

"My God!" Saxon breathed. "And you—" She shut her lips, then began anew. "Come along to the house," she said.

"If you're ashamed to be seen with me—" Mary blurted, with one of her old quick angers.

"No, no," Saxon disclaimed. "It's the driftwood and the clams. I don't want the neighbors to know. Come along."

"No; I can't, Saxon. I'd like to, but I can't. I've got to catch the next train to Frisco. I've been waiting around. I knocked at your back door. But the house was dark. Billy's still in, ain't he?"

"Yes, he gets out to-morrow."

"I read about it in the papers," Mary went on hurriedly, looking behind her. "I was in Stockton when it happened." She turned upon Saxon almost savagely. "You don't blame me, do you? I just couldn't go back to work after bein' married. I was sick of work. Played out, I guess, an' no good anyway. But if you only knew how I hated the laundry even before I got married. It's a dirty world. You don't dream, Saxon, honest to God you could never guess a hundredth part of its dirtiness. Oh, I wish I was dead; I wish I was dead an' out of it all. Listen—no, I can't now. There's the down-train puffin' at Adeline. I'll have to run for it. Can I come——"

"Aw, get a move on, can't you?" a man's voice interrupted.

Behind her the speaker had partly emerged from the darkness. No working-man, Saxon could see that—lower in the world scale, despite his good clothes, than any workingman.

"I'm comin', if you'll only wait a second," Mary placated.

And by her answer and its accents Saxon knew that Mary was afraid of this man who prowled on the rim of light.

Mary turned to her. "I got to beat it; good-by," she said, fumbling in the palm of her glove.

She caught Saxon's free hand, and Saxon felt a small hot coin pressed into it. She tried to resist, to force it back.

"No, no," Mary pleaded. "For old times. You can do as much for me some day. I'll see you again. Good-by."

Suddenly sobbing, she threw her arms around Saxon's waist, crushing the feathers of her hat against the load of wood as she pressed her face against Saxon's breast. Then she tore herself away to arm's length, passionate, quivering, and stood gazing at Saxon.

"Aw, get a hustle, get a hustle," came from the darkness the peremptory voice of the man.

"Oh, Saxon!" Mary sobbed, and was gone.

In the house, the lamp lighted, Saxon looked at the coin. It was a five-dollar piece—to her, a fortune. Then she thought of Mary, and of the man of whom she was afraid. Saxon registered another black mark against Oakland. Mary was one more destroyed. She looked at the coin and tossed it into the kitchen sink. When she cleaned the clams, she heard the coin tinkle down the vent pipe.

It was the thought of Billy, next morning, that led Saxon to go under the sink, unscrew the cap to the catch-trap, and rescue the five-dollar piece. Prisoners were not well fed, she had been told; and the thought of placing clams and dry bread before Billy, after thirty days of prison fare, was too appalling for her to contemplate. She knew how he liked to spread his butter on thick, how he liked thick, rare steak fried on a dry, hot pan, and how he liked coffee that was coffee and plenty of it.

Not until after nine o'clock did Billy arrive, and she was dressed in her prettiest house-gingham to meet him. She peeped on him as he came slowly up the front steps, and she would have run out to him except for a group of neighborhood children who were staring from across the street. The door opened before him as his hand reached for the knob, and, inside, he closed it by backing against it, for his arms were filled with Saxon. No, he had not had breakfast, or did he want any now that he had her. He had only stopped for a shave. He had stood the barber off, and he had walked all the way from the City Hall because of lack of the nickel car fare. But he'd like a bath most mighty well, and a change of clothes. She mustn't come near him until he was clean.

When all this was accomplished, he sat in the kitchen and watched her cook, noting

Saxon looked at her old friend curiously, with a swift glance that sketched all the tragedy

97

the driftwood she put in the stove and asking about it. While she moved about, she told how she had gathered the wood, how she had managed to live and not be beholden to the union, and by the time they were seated at the table she was telling him about her meeting with Mary the night before. She did not mention the five dollars.

Billy stopped chewing the first mouthful of steak. His expression frightened her. He spat the meat out on his plate.

"You got the money to buy the meat from her," he accused slowly. "You had no money, no more tick with the butcher, yet here's meat. Am I right?"

Saxon could only bend her head.

A terrifying, ageless look had come into his face, a bleak and passionless glaze in his eyes. "What else did you buy?" he demanded—not roughly, not angrily, but with the fearful coldness of a rage that words could not express.

To her surprise, she had grown calm. What did it matter? It was merely what one must expect, living in Oakland—something to be left behind when Oakland was a thing behind, a place started from.

"The coffee," she answered. "And the butter."

He emptied his plate of meat and her plate into the frying-pan, likewise the roll of butter and the slice on the table, and on top he poured the contents of the coffee canister. All this he carried into the back yard and dumped in the garbage-can. The coffee-pot he emptied into the sink.

"How much of the money you got left?" he next wanted to know.

Saxon had already gone to her purse and taken it out.

"Three dollars and eighty cents," she counted, handing it to him. "I paid forty-five cents for the steak."

He ran his eye over the money, counted it, and went to the front door. She heard the door open and close, and knew that the silver had been flung into the street. When he came back to the kitchen, Saxon was already serving him fried potatoes on a clean plate.

He glanced at the fried potatoes, the fresh slice of dry bread, and the glass of water she placed by his plate.

"It's all right," she smiled, as he hesitated. "There's nothing left that's tainted."

He shot a swift glance at her face, as if for sarcasm, then sighed and sat down. Almost immediately he was up again and holding out his arms to her. "I'm goin' to eat in a minute, but I want to talk to you first," he said, sitting down and holding her closely. "Besides, that water ain't like coffee. Gettin' cold won't spoil it none. Now, listen. You're the only person I got in this world. You wasn't afraid of me an' what I just done, an' I'm glad of that. Now we'll forget all about Mary. I got charity enough. I'm just as sorry for her as you. I'd do anything for her. I'd wash her feet for her like Christ did. I'd let her eat at my table, an' sleep under my roof. But all that ain't no reason I should touch anything she's responsible for. Now forget her. It's you an' me, Saxon, only you an' me an' to hell with the rest of the world. Nothing else counts. You won't never have to be afraid of me again. Whiskey an' I don't mix very well, so I'm going to cut whiskey out. I've been clean off my nut, an' I ain't treated you altogether right. But that's all past. It won't never happen again. I'm goin' to start out fresh.

"Now take this thing. I oughtn't to acted so hasty. But I did. I oughta talked it over. But I didn't. My temper got the best of me, an' you know I got one. If a fellow can keep his temper in boxin', why he can keep it in bein' married, too. Only this got me too sudden-like. It's something I can't stomach, that I never could stomach. An' you wouldn't want me to any more 'n I'd want you to stomach something you just couldn't."

She sat up straight on his knees and looked at him, afire with an idea. "You mean that, Billy?"

"Sure I do."

"Then I'll tell you something I can't stomach any more. I'll die if I have to."

"Well?" he questioned, after a searching pause.

"It's up to you," she said.

"Then fire away."

"You don't know what you're letting yourself in for," she warned. "Maybe you'd better back out before it's too late."

He shook his head stubbornly. "What you don't want to stomach you ain't goin' to stomach. Let her go."

"First," she commenced, "no more slugging of scabs."

His mouth opened, but he checked the involuntary protest.

"And, second, no more Oakland."

"I don't get that last."

"No more Oakland. No more living in Oakland. I'll die if I have to. It's pull up stakes and get out."

He digested this slowly. "Where?" he asked finally.

"Anywhere. Everywhere. Smoke a cigarette and think it over."

He shook his head and studied her.

"You mean that?" he asked at length.

"I do. I want to chuck Oakland just as hard as you wanted to chuck the beefsteak, the coffee, and the butter."

She could see him brace himself. She could feel him brace his very body ere he answered.

"All right then, if that's what you want. We'll quit Oakland. We'll quit it cold. It never done nothin' for me, an' I guess I'm husky enough to scratch for us both anywheres."

Billy stood up, still holding her. He glanced at the fried potatoes. "Stone cold," he said. "Come on. Put on your prettiest. We're goin' up-town for something to eat an' to celebrate. I guess we got a celebration comin', seein' as we're going to pull up stakes an' pull our freight from the old burg. An' we won't have to walk. I can borrow a dime from the barber, an' I got enough junk to hock for a blowout."

His junk proved to be several gold medals won in his amateur days at boxing tournaments. Once up-town and in the pawnshop, Uncle Sam seemed thoroughly versed in the value of the medals, and Billy jingled a handful of silver in his pocket as they walked out.

He was as hilarious as a boy, and she joined in his good spirits. When he stopped at a corner cigar-store to buy a sack of tobacco, he changed his mind and bought cigars.

"Oh, I'm a regular devil," he laughed. "Nothing's too good to-day. It's Barnum's."

They strolled to the restaurant at Seventh and Broadway where they had had their wedding supper.

"Let's make believe we're not married," Saxon suggested.

"Sure," he agreed, "an' take a private room so as the waiter'll have to knock on the door each time he comes in."

Saxon demurred at that. "It will be too expensive, Billy. You'll have to tip him for the knocking. We'll take the regular dining-room."

"Order anything you want," Billy said largely, when they were seated. "Here's family porterhouse, a dollar an' a half. What d'ye say?"

"And hash browned," she abetted, "and coffee extra special, and some oysters first— I want to compare them with the Rock oysters."

Billy nodded, and looked up from the bill of fare. "Here's mussels bordelay. Try an order of them, too, an' see if they beat your Rock Wall ones."

"Why not?" Saxon cried, her eyes dancing. "The world is ours. We're just travelers through this town."

"Yep, that's the stuff," Billy muttered absently. He was looking at the theater column. He lifted his eyes from the paper. "Matinee at Bell's. We can get reserved seats for a quarter. Dog-gone the luck anyway!"

His exclamation was so aggrieved and violent that it brought alarm into her eyes.

"If I'd only thought," he regretted, "we could a' gone to the Forum for grub. That's the swell joint where fellows like Roy Blanchard hangs out, blowin' the money we sweat for them."

They bought reserved tickets at Bell's Theater; but it was too early for the performance, and they went down Broadway and into the Electric Theater to while away the time on a moving-picture show. A cowboy film was run off, and a French comic; then came a rural drama situated somewhere in the Middle West. It began with a farmyard scene. The sun blazed down on a corner of the barn and on a rail fence where the ground lay in the mottled shade of large trees overhead. There were chickens, ducks, and turkeys, scratching, waddling, moving about. A big sow, followed by a roly-poly litter of seven little ones, marched majestically through the chickens, rooting them out of the way. The hens, in turn, took it out on the little porkers, pecking them when they strayed too far from their mother. And over the top rail a horse looked drowsily on, ever and anon, at mathematically precise intervals, switching a lazy tail that flashed high lights in the sunshine.

A dog ran upon the scene. The mother pig turned tail and with short ludicrous jumps, followed by her progeny and pursued by the dog, fled out of the film. A young girl came on, a sunbonnet hanging down her back, her apron caught up in front and filled with grain which she threw to the fluttering fowls.

A young man entered, his errand immediately known to an audience educated in moving pictures. But Saxon had no eyes for the love-making, the pleading forceful-ness, the shy reluctance, of man and maid. Ever her gaze wandered back to the chick-ens, to the mottled shade under the trees, to the warm wall of the barn, to the sleepy horse with its ever-recurrent whisk of tail.

She drew closer to Billy, and her hand, passed around his arm, sought his hand.

"Oh, Billy," she sighed. "I'd just die of happiness in a place like that." And, when the film was ended: "We got lots of time for Bell's. Let's stay and see that one over again."

They sat through a repetition of the per-formance, and when the farmyard scene appeared, the longer Saxon looked at it the more it affected her. And this time she took in further details. She saw fields beyond, rolling hills in the background, and a cloud-flecked sky. She identified some of the chickens, especially an obstreperous old hen who resented the thrust of the sow's muzzle, particularly pecked at the little pigs, and laid about her with a vengeance when the grain fell. Saxon looked back across the fields to the hills and sky, breathing the spaciousness of it, the freedom, the content. Tears welled into her eyes, and she wept silently, happily.

"Now I know where we're going when we leave Oakland," she informed him.

"Where?"

"There."

He looked at her, and followed her gaze to the screen.

"Oh," he said, and cogitated. "An' why shouldn't we?" he added.

"Oh, Billy, will you?"

Her lips trembled in her eagerness, and her whisper broke and was almost inaudible.

"Sure," he said. It was his day of royal largess. "What you want is yourn, an' I'll scratch my fingers off for it. An' I've always had a hankerin' for the country myself."

XXVIII

It was early evening when they got off the car at Seventh and Pine on their way home from Bell's Theater. Billy and Saxon did their little marketing together, then separated at the corner, Saxon to go on to the house and prepare supper, Billy to go and see the boys—the teamsters who had fought on in the strike during his month of retirement.

"Take care of yourself, Billy," she called, as he started off.

"Sure," he answered, turning his face to her over his shoulder.

Her heart leaped at the smile. It was his old, unsullied love-smile which she wanted always to see on his face—for which she would wage the utmost woman's war to possess. A thought of this flashed brightly through her brain, and it was with a proud little smile that she remembered all her pretty equipment stored at home.

Three-quarters of an hour later, supper ready, all but the putting on of the lamb-chops at the sound of his step, Saxon waited. She heard the gate click, but instead of his step she heard a curious and confused scrap-ing of many steps. She flew to open the door. Billy stood there, but a different Billy from the one she had parted from so short a time before. A small boy, beside him, held his hat. His face had been fresh-washed, or, rather, drenched, for his shirt and shoulders were wet. His hair lay damp and plastered against his forehead, and was darkened by oozing blood. Both arms hung limply by his side. But his face was composed, and he even grinned.

"It's all right," he reassured Saxon. "The joke's on me. Somewhat damaged but still in the ring." He stepped gingerly across the threshold. "Come on in, you fellows. We're all mutts together."

He was followed in by the boy with his hat, by Bud Strothers and another teamster she knew, and by two strangers. The lat-ter were big, hard-featured, sheepish-faced men, who stared at Saxon as if afraid of her.

"It's all right, Saxon," Billy began, but was interrupted by Bud.

"First thing is to get him on the bed an' cut his clothes off him. Both arms is broke, and here are the ginks that done it."

He indicated the two strangers, who shuffled their feet with embarrassment and looked more sheepish than ever.

Billy sat down on the bed, and while Saxon held the lamp, Bud and the strangers proceeded to cut coat, shirt, and undershirt from him.

"He wouldn't go to the receivin' hospi-tal," Bud said to Saxon.

"Not on your life," Billy concurred. "I had 'em send for Doc Hentley. He'll be here any minute. Them two arms is all I got. They've done pretty well by me, an'

I gotta do the same by them. No medical students a-learnin' their trade on me."

"But how did it happen?" Saxon demanded, looking from Billy to the strangers, puzzled by the amity that so evidently existed among them all.

"Oh, they're all right," Billy dashed in. "They done it through mistake. They're Frisco teamsters, an' they come over to help us—a lot of 'em."

The two teamsters seemed to cheer up at this, and nodded their heads.

"Yes, missus," one of them rumbled hoarsely. "It's all a mistake, an'—well, the joke's on us."

"The drinks, anyway," Billy grinned.

Not only was Saxon not excited, but she was scarcely perturbed. What had happened was only to be expected. It was in line with all that Oakland had already done to her and hers, and, besides, Billy was not dangerously hurt. Broken arms and a sore head would heal. She brought chairs and seated everybody.

"Now tell me what happened," she begged. "I'm all at sea, what of you two burleys breaking my husband's arms, then seeing him home and holding a love-feast with him."

"An' you got a right," Bud Strothers assured her. "You see, it happened this way——"

"You shut up, Bud," Billy broke in. "You didn't see anything of it."

Saxon looked to the San Francisco teamsters.

"We'd come over to lend a hand, seein' as the Oakland boys was gettin' some the short end of it," one spoke up, "an' we've sure learned some scabs there's better trades than drivin' team. Well, me an' Jackson here was nosin' around to see what we can see, when your husband comes moseyin' along. When he——"

"Hold on," Jackson interrupted. "Get it straight as you go along. We reckon we know the boys by sight. But your husband we ain't never seen around, him bein'——"

"As you might say, put away for a while," the first teamster took up the tale. "So, when we sees what we thinks is a scab dodgin' away from us an' takin' the short cut through the alley——"

"The alley back of Campbell's grocery," Billy elucidated.

"Yep, back of the grocery," the first teamster went on; "why, we're sure he's a scab makin' a sneak to get into the stables over the back fences."

"We caught one there, Billy an' me," Bud interpolated.

"So we don't waste any time," Jackson said, addressing himself to Saxon. "We've done it before, an' we know how to do 'em up brown an' tie 'em with baby ribbon. So we catch your husband right in the alley."

"I was lookin' for Bud," said Billy. "The boys told me I'd find him somewhere around the other end of the alley. An' the first thing I know, Jackson, here, asks me for a match."

"An' right there's where I get in my fine work," resumed the first teamster.

"What?" asked Saxon.

"That." The man pointed to the wound in Billy's scalp. "I laid 'm out. He went down like a steer, an' got up on his knees dippy, a-gabblin' about somebody standin' on their foot. He didn't know where he was at, you see; clean groggy. An' then we done it."

The man paused, the tale told.

"Broke both his arms with the crowbar," Bud supplemented.

"That's when I come to myself, when the bones broke," Billy corroborated. "An' there was the two of 'em givin' me the ha-ha. 'That'll last you some time,' Jackson was sayin'. An' Anson says, 'I'd like to see you drive horses with them arms.' An' then Jackson says, 'Let's give 'm something for luck.' An' with that he fetched me a wallop on the jaw."

"No," corrected Anson. "That wallop was mine."

"Well, it sent me into dreamland over again," Billy sighed. "An' when I come to, here was Bud an' Anson an' Jackson sousin' me at a water-trough. An' then we dodged a reporter an' all come home together."

Bud Strothers held up his fist and indicated freshly abraded skin. "The reporter guy just insisted on samplin' it," he said. Then, to Billy, "That's why I cut around Ninth an' caught up with you down on Sixth."

A few minutes later Doctor Hentley arrived and drove the men from the room. They waited till he had finished, to assure themselves of Billy's well-being, and then departed. In the kitchen, Doctor Hentley washed his hands and gave Saxon final instructions.

"If it wouldn't drive a man to drink," Billy groaned, when Saxon returned to him. "Did you ever dream such luck? Look at all my fights in the ring, an' never a broken bone, an' here, snap, snap, just like that, two arms smashed."

"Oh, it might be worse," Saxon smiled cheerfully.

"I'd like to know how."

"It might have been your neck."

"An' a good job. I tell you, Saxon, you gotta show me anything worse."

"I can," she said confidently.

"Well?"

"Well, wouldn't it be worse if you intended staying on in Oakland where it might happen again?"

"I can see myself becomin' a farmer an' plowin' with a pair of pipe-stems like these," he persisted.

"Doctor Hentley says they'll be stronger at the break than ever before. And you know yourself that's true of clean-broken bones. Now you close your eyes and go to sleep. You're all done up, and you need to keep your brain quiet and stop thinking."

He closed his eyes obediently. She slipped a cool hand under the nape of his neck and let it rest.

"That feels good," he murmured. "You're so cool, Saxon. Your hand, and you, all of you. Bein' with you is like comin' out into the cool night after dancin' in a hot room."

After several minutes of quiet, he began to giggle.

"What is it?" she asked.

"Oh, nothin'. I was just thinkin'—thinkin' of them mutts doin' me up."

Next morning Billy awoke with his blues dissipated. From the kitchen Saxon heard him painfully wrestling with strange vocal acrobatics.

"I got a new song you never heard," he told her when she came in with a cup of coffee. "I only remember the chorus, though. It's the old man talkin' to some hobo of a hired man that wants to marry his daughter. Mamie, that Billy Murphy used to run with before he got married, used to sing it. It's a kind of a sobby song. It used to always give Mamie the weeps. Here's the way the chorus goes—an' remember, it's the old man spielin'."

And with great solemnity and excruciating flatting, Billy sang:

"'O treat my daughter kind-i-ly,
   An' say you'll do no harm,
   An' when I die I'll will to you
      My little house an' farm—
   My horse, my plow, my sheep, my cow,
   An' all them little chickens in the ga-a-rden.'"

"It's them little chickens in the garden that gets me," he explained. "That's how I remembered it—from the chickens in the movin' pictures yesterday. An some day we'll have little chickens in the garden, won't we, old girl?"

"And a daughter, too," Saxon amplified.

"An' I'll be the old geezer sayin' them same words to the hired man," Billy carried the fancy along. "It don't take long to raise a daughter if you ain't in a hurry."

Saxon took her long-neglected ukulélé from its case and strummed it into tune.

"And I've a song you never heard, Billy. Tom's always singing it. He's crazy about taking up government land and going farming, only Sarah won't think of it. He sings it something like this:

"'We'll have a little farm,
   A pig, a horse, a cow,
And you will drive the wagon,
And I will drive the plow.'"

"Only in this case I guess it's me that'll do the plowin'," Billy approved, "Say, Saxon, sing 'Harvest Days.' That's a farmer's song, too."

After that, she feared the coffee was growing cold and compelled Billy to take it. In the helplessness of two broken arms he had to be fed like a baby.

"I'll tell you one thing," Billy said, between mouthfuls. "Once we get settled down in the country you'll have that horse you've been wishin' for all your life. An' it'll be all your own, to ride, drive, sell, or do anything you want with."

And, again, he ruminated: "One thing that'll come handy in the country is that I know horses. That's a big start. I can always get a job at that—if it ain't at union wages. An' the other things about farmin' I can learn fast enough. Say, d'ye remember that day you first told me about wantin' a horse to ride all your life?"

Saxon remembered, and it was only by a severe struggle that she was able to keep the tears from welling into her eyes. She seemed bursting with happiness, and she was remembering many things—all the warm promise of life with Billy that had been hers in the days before hard times. And now the promise was renewed again. Since its fulfilment had not come to them, they were going away to fulfil it for themselves and make the moving pictures come true.

The Valley of the Moon

THE STORY OF A FIGHT AGAINST ODDS FOR LOVE AND A HOME

By Jack London

Author of "Martin Eden," "Burning Daylight," "Smoke Bellew," etc.

Illustrated by Howard Chandler Christy

SYNOPSIS:—Is this the man? So Saxon questioned of herself when she had met "Big Bill" Roberts, one-time prize-fighter, on the dancing-floor at Weasel Park, whither she and Mary, ironers of fancy starch, had gone for a Sunday outing. Never had she come so near to losing her heart as Billy, blue eyed, boyish, gentlemanly, had come to winning it after a few hours' acquaintance. Planned by Mary and Bert Wanhope, the meeting had taken a happy turn, for both Saxon and Billy had seized the future in the present and grasped at its chance for happiness. Billy was a teamster and knew what hard work meant, so they went home early, Saxon glorying in his refusal to "make a time of it," as Bert suggested. He kissed her good-night at the gate with Wednesday night's dance as their next meeting. Friday's dance was next arranged for, but on Thursday night Charley Long, a rebuffed suitor, met her outside the laundry and warned her that if she did not go with him "somebody'll get hurt." But Saxon bore the notion that Billy, at least, could take care of himself.
Billy did, and Saxon experienced the delightful sensation of knowing that this big boy cared enough for her to risk a fight—which wasn't needed. Finally there came Billy's frank proposal, and Saxon, countering only with the objection that she was the elder—an objection overruled by Billy's statement that "Love's what counts"—accepted him.
Saxon married Billy at the promised time, in spite of all family objections. They and Mary and Bert ate the wedding supper at Barnum's, and then Saxon and Billy went to their Pine Street cottage. Later Mary and Bert married and became their neighbors. The winter passed without an event to mar their happiness, though Billy's wages were cut. But in the spring came a strike in the railroad shops, and it threw a pall over the whole neighborhood. To Saxon, approaching mother-hood, the passing days bore a menace.
The strike proved to be very serious. The neighborhood was full of rioting. In one encounter Bert was killed, and several of Billy's friends are at length responsible for the death of scabs. In the midst of the excitement, Saxon's baby—a girl—is born and dies. Billy was compelled to go on strike, and this brought much hardship to the Pine Street cottage; funds and provisions gave out. Harmon, a railroad fireman, was taken as a lodger. Saxon stood stoutly by her husband and refused to let him take any job that would "throw the other fellows down." Billy began to drink. One night he came home terribly bruised, after a boxing bout with the "Chicago Terror." But he brought twenty dollars, the loser's end.
Much discouraged, Billy continues his intemperate habits. One day, in a fit of absolutely unwarranted jealousy, he attacks Harmon, the lodger, for which he receives a thirty-day jail sentence. During that time Saxon struggles along as best she can, and in her loneliness has much time for reflection. She realizes that out of their present condition and mode of life no happiness can come. She is shocked one day to discover that Mary, her old friend and Bert's widow, has been driven upon the streets. She must get away from it all. Billy's release is celebrated by a theater treat, for which his precious amateur athletic medals are pawned. At the moving pictures they see a film depicting farm life. This determines them. They will seek a home in the country. Their plans are interrupted by an accident to Billy. He is mistaken for a scab and terribly beaten. Both arms are broken; but he is soon on the mend.

BETWEEN feeding and caring for Billy, doing the housework, making plans, and selling her store of pretty needlework, the days flew happily for Saxon. Billy's consent to sell her pretties had been hard to get, but at last she succeeded in coaxing it out of him.

"It's only the ones I haven't used," she urged; "and I can always make more when we get settled somewhere."

What she did not sell, along with the household linen and her and Billy's spare clothing, she arranged to store with Tom.

"Go ahead," Billy said. "This is your picnic. What you say goes. You're Robinson Crusoe, an' I'm your man Friday. Made up your mind yet which way you're goin' to travel?"

Saxon shook her head.

"Or how?"

"The way our people came into the West," she said proudly, and held up one foot and then the other, encased in stout walking-shoes which she had begun that morning to break in about the house.

After a few days, Billy was able to be up and about. He was still quite helpless, however, with both his arms in splints.

Doctor Hentley not only agreed, but himself suggested, that his bill should wait against better times for settlement. Of government land, in response to Saxon's eager questioning, he knew nothing, except that he had a hazy idea that the days of government land were over.

Tom, on the contrary, was confident that there was plenty of government land. He talked of Honey Lake, of Shasta County, and of Humboldt. "But you can't tackle it at this time of year, with winter comin' on," he advised Saxon. "The thing for

103

The farmer crossed the plowed strip to Saxon, and joined her on the rail. "He's plowed before, a little mite, ain't he?" Saxon shook her head. "Never in his life. But he knows how to drive horses"

you two to do is to head south for warmer weather—say along the coast. It don't snow down there. I tell you what you do. Go down by San José and Salinas an' come out on the coast at Monterey. South of that you'll find government land mixed up with forest reserves and Mexican rancheros. It's pretty wild, without any roads to speak of. All they do is handle cattle. But there's some fine redwood canyons, with good patches of farming ground, that run right down to the ocean. I was talkin' last year with a fellow that's been all through there. An' I'd 'a' gone, like you an' Billy, only Sarah wouldn't hear of it. There's gold down there, too. Quite a bunch is in there prospectin', an' two or three good mines have opened. But that's farther along and in a ways from the coast. You might take a look."

Saxon shook her head. "We're not looking for gold, but for chickens and a place to grow vegetables. Our folks had all the chance for gold in the early days, and what have they got to show for it?"

"I guess you're right," Tom conceded. "They always played too big a game, an' missed the thousand little chances right under their nose."

Not until Doctor Hentley gave the word did the splints come off Billy's arms, and Saxon insisted upon an additional two weeks' delay so that no risk would be run. These two weeks would complete another month's rent, and the landlord had agreed to wait payment for the last two months until Billy was on his feet again. Salinger's awaited the day set by Saxon for taking back their furniture. Also, they had returned to Billy seventy-five dollars.

"The rest you've paid will be rent," the collector told Saxon. "And the furniture's second hand now, too. The deal will be a loss to Salinger's, and they didn't have to do it, either; you know that. So just remember they've been pretty square with you, and if you start over again, don't forget them."

Out of this sum, and out of what was realized from Saxon's pretties, they were able to pay all their small bills and yet have a few dollars remaining in pocket.

"I hate owin' things worse 'n poison," Billy said to Saxon. "An' now we don't owe a soul in this world except the landlord an' Doc Hentley."

"And neither of them can afford to wait longer than they have to," she said.

"And they won't," Billy answered quietly.

Salinger's wagon was at the house, taking out the furniture, the morning they left. The landlord, standing at the gate, received the keys, shook hands with them, and wished them luck.

"You're goin' at it right," he congratulated them. "Sure an' wasn't it under me roll of blankets I tramped into Oakland meself, forty year ago? Buy land, like me, when it's cheap. It'll keep you from the poorhouse in your old age. There's plenty of new towns springin' up. Get in on the ground floor. The work of your hands'll keep you in food an' under a roof, an' the land'll make you well-to-do. An' you know me address. When you can spare it send along that small bit of rent. An' good luck. An' don't mind what people think. 'Tis them that looks that finds."

Curious neighbors peeped from behind the blinds as Billy and Saxon strode up the street, while the children gazed at them in gaping astonishment. On Billy's back, inside a painted canvas tarpaulin, was slung the roll of bedding. Inside the roll were changes of underclothing and odds and ends of necessities. Outside, from the lashings, depended a frying-pan and cooking-pail. In his hand he carried the coffee-pot. Saxon carried a small telescope basket protected by black oilcloth.

"We must look like holy frights," Billy grumbled, shrinking from every gaze that was bent upon him.

"It'd be all right, if we were going camping," Saxon consoled.

"Only we're not."

"But they don't know that," she continued. "It's only you know that, and what you think they're thinking isn't what they're thinking at all. Most probably they think we're going camping. And the best of it is, we are going camping. We are! We are!"

At this Billy cheered up, though he muttered his firm intention to knock the block off of any guy that got fresh. He stole a glance at Saxon. Her cheeks were red, her eyes glowing.

"It's a sporting proposition all right, all right," he considered. "But just the same, let's turn off an' go around the block.

There's some fellows I know, standin' up there on the next corner, an' I don't want to knock *their* blocks off."

XXX

The electric car ran as far as Haywards, but at Saxon's suggestion they got off at San Leandro. "It doesn't matter where we start walking," she said, "for start to walk somewhere we must. And as we're looking for land and finding out about land, the quicker we begin to investigate the better. Besides, we want to know all about all kinds of land, close to the big cities as well as back in the mountains."

"Gee! This must be the Porchugeeze headquarters," was Billy's reiterated comment, as they walked through San Leandro. "It looks as though they'd crowded our kind out," Saxon adjudged.

"Some tall crowdin', I guess," Billy grumbled. "It looks like the free-born American ain't got no room left in his own land."

"Then it's his own fault," Saxon said, with vague asperity, resenting conditions she was just beginning to grasp.

"Oh, I don't know about that. I reckon the American could do what the Porchugeeze do if he wanted to. Only he don't want to, thank God. He ain't much given to livin' like a pig offen leavin's."

"Not in the country, maybe," Saxon controverted. "But I've seen an awful lot of Americans living like pigs in the cities."

Billy grunted unwilling assent. "I guess they quit the farms an' go to the city for something better, an' get it in the neck."

"Look at all the children!" Saxon cried. "School's letting out. And nearly all are Portuguese, Billy."

"They never wore glad rags like them in the old country," Billy sneered. "They had to come over here to get decent clothes and decent grub. They're as fat as butterballs."

Saxon nodded affirmation, and a great light seemed suddenly to kindle in her understanding. "That's the very point, Billy. They're doing it—doing it farming, too. Strikes don't bother *them*."

"You don't call that dinky gardenin' farming," he objected, pointing to a piece of land barely the size of an acre, which they were passing.

"Oh, your ideas are still big," she laughed. "You're like Uncle Will, who owned thousands of acres and wanted to own a million, and who wound up as night watchman. That's what was the trouble with all us Americans. Everything large scale. Anything less than one hundred and sixty acres was small scale."

"Just the same," Billy held stubbornly, "large scale's a whole lot better'n small scale, like all these dinky gardens."

Saxon sighed. "I don't know which is the dinkier," she observed finally, "owning a few little acres and the team you're driving, or not owning any acres and driving for wages a team somebody else owns."

Billy winced. "Go on, Robinson Crusoe," he growled good-naturedly. "Rub it in good an' plenty. An' the worst of it is, it's correct. A hell of a free-born American I've been, a-drivin' other folkses' teams for a livin', a-strikin' and a-sluggin' scabs, an' not bein' able to keep up with the instalments for a few sticks of furniture. Just the same I was sorry for one thing. I hated worse'n Sam Hill to see that Morris chair go back—you liked it so. We did a lot of honeymoonin' in that chair."

They were well out of San Leandro, walking through a region of tiny holdings.

"Now, Billy, remember we're not going to take up with the first piece of land we see," cautioned Saxon, the new home uppermost in her mind. "We've got to go into this with our eyes open."

"An' they ain't open yet," he agreed.

"And we've got to get them open. 'Tis them that looks that finds.' There's lots of time to learn things. We don't care if it takes months and months. We're footloose. A good start is better than a dozen bad ones. We've got to talk and find out. We'll talk with everybody we meet. Ask questions. Ask everybody. It's the only way to find out."

"I ain't much of a hand at askin' questions," Billy demurred.

"Then I'll ask," she cried. "We've got to win out at this game, and the way is to know. Look at all these Portuguese. Where are all the Americans? They owned the land first, after the Mexicans. What made the Americans clear out? How do the Portuguese make it go? Don't you see? We've got to ask millions of questions."

Beside the road they came upon a lineman eating his lunch.

"Stop and talk," Saxon whispered.

"Aw, what's the good? He's a lineman. What'd he know about farmin'?"

"You can never tell. He's our kind. Go ahead, Billy. You just speak to him. He isn't working now, anyway, and he'll be more likely to talk. See that tree in there, just inside the gate, an' the way the branches are grown together. It's a curiosity. Ask him about it. That's a good way to get started."

Billy stopped, when they were alongside. "How do you do?" he said gruffly. The lineman, a young fellow, paused in the cracking of a hard-boiled egg to stare up at the couple. "How do you do?" he said.

Billy swung his pack from his shoulders to the ground, and Saxon rested her telescope basket.

"Peddlin'?" the young man asked, too discreet to put his question directly to Saxon, yet dividing it between her and Billy, and cocking his eye at the covered basket.

"No," she spoke up quickly. "We're looking for land. Do you know of any around here?"

Again he desisted from the egg, studying them with sharp eyes as if to fathom their financial status. "Do you know what land sells for around here?" he asked.

"No," Saxon answered. "Do you?"

"I guess I ought to. I was born here. And land like this all around you runs at from two to three hundred to four an' five hundred dollars an acre."

"Whew!" Billy whistled. "I guess we don't want none of it."

"But what makes it that high?—town lots?" Saxon wanted to know.

"Nope. The Porchugeeze make it that high, I guess."

"I thought it was pretty good land that fetched a hundred an acre," Billy said.

"Oh, them times is past. They used to give away land once, an' if you was good, throw in all the cattle runnin' on it."

"How about government land around here?" was Billy's next query.

"Ain't none, an' never was. This was old Mexican grants. My grandfather bought sixteen hundred of the best acres around here for fifteen hundred dollars—five hundred down an' the balance in five years without interest. But that was in the early days. He come West in '48, tryin' to find a country without chills an' fever."

"He found it all right," said Billy.

"You bet he did. An' if him an' father'd held onto the land it'd been better than a gold mine, an' I wouldn't be workin' for a livin'. What's your business?"

"Teamster."

"Been in the strike in Oakland?"

"Sure thing. I've teamed there most of my life."

Here the two men wandered off into a discussion of union affairs and the strike situation; but Saxon refused to be balked, and brought back the talk to the land.

"How was it that the Portuguese ran up the price of land?" she asked.

The young fellow broke away from union matters with an effort, and for a moment regarded her with lack-luster eyes, until the question sank into his consciousness.

"Because they worked the land overtime. Because they worked mornin', noon, an' night, all hands, women an' kids. Because they could get more out of twenty acres than we could out of a hundred an' sixty. Look at old Silva—Antonio Silva. I've known him ever since I was a shaver. He didn't have the price of a square meal when he hit this section and begun leasin' land from my folks. Look at him now—worth two hundred an' fifty thousan' cold, an' I bet he's got credit for a million, an' there's no tellin' what the rest of his family owns."

"And he made all that out of your folks' land?" Saxon demanded.

The young lineman nodded his head with evident reluctance.

"Then why didn't your folks do it?" she pursued.

The lineman shrugged his shoulders. "Search me," he said.

"But the money was in the land," she persisted.

"Blamed if it was," came the retort, tinged slightly with choler. "We never saw it stickin' out so as you could notice it. The money was in the heads of the Porchugeeze, I guess. They knew a few more'n we did, that's all."

Saxon showed such dissatisfaction with his explanation that he was stung to action. He got up wrathfully.

"Come on, an' I'll show you," he said. "I'll show you why I'm workin' for wages when I might 'a' been a millionaire if my folks hadn't been mutts. That's what we old Americans are, Mutts, with a capital M."

He led them inside the gate, to the fruit-tree that had first attracted Saxon's attention.

"Say," Billy remarked, while they waited for the water to boil, "d'ye know what this reminds

me of?" Saxon was certain she did know, but she shook her head. She wanted to hear him say it

From the main crotch diverged the four main branches of the tree. Two feet above the crotch, the branches were connected, each to the ones on both sides, by braces of living wood. "You think it growed that way, eh? Well, it did. But it was old Silva that made it just the same—caught two sprouts, when the tree was young, an' twisted 'em together. Pretty slick, eh? You bet. That tree'll never blow down. It's a natural, springy brace, an' beats iron braces stiff. Look along all the rows. Every tree's that way. See? An' that's just one trick of the Porchugeeze. They got a million like it.

"Figure it out for yourself. They don't need props when the crop's heavy. Why, when we had a heavy crop, we used to use five props to a tree. Now take ten acres of trees. That'd be several thousan' props. Which cost money, an' labor to put in an' take out every year. These here natural braces don't have to have a thing done. They're Johnny-on-the-spot all the time. Why, the Porchugeeze has got us skinned a mile. Come on, I'll show you."

Billy, with city notions of trespass, betrayed perturbation at the freedom they were making of the little farm.

"Oh, it's all right, as long as you don't step on nothin'," the lineman reassured him. "Besides, my grandfather used to own this. They know me. Forty years ago old Silva come from the Azores. Went sheep herdin' in the mountains for a couple of years, then blew into San Leandro. These five acres was the first land he leased. That was the beginnin'. Then he begun leasin' by the hundreds of acres, an' by the hundred-an'-sixties. An' his sisters an' his uncles an' his aunts begun pourin' in from the Azores—they're all related there, you know—an' pretty soon San Leandro was a regular Porchugeeze settlement.

"An' old Silva wound up by buyin' these five acres from grandfather. Pretty soon— an' father by that time was in the hole to the neck—he was buyin' father's land by the hundred-an'-sixties. An' all the rest of his relations was doin' the same thing. Father was always gettin' rich quick, an' *he* wound up by dyin' in debt. But old Silva never overlooked a bet, no matter how dinky. An' all the rest are just like him. You see outside the fence there, clear to the wheel-tracks in the road— horse-beans. We'd 'a' scorned to do a picayune thing like that. Not Silva. Why, he's got a town house in San Leandro now. An' he rides around in a four-thousan'-dollar tourin'-car. An' just the same his front dooryard grows onions clear to the sidewalk. He clears three hundred a year on that patch alone. I know ten acres of land he bought last year—a thousan' an acre they asked 'm, an' he never batted an eye. He knew it was worth it, that's all. He knew he could make it pay. Back in the hills there, he's got a ranch of five hundred an' eighty acres, bought it dirt cheap, too; an' I want to tell you I could travel around in a different tourin'-car every day in the week just outa the profits he makes on that ranch, from the horses all the way from heavy drafts to fancy steppers."

"But how? How did he get it all?" Saxon clamored.

"By bein' wise to farmin'. Why, the whole blame family works. They ain't ashamed to roll up their sleeves an' dig— sons an' daughters an' daughter-in-laws, old man, old woman, an' the babies. They have a sayin' that a kid four years old that can't pasture one cow on the county road an' keep it fat ain't worth his salt. Why, the Silvas, the whole tribe of 'em, works a hundred acres in peas, eighty in tomatoes, thirty in asparagus, ten in pie-plant, forty in cucumbers, an'—oh, stacks of other things."

"But how do they do it?" Saxon continued to demand. "We've never been ashamed to work. We've worked hard all our lives. I can outwork any Portuguese woman ever born. And I've done it, too, in the jute-mills. There were lots of Portuguese girls working at the looms all around me, and I could outweave them every day, and I did, too. It isn't a case of work. What is it?"

The lineman looked at her in a troubled way. "Many's the time I've asked myself that same question. 'We're better'n these cheap immigrants,' I'd say to myself. 'We was here first, an' owned the land. I can lick any dago that ever hatched in the Azores. I got a better education. Then how in thunder do they put it all over us, get our land, an' start accounts in the banks?' An' the only answer I ever got is that we ain't got the *sabe*. We don't use our head-pieces right. Something's wrong with us. Anyway, we wasn't wised up to farming. We played at it. Show you? That's what I brung you in for—the way old Silva an' all his tribe farms. Look at this place. Some cousin of his, just out from the Azores, is makin' a start on it, an' payin' good rent to Silva. Pretty soon he'll be up to snuff an' buyin' land for himself from some perishin' American farmer. "Look at that, though you ought to see it in summer. Not an inch wasted. Where we get one thin crop, they get four fat crops. An' look at the way they crowd it—currants between the tree rows, beans between the currant rows, a row of beans close on each side the trees, an' rows of beans along the ends of the tree rows. Why, Silva wouldn't sell these five acres for five hundred an acre, cash down. He gave grandfather fifty an acre for it on long time, an' here am I workin' for the telephone company an' puttin' in a telephone for old Silva's cousin from the Azores that can't speak American yet."

Saxon talked with the lineman, following him about, till one o'clock, when he looked at his watch, said good-by, and returned to his task of putting in a telephone for the latest immigrant from the Azores.

When in town, Saxon carried her oil-cloth-wrapped telescope in her hand; but it was so arranged with loops that, once on the road, she could thrust her arms through the loops and carry it on her back.

A mile on from the lineman they stopped where a small creek, fringed with brush, crossed the county road. Billy was for the cold lunch, which was the last meal Saxon had prepared in the Pine Street cottage; but she was determined upon building a fire and boiling coffee. Not that she desired it for herself, but that she was impressed with the idea that everything at the start of their strange wandering must be as comfortable as possible for Billy's sake. Bent on inspiring him with enthusiasm equal to her own, she declined to dampen what sparks he had caught by anything so uncheerful as a cold meal.

"Now one thing we want to get out of our heads right at the start, Billy, is that we're in a hurry. We're not in a hurry, and we don't care whether school keeps or not. We're out to have a good time, a regular adventure like you read about in books. And right here's where we stop and boil coffee. You get the fire going, Billy, and I'll get the water and the things ready to spread out."

"Say," Billy remarked, while they waited for the water to boil, "d'ye know what this reminds me of?"

Saxon was certain she did know, but she shook her head. She wanted to hear him say it.

"Why, the second Sunday I knew you, when we drove out to Moraga Valley behind Prince and King. You spread the lunch that day."

"Only it was a more scrumptious lunch," she added, with a happy smile.

"But I wonder why we didn't have coffee that day," he went on.

"Perhaps it would have been too much like housekeeping," she laughed.

"I know something else that happened that day which you'd never guess," Billy reminisced. "I bet you couldn't."

"I wonder," Saxon murmured, and guessed it with her eyes.

Billy's eyes answered, and quite spontaneously he reached over, caught her hand, and pressed it caressingly to his cheek. "It's little, but oh, my," he said, addressing the imprisoned hand. Then he gazed at Saxon, and she warmed with his words. "We're beginnin' courtin' all over again, ain't we?"

Both ate heartily, and Billy was guilty of three cups of coffee.

"Say, this country air gives some appetite," he mumbled, as he sank his teeth into his fifth bread-and-meat sandwich.

Saxon's mind had reverted to all the young lineman had told her, and she completed a sort of general résumé of the information. "My!" she exclaimed, "but we've learned a lot!"

"An' we've sure learned one thing," Billy said. "An' that is that this is no place for us, with land a thousan' an acre an' only twenty dollars in our pockets."

"Oh, we're not going to stop here," she hastened to say. "But just the same it's the Portuguese that gave it its price, and they make things go on it."

"An' I take my hat off to them," Billy responded. "But all the same, I'd sooner have forty acres at a hundred an acre than four at a thousan' an acre. Somehow, you know, I'd be scared stiff on four acres—scared of fallin' off, you know."

She was in full sympathy with him. In her heart of hearts the forty acres tugged much the harder. In her way, allowing for the difference of a generation, her desire for spaciousness was as strong as her Uncle Will's.

"Well, we're not going to stop here," she assured Billy. "We're going in, not for forty acres, but for a hundred and sixty acres free from the government."

"An' I guess the government owes it to us for what our fathers an' mothers done. I tell you, Saxon, when a woman walks across the plains like your mother done, an' a man an' wife gets massacred by the Indians like my grandfather an' -mother done, the government does owe them something."

"Well, it's up to us to collect."

"An' we'll collect all right, all right, somewhere down in them redwood mountains south of Monterey."

XXXI

It was a good afternoon's tramp to Niles, passing through the town of Haywards; yet Saxon and Billy found time to diverge from the main county road and take the parallel roads through acres of intense cultivation where the land was farmed to the wheel-tracks. Saxon looked with amazement at these small, brown-skinned immigrants who came to the soil with nothing and yet made the soil pay for itself to the tune of two hundred, five hundred, even a thousand dollars an acre. On every hand was activity. Women and children were in the fields as well as men. The land was turned endlessly over and over. They seemed never to let it rest. And it rewarded them.

"Look at their faces," Saxon said. "They are happy and contented. They haven't faces like the people in our neighborhood after the strikes began."

"Oh, sure, they got a good thing," Billy agreed. "You can see it stickin' out all over them. But they needn't get chesty with *me*, I can tell them that much—just because they've jiggerooed us out of our land an' everything."

"But they're not showing any signs of chestiness," Saxon demurred.

"No, they're not, come to think of it. All the same, they ain't so wise. I bet I could tell 'em a few about horses."

It was sunset when they entered the little town of Niles. Billy, who had been silent for the last half-mile, hesitantly ventured a suggestion.

"Say, I could put up for a room in the hotel just as well as not. What d'ye think?"

But Saxon shook her head emphatically. "How long do you think our twenty dollars will last at that rate? Besides, the only way to begin is to begin at the beginning. We didn't plan sleeping in hotels."

"All right," he gave in. "I'm game. I was just thinkin' about you."

"Then you'd better think I'm game, too," she flashed forgivingly. "And now we'll have to see about getting things for supper."

They bought a round steak, potatoes, onions, and a dozen eating-apples, then went out from the town to the fringe of trees and brush that advertised a creek. Beside the trees, on a sand bank, they pitched camp. Plenty of dry wood lay about, and Billy whistled genially while he gathered and chopped. Saxon, keen to follow his every mood, was cheered by the atrocious discord on his lips. She smiled to herself as she spread the blankets, with the tarpaulin underneath, for a table, having first removed all twigs from the sand. She had much to learn in the matter of cooking over a camp-fire, and made fair progress, discovering, first of all, that control of the fire meant far more than the size of it. When the coffee was boiled, she settled the grounds with a part-cup of cold water and placed the pot on the edge of the coals where it would keep hot and yet not boil. She fried potato dollars and onions in the same pan, but separately, and set them on top of the coffee-pot in the tin plate she was to eat from, covering it with Billy's inverted plate. On the dry hot pan, in the way that delighted Billy, she fried the steak. This completed, and while Billy poured the coffee, she served the steak, putting the dollars and onions back into the frying-pan for a moment to make them piping hot again.

"What more d'ye want than this?" Billy challenged, with deep-toned satisfaction, in the pause after his final cup of coffee, while he rolled a cigarette. He lay on his side, full length, resting on his elbow. The fire was burning brightly, and Saxon's color was heightened by the flickering flames. "Now our folks, when they was on the move, had to be afraid for Indians and wild animals and all sorts of things; an' here we are, as safe as bugs in a rug. Take this sand. What better bed could you ask?

Soft as feathers. Say, you look good to me, heap little squaw. I bet you don't look an inch over sixteen right now, Mrs. Babe-in-the-Woods."

"Don't I?" she glowed, with a flirt of the head sideways and a white flash of teeth. "If you weren't smoking a cigarette I'd ask you if your mother knew you're out, Mr. Babe-on-the-Sandbank."

"Say," he began, with transparently feigned seriousness, "I want to ask you something, if you don't mind. Now, of course, I don't want to hurt your feelin's or nothin', but just the same there's something important I'd like to know."

"Well, what is it?" she inquired, after a fruitless wait.

"Well, it's just this, Saxon. I like you like anything an' all that, but here's night come on, an' we're a thousand miles from anywhere, and—well, what I wanta know is: are we really an' truly married, you an' me?"

"Really and truly," she assured him. "Why?"

"Oh, nothing; but I'd kind a-forgotten, an' I was gettin' embarrassed, you know, because if we wasn't, seein' the way I was brought up, this'd be no place—"

"That will do you," she said severely. "And this is just the time and place for you to get in the firewood for morning, while I wash up the dishes and put the kitchen in order."

He started to obey, but paused to throw his arm about her and draw her close. Neither spoke, but when he went his way Saxon's breast was fluttering, and a song of thanksgiving breathed on her lips.

The night had come on, dim with the light of faint stars. But these had disappeared behind clouds that seemed to have arisen from nowhere. It was the beginning of California's Indian summer. The air was warm, with just the first hint of evening chill, and there was no wind.

"I've a feeling as if we've just started to live," Saxon said, when Billy, his firewood collected, joined her on the blankets before the fire. "I've learned more to-day than in ten years in Oakland." She drew a long breath and braced her shoulders. "Farming's a bigger subject than I thought."

Billy said nothing. With steady eyes he was staring into the fire, and she knew he was turning something over in his mind.

"What is it?" she asked, when she saw

he had reached a conclusion, at the same time resting her hand on the back of his.

"Just been framin' up that ranch of ourn," he answered. "It's all well enough, these dinky farmlets. They'll do for foreigners. But we Americans just gotta have room. I want to be able to look at a hilltop an' know it's my land, and know it's my land down the other side an' up the next hilltop, an' know that over beyond that, down alongside some creek, my mares are most likely grazin', an' their little colts grazin' with 'em or kickin' up their heels. You know, there's money in raisin' horses—especially the big workhorses that run to eighteen hundred an' two thousand pounds. They're payin' for 'em, in the cities, every day in the year, seven an' eight hundred a pair, matched geldings, four years old. Good pasture an' plenty of it, in this kind of a climate, is all they need, along with some sort of shelter an' a little hay in long spells of bad weather. I never thought of it before, but let me tell you that this ranch proposition is beginnin' to look good to *me*."

Saxon was all excitement. Here was new information on the cherished subject, and, best of all, Billy was the authority. Still better, he was taking an interest himself.

"There'll be room for that and for everything on a quarter-section," she encouraged.

"Sure thing. Around the house we'll have vegetables an' fruit and chickens an' everything, just like the Porchugeeze, an' plenty of room, beside, to walk around an' range the horses."

"But won't the colts cost money, Billy?"

"Not much. The cobblestones eat horses up fast. That's where I'll get my brood-mares, from the ones knocked out by the city. I know *that* end of it. They sell 'em at auction, an' they're good for years an' years, only no good on the cobbles any more."

There ensued a long pause. In the dying fire both were busy visioning the farm to be.

"It's pretty still, ain't it?" Billy said, rousing himself at last. He gazed about him. "An' black as a stack of black cats." He shivered, buttoned his coat, and tossed several sticks on the fire. "Just the same, it's the best kind of a climate in the world. Many's the time, when I was a little kid, I've heard father brag about California's bein' a blanket climate. He went East, once, an' stayed a summer an' a winter,

"I found this place in a delightful climate, close to San José—and I bought it. I paid two thou-

sand cash and gave a mortgage for two thousand. It cost two hundred an acre, you see"

an' got all he wanted. Never again for him."

"My mother said there never was such a land for climate. How wonderful it must have seemed to them after crossing the deserts and mountains. They called it the land of milk and honey. The ground was so rich that all they needed to do was scratch it, Cady used to say."

"And wild game everywhere," Billy contributed. "Mr. Roberts, the one that adopted my father, he drove cattle from the San Joaquin to the Columbia River. He had forty men helpin' him, an' all they took along was powder an' salt. They lived off the game they shot."

"The hills were full of deer, and my mother saw whole herds of elk around Santa Rosa. Sometime we'll go there, Billy. I've always wanted to."

By this time the fire had died down, and Saxon had finished brushing and braiding her hair. Their bed-going preliminaries were simple, and in a few minutes they were side by side under the blankets. Saxon closed her eyes, but could not sleep. On the contrary, she had never been more wide awake. She had never slept out of doors in her life, and by no exertion of will could she overcome the strangeness of it. In addition, she was stiffened from the long trudge, and the sand, to her surprise, was anything but soft. An hour passed. She tried to believe that Billy was asleep, but felt certain he was not. The sharp crackle of a dying ember startled her. She was confident that Billy had moved slightly.

"Billy," she whispered, "are you awake?"

"Yep," came his low answer, "an' thinkin' this sand is harder'n a cement floor. It's one on me, all right. But who'd 'a' thought it?"

Both shifted their postures slightly, but vain was the attempt to escape from the dull, aching contact of the sand.

An abrupt, metallic, whirring noise of some near-by cricket gave Saxon another startle. She endured the sound for some minutes, until Billy broke forth.

"Say, that gets my goat, whatever it is."

"Do you think it's a rattlesnake?" she asked, maintaining a calmness she did not feel.

"Just what I've been thinkin'."

"I saw two, in the window of Bowman's drug store. An' you know, Billy, they've got a hollow fang, and when they stick it into you the poison runs down the hollow."

"Br-r-r-," Billy shivered, in fear that was not altogether mockery. "Certain death, everybody says, unless you're a Bosco. Remember him?"

"He eats 'em alive! He eats 'em alive! Bosco! Bosco!" Saxon responded, mimicking the cry of a side-show barker.

"Just the same, all Bosco's rattlers had the poison-sacks cut outa them. They must 'a' had. Gee! It's funny I can't get asleep. I wish that thing'd close its trap. I wonder if it is a rattlesnake."

"No; it can't be," Saxon decided. "All the rattlesnakes were killed off long ago."

"Then where did Bosco get his?" Billy demanded, with unimpeachable logic. "An' why don't you go to sleep?"

"Because it's all new, I guess," was her reply. "You see, I never camped out in my life."

"Neither did I. An' until now I always thought it was a lark." He changed his position on the maddening sand and sighed heavily. "But we'll get used to it in time, I guess. What other folks can do, we can, an' a mighty lot of 'em has camped out. It's all right. Here we are, free an' independent, no rent to pay, our own bosses—"

He stopped abruptly. From somewhere in the brush came an intermittent rustling. When they tried to locate it, it mysteriously ceased, and when the first hint of drowsiness stole upon them, the rustling as mysteriously recommenced.

"It sounds like something creeping up on us," Saxon suggested, snuggling closer to Billy.

"Well, it ain't a wild Indian, at all events," was the best he could offer in the way of comfort. He yawned deliberately. "Aw, shucks! What's there to be scared of? Think of what all the pioneers went through."

Again Saxon was drowsing, when the rustling sound was heard, this time closer. To her excited apprehension there was something stealthy about it, and she imagined a beast of prey creeping upon them. "Billy," she whispered. "Yes, I'm a-listenin' to it," came his wide-awake answer.

"Mightn't that be a panther, or maybe a—wildcat?"

"It can't be. All the varmints was killed off long ago. This is peaceable farmin' country."

A vagrant breeze sighed through the trees and made Saxon shiver. The mysterious cricket-noise ceased with suspicious abruptness. Then, from the rustling noise, ensued a dull but heavy thump that caused both Saxon and Billy to sit up in the blankets. There were no further sounds, and they lay down again, though the very silence now seemed ominous.

"Huh," Billy muttered with relief. "As though I don't know what it was. It was a rabbit. I've heard tame ones bang their hind feet down on the floor that way."

In vain Saxon tried to win sleep. The sand grew harder with the passage of time. Her flesh and her bones ached from contact with it. And though her reason flouted any possibility of wild dangers, her fancy went on picturing them with unflagging zeal.

A new sound commenced. It was neither a rustling nor a rattling, and it tokened some large body passing through the brush. Sometimes twigs crackled and broke, and, once, they heard bush-branches pressed aside and spring back into place.

"If that other thing was a panther, this is an elephant," was Billy's uncheering opinion. "It's got weight. Listen to that. An' it's comin' nearer."

There were frequent stoppages, then the sounds would begin again, always louder, always closer. Billy sat up in the blankets once more, passing one arm around Saxon, who had also sat up.

"I ain't slept a wink," he complained. "There it goes again. I wish I could see."

"It makes a noise big enough for a grizzly," Saxon chattered, partly from nervousness, partly from the chill of the night.

"It ain't no grasshopper, that's sure."

Billy started to leave the blankets, but Saxon caught his arm.

"What are you going to do?"

"Oh, I ain't scairt none," he answered. "But honest to' God this is gettin' on my nerves. If I don't find what that thing is, it'll give me the willies. I'm just goin' to reconnoiter. I won't go close."

So intensely dark was the night that the moment Billy crawled beyond the reach of her hand he was lost to sight. She sat and waited. The sounds had ceased, though she could follow Billy's progress by the cracking of dry twigs and limbs. After a few moments he returned and crawled under the blankets.

"I scared it away, I guess. It's got better ears, an' when it heard me comin'

it skinned out, most likely. I did my dangdest, too, not to make a sound. Oh, Lord, there it goes again!"

They sat up. Saxon nudged Billy.

"There," she warned, in the faintest of whispers. "I can hear it breathing. It almost made a snort."

A dead branch cracked loudly, and so near at hand that both of them jumped shamelessly.

"I ain't goin' to stand any more of its foolin'," Billy declared wrathfully. "It'll be on top of us if I don't."

"What are you going to do?" she queried anxiously.

"Yell the top of my head off. I'll get a fall outa whatever it is."

He drew a deep breath and emitted a wild yell.

The result far exceeded any expectation he could have entertained, and Saxon's heart leaped up in sheer panic. On the instant the darkness erupted into terrible sound and movement. There were crashings of underbrush and lunges and plunges of heavy bodies in different directions. Fortunately for their ease of mind, all these sounds receded and died away.

"An' what d'ye think of that?" Billy broke the silence. "Gee! all the fight fans used to say I was scairt of nothin'. Just the same I'm glad they ain't seein' me to-night." He groaned. "I've got all I want of that blamed sand. I'm goin' to get up and start the fire."

This was easy. Under the ashes were live embers which quickly ignited the wood he threw on. A few stars were peeping out in the misty zenith. He looked up at them, deliberated, and started to move away.

"Where are you going now?" Saxon called.

"Oh, I've an idea," he replied noncommittally, and walked boldly away beyond the circle of the firelight.

Saxon sat with the blankets drawn closely under her chin, and admired his courage. He had not even taken the hatchet, and he was going in the direction in which the disturbance had died away.

Ten minutes later he came back chuckling. "The sons-of-guns, they got my goat all right. I'll be scairt of my own shadow next. What was they? Huh! You couldn't guess in a thousand years. A bunch of half-grown calves, an' they was worse scairt than us."

He smoked a cigarette by the fire, then rejoined Saxon under the blankets.

"A fine farmer I'll make," he chafed, "when a lot of little calves can scare the stuffin' outa me. I bet your father or mine wouldn't 'a' batted an eye. The stock has gone to seed, that's what it has."

"No, it hasn't," Saxon defended. "The stock is all right. We're just as able as our folks ever were, and we're healthier on top of it. We've been brought up different, that's all. We've lived in cities all our lives. We know the city sounds and things, but we don't know the country ones. Our training has been unnatural, that's the whole thing in a nutshell. Now we're going in for natural training. Give us a little time, and we'll sleep as sound out of doors as ever your father or mine did."

"But not on sand," Billy groaned.

"We won't try. That's one thing, for good and all, we've learned the very first time. And now hush up and go to sleep."

Their fears had vanished, but the sand, receiving now their undivided attention, multiplied its unyieldingness. Billy dozed off first, and roosters were crowing somewhere in the distance when Saxon's eyes closed. But they could not escape the sand, and their sleep was fitful.

At the first gray of dawn Billy crawled out and built a roaring fire. Saxon drew up to it shiveringly. They were hollow-eyed and weary. Saxon began to laugh. Billy joined sulkily, then brightened up as his eyes chanced upon the coffee-pot, which he immediately put on to boil.

XXXII

It is forty miles from Oakland to San José, and Saxon and Billy accomplished it in three easy days. No more obliging and angrily garrulous linemen were encountered, and few were the opportunities for conversation with chance wayfarers. Numbers of tramps, carrying rolls of blankets, were met, traveling both north and south on the county road; and from talks with them Saxon quickly learned that they knew little or nothing about farming. They were mostly old men, feeble or besotted, and all they knew was work—where jobs might be good, where jobs had been good; but the places they mentioned were always a long way off. One thing she did glean from them, and that was that the district she and

Billy were passing through was "small farmer" country in which outside labor was rarely hired, and that when it was it was generally Portuguese.

The farmers themselves were unfriendly. They drove by Billy and Saxon, often with empty wagons, but never invited them to ride. When chance offered and Saxon did ask questions, they looked her over curiously or suspiciously, and gave ambiguous and facetious answers.

"They ain't Americans," Billy fretted. "Why, in the old days everybody was friendly to everybody."

"It's the spirit of the times, Billy. The spirit has changed. Besides, these people are too near. Wait till we get farther away from the cities, then we'll find them more friendly."

"A measly lot these ones are," he sneered.

"Maybe they've a right to be," she laughed. "For all you know, more than one of the scabs you've slugged were sons of theirs."

"If I could only hope so," Billy said fervently. "But I don't care if I owned ten thousand acres, any man hikin' with his blankets might be just as good a man as me, an' maybe better, for all I'd know. I'd give 'm the benefit of the doubt, anyway."

Billy asked for work, at first indiscriminately, later only at the larger farms. The unvarying reply was that there was no work. A few said there would be plowing after the first rains. Here and there, in a small way, dry plowing was going on. But, in the main, the farmers were waiting.

"But do you know how to plow?" Saxon asked Billy.

"No; but I guess it ain't much of a trick to turn. Besides, next man I see plowing I'm goin' to get a lesson from."

In the mid-afternoon of the second day his opportunity came. He climbed on top of the fence of a small field and watched an old man plow round and round it.

"Aw, shucks, just as easy as easy," Billy commented scornfully. "If an old codger like that can handle one plow, I can handle two."

"Go on and try it," Saxon urged.

"What's the good?"

"Cold feet," she jeered, but with a smiling face. "All you have to do is ask him. All he can do is say no. And what if he does? You faced the Chicago Terror twenty rounds without flinching."

"Aw, but it's different," he demurred, then dropped to the ground inside the fence. "Two to one the old geezer turns me down."

"No, he won't. Just tell him you want to learn, and ask him if he'll let you drive around a few times. Tell him it won't cost him anything."

"Huh! If he gets chesty I'll take his blamed plow away from him."

From the top of the fence, but too far away to hear, Saxon watched the colloquy. After several minutes, the lines were transferred to Billy's neck, the handles to his hands. Then the team started, and the old man, delivering a rapid fire of instructions, walked alongside of Billy. When a few turns had been made, the farmer crossed the plowed strip to Saxon, and joined her on the rail.

"He's plowed before, a little mite, ain't he?"

Saxon shook her head. "Never in his life. But he knows how to drive horses."

"He showed he wa'n't all greenhorn, an' he learns pretty quick." Here the farmer chuckled and cut himself a chew from a plug of tobacco. "I reckon he won't tire me out a-settin' here."

The unplowed area grew smaller and smaller, but Billy evinced no intention of quitting, and his audience on the fence was deep in conversation. Saxon's questions flew fast and furious, and she was not long in concluding that the old man bore a striking resemblance to the description the lineman had given of his father.

Billy persisted till the field was finished, and the old man invited him and Saxon to stop the night. There was a disused outbuilding where they would find a small cook-stove, he said, and also he would give them fresh milk. Further, if Saxon wanted to test her desire for farming, she could try her hand on the cow.

The milking lesson did not prove as successful as Billy's plowing; but when he had mocked sufficiently, Saxon challenged him to try, and he failed as grievously as she. Saxon had eyes and questions for everything, and it did not take her long to realize that she was looking upon the other side of the farming shield. Farm and farmer were old fashioned. There was no intensive cultivation. There was too much land too little farmed: Everything was slipshod. House and barn and outbuild-

ings were fast falling into ruin. The front yard was weed-grown. There was no vegetable garden. The small orchard was old, sickly, and neglected. The trees were twisted, spindling, and overgrown with a gray moss. The sons and daughters were away in the cities, Saxon found out. One daughter had married a doctor, the other was a teacher in the state normal school; one son was a locomotive engineer, the second was an architect, and the third was a police-court reporter in San Francisco. On occasion, the father said, they helped out the old folks.

"What do you think?" Saxon asked Billy, as he smoked his after-supper cigarette.

His shoulders went up in a comprehensive shrug. "Huh! That's easy. The old geezer's like his orchard—covered with moss. It's plain as the nose on your face, after San Leandro, that he don't know the first thing. An' them horses. It'd be a charity to him, an' a savin' of money for him, to take 'em out an' shoot 'em both. You bet you don't see the Porchugeeze with horses like them. An' it ain't a case of bein' proud, or puttin' on side, to have good horses. It's brass tacks an' business. It pays. That's the game. You oughta see the way they work an' figure horses in the city."

They slept soundly, and, after an early breakfast, prepared to start.

"I'd like to give you a couple of days' work," the old man regretted, at parting; "but I can't see it. The ranch just about keeps me and the old woman, now that the children are gone. An' then it don't always. Seems times have been bad for a long spell now. Ain't never been the same since Grover Cleveland."

Early in the afternoon, on the outskirts of San José, Saxon called a halt. "I'm going right in there and talk," she declared, "unless they set the dogs on me. That's the prettiest place yet, isn't it?"

Billy, who was always visioning hills and spacious ranges for his horses, mumbled unenthusiastic assent.

"And the vegetables! Look at them! And the flowers growing along the borders! That beats tomato plants in wrapping-paper."

"Don't see the sense of it," Billy objected. "Where's the money come in from flowers that take up the ground that good vegetables might be growin' on?"

"And that's what I'm going to find out."
She pointed to a woman, stooped to the
ground and working with a trowel, in front
of the tiny bungalow. "I don't know what
she's like, but at the worst she can only
be mean. See! She's looking at us now.
Drop your load alongside of mine, and
come on in."

Billy slung the blankets from his shoulder
to the ground, but elected to wait. As
Saxon went up the narrow, flower-bordered
walk, she noted two men at work among
the vegetables—one an old Chinese, the other
old and of some dark-eyed foreign breed.
Here were neatness, efficiency, and intensive
cultivation with a vengeance—even her un-
trained eye could see that. The woman
stood up and turned from her flowers, and
Saxon saw that she was middle-aged, slender,
and simply but nicely dressed. She wore
glasses, and Saxon's reading of her face was
that it was kind but nervous looking.

"I don't want anything to-day," she
said before Saxon could speak, adminis-
tering the rebuff with a pleasant smile.

Saxon groaned inwardly over the black-
covered telescope basket. Evidently the
woman had seen her put it down. "We're
not peddling," she explained quickly.

"Oh, I am sorry for the mistake."

This time the woman's smile was even
pleasanter, and she waited for Saxon to
state her errand. Nothing loath, Saxon
took it at a plunge.

"We're looking for land. We want to
be farmers, you know, and before we get
the land we want to find out what kind
of land we want. And seeing this pretty
place has just filled me up with questions.
You see, we don't know anything about
farming. We've lived in the city all our
lives, and now we've given it up and are
going to live in the country and be happy."

She paused. The woman's face seemed
to grow quizzical.

"But how do you know you will be
happy in the country?" she asked.

"I don't know. All I do know is that
poor people can't be happy in the city
where they have labor troubles all the
time. If they can't be happy in the
country, then there's no happiness anywhere, and that doesn't seem fair, does it?"

"It is sound reasoning, my dear, as far
as it goes. But you must remember that
there are many poor people in the country
and many unhappy people."

"You look neither poor nor unhappy,"
Saxon challenged.

"But I may be peculiarly qualified to live
and succeed in the country. You've spent
your life in the city. You don't know the
first thing about the country. It might
even break your heart."

Saxon's mind went back to the terrible
months in the Pine Street cottage. "I
know already that the city will break my
heart. Maybe the country will, too, but
just the same it's my only chance. It's
that or nothing. Besides, our folks before
us were all of the country. It seems the
more natural way. And better, here I am,
which proves that 'way down inside I must
want the country, must, as you call it, be
peculiarly qualified for the country, or else
I wouldn't be here."

The other nodded approval, and looked
at her with growing interest.

"That young man—" she began.

"Is my husband. He was a teamster
until the big strike. My name is Roberts,
Saxon Roberts, and my husband is William
Roberts."

"And I am Mrs. Mortimer," the other
said, with a bow of acknowledgment. "I
am a widow. And now, if you will ask
your husband in I shall try to answer some
of your many questions. Tell him to put
the bundles inside the gate. And now
what are all your questions?"

"Oh, all kinds. How does it pay? How
did you manage it all? How much did
the land cost? Did you build that beautiful house? How much do you pay the
men? How did you learn all the different
kinds of things, and which grew best and
which paid best? What is the best way to
sell them? How do you sell them?"
Saxon paused and laughed. "Oh, I haven't
begun yet. Why do you have flowers on
the borders everywhere? I looked over the
Portuguese farms around San Leandro, but
they never mixed flowers and vegetables."

Mrs. Mortimer held up her hand. "Let
me answer the last first. It is the key to
almost everything."

But Billy arrived, and the explanation
was deferred until after his introduction.

"The flowers caught your eyes, didn't
they, my dear?" Mrs. Mortimer resumed.
"And brought you in through my gate and
right up to me. And that's the very reason
they were planted with vegetables—to
catch eyes. You can't imagine how many

eyes they have caught, or how many owners of eyes they have lured inside my gate. This is a good road, and is a very popular, short, country drive for townsfolk. Oh, no; I've never had any luck with automobiles. They can't see anything for dust. But I began when nearly everybody still used carriages. The townswomen would drive by. My flowers, and then my place, would catch their eyes. They would tell their drivers to stop. And—well, somehow, I managed to be in the front within speaking distance. Usually I succeeded in inviting them in to see my flowers—and vegetables, of course. Everything was sweet, clean, pretty. It all appealed. And," Mrs. Mortimer shrugged her shoulders, "it is well known that the stomach sees through the eyes. The thought of vegetables growing among flowers pleased their fancy. They wanted my vegetables. They must have them. And they did, at double the market price, which they were only too glad to pay. You see, I became the fashion, or a fad, in a small way. Nobody lost. The vegetables were certainly good, as good as any on the market and often fresher. And besides, my customers killed two birds with one stone; for they were pleased with themselves for philanthropic reasons. Not only did they obtain the finest and freshest possible vegetables, but at the same time they were happy with the knowledge that they were helping a deserving widow. Yes, and it gave a certain tone to their establishments to be able to say they bought Mrs. Mortimer's vegetables. But that's too big a side to go into. In short, my little place became a show place—anywhere to go, for a drive or anything, you know, when time has to be killed. And it became noised about who I was, who my husband had been, what I had been. Some of the towns-ladies I had known personally in the old days. They actually worked for my success. And then, too, I used to serve tea. My patrons became my guests for the time being. I still serve it, when they drive out to show me off to their friends. So, you see, the flowers are one of the ways I succeeded."

Saxon was glowing with appreciation, but Mrs. Mortimer, glancing at Billy, noted not entire approval. His blue eyes were clouded.

"Well, out with it!" she encouraged. "What are you thinking?"

To Saxon's surprise, he answered directly, and to her double surprise, his criticism was of a nature which had never entered her head.

"It's just a trick," Billy expounded. "That's what I was gettin' at."

"But a paying trick," Mrs. Mortimer interrupted, her eyes dancing and vivacious behind their glasses.

"Yes, and no," Billy said stubbornly, speaking in his slow, deliberate fashion. "If every farmer was to mix flowers an' vegetables, then every farmer would get double the market price, an' then there wouldn't be any double market price. Everything'd be as it was before."

"You are opposing a theory to a fact," Mrs. Mortimer stated. "The fact is that all farmers do not do it. The fact is that I do receive double the price. You can't get away from that."

Billy was unconvinced, though unable to reply. "Just the same," he muttered, with a slow shake of the head, "I don't get the hang of it. There's something wrong so far as we're concerned—my wife an' me, I mean. Maybe I'll get hold of it after a while."

"And in the mean time, we'll look around," Mrs. Mortimer invited. "I want to show you everything, and tell you how I make it go. Afterward; we'll sit down, and I'll tell you about the beginning. You see," she bent her gaze on Saxon, "I want you thoroughly to understand that you can succeed in the country if you go about it right. I didn't know a thing about it when I began, and I didn't have a fine big man like yours. I was all alone. But I'll tell you about that."

For the next hour, among vegetables, berry-bushes and fruit-trees, Saxon stored her brain with a huge mass of information to be digested at her leisure. Billy, too, was interested, but he left the talking to Saxon, himself rarely asking a question. At the rear of the bungalow, where everything was as clean and orderly as at the front, they were shown through the chicken-yard. Here, in different runs, were kept several hundred small and snow-white hens. "White Leghorns," said Mrs. Mortimer. "You have no idea what they netted me this year. I never keep a hen a moment past the prime of her laying period."

"Just what I was tellin' you about horses, Saxon," Billy broke in.

Ten minutes later he came back chuckling. "They got my goat all right. I'll be scairt
of my own shadow next"

"And by the simple method of hatching
them at the right time, which not one
farmer in ten thousand ever dreams of
doing, I have them laying in the winter,
when most hens stop laying and when eggs
are highest. Another thing: I have my
special customers. They pay me ten cents a
dozen more than the market price, because
my specialty is one-day eggs."

Here she chanced to glance at Billy, and
guessed that he was still wrestling with
his problem.

"Same old thing?" she queried.

He nodded. "Same old thing. If every
farmer delivered day-old eggs, there would
be no ten cents higher'n the top price.
They'd be no better off than they was
before."

"But the eggs would be one-day eggs,
all the eggs would be one-day eggs, you
mustn't forget that," Mrs. Mortimer
pointed out.

"But that don't butter no toast for my
wife an' me," he objected. "An' that's
what I've been tryin' to get the hang of,
an' now I got it. You talk about theory
an' fact. Ten cents higher than top price

is a theory to Saxon an' me. The fact is
we ain't got no eggs, no chickens, an' no
land for the chickens to run an' lay eggs
on."

Their hostess nodded sympathetically.

"An' there's something else about this
outfit of yourn that I don't get the hang
of," he pursued. "I can't just put my
finger on it, but it's there all right."

They were shown over the cattery, the
piggery, the milkery, and the kennelry,
as Mrs. Mortimer called her live-stock
departments. None was large. All were
money-makers, she assured them, and
rattled off her profits glibly. She took
their breaths away by the prices given and
received for pedigreed Persians, pedigreed
Ohio Improved Chesters, pedigreed Scotch
collies, and pedigreed Jerseys. For the
milk of the last she also had a special private market, receiving five cents more a
quart than was fetched by the best dairy-
milk. Billy was quick to point out the
difference between the look of her orchard
and the look of the orchard they had
inspected the previous afternoon, and Mrs.
Mortimer showed him scores of other

differences, many of which he was compelled to accept on faith.

Then she told them of another industry, her home-made jams and jellies, always contracted for in advance and at prices dizzyingly beyond the regular market. They sat in comfortable rattan chairs on the veranda, while she told the story of how she had drummed up the jam and jelly trade, dealing only with the one best restaurant and one best club in San José. To the proprietor and the steward she had gone with her samples, in long discussions beaten down their opposition, overcome their reluctance, and persuaded them to make a "special" of her wares, to boom them quietly with their patrons, and, above all, to charge stiffly for dishes and courses in which they appeared.

Throughout the recital Billy's eyes were moody with dissatisfaction. Mrs. Mortimer saw, and waited.

"And now, begin at the beginning," Saxon begged.

But Mrs. Mortimer refused unless they agreed to stop for supper. Saxon frowned Billy's reluctance away, and accepted for both of them.

"Well, then," Mrs. Mortimer took up her tale, "in the beginning I was a greenhorn, city born and bred. All I knew of the country was that it was a place to go to for vacations, and I always went to springs and mountain and seaside resorts. I had lived among books almost all my life. I was head librarian of the Doncaster Library for years. Then I married Mr. Mortimer. He was a book man, a professor in San Miguel University. He had a long sickness, and when he died there was nothing left. Even his life insurance was eaten into before I could be free of creditors. As for myself, I was worn out, on the verge of nervous prostration, fit for nothing. I had five thousand dollars left, however, and, without going into the details, I decided to go to farming. I found this place in a delightful climate, close to San José—the end of the electric line is only a quarter of a mile on—and I bought it. I paid two thousand cash and gave a mortgage for two thousand. It cost two hundred an acre, you see."

"Twenty acres!" Saxon cried.

"Wasn't that pretty small?" Billy ventured.

"Too large, oceans too large. I leased ten acres of it the first thing. And it's still leased after all this time. Even the ten I'd retained was much too large for a long, long time. It's only now that I'm beginning to feel a tiny mite crowded."

"And ten acres has supported you an' two hired men?" Billy demanded, amazed.

Mrs. Mortimer clapped her hands delightedly. "Listen. I had been a librarian. I knew my way among books. First of all I'd read everything written on the subject, and subscribed to some of the best farm magazines and papers. And you ask if my ten acres have supported me and two hired men. Let me tell you. I have four hired men. The ten acres certainly must support them, as it supports Hannah—she's a Swedish widow who runs the house and who is a perfect Trojan during the jam and jelly season—and Hannah's daughter, who goes to school and lends a hand, and my nephew, whom I have taken to raise and educate. Also, the ten acres have come pretty close to paying for the whole twenty, as well as for this house and all the outbuildings and all the pedigreed stock."

Saxon remembered what the young lineman had said about the Portuguese. "The ten acres didn't do a bit of it," she cried. "It was your head that did it all, and you know it."

"And that's the point, my dear. It shows the right kind of person can succeed in the country. Remember, the soil is generous. But it must be treated generously, and that is something the old-style American farmer can't get into his head. So it is head that counts. Even when his starving acres have convinced him of the need for fertilizing, he can't see the difference between cheap fertilizer and good fertilizer."

"And that's something I want to know about," Saxon exclaimed.

"And I'll tell you all I know, but first, you must be very tired. I noticed you were limping. Let me take you in—never mind your bundles; I'll send Chang for them."

To Saxon, with her innate love of beauty and charm in all personal things, the interior of the bungalow was a revelation. Never before had she been inside a middle-class home, and what she saw not only far exceeded anything she had imagined, but was vastly different from her imaginings. Mrs. Mortimer noted her sparkling glances which took in everything, and went out of her way to show Saxon around, doing it under the guise of gleeful boasting, stating the costs of the different materials, explaining how she had done things with her own hands, such as staining the floors, weathering the bookcases, and putting together the big Mission Morris chair. Billy stepped gingerly behind, and though it never entered his mind to ape to the manner born, he succeeded in escaping conspicuous awkwardnesses, even at the table, where he and Saxon had the unique experience of being waited on in a private house by a servant.

"If you'd only come along next year," Mrs. Mortimer mourned; "then I should have had the spare room I had planned."

"That's all right," Billy spoke up; "thank you just the same. But we'll catch the electric car into San José an' get a room."

Mrs. Mortimer was still disturbed at her inability to put them up for the night, and Saxon changed the conversation by pleading to be told more.

"You remember, I told you I'd paid only two thousand down on the land," Mrs. Mortimer complied. "That left me three thousand to experiment with. Of course all my friends and relatives prophesied failure. And of course I made my mistakes, plenty of them, but I was saved from still more by the thorough study I had made and continued to make." She indicated shelves of farm books and files of farm magazines that lined the walls. "And I continued to study. I was resolved to be up to date, and I sent for all the experiment-station reports. I went almost entirely on the basis that whatever the old-type farmer did was wrong, and, do you know, in doing that I was not so far wrong myself. It's almost unthinkable, the stupidity of the old-fashioned farmers. Oh, I consulted with them, talked things over with them, challenged their stereotyped ways, demanded demonstration of their dogmatic and prejudiced beliefs, and quite succeeded in convincing the last of them that I was a fool and doomed to come to grief."

"But you didn't! You didn't!"

Mrs. Mortimer smiled gratefully. "Sometimes, even now, I'm amazed that I didn't. But I came of a hard-headed stock which had been away from the soil long enough to gain a new perspective. When a thing satisfied my judgment, I did it forthwith

and downright, no matter how extravagant it seemed. Take the old orchard. Worthless! Worse than worthless! Old Calkins nearly died of heart-disease when he saw the devastation I had wreaked upon it. And look at it now. There was an old rattletrap ruin where the bungalow now stands. I put up with it, but I immediately pulled down the cow-barn, the pigsties, the chicken-houses, everything—made a clean sweep. They shook their heads and groaned when they saw such wanton waste by a widow struggling to make a living. But worse was to come. They were paralyzed when I told them the price of the beautiful O. I. C.'s—pigs, you know, Chesters—which I bought. Sixty dollars for the three, and only just weaned. Then I hustled the nondescript chickens to market, replacing them with the White Leghorns. The two scrub cows that came with the place I sold to the butcher for thirty dollars each, paying two hundred and fifty each for two blue-blooded Jersey heifers—and coined money on the exchange, while Calkins and the rest went right on with their scrubs that couldn't give enough milk to pay for their board."

Billy nodded approval. "Remember what I told you about horses," he reiterated to Saxon; and, assisted by his hostess, he gave a very creditable disquisition on horseflesh and its management from a business point of view.

Mrs. Mortimer saw them to the county road. "You are brave young things," she said at parting. "I only wish I were going with you, my pack upon my back. You're perfectly glorious, the pair of you. If ever I can do anything for you, just let me know. You're bound to succeed, and I want a hand in it myself. Let me know how that government land turns out, though I warn you I haven't much faith in its feasibility. It's sure to be too far away from markets."

She shook hands with Billy; Saxon she caught into her arms and kissed.

"Be brave," she said, with low earnestness, in Saxon's ear. "You'll win. You are starting with the right ideas. You're young yet, both of you. Don't be in a hurry. Any time you stop anywhere for a while, let me know, and I'll mail you heaps of agricultural reports and farm publications. Good-by. Heaps and heaps and heaps of luck."

The Valley of the Moon

THE STORY OF A FIGHT AGAINST ODDS FOR LOVE AND A HOME

By Jack London

Author of "Martin Eden," "Burning Daylight," "Smoke Bellew," etc.

Illustrated by Howard Chandler Christy

SYNOPSIS:—Is this the man? So Saxon questioned of herself when she had met "Big Bill" Roberts, one-time prize-fighter, on the dancing-floor at Weasel Park, whither she and Mary, ironers of fancy starch, had gone for a Sunday outing. Never had she come so near to losing her heart as Billy, blue eyed, boyish, gentlemanly, had come to winning it after a few hours' acquaintance. Planned by Mary and Bert Wanhope, the meeting had taken a happy turn, for both Saxon and Billy had seized the future in the present and grasped at its chance for happiness. Billy was a teamster and knew what hard work meant, so they went home early, Saxon glorying in his refusal to "make a time of it," as Bert suggested. He kissed her good-night at the gate with Wednesday night's dance as their next meeting. Friday's dance was next arranged for, but on Thursday night Charley Long, a rebuffed suitor, met her outside the laundry and warned her that if she did not go with him "somebody'll get hurt." But Saxon bore the notion that Billy, at least, could take care of himself.

Billy did, and Saxon experienced the delightful sensation of knowing that this big boy cared enough for her to risk a fight—which wasn't needed. Finally there came Billy's frank proposal, and Saxon, countering only with the objection that she was the elder—an objection overruled by Billy's statement that "Love's what counts"—accepted him.

Saxon married Billy at the promised time, in spite of all family objections. They and Mary and Bert ate the wedding supper at Barnum's, and then Saxon and Billy went to their Pine Street cottage. Later Mary and Bert married and became their neighbors. The winter passed without an event to mar their happiness, though Billy's wages were cut. But in the spring came a strike in the railroad shops, and it threw a pall over the whole neighborhood. To Saxon, approaching mother-hood, the passing days bore a menace.

The strike proved to be very serious. The neighborhood was full of rioting. In one encounter Bert was killed, and several of Billy's friends are at length responsible for the death of scabs. In the midst of the excitement, Saxon's baby—a girl—is born and dies. Billy was compelled to go on strike, and this brought much hardship to the Pine Street cottage; funds and provisions gave out. Harmon, a railroad fireman, was taken as a lodger. Saxon stood stoutly by her husband and refused to let him take any job that would "throw the other fellows down." Billy began to drink. One night he came home terribly bruised, after a boxing bout with the "Chicago Terror." But he brought twenty dollars, the loser's end. ·

Much discouraged, Billy continues his intemperate habits. One day, in a fit of absolutely unwarranted jealousy, he attacks Harmon, the lodger, for which he receives a thirty-day jail sentence. During that time Saxon struggles along as best she can, and in her loneliness has much time for reflection. She realizes that out of their present condition and mode of life no happiness can come. She is shocked one day to discover that Mary, her old friend and Bert's widow, has been driven upon the streets. She must get away from it all. Billy's release is celebrated by a theater treat, for which his precious amateur athletic medals are pawned. At the moving pictures they see a film depicting farm life. This determines them. They will seek a home in the country.

As soon as possible they start, equipped for camping, to seek government land in the southern part of the state. From chance acquaintances they learn much of the farming practises of the foreign element. In three days they are at San José, where they come to the small farm of a widow, Mrs. Mortimer, who receives them kindly, and they become much interested in what she has accomplished with slight outlay.

BILLY sat motionless on the edge of the bed in their little room in San José that night, a musing expression in his eyes.

"Well," he remarked at last, with a long-drawn breath, "all I've got to say is there's some pretty nice people in this world after all. Take Mrs. Mortimer. Now she's the real goods—regular old American."

"A fine educated lady," Saxon agreed, "and not a bit ashamed to work at farming herself. And she made it go, too."

"On twenty acres—no, ten; and paid for 'em an' all improvements, an' supported herself, four hired men, a Swede woman an' daughter, an' her own nephew. It gets me. Ten acres! Why, my father never talked less 'n one hundred an' sixty acres. Even your brother Tom still talks in quarter sections. An' she was only a woman, too. We was lucky in meetin' her."

"Wasn't it an adventure!" Saxon cried. "That's what comes of traveling. You never know what's going to happen next. It jumped right out at us, just when we were tired and wondering how much farther to San José. We weren't expecting it at all. And she didn't treat us as if we were tramping. And that house—so clean and beautiful. You could eat off the floor. I never dreamed of anything so sweet and lovely as the inside of that house."

The next morning they were early afoot, seeking through the suburbs of San José the road to San Juan and Monterey. Saxon's limp had increased. Beginning with a burst blister, her heel was skinning rapidly. Billy remembered his father's talks about care of the feet, and stopped at a butcher shop to buy five cents' worth of mutton tallow.

"That's the stuff," he told Saxon. "We'll put some on as soon as we're clear of town. An' we might as well go easy for a couple of days. Now if I could get a little work so as you could rest up several days, it'd be just the thing."

Almost on the outskirts of town, he left Saxon on the county road and went up a long driveway to what appeared a large farm. He came back beaming.

"It's all hunky-dory," he called, as he approached. "We'll just go down to that clump of trees by the creek an' pitch camp. I start work in the mornin', two dollars a day an' board myself. It'd ben a dollar an' a half if he furnished the board. I told 'm I liked the other way best, an' that I had my camp with me."

"How did you get the job?" Saxon asked, as they cast about, determining their camp site.

"Wait till we get fixed, an' I'll tell you all about it. It was a dream, a cinch."

Not until the bed was spread, the fire built, and a pot of beans boiling, did Billy throw down the last armful of wood and begin.

"In the first place, Benson's no old-fashioned geezer. You wouldn't think he was a farmer to look at 'm. He's up to date, sharp as tacks, talks an' acts like a business man. I could see that, just by lookin' at his place, before I seen *him*. He took about fifteen seconds to size me up.

"'Can you plow?' says he.

"'Sure thing,' I told 'm.

"'Know horses?'

"'I was hatched in a box stall,' says I.

"An' just then—you remember that four-horse load of machinery that come in after me?—just then it drove up.

"'How about four horses?' he asks, casual-like.

"'Right to home. I can drive 'm to a plow, a sewin' machine, or a merry-go-round.'

"'Jump up an' take them lines, then,' he says, quick an' sharp, not wastin' seconds. 'See that shed. Go round the barn to the right an' back for unloadin'.'"

"An' right here I wanta tell you it was some nifty drivin' he was askin'. I could see by the tracks the wagons 'd all ben goin' around the barn to the left. What he was askin' was too close work for comfort—a double turn, like an S, between a corner of a paddock an' around the corner of the barn to the last swing. An' to eat into the little room there was, there was piles of manure

just thrown outa the barn an' not hauled away yet. But I wasn't lettin' on nothin'. The driver gave me the lines, an' I could see he was grinnin' sure I'd make a mess of it. I bet he couldn't 'a' done it himself. I never let on, an' away we went, me not even knowin' the horses—but, say, if you'd seen me throw them leaders clean to the top of the manure till the nigh horse was scrapin' the side of the barn to make it, an' the off hind hub was cuttin' the corner post of the paddock to miss by six inches. It was the only way. An'. them horses was sure beauts. The leaders slacked back an' darn near sat down on their singletrees when I threw the back into the wheelers an' slammed on the brake an' stopped on the very precise spot.

"'You'll do,' Benson says. 'That was good work.'

"'Aw, shucks,' I says; 'gimme something real hard.'

"He smiles an' understands.

"'You done that well,' he says. 'An' I'm particular about who handles my horses. The road ain't no place for you. You must be a good man gone wrong. Just the same you can plow with my horses, startin' in to-morrow mornin'.'

"Which shows how wise he wasn't. I hadn't showed I could plow."

When Saxon had served the beans and Billy the coffee, the girl stood still a moment and surveyed the spread meal on the blankets—the canister of sugar, the condensed-milk tin, the sliced corned beef, the lettuce salad and sliced tomatoes, the slices of fresh French bread, and the steaming plates of beans and mugs of coffee.

"What a difference from last night!" Saxon exclaimed, clapping her hands. "It's like an adventure out of a book. Think of that beautiful table and beautiful house last night, and then look at this! Why, we could have lived a thousand years on end in Oakland and never met a woman like Mrs. Mortimer or dreamed a house like hers existed. And, Billy, just to think, we've only just started!"

Billy worked for three days, and while insisting that he was doing very well, he freely admitted that there was more in plowing than he had thought. Saxon experienced quiet satisfaction when she learned he was enjoying it.

The last day Billy worked, the sky clouded over, the air grew damp, a strong wind began to blow from the southeast, and all the signs were present of the first winter rain. Billy came back in the evening with a small roll of old canvas he had borrowed, which he proceeded to arrange over their bed on a framework so as to shed rain.

He went ahead with storm preparations, elevating the bed on old boards which he lugged from a disused barn falling to decay on the opposite bank of the creek. Upon the boards he heaped dry leaves for a mattress. He concluded by reinforcing the canvas with additional guys of odd pieces of rope and baling wire.

When the first splashes of rain arrived, Saxon was delighted. But a terrific blast of wind parted several of the guys, collapsed the framework, and for a moment buried them under the canvas. The next moment, canvas, framework, and trailing guys were whisked away into the darkness, and Saxon and Billy were deluged with rain.

"Only one thing to do," he yelled in her ear. "Gather up the things an' get into that old barn."

They accomplished this in the drenching darkness, making two trips across the stepping-stones of the shallow creek and soaking themselves to the knees. The old barn leaked like a sieve, but they managed to find a dry space on which to spread their anything but dry bedding.

They were undisturbed until past midnight, when, from the open doorway, came a flash of electric light, like a tiny searchlight, which quested about the barn and came to rest on Saxon and Billy. From the source of light a harsh voice said:

"Ah! ha! I've got you! Come out of that!"

Billy sat up, his eyes dazzled by the light. The voice behind the light was approaching and reiterating its demand that they come out of that.

"What's up?" Billy asked.

"Me," was the answer; "an' wide awake, you bet."

The voice was now beside them, scarcely a yard way, yet they could see nothing on account of the light, which was intermittent, frequently going out for an instant as the operator's thumb tired on the switch.

"Come on; get a move on," the voice went on. "Roll up your blankets an' trot along. I want you."

"Who are you?" Billy demanded.

"I'm the constable. Come on."

"Well, what do you want?"

"You, of course, the pair of you."

"What for?"

"Vagrancy. Now hustle. I ain't goin' to loaf here all night."

"Aw, chase yourself," Billy advised. "I ain't a vag. I'm a workingman."

"Maybe you are an' maybe you ain't," said the constable; "but you can tell all that to Judge Neusbaumer in the mornin'."

"Why you—you stinkin', dirty cur; you think you're goin' to pull me," Billy began. "Turn that light on yourself. I want to see what kind of an ugly mug you got. Pull me, eh? Pull *me?* For two cents I'd get up there an' beat you to a jelly, you—"

"No, no, Billy," Saxon pleaded. "Don't make trouble. It would mean jail."

"That's right," the constable approved; "listen to your woman."

"She's my wife, an' see you speak of her as such," Billy warned. "Now get out, if you know what's good for yourself."

"I've seen your kind before," the constable retorted. "An' I've got my little persuader with me. Take a squint."

The shaft of light shifted, and out of the darkness, illuminated with ghastly brilliance, they saw thrust a hand holding a revolver. This hand seemed a thing apart, self-existent, with no corporeal attachment, and it appeared and disappeared like an apparition as the thumb-pressure wavered on the switch. One moment they were staring at the hand and revolver, the next moment at impenetrable darkness, and the next moment again at the hand and revolver.

"Now I guess you'll come," the constable gloated.

"You got another guess comin'," Billy began.

But at that moment the light went out. They heard a quick movement on the officer's part and the thud of the light-stick on the ground. Both Billy and the constable fumbled for it, but Billy found it and flashed it on the other. They saw a gray-bearded man clad in streaming oilskins. He was an old man, and reminded Saxon of the sort she had often seen in Grand Army processions on Decoration Day.

"Give me that stick," he bullied.

Billy sneered a refusal.

"Then I'll put a hole through you, by criminy."

He leveled the revolver directly at Billy, whose thumb on the switch did not waver,

She felt very small beside the two young giants, and very proud, withal, that she belonged to the race that
for half an hour," Hazard said.   "You could teach me a lot.   Are you going to
the same, I could teach you a few, and there s one

gave them birth. She could only listen to them talk. "I'd like to put on the gloves with you every day
stay around here?" "No. We're goin' on down the coast, lookin' for land. Just
thing you could teach me—surf swimmin'"

and they could see the gleaming bullet-tips in the chambers of the cylinder.

"Why, you whiskery old skunk, you ain't got the grit to shoot sour apples," was Billy's answer. "I know your kind—brave as lions when it comes to pullin' miserable broken-spirited bindle-stiffs, but as leary as a yellow dog when you face a man. Pull that trigger! Why, you pusillanimous piece of dirt, you'd run with your tail between your legs if I said boo!"

Suiting action to the word, Billy let out an explosive "boo!" and Saxon giggled involuntarily at the startle it caused in the constable.

"I'll give you a last chance," the latter grated through his teeth. "Turn over that light-stick an' come along peaceable, or I'll lay you out."

Saxon was frightened for Billy's sake, and yet only half frightened. She had a faith that the man dared not fire, and she felt the old familiar thrills of admiration for Billy's courage. She could not see his face, but she knew in all certitude that it was bleak and passionless in the terrifying way she had seen it when he fought the three Irishmen.

"You ain't the first man I killed," the constable threatened. "I'm an old soldier, an' I ain't squeamish over blood—"

"And you ought to be ashamed of yourself," Saxon broke in, "trying to shame and disgrace peaceable people who've done no wrong."

"You've done wrong sleepin' here," was his vindication. "This ain't your property. It's agin the law. An' folks that go agin the law go to jail, as the two of you'll go. I've sent many a tramp up for thirty days for sleepin' in this very shack. Why, it's a regular trap for 'em. I got a good glimpse of your faces an' could see you was tough characters." He turned on Billy. "I've fooled enough with you. Are you goin' to give in an' come peaceable?"

"I'm goin' to tell you a couple of things, old hoss," Billy answered. "Number one: you ain't goin' to pull us. Number two: we're goin' to sleep the night out here."

"Gimme that light-stick," the constable demanded peremptorily.

"Gwan, Whiskers. You're standin' on your foot. Beat it. Pull your freight. As for your torch, you'll find it outside in the mud."

Billy shifted the light until it illuminated the doorway, and then threw the stick as he

would pitch a baseball. They were now in total darkness, and they could hear the intruder gritting his teeth in rage.

"Now start your shootin' an' see what'll happen to you," Billy advised menacingly.

Saxon felt for Billy's hand and squeezed it proudly. The constable grumbled some threat.

"What's that?" Billy demanded sharply. "Ain't you gone yet? Now listen to me, Whiskers. I've put up with all your shannanigan I'm goin' to. Now get out or I'll throw you out. An' if you come monkeyin' around here again you'll sure get yours. Now get!"

So great was the roar of the storm that they could hear nothing. Billy rolled a cigarette. When he lighted it, they saw the barn was empty. Billy chuckled.

"There is no use moving till morning," Saxon said. "Then, just as soon as it's light, we'll catch a car into San José, rent a room, and get a hot breakfast."

"But Benson," Billy demurred.

"I'll telephone him from town. It will only cost five cents. I saw he had a wire. And you couldn't plow on account of the rain. My heel will be all right by the time it clears up, and then we can start traveling."

XXXIV

EARLY on Monday morning, three days later, Saxon and Billy took an electric car to the end of the line and started a second time for San Juan. Puddles were standing in the road, but the sun shone from a blue sky, and everywhere, on the ground, was a faint hint of budding green. At Benson's, Saxon waited while Billy went in to get his six dollars for the three-days' plowing.

"Kicked like a steer because I was quittin'," he told her, when he came back.

An hour afterward, with a good three miles to their credit, they edged to the side of the road at the sound of an automobile behind them. But the machine did not pass. Benson was alone in it, and he came to a stop alongside.

"Where are you bound?" he inquired of Billy, with a quick, measuring glance at Saxon.

"Monterey—if you're goin' that far," Billy answered, with a chuckle.

"I can give you a lift as far as Watsonville. It would take you several days on shank's mare with those loads. Climb in."

He addressed Saxon directly. "Do you want to ride in front?"

Saxon glanced to Billy.

"Go on," he approved. "It's fine in front. This is my wife, Mr. Benson—Mrs. Roberts."

"Oh, ho! so you're the one that took your husband away from me," Benson accused, good humoredly, as he tucked the robe around her.

Saxon shouldered the responsibility and became absorbed in watching him start the car.

"I'd be a mighty poor farmer if I owned no more land than you'd plowed before you came to me," Benson, with a twinkling eye, jerked over his shoulder to Billy.

"I'd never had my hands on a plow but once before," Billy confessed. "But a fellow has to learn some time."

"At two dollars a day?"

"If he can get some alfalfa artist to put up for it," Billy met him complacently.

Benson laughed heartily.

"You're a quick learner," he complimented. "I could see that you and plows weren't on speaking acquaintance. But you took hold right. There isn't one man in ten I could hire off the county road that could do as well as you were doing on the third day. But your big asset is that you know horses. It was half a joke when I told you to take the lines that morning. You're a trained horseman, and a born horseman as well."

"He's very gentle with horses," Saxon said.

"But there's more than that to it," Benson took her up. "Your husband's got the *way* with him. It's hard to explain. But that's what it is—the *way*. It's an instinct, almost. Kindness is necessary. But *grip* is more so. Your husband grips his horses. Kindness couldn't have done it."

Benson paused, and added, with a short laugh:

"Horseflesh is a hobby of mine. Don't think otherwise because I am running a stink engine. I'd rather be streaking along here behind a pair of fast steppers. But I'd lose time on them, and, worse than that, I'd be too anxious about them all the time. As for this thing, why, it has no nerves, no delicate joints or tendons; it's a case of let her rip."

The miles flew past, and Saxon was soon deep in talk with her host. In response to his direct querying, she told him her and Billy's plans, sketching the Oakland life vaguely, and dwelling at length on their future intentions.

Almost as in a dream, when they passed the nurseries at Morgan Hill, she learned they had come twenty miles, and realized that it was a longer stretch than they had planned to walk that day. And still the machine hummed on, eating up the distance as ever it flashed into view.

"I wondered what so good a man as your husband was doing on the road," Benson told her.

"Yes," she smiled. "He said you said he must be a good man gone wrong."

"But you see, I didn't know about *you*. Now I understand. And before I forget it, I want to tell you one thing." He turned to Billy. "I am just telling your wife that there's an all-the-year job waiting for you on my ranch. And there's a tight little cottage of three rooms the two of you can housekeep in. Don't forget."

Among other things, Saxon discovered that Benson had gone through the College of Agriculture at the University of California—a branch of learning she had not known existed. He gave her small hope in her search for government land.

"The only government land left," he informed her, "is what is not good enough to take up for one reason or another. If it's good land down there where you're going, then the market is inaccessible. I know no railroads tap in there."

"Wait till we strike Pajaro Valley," he said, when they had passed Gilroy and were booming on toward Sargent's. "I'll show you what can be done with the soil—and not by cow-college graduates but by uneducated foreigners that the high and mighty American has always sneered at. I'll show you. It's one of the most wonderful demonstrations in the state."

At Sargent's, he left them in the machine a few minutes while he transacted business.

"Whew! It beats hikin'," Billy said. "Just the same, when we get settled an' well-off, I guess I'll stick by horses. They'll always be good enough for me."

"A machine's only good to get somewhere in a hurry," Saxon agreed. "Of course, if we got very, very rich—"

"Say, Saxon," Billy broke in, suddenly struck with an idea. "I've learned one thing: I ain't afraid any more of not gettin' work in the country. I was at first, but I didn't tell you. Just the same, I was dead leary when we pulled out on the San Leandro pike. An' here, already, is two places open —Mrs. Mortimer's an' Benson's—an' steady jobs, too. Yep, a man can get work in the country."

"It's the wrong time of the year to see Pajaro Valley," Benson said, when he again sat beside Saxon, and Sargent's was a thing of the past. "Just the same, it's worth seeing any time. Think of it—twelve thousand acres of apples! Do you know what they call Pajaro Valley now? New Dalmatia. We're being squeezed out. We Yankees thought we were smart. Well, the Dalmatians came along and showed they were smarter. They were miserable immigrants—poorer than Job's turkey. First, they worked by day labor in the fruit harvest. Next, they began, in a small way, buying the apples on the trees. The more money they made the bigger became their deals. Pretty soon they were renting the orchards on long leases. And now they are beginning to buy the land. It won't be long before they own the whole valley, and the last American will be gone.

"Oh, our smart Yankees! Why, those first ragged Slavs in their first little deals with us only made something like two and three thousand per cent. profit. And now they're satisfied to make a hundred per cent. It's a calamity if their profits sink to twenty-five or fifty per cent. Lots of them, like Luke Scurich, are in it on a large scale. Several of them are worth a quarter of a million already. They *know* trees in much the same way your husband knows horses. They can tell if a tree's feeling as well to-day as it felt yesterday. And if it isn't, they know why and proceed to remedy matters for it. They can look at a tree in bloom and tell how many boxes of apples it will pack, and not only that—they'll know what the quality and grades of those apples are going to be. They're coining money hand over fist."

"What do they do with all the money?" Saxon queried.

"Buy the Americans of Pajaro Valley out, of course, as they are already doing."

"And then?" she questioned.

"Then they'll start buying the Americans out of some other valley. And the Americans will spend the money and by the second generation start rotting in the cities, as you

and your husband would have rotted if you hadn't got out."

Saxon could not repress a shudder. As Mary had rotted, she thought; as Bert and all the rest had rotted; as Tom and all the rest were rotting.

"Oh, it's a great country," Benson was continuing. "But we're not a great people. Kipling is right. We're crowded out and sitting on the stoop. And the worst of it is there's no reason we shouldn't know better. We're teaching it in all our agricultural colleges, experiment stations, and demonstration trains. But the people won't take hold, and the immigrant, who has learned in a hard school, beats them out. Why, after I graduated, and before my father died—he was of the old school and laughed at what he called my theories—I traveled for a couple of years. I wanted to see how the old countries farmed. Oh, I saw.

"We'll soon enter the valley. You bet I saw. First thing, in Japan, the terraced hillsides. Take a hill so steep you couldn't drive a horse up it. No bother to them. They terraced it—a stone wall, and good masonry, six feet high; a level terrace, six feet wide; up and up, walls and terraces, same thing all the way, straight into the air, walls upon walls, terraces upon terraces, until I've seen ten-foot walls built to make three-foot terraces, and twenty-foot walls for four or five feet of soil they could grow things on. And that soil packed up the mountainsides in baskets on their backs!

"Same thing everywhere I went, in Greece, in Ireland, in Dalmatia—I went there, too. They went around and gathered every bit of soil they could find, gleaned it, and even stole it by the shovelful or handful, and carried it up the mountains on their backs and built farms—*built* them, *made* them, on the naked rock. Why, in France, I've seen hill peasants mining their stream-beds for soil, as our fathers mined the streams of California for gold. Only our gold's gone, and the peasants' soil remains, turning over and over, doing something, growing something, all the time. Now I guess I'll hush."

"My God!" Billy muttered, in awe-stricken tones. "Our folks never done that. No wonder they lost out."

"There's the valley now," Benson said.

It was not a large valley that Saxon saw. But everywhere, across the flat lands and up the low, rolling hills, the industry of the

DRAWN BY HOWARD CHANDLER CHRISTY

Delighted with the result, she leaned over the railing, gradually increasing
her voice to its full strength as she sang

133

Dalmatians was evident. As she looked she listened to Benson.

"Do you know what the old settlers did with this beautiful soil? Planted the flats in grain and pastured cattle on the hills. And now twelve thousand acres of it are in apples. Take Matteo Lettunich—he's one of the originals. Entered through Castle Garden and became a dishwasher. When he laid eyes on this valley he knew it was his Klondike. To-day he leases seven hundred acres and owns a hundred and thirty of his own—the finest orchard in the valley, and he packs from forty to fifty thousand boxes of export apples from it every year. And he won't let a soul but a Dalmatian pick a single apple of all those apples. One day, in a banter, I asked him what he'd sell his hundred and thirty acres for. He answered seriously. He told me what it had netted him, year by year, and struck an average. He told me to calculate the principal from that at six per cent. I did. It came to over three thousand dollars an acre."

"What are all the Chinks doin' in the valley?" Billy asked. "Growin' apples, too?"

Benson shook his head.

"But that's another point where we Americans lose out. There isn't anything wasted in this valley, not a core or a paring; and it isn't the Americans who do the saving. There are fifty-seven apple-evaporating furnaces, to say nothing of the apple canneries and cider and vinegar factories. And Mr. John Chinaman owns them. They ship fifteen thousand barrels of cider and vinegar each year."

"It was our folks that made this country," Billy reflected. "Fought for it, opened it up, did everything—"

"But develop it," Benson caught him up. "We did our best to destroy it, as we destroyed the soil of New England." He waved his hand, indicating some place beyond the hills. "Salinas lies over that way. If you went through there you'd think you were in Japan. And more than one fat little fruit valley in California has been taken over by the Japanese. Their method is somewhat different from the Dalmatians'. First they drift into fruit picking at day's wages. They give better satisfaction than the American fruit-pickers, too, and the Yankee grower is glad to get them. Next, as they get stronger, they form in Japanese unions and proceed to run the American

labor out. Still the fruit-growers are satisfied. The next step is when the Japs won't pick. The American labor is gone. The fruit-grower is helpless. The crop perishes. Then in step the Jap labor bosses. They're the masters already. They contract for the crop. The fruit-growers are at their mercy, you see. Pretty soon the Japs are running the valley. The fruit-growers have become absentee landlords and are busy learning higher standards of living in the cities or making trips to Europe. Remains only one more step. The Japs buy them out."

"But if this goes on, what is left for us?" asked Saxon.

"What is happening. Those of us who haven't anything, rot in the cities. Those of us who have land, sell it and go to the cities. Some become larger capitalists; some go into the professions; the rest spend the money and start rotting when it's gone, and if it lasts their lifetime their children do the rotting for them."

Their long ride was soon over, and at parting Benson reminded Billy of the steady job that awaited him any time he gave the word.

"I guess we'll take a peep at that government land first," Billy answered.

Billy and Saxon, their packs upon their backs, trudged along a hundred yards. He was the first to break silence.

"An' I tell you another thing, Saxon. We'll never be goin' around smellin' out an' swipin' bits of soil an' carryin' it up a hill in a basket. The United States is big yet. I don't care what Benson or any of 'em says; the United States ain't played out. There's millions of acres untouched an' waitin', an' it's up to us to find 'em."

"And I'll tell you one thing," Saxon said. "We're getting an education. Tom was raised on a ranch, yet he doesn't know right now as much about farming conditions as we do. And I'll tell you another thing: the more I think of it, the more it seems we are going to be disappointed about that government land."

"Ain't no use believin' what everybody tells you," he protested.

"Oh, it isn't that. It's what I think. I leave it to you. If this land around here is worth three thousand an acre, why is it that government land, if it's any good, is waiting there, only a short way off, to be taken for the asking?"

Billy pondered this for a quarter of a mile, but could come to no conclusion.

XXXV

THEY had taken the direct county road across the hills from Monterey, instead of the Seventeen Mile Drive around by the coast, so that Carmel Bay came upon them without any foreglimmerings of its beauty. Dropping down through the pungent pines, they passed woods-embowered cottages, quaint and rustic, of artists and writers, and went on across wind-blown rolling sandhills held to place by sturdy lupins, and nodding with pale California poppies. Saxon screamed in sudden wonder of delight, then caught her breath and gazed at the amazing peacock-blue of a breaker, shot through with golden sunlight, overfalling in a mile-long sweep and thundering into white ruin of foam on a crescent beach of sand scarcely less white.

How long they stood and watched the stately procession of breakers, rising from out the deep and wind-capped sea to froth and thunder at their feet, Saxon did not know. She was recalled to herself when Billy, laughing, tried to remove the telescope basket from her shoulders.

"You kind of look as though you was goin' to stop a while," he said. "So we might as well get comfortable."

"I never dreamed it, I never dreamed it," she repeated, with passionately clasped hands.

At last she was able to take her eyes from the surf and gaze at the sea-horizon of deepest peacock-blue and piled with cloud masses, at the curve of the beach south to the jagged point of rocks, and at the rugged blue mountains seen across soft, low hills, landward, up Carmel Valley.

"Might as well sit down an' take it easy," Billy indulged her. "This is too good to want to run away from all at once."

Saxon assented, but began immediately to unlace her shoes.

"You ain't a-goin' to?" Billy asked in surprised delight, then began unlacing his own.

But before they were ready to run barefooted on the perilous fringe of cream-wet sand where land and ocean met, a new and wonderful thing attracted their attention. Down from the dark pines and across the sand-hills ran a man, naked save for narrow trunks. He was smooth and rosy-skinned, cherubic-faced, with a thatch of curly yellow hair, but his body was hugely thewed as a Hercules.

"Gee!—must be Sandow," Billy muttered low to Saxon.

But she was thinking of the engraving in her mother's scrap-book, and of the vikings on the wet sands of England.

The runner passed them a dozen feet away, crossed the wet sand, never pausing till the froth-wash was to his knees, while above him upreared a wall of overtopping water. Huge and powerful as his body had seemed, it was now white and fragile in the face of that imminent, great-handed buffet of the sea. Saxon gasped with anxiety, and she stole a look at Billy to note that he was tense with watching.

But the stranger sprang to meet the blow, and just when it seemed he must be crushed, he dived into the face of the breaker and disappeared. The mighty mass of water fell in thunder on the beach, but beyond appeared a yellow head, one arm outstretching, and a portion of a shoulder. Only a few strokes was he able to make ere he was compelled to dive through another breaker. This was the battle—to win seaward against the sweep of the shoreward-hastening sea. Each time he dived and was lost to view Saxon caught her breath and clenched her hands. Often it seemed he must fail and be thrown upon the beach, but at the end of half an hour he was beyond the outer edge of the surf and swimming strong, no longer diving, but topping the waves. Soon he was so far away that only at intervals could they find the speck of him. That, too, vanished, and Saxon and Billy looked at each other, she with amazement at the swimmer's valor, Billy with blue eyes flashing.

"Some swimmer, that boy, some swimmer," he praised. "Say, I only know tank swimmin', an' bay swimmin', but now I'm goin' to learn ocean swimmin'. If I could do that I'd be so proud you couldn't come within forty feet of me. Why, Saxon, honest to God, I'd sooner do what he done than own a thousan' farms! I never seen anything like that guy in the swimmin' line. An' I'm not goin' to leave this beach until he comes back. All by his lonely out there in a mountain sea, think of it! He's got his nerve all right, all right."

Saxon and Billy ran barefooted up and down the beach, pursuing each other with brandished snakes of seaweed and playing like children for an hour. Then they sighted the yellow head bearing shoreward. Billy was at the edge of the surf to meet him,

DRAWN BY HOWARD CHANDLER CHRISTY

Billy came back and sat beside her, lazying in the sea-cool sunshine, and together they watched the sun sink
a while. "Oh, I don't know, Billy. Perhaps that it wa

into the horizon where the ocean was deepest peacock-blue. "What was you thinkin' of?" he asked, after better, one day like this, than ten thousand years in Oakland"

emerging, not white-skinned as he had entered, but red from the pounding he had received at the hands of the sea.

"You're a wonder, and I just got to hand it to you," Billy greeted him, in outspoken admiration.

"It *was* a big surf to-day," the young man replied, with a nod of acknowledgment.

"It don't happen that you are a fighter I never heard of?" Billy queried, striving to get some inkling of the identity of the physical prodigy.

The other laughed and shook his head, and Billy could not guess that he was an ex-captain of a 'varsity eleven, and incidentally the father of a family and the author of many books. He looked Billy over with an eye trained in measuring freshmen aspirants for the gridiron.

"You're some body of a man," he appreciated. "You'd strip with the best of them. Am I right in guessing that you know your way about in the ring?"

Billy nodded. "My name's Roberts."

The swimmer scowled with a futile effort at recollection.

"Bill—Bill Roberts," Billy supplemented.

"Oh, ho! . . . Not *Big* Bill Roberts? Why, I saw you fight, before the earthquake, in the Mechanics' Pavilion. You're a two-handed fighter—I remember that—with an awful wallop, but slow. You were slow that night, but you got your man." He put out a wet hand. "My name's Hazard—Jim Hazard."

"An' if you're the football coach that was, a couple of years ago, I've read about you in the papers. Am I right?"

They shook hands heartily, and Saxon was introduced. She felt very small beside the two young giants, and very proud, withal, that she belonged to the race that gave them birth. She could only listen to them talk.

"I'd like to put on the gloves with you every day for half an hour," Hazard said. "You could teach me a lot. Are you going to stay around here?"

"No. We're goin' on down the coast, lookin' for land. Just the same, I could teach you a few, and there's one thing you could teach me—surf swimmin'."

"I'll swap lessons with you any time," Hazard offered. He turned to Saxon. "Why don't you stop in Carmel for a while? It isn't so bad."

"It's beautiful," she acknowledged, with a grateful smile, "but—" She turned and pointed to their packs on the edge of the lupins. "We're on the tramp, and looking for government land."

"If you're looking down past the Sur for it, it will keep," he laughed. "Well, I've got to run along and get some clothes on. If you come back, look me up. Anybody will tell you where I live. So long."

And as he had first arrived, he departed, crossing the sand-hills on the run.

Billy followed him with admiring eyes.

"Some boy, some boy," he murmured. "Why, Saxon, he's famous! An' he ain't a bit stuck on himself. Just man to man. Say!—I'm beginnin' to have faith in the old stock again."

They turned their backs on the beach, and in the tiny main street bought meat, vegetables, and half a dozen eggs. Billy had to drag Saxon away from the window of a fascinating shop where were iridescent pearls of abalone, set and unset.

"Abalones grow here, all along the coast," Billy assured her; "an' I'll get you all you want. Low tide's the time."

They turned south. Everywhere from among the pines peeped the quaint, pretty houses of the artist folk, and they were not prepared, where the road dipped to Carmel River, for the building that met their eyes.

"I know what it is," Saxon almost whispered. "It's an old Spanish Mission. It's the Carmel Mission, of course."

Hidden from the sea by low hillocks, forsaken by human being and human habitation, the church of sun-baked clay and straw stood hushed and breathless in the midst of the adobe ruins which once had housed its worshiping thousands. The spirit of the place descended upon Saxon and Billy, and they walked softly, speaking in whispers, almost afraid to go in through the open portal. There was neither priest nor worshiper, yet they found all the evidences of use by a congregation, which Billy judged must be small from the number of the benches. Later they climbed the earthquake-cracked belfry, noting the hand-hewn timbers; and in the gallery, discovering the pure quality of their voices, Saxon, trembling at her own temerity, softly sang the opening bars of "Jesus, Lover of My Soul." Delighted with the result, she leaned over

the railing, gradually increasing her voice to
its full strength as she sang:

> Jesus, Lover of my soul,
>   Let me to Thy bosom fly,
> While the nearer waters roll,
>   While the tempest still is nigh.
> Hide me, O my Saviour, hide,
>   Till the storm of life is past;
> Safe into the haven guide;
>   Oh, receive my soul at last.

Billy leaned against the ancient wall and
loved her with his eyes, and when she had
finished he murmured, almost in a whisper:
"That was beautiful—just beautiful.
An' you ought to 'a'seen your face when you
sang. It was as beautiful as your voice.
Ain't it funny? I never think of religion
except when I think of you."

They camped in the willow bottom,
cooked dinner, and spent the afternoon on
the point of low rocks north of the mouth of
the river. They had not intended to spend
the afternoon, but found themselves too fas-
cinated to turn away from the breakers
bursting upon the rocks and from the many
kinds of colorful sea life—starfish, crabs,
mussels, sea-anemones, and, once, in a rock-
pool, a small devil-fish that chilled their
blood when it cast the hooded net of its body
around the small crabs they tossed to it.
As the tide grew lower, they gathered a mess
of mussels—huge fellows, five and six inches
long and bearded like patriarchs. Then,
while Billy wandered in a vain search for
abalones, Saxon lay and dabbled in the
crystal-clear water of a rock pool, dipping up
handfuls of glistening jewels—ground bits of
shell and pebbles of flashing rose and blue
and green and violet. Billy came back and
sat beside her, lazying in the sea-cool sunshine, and together they watched the sun
sink into the horizon where the ocean was
deepest peacock-blue.

"What was you thinkin' of?" he asked,
after a while.

"Oh, I don't know, Billy. Perhaps that
it was better, one day like this, than ten
thousand years in Oakland."

XXXVI

SAXON and Billy were gone weeks on the
trip south, but in the end they came back to
Carmel. They had stopped with Hafler,
the poet, in the marble house which he had
built with his own hands. This queer
dwelling was all in one room, built almost
entirely of white marble. Hafler cooked, as

over a camp-fire, in the huge marble fireplace,
which he used in all ways as a kitchen.
The poet was on the verge of departing for
San Francisco and New York, but remained
a day over with them to explain the country
and run over the government land with
Billy. Hafler left the next day to catch the
train at Monterey. He gave them the freedom of the marble house, and told them to
stay the whole winter if they wanted.

They spent days in going over the government land, and in the end reluctantly decided against taking it up. The redwood
canyons and great cliffs of the Santa Lucia
Mountains fascinated Saxon; but she remembered what Hafler had told her of the
summer fogs which hid the sun sometimes
for a week or two at a time, and which lingered for months. Then, too, there was no
access to market. It was many miles to
where the nearest wagon-road began at
Post's, and from there on, past Point Sur to
Carmel, it was a weary and perilous way.
Billy, with his teamster judgment, admitted
that for heavy hauling it was anything but a
picnic.

Billy visioned the grassy slopes pastured
with his horses and cattle, and found it hard
to turn his back; but he listened with a willing ear to Saxon's arguments in favor of a
farm-home like the one they had seen in the
moving pictures in Oakland.

"But it must have redwoods on it," Saxon
hastened to stipulate. "I've fallen in love
with them. And there must be good wagon-
roads, and a railroad not more than a
thousand miles away."

Heavy winter rains held them prisoners
for two weeks in the marble house. Saxon
browsed among Hafler's books, though most
of them were depressingly beyond her, while
Billy hunted with Hafler's guns. But he
was a poor shot and a worse hunter. His
only success was with rabbits, which he
managed to kill on occasions when they
stood still. Despite the way he grumbled at
himself, Saxon could see the keen joy he was
taking. This belated arousal of the hunting
instinct seemed to make almost another
man of him. He was out early and late,
compassing prodigious climbs and tramps—
once reaching as far as the gold mines Tom
had spoken of, and being away two days.

"Talk about pluggin' away at a job in the
city, an' goin' to movin' pictures and Sunday picnics for amusement!" he would
burst out. "I can't see what was eatin' me

that I ever put up with such truck. Here's where I oughta ben all the time."

After they left Post's on the way back to Carmel, the condition of the road proved the wisdom of their rejection of the government land. They passed a rancher's wagon over-turned, a second wagon with a broken axle, and the stage a hundred yards down the mountainside where it had fallen, pas-sengers, horses, road, and all.

"I guess they just about quit tryin' to use this road in the winter," Billy said.

Settling down at Carmel was an easy matter. A poet named Mark Hall had offered them the free use of a "shack," and it turned out to be a three-roomed house comfortably furnished for housekeeping. Hall put Billy immediately to work on his potato-patch—a matter of three acres which the poet farmed erratically to the huge de-light of his crowd. He planted at all sea-sons, and it was accepted by the community that what did not rot in the ground was evenly divided between the gophers and trespassing cows. A plow was borrowed, a team of horses hired, and Billy took hold. Also he built a fence around the patch, and after that was set to staining the shingled roof of the bungalow.

From a financial standpoint, Saxon and Billy were putting aside much money. They paid no rent; their simple living was cheap, and Billy had all the work he cared to accept. The various members of the crowd seemed in a conspiracy to keep him busy. It was all odd jobs, but he preferred it so, for it enabled him to suit his time to Jim Hazard's. Each day they boxed and took a long swim through the surf. When Hazard finished his morning's writing, he would whoop through the pines to Billy, who dropped whatever work he was doing. After the swim, they would take a fresh shower at Hazard's house, rub each other down in training-camp style, and be ready for the noon meal. In the afternoon, Haz-ard returned to his desk, and Billy to his outdoor work, although, still later, they often met for a few miles' run over the hills. Training was a matter of habit to both men. Hazard, when he had finished with seven years of football, knowing the dire death that awaits the big-muscled athlete who ceases training abruptly, had been com-pelled to keep it up. Not only was it a ne-cessity, but he had grown to like it. Billy

also liked it, for he took great delight in the silk of his body.

Often, in the early morning, gun in hand, he was off with Mark Hall, who taught him to shoot and hunt. This part of the coun-try was too settled for large game, but Billy kept Saxon supplied with squirrels and quail, cottontails and jackrabbits, snipe and wild ducks. As he became expert with shotgun and rifle, he began to regret the deer and the mountain lion he had missed down below the Sur; and to the requirements of the farm he and Saxon sought, he added plenty of game.

"There must be hills and valleys, and rich land, and streams of clear water, good wagon-roads and a railroad not too far away, plenty of sunshine, and cold enough at night to need blankets, and not only pines but plenty of other kinds of trees, with open spaces to pasture Billy's horses and cattle, and deer and rabbits for him to shoot, and lots and lots of redwood trees, and——and ——well, and no fog," Saxon concluded the description of the farm she and Billy sought. Mark Hall laughed delightedly.

"And nightingales roosting in all the trees," he cried, "flowers that neither fail nor fade, bees without stings, honeydew every morning, showers of manna between-whiles, fountains of youth, and quarries of philosopher's stones—why, I know the very place. Let me show you."

She waited while he pored over road-maps of the state. Failing in them, he got out a big atlas, and though all the countries of the world were in it, he could not find what he was after.

"Never mind," he said. "Come over to-night and I'll be able to show you."

That evening he led her out on the ver-anda to the telescope, and she found herself looking through it at the full moon.

"Somewhere up there in some valley you'll find that farm," he teased.

Mrs. Hall looked inquiringly at them as they returned inside.

"I've been showing her a valley in the moon where she expects to go farming," he laughed.

"We started out prepared to go any dis-tance," Saxon said. "And if it's to the moon, I expect we can make it."

"But, my dear child, you can't ex-pect to find such a paradise on the earth," Hall continued. "For instance, you can't have redwoods without fog. They go

They called her Venus and made her assume different poses

together. The redwoods only grow in the fog belt."

Saxon debated a while.

"Well, we could put up with a little fog," she conceded, "—almost anything to have redwoods."

A little later in the evening, the subject of farming having remained uppermost, Hall swept off into a diatribe against the "gambler's paradise," which was his epithet for the United States.

"When you think of the glorious chance," he said "—a new country, bounded by the oceans, situated just right in latitude, with the richest land and vastest natural resources of any country in the world, settled by immigrants who had thrown off all the leading-strings of the Old World and were in the humor for democracy. There was only one thing to stop them from perfecting the democracy they started, and that thing was greediness.

"They started gobbling everything in sight like a lot of swine, and while they gobbled, democracy went to smash. Gobbling became gambling. It was a nation of tin-horns. Whenever a man lost his stake, all he had to do was to chase the frontier west a few miles and get another stake. They moved over the face of the land like so many locusts. They destroyed everything —the Indians, the soil, the forests, just as they destroyed the buffalo and the passenger-pigeon. Their morality in business and politics was gambler morality. Their laws were gambling laws—how to play the game. Everybody played. Therefore, hurrah for the game! Nobody objected, because nobody was unable to play.

"So they gobbled and gambled from the Atlantic to the Pacific, until they'd swined a whole continent. When they'd finished with the lands and forests and mines, they turned back, gambling for any little stakes they'd overlooked, gambling for franchises and monopolies, using politics to protect their crooked deals and brace games. And democracy went clean to smash!

"And then was the funniest time of. all. The losers couldn't get any more stakes, while the winners went on gambling among themselves. The losers could only stand around with their hands in their pockets and look on. When they got hungry, they went, hat in hand, and begged the successful gamblers for a job. The losers went to work for the winners, and they've been working for

them ever since, and democracy sidetracked up Salt Creek. You, Billy Roberts, have never had a hand in the game in your life. That's because your people were among the also-rans."

"How about yourself?" Billy asked. "I ain't seen you holdin' any hands."

"I don't have to. I don't count. I am a parasite."

"What's that?"

"A flea, a wood-tick, anything that gets something for nothing. I batten on the mangy hides of the workingmen. I don't have to gamble. I don't have to work. My father left me enough of his winnings. Oh, don't preen yourself, my boy. Your folks were just as bad as mine. But yours lost, and mine won, and so you plow in my potato-patch."

"I don't see it," Billy contended stoutly. "A man with gumption can win out to-day—"

"On government land?" Hall asked quickly.

Billy swallowed and acknowledged the stab. "Just the same he can win out," he reiterated.

"Surely—he can win a job from some other fellow? A young husky with a good head like yours can win jobs anywhere. But think of the handicaps on the fellows who lose. How many tramps have you met along the road who could get a job driving four horses for the Carmel livery stable? And some of them were as husky as you when they were young. And on top of it all you've got no shout coming. It's a mighty big come-down from gambling for a continent to gambling for a job."

"Just the same—" Billy recommenced.

"Oh, you've got it in your blood," Hall cut him off cavalierly. "And why not? Everybody in this country has been gambling for generations. It was in the air when you were born. You've breathed it all your life. You, who've never had a white chip in the game, still go on shouting for it and capping for it."

"But what are all of us losers to do?" Saxon inquired.

"Call in the police and stop the game," Hall recommended. "It's crooked."

Saxon frowned.

"Do what your forefathers didn't do," he amplified. "Go ahead and perfect democracy."

She remembered a remark of Mercedes.

"A friend of mine says that democracy is an enchantment."

"It is—in a gambling-joint. There are a million boys in our public schools right now swallowing the gump of 'canal-boy to President,' and millions of worthy citizens who sleep sound every night in the belief that they have a say in running the country."

"You talk like my brother Tom," Saxon said, failing to comprehend. "If we all get into politics and work hard for something better, maybe we'll get it after a thousand years or so. But I want it now. I can't wait; I want it now."

"But that is just what I've been telling you, my dear girl. That's what's the trouble with all the losers. They can't wait. They want it now—a stack of chips and a fling at the game. Well, they won't get it now. That's what's the matter with you, chasing a valley in the moon. That's what's the matter with Billy, aching right now for a chance to win ten cents from me at pedro and cussing wind-chewing under his breath."

"Gee!—you'd make a good soap-boxer," commented Billy.

"And I'd be a soap-boxer if I didn't have the spending of my father's ill-gotten gains. It's none of my affair. Let them rot. They'd be just as bad if they were on top. It's all a mess—blind bats, hungry swine, and filthy buzzards—"

Here Mrs. Hall interfered.

"Now, Mark, you stop that, or you'll be getting the blues."

He tossed his mop of hair and laughed with an effort.

"No, I won't," he denied. "I'm going to get ten cents from Billy at a game of pedro. He won't have a look in."

Saxon and Billy flourished in the genial, human atmosphere of Carmel. They appreciated in their own estimation. Saxon felt that she was something more than a laundry girl and the wife of a union teamster. She was no longer pent in the narrow, working-class environment of a Pine Street neighborhood. Life had grown opulent. They fared better physically, materially, and spiritually; and all this was reflected in their features, in the carriage of their bodies. She knew Billy had never been handsomer or in more splendid bodily condition. And she demurely confessed to him that Mrs.

Hall and several other of the matrons had enthusiastically admired her form one day when in for a cold dip in the Carmel River. They called her Venus, and made her assume different poses.

The men in the crowd were open in their admiration of Saxon, in an aboveboard manner. But she made no mistake. She did not lose her head. There was no chance of that, for her love for Billy beat more strongly than ever. Nor was she guilty of overappraisal. She knew him for what he was, and loved him with open eyes. He had no book-learning, no art, like the other men. His grammar was bad; she knew that, just as she knew that he would never mend it. Yet she would not have exchanged him for any of the others, not even for Mark Hall with the princely heart, whom she loved much in the same way that she loved his wife.

For that matter, she found in Billy a certain health and rightness, a certain essential integrity, which she prized more highly than all book-learning and bank-accounts.

Were Saxon driven to speech to attempt to express what he meant to her, she would have done it with the simple word "man." Always he was that to her. Always in glowing splendor, that was his connotation—MAN. Sometimes, by herself, she would all but weep with joy at recollection of his way of informing some truculent male that he was standing on his foot. "Get off your foot. You're standin' on it." It was Billy! It was magnificently Billy! And it was this Billy who loved her. She knew it. She knew it by the pulse that only a woman knows how to gage. He loved her less wildly, it was true; but more fondly, more maturely. It was the love that lasted—if only they did not go back to the city where the beautiful things of the spirit perished and the beast bared its fangs.

They planned to leave Carmel with the first days of summer. Much to Saxon's gratification, the crowd was loth to see them depart. The owner of the Carmel stable offered to put Billy in charge at ninety dollars a month. Also, he received a similar offer from the stable in Pacific Grove.

"Whither away?" an acquaintance hailed them on the station platform at Monterey.

"To a valley in the moon," Saxon answered gaily.

As she opened the front door, she was expectant of any sort of a terrible husband-wreck. But the Billy she sa
was precisely the Billy she had parted from. "There was no fight?" she cried, in such evident
disappointment that he laughed. "They was all yellin' 'Fake! Fake!' when I
left, an' wantin' their money back"

The Valley of the Moon

THE STORY OF A FIGHT AGAINST ODDS FOR LOVE AND A HOME

By Jack London

Author of "Martin Eden," "Burning Daylight," "Smoke Bellew," etc.

Illustrated by Howard Chandler Christy

SYNOPSIS:—Is this the man? So Saxon questioned of herself when she had met "Big Bill" Roberts, one-time prize-fighter, on the dancing-floor at Weasel Park, whither she and Mary, ironers of fancy starch, had gone for a Sunday outing. Never had she come so near to losing her heart as Billy, blue eyed, boyish, gentlemanly, had come to winning it after a few hours' acquaintance. Planned by Mary and Bert Wanhope, the meeting had taken a happy turn, for both Saxon and Billy had seized the future in the present and grasped at its chance for happiness. Billy was a teamster and knew what hard work meant, so they went home early, Saxon glorying in his refusal to "make a time of it," as Bert suggested. He kissed her good-night at the gate with Wednesday night's dance as their next meeting. Friday's dance was next arranged for, but on Thursday night Charley Long, a rebuffed suitor, met her outside the laundry and warned her that if she did not go with him "somebody'll get hurt." But Saxon bore the notion that Billy, at least, could take care of himself.

Billy did, and Saxon experienced the delightful sensation of knowing that this big boy cared enough for her to risk a fight—which wasn't needed. Finally there came Billy's frank proposal, and Saxon, countering only with the objection that she was the elder—an objection overruled by Billy's statement that "Love's what counts"—accepted him.

Saxon married Billy at the promised time, in spite of all family objections. They and Mary and Bert ate the wedding supper at Barnum's, and then Saxon and Billy went to their Pine Street cottage. Later Mary and Bert married and became their neighbors. The winter passed without an event to mar their happiness, though Billy's wages were cut. But in the spring came a strike in the railroad shops, and it threw a pall over the whole neighborhood. To Saxon, approaching mother-hood, the passing days bore a menace.

The strike proved to be very serious. The neighborhood was full of rioting. In one encounter Bert was killed, and several of Billy's friends are at length responsible for the death of scabs. In the midst of the excitement, Saxon's baby—a girl—is born and dies. Billy was compelled to go on strike, and this brought much hardship to the Pine Street cottage; funds and provisions gave out. Harmon, a railroad fireman, was taken as a lodger. Saxon stood stoutly by her husband and refused to let him take any job that would "throw the other fellows down." Billy began to drink. One night he came home terribly bruised, after a boxing bout with the "Chicago Terror." But he brought twenty dollars, the loser's end.

Much discouraged, Billy continues his intemperate habits. One day, in a fit of absolutely unwarranted jealousy, he attacks Harmon, the lodger, for which he receives a thirty-day jail sentence. During that time Saxon struggles along as best she can, and in her loneliness has much time for reflection. She realizes that out of their present condition and mode of life no happiness can come. She is shocked one day to discover that Mary, her old friend and Bert's widow, has been driven upon the streets. She must get away from it all. Billy's release is celebrated by a theater treat, for which his precious amateur athletic medals are pawned. At the moving pictures they see a film depicting farm life. This determines them. They will seek a home in the country.

As soon as possible they start, equipped for camping, to seek government land in the southern part of the state. From chance acquaintances they learn much of the farming practises of the foreign element. In three days they are at San José, where they come to the small farm of a widow, Mrs. Mortimer, who receives them kindly, and they become much interested in what she has accomplished with slight outlay. The trip south does not result in their finding what they want, and they return to spend the winter in the literary and artist colony at Carmel, where they make many friends. Saxon's requirements for her future home are so many that a poet tells her that what she wants can be found nowhere short of a valley in the moon. With the coming of summer, Billy and Saxon set out again, this time toward the north, on their search for the "valley of the moon."

"WE hiked into Monterey last winter, but we're ridin' out now, b'gosh!" Billy said, as the train pulled out.

They had decided against retracing their steps over the ground already traveled, and took the train to San Francisco, bound north for their blanket climate. Their intention was to cross the bay to Sausalito and wander up through the coast counties. Here, they had been told, they would find the true home of the redwood. But Billy, in the smoking-car for a cigarette, seated himself beside a man who was destined to deflect them from their course. He was a keen-faced, dark-eyed man, undoubtedly a Jew; and Billy, remem-bering Saxon's admonition always to ask questions, watched his opportunity and started a conversation. It took but a little while to learn that Gunston was a commis-sion merchant, and to realize that the con-tent of his talk was too valuable for Saxon to lose. Promptly when he saw that the other's cigar was finished, Billy invited him into the next car to meet Saxon. Billy would have been incapable of such an act prior to his sojourn in Carmel. That much, at least, he had acquired of social facility.

"He's just ben tellin' me about the potato kings, and I wanted him to tell you," Billy explained to Saxon, after the introduction. "Go on and tell her, Mr. Gunston, about that fan-tan sucker that made nineteen thousan' last year in celery an' asparagus."

145

"I was just telling your husband about the way the Chinese make things go up the San Joaquin River. It would be worth your while to go up there and look around. It's the good season now—too early for mosquitoes."

"Tell her about Chow Lam," Billy urged.

The commission merchant leaned back and laughed.

"Chow Lam, seven years ago, was a broken-down fan-tan player. He hadn't a cent, and his health was going back on him. He had worn out his back with twenty years' work in the gold mines, washing over the tailings of the early miners. And whatever he'd made he'd lost at gambling. Also, he was in debt three hundred dollars to the Six Companies—you know, they're Chinese affairs. And remember, this was only seven years ago—health breaking down, three hundred in debt, and no trade. Chow Lam blew into Stockton and got a job on the peat lands at day's wages. It was a Chinese company, down on Middle River, that farmed celery and asparagus. This was when he got onto himself and took stock of himself.

"He saved his wages for two years, and bought one share in a thirty-share company. That was only five years ago. They leased three hundred acres of peat land from a white man who preferred traveling in Europe. Out of the profits of that one share in the first year, he bought two shares in another company. And in a year more, out of the three shares, he organized a company of his own. One year of this, with bad luck, and he just broke even. That brings it up to three years ago. The following year, bumper crops, he netted four thousand. The next year it was five thousand. And last year he cleaned up nineteen thousand dollars!"

"My!" was all Saxon could say.

Her eager interest, however, incited the commission merchant to go on.

"Look at Sing Kee—the potato king of Stockton. I know him well. I've had more large deals with him and made less money than with any man I know. He was only a coolie, and he smuggled himself into the United States thirty years ago. Started at day's wages, then peddled vegetables in a couple of baskets slung on a stick, and after that opened up a store in Chinatown in San Francisco. But he had a head on him, and he was soon onto the curves of the Chinese farmers that dealt at his store. The store couldn't make money fast enough to suit him. He headed up the San Joaquin. Didn't do much for a couple of years except keep his eyes peeled. Then he jumped in and leased twelve hundred acres at seven dollars an acre—"

"Whew!" Billy said. "Eight thousan', four hundred dollars just for rent the first year. I know five hundred acres I can buy for three dollars an acre."

"Will it grow potatoes?" Gunston asked.

Billy shook his head. "Nor nothin' else, I guess."

All three laughed heartily, and the commission merchant resumed:

"That seven dollars was only for the land. Possibly you know what it costs to plow twelve hundred acres?"

Billy nodded solemnly.

"And he got a hundred and sixty sacks to the acre that year," Gunston continued. "Potatoes were selling at fifty cents. My father was at the head of our concern at the time, so I know for a fact. And Sing Kee could have sold at fifty cents and made money. But did he? Trust a Chinaman to know the market. They can skin the commission merchants at it. Sing Kee held on. When 'most everybody else had sold, potatoes began to climb. He laughed at our buyers when we offered him sixty cents, seventy cents, a dollar. Do you want to know what he finally did sell for? One dollar and sixty-five a sack. Suppose they actually cost him forty cents. A hundred and sixty times twelve hundred— let me see—twelve times naught is naught, and twelve times sixteen is a hundred and ninety-two. A hundred and ninety-two thousand sacks at a dollar and a quarter net—four into a hundred and ninety-two is forty-eight, plus, is two hundred and forty—there you are: two hundred and forty thousand dollars clear profit on that year's deal.

"But of course that was unusual," Gunston hastened to qualify. "There was a failure of potatoes in other districts, and a corner, and in some strange way Sing Kee was dead on. He never made profits like that again. But he goes ahead steadily. Last year he had four thousand acres in potatoes, a thousand in asparagus, five hundred in celery, and five hundred in beans. And he's running six hundred acres in seeds.

No matter what happens to one or two crops, he can't lose on all of them."

"Why don't Americans succeed like that?" asked Saxon.

"Because they won't, I guess. There's nothing to stop them except themselves. I'll tell you one thing, though—give me the Chinese to deal with. He's honest. His word is as good as his bond. If he says he'll do a thing, he'll do it. And anyway, the white man doesn't know how to farm. Even the up-to-date white farmer is content with one crop at a time and rotation of crops. Mr. John Chinaman goes him one better, and grows two crops at one time on the same soil. I've seen it—radishes and carrots, two crops, sown at one time."

"Which don't stand to reason," Billy objected; "they'd be only a half-crop to each."

"Another guess coming," Gunston jeered. "Carrots have to be thinned when they're so far along. So do radishes. But carrots grow slow. Radishes grow fast. The slow-going carrots serve the purpose of thinning the radishes. And when the radishes are pulled, ready for market, that thins the carrots, which come along later. You can't beat the Chink."

"Don't see why a white man can't do what a Chink can," protested Billy.

"That sounds all right," Gunston replied. "The only objection is that the white man doesn't. The Chink is busy all the time, and he keeps the ground just as busy. He has organization, system. Who ever heard of white farmers keeping books? The Chink does. No guesswork with him. He knows just where he stands, to a cent, on any crop at any moment. And he knows the market. He plays both ends. How he does it is beyond me, but he knows the market better than we commission merchants."

The conversation with Gunston lasted hours, and the more he talked of the Chinese and their farming ways the more Saxon became aware of a growing dissatisfaction. She did not question the facts. The trouble was that they were not alluring. Somehow, she could not find place for them in her valley of the moon. It was not until the genial Jew left the train that Billy gave definite statement to what was vaguely bothering her.

"Huh! We ain't Chinks. We're white folks. Does a Chink ever want to ride a horse, hell-bent for election an' havin' a

good time of it? Did you ever see a Chink go swimmin' out through the breakers at Carmel?—or boxin', wrestlin',' runnin',' an' jumpin,' for the sport of it? Did you ever see a Chink take a shotgun on his arm, tramp six miles, an' come back happy with one measly rabbit? What does a Chink do? Work his head off. But what's the good? If they's one thing I've learned solid since you an' me hit the road, Saxon, it is that work's the least part of life. God —if it was all of life I couldn't cut my throat quick enough to get away from it! Look at Rockefeller. Has to live on milk. I want porterhouse and a stomach that can bite sole-leather. An' I want you, an' plenty of time along with you, an' fun for both of us. What's the good of life if they ain't no fun?"

"Oh, Billy!" Saxon cried. "It's just what I've been trying to get straightened out in my head. It's been worrying me for ever so long. I was afraid there was something wrong with me—that I wasn't made for the country, after all. All the time I didn't envy the San Leandro Portuguese. I didn't want to be one, or a Pajaro Valley Dalmatian, or even a Mrs. Mortimer. And you didn't, either. What we want is a valley of the moon, with not too much work, and all the fun we want. And we'll just keep on looking until we find it. And if we don't find it, we'll go on having the fun just as we have ever since we left Oakland. And, Billy, we're never, never going to work our heads off, are we?"

"Not on your life," Billy growled, in fierce affirmation.

They walked into Black Diamond with their packs on their backs. It was a scattered village of shabby little cottages, with a main street that was a wallow of black mud from the last late spring rain. The sidewalks bumped up and down in uneven steps and landings. Everything seemed un-American. The names on the strange, dingy shops were unspeakably foreign. The one dingy hotel was run by a Greek.

"Huh!—this ain't the United States," Billy muttered.

At the steamboat wharf, they watched the bright-painted Greek boats arriving, discharging their loads of glorious salmon, and departing. New York Cut-off, as the slough was called, curved to the west and north and flowed into a vast body of water which was the united Sacramento and San Joaquin rivers.

Billy pointed out the mouth of the slough and across the broad reach of water to a cluster of tiny white buildings, behind which, like a glimmering mirage, rolled the low Montezuma Hills. "Those houses is Collinsville," he informed her. "The Sacramento River comes in there, and you go up it to Rio Vista an' Isleton and Walnut Grove and all those places Mr. Gunston was tellin' us about. It's all islands an' sloughs, connectin' clear across to the San Joaquin."

Now and again an overland passenger train rushed by in the distance, echoing along the background of foothills of Mt. Diablo, which bulked, twin-peaked, green-crinkled, against the sky. Then the slumbrous quiet would fall, to be broken by the far call of a foreign tongue or by a gasoline fishing-boat chugging in through the mouth of the slough.

Not a hundred feet away, anchored close in the tules, lay a beautiful white yacht. Despite its tininess, it looked broad and comfortable. Smoke was rising for'ard from its stovepipe. On its stern, in gold letters, they read "Roamer." On top of the cabin, basking in the sunshine, lay a man and woman, the latter with a pink scarf around her head. The man was reading aloud from a book while she sewed. Beside them sprawled a fox-terrier. "Gosh—they don't have to stick around cities to be happy!" Billy commented.

A Japanese came on deck from the cabin, sat down for'ard, and began picking a chicken. The feathers floated away in a long line toward the mouth of the slough. "Oh, look!" Saxon pointed in her excitement. "He's fishing! And the line is fast to his toe!"

The man had dropped the book face-downward on the cabin and reached for the line, while the woman looked up from her sewing and the terrier began to bark. In came the line, hand under hand, and at the end a big catfish. When this was removed, and the line rebaited and dropped overboard, the man took a turn around his toe and went on reading.

A Japanese came down on the landing-stage beside Saxon and Billy and hailed the yacht. He carried parcels of meat and vegetables; one coat pocket bulged with letters, the other with morning papers. In response to his hail, the Japanese on the yacht stood up with the part-plucked chicken. The man said something to him, put aside the book, got into the white skiff lying astern, and rowed to the landing. As he came alongside the stage, he pulled in his oars, caught hold, and said good-morning genially.

"Why, I know you," Saxon said impulsively, to Billy's amazement. "You are—" Here she broke off in confusion.

"Go on," the man said, smiling.

"You are Jack Hastings, I'm sure of it. I used to see your photograph in the papers all the time you were war correspondent in the Japanese-Russian War."

"Right you are," he ratified. "And what's your name?"

Saxon introduced herself and Billy, and, when she noted the writer's observant eye on their packs, she sketched the pilgrimage they were on. The farm in the valley of the moon evidently caught his fancy, and, though the Japanese and his parcels were safely in the skiff, Hastings still lingered. When Saxon spoke of Carmel, he seemed to know everybody in Hall's crowd, and when he heard they were intending to go to Rio Vista, his invitation was immediate.

"Why, we're going that way ourselves, inside an hour, as soon as slack water comes," he exclaimed. "It's just the thing. Come on on board. We'll be there by four this ꞏafternoon if there's any wir　at all. Come on. My wife's on board, and Mrs. Hall is one of her best chums. We've been away to South America; just got back, or you'd have seen us in Carmel."

It was the second time in her life that Saxon had been in a small boat, and the Roamer was the first yacht she had ever been on board. The writer's wife, whom he called Clara, welcomed them heartily, and Saxon lost no time in falling in love with her and in being fallen in love with in return. So strikingly did they resemble each other that Hastings was not many minutes in calling attention to it. He placed them side by side, studied their eyes and mouths and ears, compared their hands, their hair, their ankles, and swore that his fondest dream was shattered—namely, that when Clara had been made the mold was broken.

Hastings decided to eat dinner—he called the midday meal by its old-fashioned name—before sailing; and down below Saxon was surprised and delighted by the measure of comfort in so tiny a cabin. There was just room for Billy to stand upright. A centerboard case divided the room in half longitudinally, and to this was attached the hinged table from which they ate. Low bunks that ran the full cabin-length, upholstered in cheerful green, served as seats. A curtain, easily attached by hooks between the centerboard case and the roof, at night screened Mrs. Hastings' sleeping quarters. On the opposite side the two Japanese bunked, while for'ard, under the deck, was the galley. So small was it that there was just room beside it for the cook, who was compelled by the low deck to squat on his hams. The other Japanese, who had brought the parcels on board, waited on the table.

"They are looking for a ranch in the valley of the moon," Hastings concluded his explanation of the pilgrimage to Clara.

"Oh!—don't you know—" she cried; but was silenced by her husband.

"Hush," he said peremptorily, then turned to their guests. "Listen. There's something in that valley-of-the-moon idea, but I won't tell you what. It is a secret. Now, we've a ranch in Sonoma Valley, and if you ever come there you'll learn the secret. Oh, believe me, it's connected with your valley of the moon. Isn't it, Mate?" This was the mutual name he and Clara had for each other.

"You might find our valley the very one you are looking for," she said.

But Hastings shook his head at her to check further speech on her part. She turned to the fox-terrier and made it speak for a piece of meat.

"Her name's Peggy," she told Saxon. "We had two Irish terriers down in the South Seas, brother and sister, but they died. We called them Peggy and Possum. So she's named after the original Peggy."

Billy was impressed by the ease with which the Roamer was operated. At a word from Hastings, the two Japanese had gone on deck, while they lingered at table. Billy could hear them throwing down the halyards, casting off gaskets, and heaving the anchor short on the tiny winch. In several minutes one called down that everything was ready, and all went on deck. Hoisting mainsail and jigger was a matter of minutes. Then the cook and cabin-boy broke out anchor, and, while one hove it up,

the other hoisted the jib. Hastings, at the wheel, trimmed the sheet. The Roamer paid off, filled her sails, slightly heeling, and slid across the smooth water and out the mouth of New York Slough. The Japanese coiled the halyards and went below for their own dinner.

The tiny white houses of Collinsville, which they were nearing, disappeared behind a low island, though the Montezuma Hills, with their long, low, restful lines, slumbered on the horizon apparently as far away as ever.

As the Roamer passed the mouth of Montezuma Slough and entered the Sacramento, they came upon Collinsville close at hand. Saxon clapped her hands.

"It's like a lot of toy houses," she said, "cut out of cardboard."

They passed many arks and houseboats of fishermen moored among the tules, and the women and children, like the men in the boats, were dark skinned, black eyed, foreign. As they proceeded up the river, they began to encounter dredgers at work, biting out mouthfuls of the sandy river bottom and heaping it on top the huge levees. Great mats of willow brush, hundreds of yards in length, were laid on top the river slope of the levees and held in place by steel cables and thousands of cubes of cement. The willows soon sprouted, Hastings told them, and by the time the mats were rotted away, the sand was held in place by the roots of the trees.

"It must cost like Sam Hill," Billy observed.

"But the land is worth it," Hastings explained. "This island land is the most productive in the world. This section of California is like Holland. You wouldn't think it, but this water we're sailing on is higher than the surface of the islands."

Except for the dredgers, the fresh-piled sand, the dense willow thickets, and always Mt. Diablo to the south, nothing was to be seen. Occasionally a river steamboat passed, and blue herons flew into the trees.

"It must be very lonely," Saxon remarked.

Hastings laughed and told her she would change her mind later. Much he related to them of the river lands, and after a while he got on the subject of tenant farming. Saxon had started him by speaking of the land-hungry Anglo-Saxons.

"Land-hogs," he snapped. "That's our record in this country. As one old Reuben

DRAWN BY HOWARD CHANDLER CHRISTY

So strikingly did they resemble each other that Hastings was not many minutes in calling attentio
their hair, their ankles, and swore that his fondest dream was shattered-

150

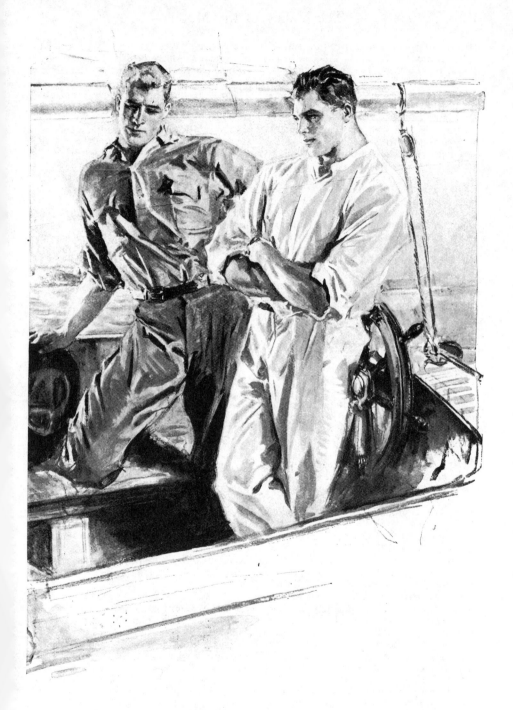

to it. He placed them side by side, studied their eyes and mouths and ears, compared their hands,
namely, that when Clara had been made the mold was broken

told a professor at an agricultural experiment station: 'They ain't no sense in tryin' to teach me farmin'. I know all about it. Ain't I worked out three farms?' It was his kind that destroyed New England. Back there, great sections are relapsing to wilderness.

"And the same thing is going on, in one way or another, the same land robbing and hogging, over the rest of the country—down in Texas, in Missouri and Kansas, out here in California. Take tenant farming. I know a ranch in my county where the land was worth a hundred and twenty-five an acre. And it gave its return at that valuation. When the old man died, the son leased it to a Portuguese and went to live in the city. In five years the Portuguese skimmed the cream and dried up the udder. The second lease, with another Portuguese for three years, gave one-quarter the former return. No third Portuguese appeared to offer to lease it. There wasn't anything left. That ranch was worth fifty thousand when the old man died. In the end the son got eleven thousand for it. Why, I've seen land that paid twelve per cent. that after the skimming of a five-years' lease paid only one and a quarter per cent."

"It's the same in our valley," Mrs. Hastings supplemented. "All the old farms are dropping into ruin. Take the Bell place, Mate." Her husband nodded emphatic endorsement. "When we used to know it, it was a perfect paradise of a farm. There were dams and lakes, beautiful meadows, lush hay-fields, red hills of grape-lands, hundreds of acres of good pasture, heavenly groves of pines and oaks, a stone winery, stone barns, grounds—oh, I couldn't describe it in hours. When Mrs. Bell died, the family scattered, and the leasing began. It's a ruin to-day."

"It's become a profession," Hastings went on. "The 'movers.' They lease, clean out, and gut a place in several years, and then move on. They're not like the foreigners, the Chinese, and Japanese, and the rest. In the main they're a lazy, vagabond, poor white sort, who do nothing else but skin the soil and move, skin the soil and move. Now, take the Portuguese and Italians in our county. They are different. They arrive in the country without a penny and work for others of their countrymen until they've learned the language and their way about. Now they're not movers. What they are after is land of their own, which they will love and care for and conserve. But in the mean time, how to get it? Saving wages is slow. There is a quicker way. They lease. In three years they can gut enough out of somebody else's land to set themselves up for life. It is sacrilege, a veritable rape of the land; but what of it? It's the way of the United States."

He turned suddenly on Billy.

"Look here, Roberts. You and your wife are looking for your bit of land. You want it bad. Now take my advice. It's cold, hard advice. Become a tenant farmer. Lease some place, where the old folks have died and the country isn't good enough for the sons and daughters. Then gut it. Wring the last dollar out of the soil, repair nothing, and in three years you'll have your own place paid for. Then turn over a new leaf, and love your soil."

"But it's wicked!" Saxon wrung out.

"It's wicked advice."

"We live in a wicked age," Hastings countered, smiling grimly. "This wholesale land skinning is the national crime of the United States to-day. Nor would I give your husband such advice if I weren't absolutely certain that the land he skins would be skinned by some Portuguese or Italian if he refrained. Help yourself. If you don't, the immigrants will."

"Oh, you don't know him," Mrs. Hastings hurried to explain. "He spends all his time on the ranch in conserving the soil. There are over a thousand acres of woods alone, and though he thins and forests like a surgeon, he won't let a tree be chopped without his permission. He's even planted a hundred thousand trees. He's always draining and ditching to stop erosion, and experimenting with pasture grasses. And every little while he buys some exhausted adjoining ranch and starts building up the soil."

"Wherefore I know what I'm talking about," Hastings broke in. "And my advice holds. I love the soil, yet to-morrow, things being as they are and if I were poor, I'd gut five hundred acres in order to buy twenty-five for myself. When you get into Sonoma Valley, look me up, and I'll put you onto the whole game, and both ends of it."

Ahead, on the left bank of the Sacramento just at the fading end of the Montezuma Hills, Rio Vista appeared. The Roamer slipped through the smooth water, past steamboat wharves, landing-stages, and warehouses. The two Japanese went for'-ard on deck. At command of Hastings, the jib ran down, and he shot the Roamer into the wind, losing way until he called, "Let go the hook!" The anchor went down, and the yacht swung to it, so close to shore that the skiff lay under overhanging willows.

"Farther up the river we tie to the bank," Mrs. Hastings said, "so that when you wake in the morning you find the branches of trees sticking down into the cabin."

She regretted the smallness of the cabin which prevented her from offering sleeping accommodations.

XXXVIII

CROSSING the Sacramento on an old-fashioned ferry, a short distance above Rio Vista, Saxon and Billy entered the river country. From the top of the levee she got her revelation. Roads ran in every direction, and she saw countless farmhouses of which she had never dreamed when sailing on the lonely river.

Three weeks they spent among the rich farm islands, which heaped up levees and pumped day and night to keep afloat. It was a monotonous land, with an unvarying richness of soil, and with only one landmark —Mt. Diablo, ever to be seen, sleeping in the midday azure, limning its crinkled mass against the sunset sky, or forming like a dream out of the silver dawn. Sometimes on foot, often by launch, they criss-crossed and threaded the river region as far as the peat lands of Middle River, down the San Joaquin to Antioch, and up Georgiana Slough to Walnut Grove on the Sacramento. And it proved a foreign land. The workers of the soil teemed by thousands, yet Saxon and Billy knew what it was to go a whole day without finding anyone who spoke English. They encountered—sometimes in whole villages—Chinese, Japanese, Italians, Portuguese, Swiss, Hindus, Koreans, Norwegians, Danes, French, Armenians, Slavs— almost every nationality save American. One American they found on the lower reaches of Georgiana who eked an illicit existence by fishing with traps. Another American, who spouted blood and destruction on all political subjects, was an itinerant bee-farmer. At Walnut Grove, bustling with life, the few Americans consisted of the storekeeper, the saloon-keeper, the butcher, the keeper of the drawbridge, and the ferry-man. Yet two thriving towns were in Walnut Grove, one Chinese, one Japanese. Most of the land was owned by Americans, who lived away from it and were continually selling it to the foreigners.

A riot, or a merrymaking—they could not tell which—was taking place in the Japanese town, as Saxon and Billy steamed out on the Apache, bound for Sacramento.

"We're settin' on the stoop," Billy railed. "Pretty soon they'll crowd us off of that."

"There won't be any stoop in the valley of the moon," Saxon cheered him.

But he was inconsolable, remarking bitterly,

"An' they ain't one of them damn foreigners that can handle four horses like me.

"But they can everlastingly farm," he added.

At Sacramento they stopped two weeks, where Billy drove team and earned the money to put them along on their travels. Also, life in Oakland and Carmel, close to the salt edge of the coast, had spoiled them for the interior. Too warm, was their verdict of Sacramento, and they followed the railroad west, through a region of swamp-land to Davisville. Here they were lured aside and to the north to pretty Woodland, where Billy drove team for a fruit-farm, and where Saxon wrung from him a reluctant consent for her to work a few days in the fruit harvest. She made an important and mystifying secret of what she intended doing with her earnings, and Billy teased her about it until the matter passed from his mind. Nor did she tell him of a money-order inclosed with a certain blue slip of paper in a letter to Bud Strothers.

They began to suffer from the heat. Billy declared they had strayed out of the blanket climate.

"There are no redwoods here," Saxon said. "We must go west toward the coast. It is there we'll find the valley of the moon."

From Woodland, they swung west and south along the county roads to the fruit paradise of Vacaville. Here Billy picked fruit, then drove team; and here Saxon received a letter and a tiny express package from Bud Strothers. When Billy came into camp from the day's work, she bade him stand still and shut his eyes. For a few seconds she fumbled and did something to the breast of his cotton work-shirt.

"Close your eyes and give me a kiss," she sang, "and then I'll show you what iss."

She kissed him, and when he looked down he saw, pinned to his shirt, the gold medals he had pawned the day they had gone to the moving-picture show and received their inspiration to return to the land.

"You darned kid!" he exclaimed, as he caught her to him. "So that's what you blew your fruit money in on? An' I never guessed! Come here to you."

And thereupon she suffered the pleasant mastery of his brawn, and was hugged and wrestled with until the coffee-pot boiled over and she darted from him to the rescue.

"I kinda always 've ben a mite proud of 'em," he confessed, as he rolled his after-supper cigarette. "They take me back to my kid days when I amateured it to beat the band. But say, d'ye know, they'd clean slipped my recollection. Oakland's a thousand years away from you an' me, an' ten thousan' miles."

"Then this will bring you back to it," Saxon said, opening Bud's letter.

Bud had taken it for granted that Billy knew the wind-up of the strike, so he devoted himself to the details as to which men had got back their jobs and which had been blacklisted. To his own amazement, he had been taken back, and was now driving Billy's horses. Still more amazing was the further information he had to impart. The old foreman of the West Oakland stables had died, and since then two other foremen had done nothing but make messes of everything. The point of all which was that the boss had spoken that day to Bud, regretting the disappearance of Billy.

"Don't make no mistake," Bud wrote; "the boss is onto all your curves. I bet he knows every scab you slugged. Just the same he says to me: 'Strothers, if you ain't at liberty to give me his address just write yourself and tell him for me to come a-running. I'll give him a hundred and twenty-five a month to take hold of the stables.'"

Saxon waited with well-concealed anxiety when the letter was finished. Billy, stretched out, leaning on one elbow, blew a meditative ring of smoke.

"Well," he uttered finally, "all you gotta do is write Bud Strothers an' tell 'm not on the boss' ugly tintype. An' while you're about it, I'll send 'm the money to get my

watch out. You work out the interest. The overcoat can stay there an' rot."

But they did not prosper in the interior heat. They lost weight. The resilience went out of their minds and bodies. As Billy expressed it, their silk was frazzled. So they shouldered their packs and headed west across the wild mountains. In the Berryessa Valley, the shimmering heat-waves made their eyes ache and their heads so that they traveled on in the early morning and late afternoon. Still west they headed, over more mountains, to beautiful Napa Valley. The next valley beyond was Sonoma, where Hastings had invited them to his ranch. And here they would have gone, had not Billy chanced upon a newspaper item which told of the writer's departure to cover some revolution that was breaking out somewhere in Mexico.

Three times in the Napa Valley, Billy refused work. Past St. Helena, Saxon hailed with joy the unmistakable redwoods they could see growing up the small canyons that penetrated the western wall of the valley. At Calistoga, at the end of the railroad they saw the six-horse stages leaving for Middletown and Lower Lake. They debated their route. That way led to Lake County and not toward the coast, so Saxon and Billy swung west through the mountains to the valley of the Russian River, coming out at Healdsburg. They lingered in the hop-fields on the rich bottoms, where Billy scorned to pick hops alongside of Indians, Japanese, and Chinese.

"I couldn't work alongside of 'em an hour before I'd be knockin' their blocks off," he explained.

So they idled their way north up the broad, fertile valley, so happy that they forgot that work was ever necessary, while the valley of the moon was a golden dream, remote, but sure some day of realization. At Cloverdale, Billy fell into luck. A combination of sickness and mischance found the stage stables short a driver. Each day the train disgorged passengers for the geysers, and Billy, as if accustomed to it all his life, took the reins of six horses and drove a full load over the mountains in stage time. The second trip he had Saxon beside him on the high box-seat. By the end of two weeks the regular driver was back. Billy declined a stable-job, took his wages, and continued north.

Saxon had adopted a fox-terrier puppy and named him Possum, after the dog Mrs. Hastings had told them about. So young was he that he quickly became footsore, and she carried him until Billy perched him on top of his pack and grumbled that Possum was chewing his back hair to a frazzle.

They passed through the painted vineyards of Asti at the end of the grape picking, and entered Ukiah, drenched to the skin by the first winter rain.

"Say," Billy said, "this summer's gone by on wheels. An' now it's up to us to find some place to winter. This Ukiah looks like a pretty good burg. We'll get a room to-night an' dry out. An' to-morrow I'll hustle around to the stables, an' if I locate anything, we can rent a shack an' have all winter to think about where we'll go next year."

XXXIX

THE winter proved much less exciting than the one spent in Carmel, and keenly as Saxon had appreciated the Carmel folk, she now appreciated them more keenly than ever. In Ukiah, she formed nothing more than superficial acquaintances. Here, people were more like those of the working class she had known in Oakland, or else they were merely wealthy and herded together in automobiles. There was no democratic artist colony that pursued fellowship disregardful of the caste of wealth.

Yet it was a more enjoyable winter than any she had spent in Oakland. Billy had failed to get regular employment; so she saw much of him, and they lived a prosperous and happy hand-to-hand existence in the tiny cottage they rented. As extra man at the biggest livery stable, Billy's spare time was so great that he drifted into horse trading. It was hazardous, and more than once he was broke, but the table never wanted for the best of steak and coffee, nor did they stint themselves for clothes.

Often Billy had Saxon out on spare saddle-horses from the stable, and his horse-deals took them on many trips into the surrounding country. Likewise, she was with him when he was driving horses to sell on commission; and in both their minds, independently, arose a new idea concerning their pilgrimage. Billy was the first to broach it. "I run into an outfit the other day that's stored in town," he said, "an' it's kept me thinkin' ever since. Ain't no use tryin' to get you to guess it, because you can't. I'll tell you—the swellest wagon-campin' outfit anybody ever heard of. First of all, the wagon's a peacherino. Strong as they make 'em. It was made to order, up on Puget Sound, an' it was tested out all the way down here. No load an' no road can strain it. The guy had consumption that had it built. A doctor an' a cook traveled with 'm till he passed in his checks here in Ukiah, two years ago. But say—if you could see it. Every kind of a contrivance—a place for everything—a regular home on wheels. Now if we could get that, an' a couple of plugs, we could travel like kings."

"Oh, Billy—it's just what I've been dreaming all winter! It would be ideal. And—well, sometimes on the road I'm sure you can't help forgetting what a nice little wife you've got—and with a wagon I could have all kinds of pretty clothes along."

Billy's blue eyes glowed a caress, cloudy and warm, as he said quietly, "I've been thinkin' about that."

"And you can carry a rifle and shotgun and fishing-poles and everything," she rushed along. "And a good, big ax, man-size, instead of that hatchet you're always complaining about. And Possum can lift up his legs and rest. And—but suppose you can't buy it? How much do they want?"

"One hundred an' fifty big bucks," he answered. "But dirt cheap at that. It's givin' it away. I tell you that rig wasn't built for a cent less than four hundred, an' I know wagon-work in the dark. Now, if I can put through that dicker with Caswell's six horses—say, I just got onto that horse-buyer to-day. If he buys 'em, who d'ye think he'll ship 'em to? To the boss, right to the West Oakland stables. I'm goin' to get you to write to him. Travelin' as we're goin' to, I can pick up bargains. An' if the boss'll talk, I can make the regular horse-buyer's commissions. He'll have to trust me with a lot of money, though, which most likely he won't, knowin' all his scabs I beat up."

"If he could trust you to run his stables, I guess he isn't afraid to let you handle his money," Saxon said.

Billy shrugged his shoulders, in modest dubiousness.

"Well, anyway, as I was sayin', if I can sell Caswell's six horses, why, we can stand off this month's bills an' buy the wagon."

Saxon visioned the picture, and shook her head slowly in a reaction of regret. "Three
hundred spot cash buys 'em," Billy went on. "An' that's bed-rock"

"But horses?" Saxon queried anxiously.

"They'll come later—if I have to take a regular job for two or three months."

Saxon saw the wagon, and was so infatuated with it that she lost a night's sleep from sheer insomnia of anticipation. Then Caswell's six horses were sold, the month's bills held over, and the wagon became theirs. One rainy morning, two weeks later, Billy had scarcely left the house, to be gone on an all-day trip into the country after horses, when he was back again.

"Come on!" he called to Saxon, from the street. "I want to show you something."

He drove down-town to a board stable, and took her through to a large, roofed enclosure in the rear. There he led to her a span of sturdy dappled chestnuts, with cream-colored manes and tails.

"Oh, the beauties! the beauties!" Saxon cried, resting her cheek against the velvet muzzle of one, while the other roguishly nozzled for a share.

"Ain't they though!" Billy reveled, leading them up and down before her admiring gaze. "Thirteen hundred an' fifty each, an' they don't look the weight, they're that slick put together. I couldn't believe it myself, till I put 'em on the scales. Say, how'd they look hooked up to that wagon of ourn?"

Saxon visioned the picture, and shook her head slowly in a reaction of regret.

"Three hundred spot cash buys 'em," Billy went on. "An' that's bed-rock. The owner wants the money so bad he's droolin' for it. Just gotta sell, an' sell quick. An' Saxon, honest to God, that pair'd fetch five hundred at auction. Both mares, full sisters, five an' six years old, registered Belgian sire, out of a heavy standard-bred mare that I know. Three hundred takes 'em, an' I got the refusal for three days."

Saxon's sadness changed to indignation.

"Oh, why did you show them to me? We haven't got three hundred, and you know it."

"Maybe you think that's all I brought you down-town for," he replied enigmatically. "Well, it ain't."

He paused, licked his lips, and shifted his weight uneasily from one leg to the other.

"Now you listen till I get all done before you say anything. Ready?"

She nodded.

"Won't open your mouth?"

This time she obediently shook her head.

"Well, it's this way," he began haltingly. "They's a youngster come up from Frisco. Young Sandow they call 'm, an' the Pride of Telegraph Hill. He's the real goods of a heavyweight, an' he was to fight Montana Red Saturday night, only Montana Red, just in a little trainin' bout, snapped his forearm yesterday. The managers has kept it quiet. Now here's the proposition: Lots of tickets sold, an' they'll be a big crowd Saturday night. At the last moment, so as not to disappoint 'em, they'll spring me to take Montana's place. I'm the dark horse. Nobody knows me—not even Young Sandow. He's come up since my time. I'll be a rube fighter. I can fight as Horse Roberts.

"Now wait a minute. The winner'll pull down three hundred big round iron dollars. Wait, I'm tellin' you! It's a lead-pipe cinch. It's like robbin' a corpse. Sandow's got all the heart in the world—regular knock-down-an'-drag-out-an'-hang-on fighter. I've followed 'm in the papers. But he ain't clever. I'm slow, all right, all right, but I'm clever, an' I got a haymaker in each arm. I got Sandow's number, an' I know it.

"Now you got the say-so in this. If you say yes, the nags is ourn. But don't look at me while you're makin' up your mind. Keep your lamps on the horses."

It was with painful indecision that she looked at the beautiful animals.

"Their names is Hazel an' Hattie," Billy put in a sly wedge. "If we get 'em we could call it the Double H outfit."

But Saxon forgot the team and could only see Billy's frightfully bruised body the night he fought the Chicago Terror. She was about to speak, when Billy, who had been hanging on her lips, broke in:

"Just hitch 'm up to our wagon in your mind an' look at the outfit. You got to go some to beat it."

"But you're not in training, Billy," she said suddenly.

"Huh!" he snorted. "I've ben in half-trainin' for the last year. My legs is like iron. They'll hold me up as long as I've got a punch left in my arms, and I always have that. Besides, I won't let 'm make a long fight. He's a man-eater, an' man-eaters is my meat. I eat 'm alive. It's the clever boys with the stamina an' endurance that I can't put away. But this Young Sandow's my meat. It's a lead-pipe cinch, I tell you. Honest to God, Saxon, it's a shame to take the money!"

"But I hate to think of you all battered up," she temporized. "If I didn't love you so, it might be different. And then, too, you might get hurt."

Billy laughed in contemptuous pride of youth and brawn.

The evening of the fight, at quarter past eight, Saxon parted from Billy. At quarter past nine, with hot water, ice, and everything ready in anticipation, she heard the gate click and Billy's step come up the porch. She had agreed to the fight much against her better judgment, and had regretted her consent every minute of the hour she had just waited; so that, as she opened the front door, she was expectant of any sort of a terrible husband-wreck. But the Billy she saw was precisely the Billy she had parted from.

"There was no fight?" she cried, in such evident disappointment that he laughed.

"They was all yellin' 'Fake! Fake!' when I left, an' wantin' their money back."

"Well, I've got you," she laughed, leading him in, though secretly she sighed farewell to Hazel and Hattie.

"I stopped by the way to get something for you that you've ben wantin' some time," Billy said casually. "Shut your eyes an' open your hand; an' when you open your eyes you'll find it grand," he chanted.

Into her hand something was laid that was very heavy and very cold, and when her eyes opened she saw it was a stack of fifteen twenty-dollar gold pieces.

"I told you it was like takin' money from a corpse," he exulted, as he emerged grinning from the whirlwind of punches, whacks, and hugs in which she had enveloped him. "They wasn't no fight at all. D'ye want to know how long it lasted? Just twenty-seven seconds—less'n half a minute. An' how many blows struck? One. An' it was me that done it. Here, I'll show you. It was just like this—a regular scream."

Billy had taken his place in the middle of the room, slightly crouching, chin tucked against the sheltering left shoulder, fists closed, elbows in so as to guard left side and abdomen, and forearms close to the body.

"It's the first round," he pictured. "Gong's sounded, an' we shook hands. Of course, seein' as it's a long fight an' we've never seen each other in action, we ain't in no rush. We're just feelin' each other out an' fiddlin' around. Seventeen seconds like that. Not a blow struck. An' then it's all off with the big Swede. It takes some time to tell it, but it happened in a jiffy, in less 'n a tenth of a second. I wasn't expectin' it myself. We're awful close together. His left glove ain't a foot from my jaw, an' my left glove ain't a foot from hisn. He feints with his right, an' I know it's a feint, an' just hunch up my left shoulder a bit an' feint with my right. That draws his guard over just about an inch, an' I see my openin'. My left ain't got a foot to travel. I don't draw it back none. I start it from where it is, corkscrewin' around his right guard an' pivotin' at the waist to put the weight of my shoulder into the punch. An' it connects! Square on the point of the chin, sideways. He drops deado. I walk back to my corner, an', honest to God, Saxon, I can't help gigglin' a little, it was that easy! The referee stands over 'm an' counts 'm out. He never quivers. The audience don't know what to make of it an' sits paralyzed. His seconds carry 'm to his corner an' set 'm on the stool. But they gotta hold 'm up. Five minutes afterward he opens his eyes—but he ain't seein' nothin. They're glassy. Five minutes more, an' he stands up. They got to help hold 'm, his legs givin' under 'm like they was sausages. An' the seconds has to help 'm through the ropes, an' they go down the aisle to his dressin'-room a-helpin' 'm. An' the crowd beginning to yell 'Fake' an' want its money back. Twenty-seven seconds—one punch—an' a spankin' pair of horses for the best wife Billy Roberts ever had in his long experience."

All of Saxon's old physical worship of her husband revived and doubled on itself many times. He was in all truth a hero, worthy to be of that wing-helmeted company leaping from the beaked boats upon the bloody English sands. The next morning he was awakened by her lips pressed on his left hand.

"Hey!—what are you doin'?" he demanded.

"Kissing Hazel and Hattie good-morning," she answered demurely. "And now I'm going to kiss you good-morning— And just where did your punch land? Show me."

Billy complied, touching the point of her chin with his knuckles. With both her hands on his arm, she shoved it back and tried to draw it forward sharply in similitude of a punch. But Billy withstrained her.

"Wait," he said. "You don't want to knock your jaw off. I'll show you. A quarter of an inch will do."

And at a distance of a quarter of an inch from her chin, he administered the slightest flick of a tap.

On the instant, Saxon's brain snapped with a white flash of light, while her whole body relaxed, numb and weak, volitionless, and her vision reeled and blurred. The next instant she was herself again, in her eyes terror and understanding.

"And it was at a foot that you struck him," she murmured, in a voice of awe.

"Yes, and with the weight of my shoulders behind it," Billy laughed. "Oh, that's nothing. Here, let me show you something else."

He searched out her solar plexus, and did no more than snap his middle finger against it. This time she experienced a single paralysis, accompanied by a stoppage of breath, but with a brain and vision that remained perfectly clear. In a moment, however, all the unwonted sensations were gone.

"Solar plexus," Billy elucidated. "Imagine what it's like when a man lifts a wallop to it all the way from his knee. That's the punch that won the championship of the world for Bob Fitzsimmons."

Saxon shuddered, then resigned herself to Billy's playful demonstration of the weak points in the human anatomy. He pressed the tip of a finger into the middle of her forearm, and she knew excruciating agony. On either side her neck, at the base, he dented gently with his thumbs, and she felt herself quickly growing unconscious.

"That's one of the death-touches of the Japs," he told her, and went on, accompanying grips and holds with a running exposition. "Here's the toe-hold that Gotch defeated Hackenschmidt with. I learned it from Farmer Burns. An' here's a half-nelson. An' here's you makin' roughhouse at a dance, an' I'm the floor-manager, an' I gotta put you out."

One hand grasped her wrist, the other hand passed around and under her forearm and grasped his own wrist. And at the first hint of pressure she felt that her arm was a pipe-stem about to break.

"That's called the 'come along.' An' here's the strong-arm. A boy can down a man with it. An' if you ever get into a scrap an' the other fellow gets your nose between his teeth—you don't want to lose your nose, do you? Well, this is what you do, quick as a flash."

Involuntarily she closed her eyes as Billy's thumb-ends pressed into them. She could feel the forerunning ache of a dull and terrible hurt.

"If he don't let go, you just press real hard, an' out pop his eyes, an' he's blind as a bat for the rest of his life. Oh, he'll let go all right, all right."

He released her and lay back laughing.

"How d'ye feel?" he asked. "Those ain't boxin' tricks, but they're all in the game in a roughhouse."

"I feel like revenge," she said, trying to apply the "come along" to his arm.

When she exerted the pressure she cried out with pain; for she had succeeded only in hurting herself. Billy grinned at her futility. She dug her thumbs into his neck in imitation of the Japanese death-touch, then gazed ruefully at the bent ends of her nails. She punched him smartly on the point of the chin and again cried out, this time to the bruise of her knuckles.

"Well, this can't hurt me," she gritted through her teeth, as she assailed his solar plexus with her doubled fists.

By this time he was in a roar of laughter. Under the sheaths of muscles that were as armor, the fatal nerve-center remained impervious.

"Go on; do it some more," he urged, when she had given up, breathing heavily. "It feels fine, like you was tickling me with a feather."

"All right, Mister Man," she threatened balefully. "You can talk about your grips and death-touches and all the rest, but that's all man's game. I know something that will beat them all, that will make a strong man as helpless as a baby. Wait a minute till I get it. There. Shut your eyes. Ready? I won't be a second."

He waited with closed eyes, and then, softly as rose petals fluttering down, he felt her lips on his mouth.

"You win," he said in solemn ecstasy, and passed his arms around her.

XL

In the morning Billy went down town to pay for Hazel and Hattie. It was due to Saxon's impatient desire to see them, that he seemed to take a remarkably long time about so simple a transaction. But she forgave him when he arrived with the two horses hitched to the camping-wagon.

"Had to borrow the harness," he said. "Pass Possum up and climb in, an' I'll show you the Double H Outfit, which is some outfit, I'm tellin' you."

Saxon's delight was unbounded and almost speechless as they drove out into the country behind the dappled chestnuts with the cream-colored tails and manes. The seat was upholstered, high-backed, and comfortable; and Billy raved about the wonders of the efficient brake. He trotted the team along the hard county road to show the standard going in them, and put them up a steep earth road almost hub-deep with mud, to prove that the Belgian sire was not wanting in their make-up.

When Saxon at last lapsed into complete silence, he studied her anxiously, with quick sidelong glances. She sighed and asked, "When do you think we'll be able to start?"

"Maybe in two weeks—or maybe in two or three months." He stopped abruptly and confusedly.

"Now, Billy, what have you got up your sleeve? I can see it in your eyes," Saxon demanded and indicted in mixed metaphors.

"Well, Saxon, you see it's like this: Sandow ain't satisfied. He's madder 'n a hatter. Never got one punch at me. Never had a chance to make a showin', an' he wants a return match. He's blattin' around town that he can lick me with one hand tied behind 'm, an' all that kind of hot air. Which ain't the point. The point is, the fight-fans is wild to see a return match. They didn't get a run for their money last time. They'll fill the house. The managers has seen me already. That was why I was so long. They's three hundred more waitin' on the tree for me to pick two weeks from last night if you'll say the word. It's just the same as I told you before. He's my meat. He still thinks I'm a rube, an' that it was a fluke punch."

Saturday night, two weeks later, Saxon ran to the door when the gate clicked. Billy looked tired. His hair was wet; his nose was swollen; one cheek was puffed; there was skin missing from his ears, and both eyes were slightly bloodshot.

"I'm darned if that boy didn't fool me," he said, as he placed the roll of gold pieces in her hand and sat down with her on his knees. "He's some boy when he gets extended. Instead of stoppin' 'm at the seventh, he kept me hustlin' till the fourteenth. Then I got 'm the way I said. It's too bad he's got a glass jaw. He's quicker 'n I thought, an' he's got a wallop that made me mighty respectful from the second round— an' the prettiest little chop-an'-come-again I ever saw. But that glass jaw! He kept it in cotton-wool till the fourteenth, an' then I connected.

"—An', say! I'm mighty glad it did last fourteen rounds. I still got all my silk. I could see that easy. I wasn't breathin' much, an' every round was fast. An' my legs was like iron. I could 'a' fought forty rounds. You see, I never said nothin', but I've ben suspicious all the time after that beatin' the Chicago Terror gave me."

"Nonsense! You would have known it long before now," Saxon cried. "Look at all your boxing and wrestling and running at Carmel."

"Nope." Billy shook his head with the conviction of utter knowledge. "That's different. It don't take it outa you. You gotta be up against the real thing, fightin' for life, round after round, with a husky you know ain't lost a thread of his silk yet— then, if you don't blow up, if your legs is steady, an' your heart ain't burstin', an' you ain't wobbly at all, an' no signs of queer street in your head—why, then you know you still got all your silk. An' I got it, I got all mine, d'ye hear me, an' I ain't goin' to risk it on no more fights. That's straight. Easy money's hardest in the end. From now on it's horse buyin' on commish, an' you an' me on the road till we find that valley of the moon."

Next morning, early, they drove out of Ukiah. Possum sat on the seat between them, his rosy mouth agape with excitement. They had originally planned to cross over to the coast from Ukiah, but it was too early in the season for the soft earth roads to be in shape after the winter rains; so they turned east, for Lake County, their route to extend north through the upper Sacra-

"He feints with his right, an' I know it's a feint, an' just hunch up my left shoulder a bit an' feint with my right. That draws his guard over just about an inch, an' I see my openin'"

mento Valley and across the mountains into Oregon.

All the land was green and flower-sprinkled, and each tiny valley, as they entered the hills, was a garden.

"Huh!" Billy remarked scornfully to the general landscape. "They say a rollin' stone gathers no moss. Just the same this looks like some outfit we've gathered. Never had so much actual property in my life at one time—an' them was the days when I wasn't rollin'. Even the furniture wasn't ourn. Only the clothes we stood up in, an' some old socks an' things,"

Saxon reached out and touched his hand, and he knew that it was a hand that loved his hand.

And Billy leaned toward her sidewise and kissed her.

The way grew hard and rocky as they began to climb, but the divide was an easy one, and they soon dropped down the canyon of the Blue Lakes among lush fields of golden poppies. In the bottom of the canyon lay a wandering sheet of water of intensest blue. Ahead, the folds of hills interlaced the distance, with a remote blue mountain rising in the center of the picture.

They asked questions of a handsome, black-eyed man with curly gray hair, who talked to them in a German accent, while a cheery-faced woman smiled down at them out of a trellised high window of the Swiss cottage perched on the bank. Billy watered the horses at a pretty hotel farther on, where the proprietor came out and talked and told them he had built it himself, according to the plans of the black-eyed man with the curly gray hair, who was a San Francisco architect.

"Goin' up, goin' up," Billy chortled, as they drove on through the winding hills past another lake of intensest blue. "D'ye notice the difference in our treatment already between ridin' an' walkin' with packs on our backs? With Hazel an' Hattie an' Saxon an' Possum an' yours truly an' this high-toned wagon, folks most likely take us for millionaires out on a lark."

Ten days later they drove into Williams, in Colusa County, and for the first time again encountered a railroad. Billy was looking for it, for the reason that at the rear of the wagon walked two magnificent work-horses which he had picked up for shipment to Oakland.

"Too hot," was Saxon's verdict, as she gazed across the shimmering level of the vast Sacramento Valley. "No redwoods. No hills. No forests. No manzanita. No madroños. Lonely and sad."

North they drove, through days of heat and dust, across the California plains, and everywhere was manifest the "new" farming—great irrigation ditches, dug and being dug, the land threaded by power lines from the mountains, and many new farmhouses on small holdings, newly fenced. The bonanza farms were being broken up. However, many of the great estates remained, five to ten thousand acres in extent, running from the Sacramento bank to the horizon, dancing in the heat waves, and studded with great valley-oaks.

"It takes rich soil to make great trees like those," a ten-acre farmer told them.

They had driven off the road a hundred feet to his tiny barn in order to water Hazel and Hattie. A sturdy young orchard covered most of his ten acres, though a goodly portion was devoted to whitewashed hen-houses and wired runways, wherein hundreds of chickens were to be seen. The farmer had just begun work on a small frame dwelling.

"I took a vacation when I bought," he explained, "and planted the trees. Then I went back to work an' stayed with it till the place was cleared. Now I'm here for keeps, an' soon as the house is finished I'll send for the wife. She's not very well, and it will do her good. We've been planning and working for years to get away from the city." He stopped in order to give a happy sigh. "And now we're free."

The water in the trough was warm from the sun.

"Hold on," the man said. "Don't let them drink that. I'll give it to them cool."

Stepping into a small shed, he turned an electric switch, and a motor the size of a fruit-box hummed into action. A five-inch stream of sparkling water splashed into the shallow main ditch of his irrigation system and flowed away across the orchard through many laterals.

"Isn't it beautiful, eh?—beautiful; beautiful!" the man chanted in an ecstasy. "It's bud and fruit. It's blood and life. Look at it. It makes a gold mine laughable, and a saloon a nightmare. I know. I—I used to be a barkeeper. In fact, I've been a barkeeper most of my life. That's how

I paid for this place. And I've hated the business all the time. I was a farm-boy, and all my life I've been wanting to get back to it. And here I am at last."

He wiped his glasses the better to behold his beloved water, then seized a hoe and strode down the main ditch to open more laterals.

"He's the funniest barkeeper I ever seen," Billy commented. "I took him for a busi-ness man of some sort. Must 'a' ben in some kind of a quiet hotel."

"Don't drive on right away," Saxon re-quested. "I want to talk with him."

He came back, polishing his glasses, his face beaming, watching the water as if fas-cinated by it. It required no more exer-tion on Saxon's part to start him than had been required on his part to start the motor.

"The pioneers settled all this in the early fifties," he said. "The Mexicans never got this far, so it was government land. Everybody got a hundred and sixty acres. And such acres! The stories they tell about how much wheat they got to the acre are almost unbelievable. Then several things happened. The sharpest and steadiest of the pioneers held what they had and added to it from the other fellows. It takes a great many quarter sections to make a bonanza farm. It wasn't long before it was 'most all bonanza farms."

"They were the successful gamblers," Saxon put in, remembering Mark Hall's words.

The man nodded appreciatively and con-tinued:

"The old folks schemed and gathered, and added the land into the big holdings, and built the great barns and mansions, and planted the house-orchards and flower-gardens. The young folks were spoiled by so much wealth and went away to the cities to spend it. And old folks and young united in one thing—in impoverishing the soil. Year after year they scratched it and took out bonanza crops. They put nothing back. Why, there's big sections they exhausted and left almost desert.

"The bonanza farmers are all gone now, thank the Lord! and here's where we small farmers come into our own. It won't be many years before the whole valley will be farmed in patches like mine. Look at what we're doing! Worked-out land that had ceased to grow wheat, and we turn the water on, treat the soil decently, and see our orchards!

"We've got the water—from the moun-tains, and from under the ground. I was reading an account the other day. All life depends on food. All food depends on water. It takes a thousand pounds of water to produce one pound of food; ten thousand pounds to produce one pound of meat. How much water do you drink in a year? About a ton. But you eat about two hundred pounds of vegetables and two hundred pounds of meat a year—which means you consume one hundred tons of water in the vegetables and one thousand tons in the meat—which means that it takes eleven hundred and one tons of water each year to keep a small woman like you going."

"Gee!" was all Billy could say.

"You see how population depends upon water," the ex-bartender went on. "Well, we've got the water, immense subterranean supplies, and in not many years this valley will be populated as thick as Belgium."

Fascinated by the five-inch stream, sluiced out of the earth and back to the earth by the droning motor, he forgot his discourse and stood and gazed, rapt and unheeding, while his visitors drove on.

"An' him a drink-slinger!" Billy mar-veled. "He can sure sling the temperance dope if anybody should ask you."

"It's lovely to think about—all that water, and all the happy people that will come here to live—"

"But it ain't the valley of the moon!" Billy laughed.

"No," she responded. "They don't have to irrigate in the valley of the moon, unless for alfalfa and such crops. What we want is the water bubbling naturally from the ground, and crossing the farm in little brooks, and on the boundary a fine, big creek—"

"With trout in it!" Billy took her up. "Gee—that valley of the moon's goin' to be some valley!" Billy meditated, flicking a fly away with his whip from Hattie's side. "Think we'll ever find it?"

Saxon nodded her head with great certi-tude.

"Just as the Jews found the Promised Land, and the Mormons Utah, and the Pioneers California. You remember the last advice we got when we left Oakland? ''Tis them that looks that finds.'"

The fish was gone. "Oh!" Saxon cried in chagrin. "Them that finds should hold," quoth Billy. "I don't care," she replied. "It was a bigger one than you ever caught, anyway." "Oh, I'm not denyin you're a peach at fishin'," he drawled. "You caught me, didn't you?"

The Valley of the Moon

THE STORY OF A FIGHT AGAINST ODDS FOR LOVE AND A HOME

By Jack London

Author of "Martin Eden," "Burning Daylight," "Smoke Bellew," etc.

Illustrated by Howard Chandler Christy

SYNOPSIS —Is this the man? So Saxon questioned of herself when she had met "Big Bill" Roberts, one-time prize-fighter, on the dancing-floor at Weasel Park, whither she and Mary, "fancy starch" ironers, had gone for a Sunday outing. Never had she come so near to losing her heart as Billy, blue eyed, boyish, gentlemanly, had come for a Sunday outing. hours' acquaintance. Planned by Mary and Bert Wanhope, the meeting had taken a happy turn, for both Saxon and Billy had seized the future in the present and grasped at its chance for happiness. Billy was a teamster and knew what hard work meant, so they went home early, Saxon glorying in his refusal to "make a time of it," as Bert suggested. He kissed her good-night at the gate with Wednesday night's dance as their next meeting. Friday's dance was next arranged for, but on Thursday night Charley Long, a rebuffed suitor, met her outside the laundry and warned her that if she did not go with him "somebody'll get hurt." But Saxon bore the notion that Billy, at least, could take care of himself.
Billy did, and Saxon experienced the delightful sensation of knowing that this big boy cared enough for her to risk a fight—which wasn't needed. Finally there came Billy's frank proposal and, Saxon, countering only with the objection that she was the elder—an objection overruled by Billy's statement that "love's what counts"—accepted him.
Saxon married Billy at the promised time, in spite of all family objections. They and Mary and Bert ate the wedding supper at Barnum's, and then Saxon and Billy went to their Pine Street cottage. Later Mary and Bert married and became their neighbors. The winter passed without an event to mar their happiness, though Billy's wages were cut. But in the spring came a strike in the railroad shops, and it threw a pall over the whole neighborhood. To Saxon, approaching mother-hood, the passing days bore a menace.
The strike proved to be very serious. The neighborhood was full of rioting. In one encounter Bert was killed, and several of Billy's friends are at length responsible for the death of scabs. In the midst of the excitement, Saxon's baby—a girl—is born and dies. Billy was compelled to go on strike, and this brought much hardship to the Pine Street cottage; funds and provisions gave out. Harmon, a railroad fireman, was taken as a lodger. Saxon stood stoutly by her husband and refused to let him take any job that would "throw the other fellows down." Billy began to drink. One night he came home terribly bruised, after a boxing bout with the "Chicago Terror." But he brought twenty dollars, the loser's end.
Much discouraged, Billy continues his intemperate habits. · One day, in a fit of absolutely unwarranted jealousy, he attacks Harmon, for which he receives a thirty-day jail sentence. During that time Saxon struggles along as best she can, and in her loneliness has much time for reflection. She realizes that out of their present condition and mode of life no happiness can come. She is shocked one day to discover that Mary, her old friend and Bert's widow, has been driven upon the streets. She must get away from it all. Billy's release is celebrated by a theater treat, for which his precious amateur athletic medals are pawned. At the moving pictures they see a film depicting farm life. This determines them. They will seek a home in the country.
As soon as possible they start, equipped for camping, to seek government land in the southern part of the state. From chance acquaintances they learn much of the farming practises of the foreign element. In three days they are at San José where they come to the small farm of a widow, Mrs. Mortimer, who receives them kindly, and they become much interested in what she has accomplished with slight outlay. The trip south does not result in their finding what they want, and they return to spend the winter in the literary and artist colony at Carmel, where they make many friends. Saxon's requirements for her future home are so many that a poet tells her that what she wants can be found nowhere short of a valley in the moon. With the coming of summer, Billy and Saxon set out again, this time toward the north, on their search for the "valley of the moon." They explore the central counties without finding any place that approaches Saxon's idea of the spot for the home. Billy earns enough money at team driving and other jobs to keep them going. They stop for the winter at Ukiah where Billy does well at horse buying and trading. He obtains a great bargain in the shape of a wagon-camping outfit, and putting on the gloves once more, comes out victor in a fight and gets money enough to buy a fine pair of mares, Hazel and Hattie. Thus equipped, spring finds them once more on the road, in high spirits and full of enthusiasm.

EVER north, through a fat and flourishing rejuvenated land, stopping at the towns of Willow, Red Bluff, and Redding, crossing the counties of Colusa, Glenn, Tehana, and Shasta, went the spruce wagon drawn by the dappled chestnuts with cream-colored manes and tails. Billy picked up only three horses for shipment, although he visited many farms; and Saxon talked with the women while he looked over the stock with the men. And Saxon grew the more convinced that the valley she sought lay not here.

At Redding, they crossed the Sacramento on a cable ferry, and made a day's scorching traverse through rolling foothills and flat table-lands. The heat grew more insupportable, and the trees and shrubs were blasted and dead. Then they came again to the Sacramento, where the great smelters of Kennett explained the destruction of the vegetation.

They climbed out of the smelting town, where eyrie houses perched insecurely on a precipitous landscape. It was a broad, well-engineered road that took them up a grade miles long and plunged down into the canyon of the Sacramento. The road, rock surfaced and easy graded, hewn out of the canyon wall, grew so narrow that Billy worried for fear of meeting opposite-bound

165

teams. Far below, the river frothed and flowed over pebbly shallows, or broke tumultuously over boulders and cascades in its race for the great valley they had left behind.

Sometimes, on the wider stretches of road, Saxon drove, and Billy walked to lighten the load. She insisted on taking her turns at walking, and when he breathed the panting mares on the steep, and Saxon stood by their heads caressing them and cheering them, Billy's joy was too deep for any turn of speech as he gazed at his beautiful horses and his glowing girl, trim and colorful in her golden-brown corduroy, the brown corduroy calves swelling sweetly under the abbreviated slim skirt. And when her answering look of happiness came to him—a sudden dimness in her straight, gray eyes—he was overmastered by the knowledge that he must say something or burst.

"Oh, you kid!" he cried.

And with radiant face she answered, "Oh, you kid!"

They camped one night in a deep dent in the canyon, where was snuggled a box-factory village, and where a toothless ancient, gazing with faded eyes at their traveling outfit, asked, "Be you showin'?"

They passed Castle Crags, mighty bastioned and glowing red against the palpitating blue sky. They caught their first glimpse of Mt. Shasta, a rose-tinted snow-peak rising, a sunset dream, between and beyond green interlacing walls of canyon—a landmark destined to be with them for many days. At unexpected turns, after mounting some steep grade, Shasta would appear again, still distant, now showing two peaks and glacial fields of shimmering white. Miles and miles and days and days they climbed, with Shasta ever developing new forms and phases in her summer snows.

"A moving picture in the sky," said Billy.

"Oh—it is all so beautiful," sighed Saxon. "But there are no moon-valleys here."

They encountered a plague of butterflies, and for days drove through untold billions of the fluttering beauties. They covered the road with uniform velvet brown. And ever the road seemed to rise under the noses of the snorting mares, filling the air with noiseless flight, drifting down the breeze in clouds of brown and yellow, soft flaked as snow, and piling in mounds against the fences, even driven to float helplessly on the irrigation ditches along the roadside. Hazel

and Hattie soon grew used to them, though Possum never ceased being made frantic.

"Huh—who ever heard of butterfly-broke horses?" Billy chaffed. "That's worth fifty bucks more on their price."

"Wait till you get across the Oregon line into the Rogue River Valley," they were told. "There's God's paradise—climate, scenery, and fruit farming; fruit ranches that yield two hundred per cent. on a valuation of five hundred dollars an acre."

"Gee!" Billy said, when he had driven on out of hearing; "that's too rich for our digestion."

And Saxon said, "I don't know about apples in the valley of the moon, but I do know that the yield is ten thousand per cent. of happiness on a valuation of one Billy, one Saxon, a Hazel, a Hattie, and a Possum."

Through Siskiyou County and across high mountains, they came to Ashland and Medford and camped beside the wild Rogue River.

"This is wonderful and glorious," pronounced Saxon, "but it is not the valley of the moon."

"Nope; it ain't the valley of the moon," agreed Billy, and he said it on the evening of the day he hooked a monster steelhead, standing to his neck in the ice-cold water of the Rogue and fighting for forty minutes with screaming reel ere he drew his finny prize to the bank, and with the scalp-yell of a Comanche jumped and clutched it by the gills.

"'Them that looks finds,'" predicted Saxon, as they drew north out of Grant's Pass, and held north across the mountains and fruitful Oregon valleys.

One day, in camp by the Umpqua River, Billy bent over to begin skinning the first deer he had ever shot. He raised his eyes to Saxon and remarked,

"If I didn't know California, I guess Oregon 'd suit me from the ground up."

In the evening, replete with deer meat, resting on his elbow, and smoking his after-supper cigarette, he said:

"Maybe they ain't no valley of the moon. An' if they ain't, what of it? We could keep on this way forever. I don't ask nothing better."

"There *is* a valley of the moon," Saxon answered soberly. "And we are going to find it. We've got to. Why, Billy, it would never do never to settle down. There would be no little Hazels and little Hatties or little—Billies—"

"Nor little Saxons," Billy interjected.

"Nor little Possums," she hurried on, nodding her head and reaching out a caressing hand to where the fox-terrier was ecstatically gnawing a deer-rib. A vicious snarl and a wicked snap that barely missed her fingers was her reward.

"Possum!" she cried in sharp reproof, again extending her hand.

"Don't," Billy warned. "He can't help it, and he's likely to get you next time."

Even more compelling was the menacing threat that Possum growled, his jaws close-guarding the bone.

"It's a good dog that sticks up for its bone," Billy championed. "I wouldn't care to own one that didn't."

"But it's my Possum," Saxon protested. "And he loves me. Besides, he must love me more than an old bone. And he must mind me. Here, you, Possum, give me that bone! Give me that bone, sir!"

Her hand went out gingerly, and the growl rose in volume and key till it culminated in a snap.

"I tell you it's instinct," Billy repeated. "He does love you, but he just can't help doin' it."

"He's got a right to defend his bones from strangers, but not from his mother," Saxon argued. "I shall make him give up that bone to me."

"Fox-terriers is awful high-strung, Saxon. You'll likely get him hysterical."

But she was obstinately set in her purpose. She picked up a short stick of firewood. "Now, sir, give me that bone!"

She threatened with the stick, and the dog's growling became ferocious. Again he snapped, then crouched back over his bone. Saxon raised the stick as if to strike him, and he suddenly abandoned the bone, rolled over on his back at her feet, four legs in the air, his ears lying meekly back, his eyes swimming and eloquent with submission and appeal.

"My God!" Billy breathed in solemn awe. "Look at it!—presenting his solar plexus to you, his vitals an' his life, all defense down, as much as sayin': 'Here I am. Stamp on me. Kick the life outa me. I love you; I am your slave, but I just can't help defendin' my bone. My instinct's stronger 'n me. Kill me, but I can't help it.'"

Saxon was melted. Tears were in her eyes as she stooped and gathered the mite of an animal in her arms. Possum was in a frenzy of agitation, whining, trembling, writhing, twisting, licking her face, all for forgiveness.

"Heart of gold with the rose in his mouth," Saxon crooned, burying her face in the soft and quivering bundle of sensibilities. "Mother is sorry. She'll never bother you again that way. There, there, little love! See? There's your bone. Take it."

She put him down, but he hesitated between her and the bone, patently looking to her for surety of permission, yet continuing to tremble in the terrible struggle between duty and desire that seemed tearing him asunder. Not until she repeated that it was all right and nodded her head consentingly, did he go to the bone.

"That Mercedes was right when she said men fought over jobs like dogs over bones," Billy enunciated slowly. "It's instinct. Why, I couldn't no more help reaching my fist to the point of a scab's jaw than could Possum from snappin' at you. They's no explainin' it. What a man has to, he has to. The fact that he does a thing shows he had to do it whether he can explain it or not. I never had no earthly reason to beat up that lodger we had, Jimmy Harmon. He was a good guy, square an' all right. But I just had to, with the strike goin' to smash, an' everything so bitter inside me that I could taste it. I never told you, but I saw 'm once after I got out—when my arms was mendin'. I went down to the round-house an' waited for 'm to come in off a run, an' I apologized to 'm. Now why did I apologize? I don't know, except for the same reason I punched 'm—I just had to."

And so Billy expounded the why of like in terms of realism, in the camp by the Umpqua River, while Possum expounded it, in similar terms of fang and appetite, on the rib of deer.

XLII

SAXON drove into the town of Roseburg. She drove at a walk. At the back of the wagon were tied two heavy young work-horses. Behind, half a dozen more marched free, and the rear was brought up by Billy, astride a ninth horse. All these he shipped from Roseburg to the West Oakland stables.

It was in the Umpqua Valley that they heard the parable of the white sparrow. The farmer who told it was elderly and flourishing. His farm was a model of

"But it's my Possum," Saxon protested. "And he loves me. Besides, he must love me more than an old

the growl rose in volume and

bone. And he must mind me. Here, you, Possum, give me that bone!" Her hand went out gingerly, and
key till it culminated in a snap

orderliness and system. Afterward, Billy
heard neighbors estimate his wealth at a
quarter of a million.

"You've heard the story of the farmer
and the white sparrow?" he asked Billy, at
dinner.

"Never heard of a white sparrow even,"
Billy answered.

"I must say they're pretty rare," the
farmer owned. "But here's the story:
Once there was a farmer who wasn't making
much of a success. Things just didn't seem
to go right, till at last, one day, he heard
about the wonderful white sparrow. It
seems that the white sparrow comes out
only just at daybreak with the first light of
dawn, and that it brings all kinds of good
luck to the farmer that is fortunate to catch
it. Next morning our farmer was up at
daybreak, and before, looking for it. And,
do you know, he sought for it continually,
for months and months, and never caught
even a glimpse of it." Their host shook his
head. "No; he never found it, but he
found so many things about the farm need-
ing attention, and which he attended to before breakfast, that before he knew it the
farm was prospering, and it wasn't so long
before the mortgage was paid off and he was
starting a bank-account."

That afternoon, as they drove along,
Billy was plunged in a deep reverie.

"Oh, I got the point all right," he said,
finally. "An' yet I ain't satisfied. Of
course they wasn't a white sparrow, but by
getting up early an' attendin' to things he'd
ben slack about before—oh, I got it all
right. An' yet, Saxon, if that's what a
farmer's life means, I don't want to find no
moon-valley. Life ain't hard work. Daylight to dark, hard at it—might just as well
be in the city. What's the difference? All
the time you've got to yourself is for sleepin'
an' when you're sleepin' you're not enjoyin'
yourself. An' what's it matter where you
sleep; you're deado. Might as well be dead
an' done with it as work your head off that
way. I'd sooner stick to the road, an' shoot
a deer an' catch a trout once in a while, an'
lie on my back in the shade, an' laugh with
you an' have fun with you, an'—an' go
swimmin'. An' I'm a willin' worker, too.
But they's all the difference in the world
between a decent amount of work an'
workin' your head off."

Saxon was in full accord. She looked
back on her years of toil, and contrasted

them with the joyous life she had lived on
the road.

"We don't want to be rich," she said.
"Let them hunt their white sparrows in the
Sacramento islands and the irrigation valleys. When we get up early in the valley of
the moon, it will be to hear the birds sing
and sing with them. And if we work hard
at times, it will be only so that we'll have
more time to play. And when you go
swimming I'm going with you. And we'll
play so hard that we'll be glad to work for
relaxation."

"I'm gettin' plumb dried out," Billy
announced, mopping the sweat from his
sunburned forehead. "What d'ye say we
head for the coast?"

West they turned, dropping down wild
mountain gorges from the height of land of
the interior valleys. So fearful was the
road, that on one stretch of seven miles they
passed ten broken-down automobiles. Billy
would not force the mares, and promptly
camped beside a brawling stream from
which he whipped two trout at a time.
Here, Saxon caught her first big trout. She
had been accustomed to landing them up to
nine and ten inches, and the screech of the
reel when the big one was hooked caused her
to cry out in startled surprise. Billy came
up the riffle to her and gave counsel. Several minutes later, cheeks flushed and eyes
dancing with excitement, Saxon dragged the
big fellow carefully from the water's edge
into the dry sand. Here it threw the hook
out and flopped tremendously until she fell
upon it and captured it in her hands.

"Sixteen inches," Billy said, as she held
it up proudly for inspection. "Hey!—
what are you goin' to do?"

"Wash off the sand, of course," was her
answer.

"Better put it in the basket," he advised,
then closed his mouth and grimly watched.

She stooped by the side of the stream and
dipped in the splendid fish. It flopped,
there was a convulsive movement on her
part, and it was gone.

"Oh!" Saxon cried in chagrin.

"Them that finds should hold," quoth
Billy.

"I don't care," she replied. "It was a
bigger one than you ever caught, anyway."

"Oh, I'm not denyin' you're a peach at
fishin'," he drawled. "You caught me,
didn't you?"

"I don't know about that," she retorted.

"Maybe it was like the man who was arrested for catching trout out of season. His defense was self-defense."

Billy pondered, but did not see.

"The trout attacked him," she explained.

Billy grinned. Fifteen minutes later he said, "You sure handed me a hot one."

The sky was overcast, and as they drove along the bank of the Coquille River the fog suddenly enveloped them.

"Whoof!" Billy exhaled joyfully. "Ain't it great! I can feel myself moppin' it up like a dry sponge. I never appreciated fog before."

Saxon held out her arms to receive it.

"I never thought I'd grow tired of the sun," she said, "but we've had more than our share the last few weeks."

"Ever since we hit the Sacramento Valley," Billy affirmed. "Too much sun ain't good. I've worked *that* out. Sunshine is like liquor. Did you ever notice how good you felt when the sun comes out after a week of cloudy weather? Well, that sunshine was just like a jolt of whisky. Had the same effect. Made you feel good all over. Now when you're swimmin', an' come out an' lay in the sun, how good you feel. That's because you're lappin' up a sun cocktail. But suppose you lay there in the sand a couple of hours. You don't feel so good. You're so slow movin' it takes you a long time to dress. You go home draggin' your legs an' feelin' rotten, with all the life sapped outa you. What's that? It's the *Katzenjammer.* You've ben soused to the ears in sunshine, like so much whisky, an' now you're payin' for it. That's why fog in the climate is best."

"Then we've been drunk for months," Saxon said. "And now we're going to sober up."

"You bet. Why, Saxon, I can do two days' work in one in this climate. Look at the mares. Blame me if they ain't perkin' up a'ready."

Vainly Saxon's eye roved the pine forest in search of her beloved redwoods. They would find them down in California, they were told in the town of Bandon.

"Then we're too far north," said Saxon. "We must go south to find our valley of the moon."

XLIII

SOUTH they held along the coast, hunting, fishing, swimming, and horse buying. Billy

shipped his purchases on the coasting steamers. Through Del Norte and Humboldt counties they went, and through Mendocino into Sonoma—counties larger than Eastern states—threading the giant woods, whipping innumerable trout-streams, and crossing countless rich valleys. Ever Saxon sought the valley of the moon. Sometimes, when all seemed fair, the lack was a railroad, sometimes madroño and manzanita trees, and, usually, there was too much fog.

"We do want a sun cocktail once in a while," she told Billy.

"Yep," was his answer. "Too much fog might make us soggy. What we're after is betwixt an' between, an' we'll have to get back from the coast a ways to find it."

This was in the fall of the year, and they turned their backs on the Pacific at old Fort Ross and entered the Russian River Valley, far below Ukiah, by way of Cazadero and Guerneville. At Santa Rosa, Billy was delayed with the shipping of several horses, so that it was not until afternoon that he drove south and east for Sonoma Valley.

"I guess we'll no more than make Sonoma Valley when it'll be time to camp," he said, measuring the sun with his eye. "This is called Bennett Valley. You cross a divide from it and come out at Glen Ellen. Now this is a mighty pretty valley if anybody should ask you. An' that's some nifty mountain over there."

Rising from rolling stubble fields, Bennett Peak towered hot in the sun, a row of bastion hills leaning against its base. But hills and mountain on that side showed bare and heated, though beautiful with the sunburnt tawniness of California.

They took a turn to the right and began crossing a series of steep foothills. As they approached the mountain there were signs of a greater abundance of water. They drove beside a running stream, and though the vineyards on the hills were summer-dry, the farmhouses in the hollows and on the levels were grouped about with splendid trees.

"Maybe it sounds funny," Saxon observed; "but I'm beginning to love that mountain already. It almost seems as if I'd seen it before, somehow; it's so all-around satisfying—oh!"

Crossing a bridge and rounding a sharp turn, they were suddenly enveloped in a mysterious coolness and gloom. All about them arose stately trunks of redwood. The forest floor was a rosy carpet of autumn fronds. Occasional shafts of sunlight, penetrating the deep shade, warmed the somberness of the grove. Alluring paths led off among the trees and into cozy nooks made by circles of red columns growing around the dust of vanished ancestors—witnessing the titanic proportions of those ancestors by the girth of the circles in which they stood.

Out of the grove they pulled to the steep divide, which was no more than a buttress of Sonoma Mountain. The way led on through rolling uplands and across small dips and canyons, all well wooded and adrip with water. In places the road was muddy from wayside springs.

"The mountain's a sponge," said Billy. "Here it is, the tail end of a dry summer, an' the ground's just leakin' everywhere."

"I know I've never been here before," Saxon communed aloud. "But it's all so familiar! So I must have dreamed it. And there's madroños—a whole grove! And manzanita! Why, I feel just as if I was coming home. Oh, Billy, if it should turn out to be our valley!"

"Plastered against the side of a mountain?" he queried, with a skeptical laugh.

"No; I don't mean that. I mean on the way to our valley. Because the way—all ways—to our valley must be beautiful. And this—I've seen it all before, dreamed it."

They passed a large and comfortable farmhouse surrounded by wandering barns and cow-sheds, went on under forest arches, and emerged beside a field with which Saxon was instantly enchanted. It flowed in a gentle concave from the road up the mountain, its farther boundary an unbroken line of timber. The field glowed like rough gold in the approaching sunset, and near the middle of it stood a solitary great redwood, with blasted top suggesting a nesting eyrie for eagles. The timber beyond clothed the mountain in solid green to what they took to be the top. But as they drove on, Saxon, looking back upon what she called *her* field, saw the real summit of Sonoma towering beyond, the mountain behind her field a mere spur upon the side of the larger mass.

Ahead and toward the right, across sheer ridges of the mountains, separated by deep green canyons and broadening lower down into rolling orchards and vineyards, they caught their first sight of Sonoma Valley and the wild mountains that rimmed its eastern side. To the left they gazed across a golden land of small hills and valleys. Beyond, to the north, they glimpsed another portion of the valley, and, still beyond, the opposing wall of the valley—a range of mountains, the highest of which reared its red and battered ancient crater against a rosy and mellowing sky. From north to southeast, the mountain rim curved in the brightness of the sun, while Saxon and Billy were already in the shadow of evening. He looked at Saxon, noted the ravished ecstasy of her face, and stopped the horses. All the eastern sky was blushing to rose, which descended upon the mountains, touching them with wine and ruby. Sonoma Valley began to fill with a purple flood, laving the mountain bases, rising, inundating, drowning them in its purple. Saxon pointed in silence, indicating that the purple flood was the sunset shadow of Sonoma Mountain. Billy nodded, then chirruped to the mares, and the descent began through a warm and colorful twilight.

On the elevated sections of the road they felt the cool, delicious breeze from the Pacific, forty miles away; while from each little dip and hollow came warm breaths of autumn earth, spicy with sunburnt grass and fallen leaves and passing flowers.

They came to the rim of a deep canyon that seemed to penetrate to the heart of Sonoma Mountain. Again, with no word spoken, merely from watching Saxon, Billy stopped the wagon. The canyon was wildly beautiful. Tall redwoods lined its entire length. On its farther rim stood three rugged knolls covered with dense woods of spruce and oak. From between the knolls, a feeder to the main canyon and likewise fringed with redwoods, emerged a smaller canyon. Billy pointed to a stubble-field that lay at the feet of the knolls.

"It's in fields like that I've seen my mares a-pasturing," he said.

They dropped down into the canyon, the road following a stream that sang under maples and alders. The sunset fires, refracted from the cloud-driftage of the autumn sky, bathed the canyon with crimson, in which ruddy-limbed madroños and wine-wooded manzanitas burned and smoldered. The air was aromatic with laurel. Wild grape-vines bridged the stream from tree to tree. Oaks of many sorts were veiled in lacy Spanish moss. Ferns and brakes grew lush beside the stream.

"I've got a hunch," said Billy.

"Let me say it first," Saxon begged.

He waited, his eyes on her face as she gazed about her in rapture.

"We've found our valley," she whispered. "Was that it?"

He nodded, but checked speech at sight of a small boy driving a cow up the road, a preposterously big shotgun in one hand, in the other as preposterously big a jack-rabbit.

"How far to Glen Ellen?" Billy asked.

"Mile an' a half," was the answer.

"What creek is this?" inquired Saxon.

"Wild Water. It empties into Sonoma Creek, half a mile down."

"Trout?"—this from Billy.

"If you know how to ketch 'em," grinned the boy.

"Deer up the mountain?"

"It ain't open season," the boy evaded.

"I guess you never shot a deer," Billy slyly baited, and was rewarded with,

"I got the horns to show."

"Deer sheds their horns," Billy teased on. "Anybody can find 'em."

"I got the meat on mine. It ain't dry yet—"

The boy broke off, gazing with shocked eyes into the pit Billy had dug for him.

"It's all right, sonny," Billy laughed, as he drove on. "I ain't the game-warden. I'm buyin' horses."

More ruddy madroños, more fairy circles of redwoods, and, still beside the singing stream, they passed a gate by the roadside. Before it stood a rural mail-box, on which was lettered "Edmund Hale." Standing under the rustic arch, leaning upon the gate, a man and woman composed a picture so arresting and beautiful that Saxon caught her breath. They were side by side, the delicate hand of the woman curled in the hand of the man, which looked as if made to confer benedictions. His face bore out this impression—a beautiful-browed countenance, with large, benevolent gray eyes under a wealth of white hair that shone like spun glass. He was fair and large; the little woman beside him was daintily wrought. She was saffron brown, as a woman of the white race can well be, with smiling eyes of bluest blue. In quaint sage-green draperies, she seemed a flower, with her small, vivid face irresistibly reminding Saxon of a springtime wake-robin.

Perhaps the picture made by Saxon and Billy was equally arresting and beautiful, as they drove down through the golden end of day. The two couples had eyes only for each other. The little woman beamed joyously. The man's face glowed into the benediction that had trembled there. To Saxon, like the field up the mountain, like the mountain itself, it seemed that she had always known this adorable pair. She knew that she loved them.

"How d'ye do," said Billy.

"You blessed children," said the man. "I wonder if you know how dear you look sitting there."

That was all. The wagon had passed by, rustling down the road which was carpeted with fallen leaves of maple, oak, and alder. Then they came to the meeting of the two creeks.

"Oh, what a place for a home," Saxon cried, pointing across Wild Water. "See, Billy, on that bench there, above the meadow."

"It's a rich bottom, Saxon, and so is the bench rich. Look at the big trees on it. An' they's sure to be springs."

"Drive over," she said.

Forsaking the main road, they crossed Wild Water on a narrow bridge and continued along an ancient, rutted road that ran beside an equally ancient worm fence of split redwood rails. They came to a gate, open and off its hinges, through which the road led out on the bench.

"This is it—I know it," Saxon said with conviction. "Drive in, Billy."

A small, whitewashed farmhouse with broken windows showed through the trees.

"Talk about your madroños—"

Billy pointed to the father of all madroños, six feet in diameter at its base, sturdy and sound, which stood before the house.

They spoke in low tones as they passed around the house under great oak trees and came to a stop before a small barn. They did not wait to unharness. Tying the horses, they started to explore. The pitch from the bench to the meadow was steep yet thickly wooded with oaks and manzanita. As they crashed through the underbrush they startled a score of quail into flight.

"How about game?" Saxon queried.

Billy grinned, and fell to examining a spring which bubbled a clear stream into the meadow. Here the ground was sunbaked and wide open in a multitude of cracks.

Disappointment leaped into Saxon's face, but Billy, crumbling a clod between his fingers, had not made up his mind.

"It's rich," he pronounced. "But—"

He broke off, stared all about, studying the configuration of the meadow, crossed it to the redwood trees beyond, then came back.

"It's no good as it is," he said. "But it's the best ever if it's handled right. All it needs is a little common sense an' a lot of drainage. This meadow's a natural basin not yet filled level. Come on; I'll show you."

They went through the redwoods and came out on Sonoma Creek. At this spot was no singing. The stream poured into a quiet pool. The willows on their side brushed the water. The opposite side was a steep bank. Billy measured the height of the bank with his eye, the depth of the water with a driftwood pole.

"Fifteen feet," he announced. "That allows all kinds of high divin' from the bank."

They followed down the pool. It emptied into a riffle, across exposed bed-rock, into another pool. As they looked, a trout flashed into the air and back, leaving a widening ripple on the quiet surface.

"This place was specially manufactured for us," Billy said. "In the morning I'll find out who owns it."

Half an hour later, feeding the horses, he called Saxon's attention to a locomotive whistle.

"You've got your railroad," he said. "That's a train pulling into Glen Ellen, an' it's only a mile from here."

Saxon was dozing off to sleep under the blankets when Billy aroused her.

"Suppose the guy that owns it won't sell?"

"There isn't the slightest doubt," Saxon answered with unruffled certainty. "This is our place. I know it."

XLIV

THEY were awakened by Possum, who was indignantly reproaching a tree-squirrel for not coming down to be killed. The squirrel chattered garrulous remarks that drove Possum into a mad attempt to climb the tree. Billy and Saxon giggled and hugged each other at the terrier's frenzy.

"If this is goin' to be our place, they'll be no shootin' of tree-squirrels," Billy said.

After a hasty breakfast, they started to explore, running the irregular boundaries of

the place and repeatedly crossing it from rail fence to creek and back again. Seven springs they found along the foot of the bench on the edge of the meadow.

"There's your water-supply," Billy said. "Drain the meadow, work the soil up, and with fertilizer and all that water you can grow crops the year round. There must be five acres of it, an' I wouldn't trade it for Mrs. Mortimer's."

They were standing in the old orchard on the bench, where they had counted twenty-seven trees, neglected but of generous girth.

"And on top the bench, back of the house, we can grow berries." Saxon paused considering a new thought. "If only Mrs. Mortimer would come up and advise us! Do you think she would, Billy?"

"Sure she would. It ain't more'n four hours' run from San José. But first we'll get our hooks into the place. Then you can write to her."

Sonoma Creek gave the long boundary to the little farm, two sides were worm-fenced, and the fourth side was the Wild Water.

"Why, we'll have that beautiful man and woman for neighbors," Saxon recollected. "Wild Water will be the dividing line between their place and ours."

"It ain't ours yet," Billy commented. "Let's go and call on 'em. They'll be able to tell us all about it."

"It's just as good as," she replied. "The big thing has been the finding. And whoever owns it doesn't care much for it. It hasn't been lived in for a long time. And— oh, Billy—are you satisfied?"

"With every bit of it," he answered frankly, "as far as it goes. But the trouble is, it don't go far enough."

The disappointment in her face spurred him to renunciation of his particular dream.

"We'll buy it—that's settled," he said. "But outside the meadow, they's so much woods that they's little pasture—not more'n enough for a couple of horses an' a cow. But I don't care. We can't have everything, an' what they is is almighty good."

"Let us call it a starter," she consoled. "Later on we can add to it—maybe the land alongside that runs up the Wild Water to the three knolls we saw yesterday—"

"Where I seen my horses pasturin'," he remembered, with a flash of eye. "Why not? So much has come true since we hit the road, maybe that'll come true, too."

Saxon drove into the town of Roseburg. At the back of the wagon were tied two heavy young work-horses. Behind, half a dozen more marched free, and the rear was brought up by Billy, astride a ninth horse. All these he shipped from Roseburg to the West Oakland stables

"We'll work for it, Billy."

They passed through the rustic gate and along a path that wound through wild woods. There was no sign of the house until they came abruptly upon it, bowered among the trees. It was eight-sided, and so justly proportioned that its two stories made no show of height. The house belonged there. It might have sprung from the soil just as the trees had. There were no formal grounds: The wild grew to the doors. The low porch of the main entrance was raised only a step from the ground. "Trilium Covert," they read, in quaint carved letters under the eave of the porch.

"Come right up-stairs, you dears," a voice called from above, in response to Saxon's knock.

Stepping back and looking up, she beheld the little lady smiling down from a sleeping-porch. Clad in a rosy-tissued and flowing house-gown, she again reminded Saxon of a flower.

"Just push the front door open and find your way," was the direction.

Saxon led, with Billy at her heels. They came into a room bright with windows, where a big log smoldered in a rough-stone fireplace. On the stone slab above stood a huge Mexican jar, filled with autumn branches and trailing fluffy smoke-vine. The walls were finished in warm, natural woods, stained but without polish. The air was aromatic with clean wood-odors. A walnut organ loomed in a shallow corner of the room. All corners were shallow in this octagonal dwelling. In another corner were many rows of books. Through the windows, across a low couch indubitably made for use, could be seen a restful picture of autumn trees and yellow grasses, threaded by well-worn paths that ran here and there over the tiny estate. A delightful little stairway wound past more windows to the upper story. Here the little lady greeted them and led them into what Saxon knew at once was her room. The two octagonal sides of the house which showed in this wide room were given wholly to windows. Under the long sill, to the floor, were shelves of books. Books lay here and there, in the disorder of use, on work-table, couch, and desk. On a sill by an open window, a jar of autumn leaves breathed the charm of the sweet brown wife, who seated herself in a tiny rattan chair, enameled a cheery red.

"A queer house," Mrs. Hale laughed, girlishly and contentedly. "But we love it. Edmund made it with his own hands—even to the plumbing, though he did have a terrible time with that before he succeeded."

"How about that hardwood floor downstairs—an' the fireplace?" Billy inquired.

"All, all," she replied proudly. "And half the furniture."

"And so," Saxon concluded, an hour later, "we've been three years searching for our valley of the moon, and we've found it."

"Valley of the moon?" Mrs. Hale queried. "Then you knew about it all the time. What kept you so long?"

"No; we didn't know. We just started on a blind search for it. Mark Hall called it a pilgrimage, and was always teasing us to carry long staffs. He said when we found the spot we'd know, because then the staffs would burst into blossom. He laughed at all the good things we wanted in our valley, and one night he took me out and showed me the moon through a telescope. He said that was the only place we could find such a wonderful valley. He meant it was moonshine, but we adopted the name and went on looking for it."

"What a coincidence!" Mrs. Hale exclaimed. "For this is the Valley of the Moon."

"I know it," Saxon said with quiet confidence. "It has everything we wanted."

"But you don't understand, my dear. This *is* the Valley of the Moon. This is Sonoma Valley. Sonoma is an Indian word, and means the Valley of the Moon."

The talk tripped along until Billy grew restless. He cleared his throat significantly and interrupted,

"We want to find out about that ranch acrost the creek—who owns it, if they'll sell, where we'll find 'em, an' such things."

Mrs. Hale stood up.

"We'll go and see Edmund," she said, leading the way.

"My!" Billy ejaculated, towering above her. "I used to think Saxon was small. But she'd make two of you."

"And you're pretty big," the little woman smiled; "but Edmund is taller than you, and broader shouldered."

They crossed a bright hall, and found the big husband lying back, reading, in a huge Mission rocker. Beside it was another tiny child's chair of red-enameled rattan. Along the length of his thigh, the head on his knee and directed toward a smoldering log in a fireplace, clung an incredibly large striped cat. Like its master, it turned its head to greet the newcomers. Again Saxon felt the loving benediction that abided in his face, his eyes, his hands—toward which she involuntarily dropped her eyes. Again she was impressed by the gentleness of them. They were hands of love. They were the hands of a type of man she had never dreamed existed. No one in that merry crowd of Carmel had prefigured him. They were artists. This was the scholar, the philosopher. In place of the passion of youth and all youth's mad revolt, was the benignity of wisdom. Those gentle hands had passed all the bitter by and plucked only the sweet of life. Dearly as she loved them, she shuddered to think what some of those Carmelites would be like when they were as old as he.

"Here are the dear children, Edmund," Mrs. Hale said. "What do you think! They want to buy the Madroño Ranch. They've been three years searching for it— I forgot to tell them we had searched ten years for Trilium Covert. Tell them all about it. Surely Mr. Naismith is still of a mind to sell."

They seated themselves in simple massive chairs, and Mrs. Hale took the tiny rattan beside the big Mission rocker, her slender hand curled like a tendril in Edmund's. And while Saxon listened to the talk, her eyes took in the grave rooms lined with books. She began to realize how a mere structure of wood and stone may express the spirit of him who conceives and makes it. Those gentle hands had made all this--the very furniture, she guessed, as her eyes roved from desk to chair, from work-table to reading-stand beside the bed in the other room, where stood a green-shaded reading-lamp and orderly piles of magazines and books.

As for the matter of Madroño Ranch, it was easy enough, Mr. Hale said. Naismith would sell. Had desired to sell for the past five years, ever since he had engaged in the enterprise of bottling mineral water at the springs lower down the valley. It was fortunate that he was the owner, for about all the rest of the surrounding land was owned by a Frenchman—an early settler. He would not part with a foot of it. He was a peasant, with all the peasant's love

of the soil, which, in him, had become an obsession, a disease. He was a land miser. With no business capacity, old and opinionated, he was land poor, and it was an open question which would arrive first, his death or bankruptcy.

Naismith owned Madroño Ranch, and had set the price for it at fifty dollars an acre. That would be a thousand dollars, for there were twenty acres. As a farming investment, using old-fashioned methods, it was not worth it. As a business investment, yes; for the virtues of the valley were on the eve of being discovered by the outside world, and no better location for a summer home could be found. As a happiness investment in joy of beauty and climate, it was worth a thousand times the price asked. And he knew Naismith would allow time on most of the amount. Edmund's suggestion was that they take a two-years' lease, with option to buy, the rent to apply to the purchase if they took it up. Naismith had done that once with a Swiss, who had paid a monthly rental of ten dollars. But the man's wife had died, and he had gone away.

Edmund soon divined Billy's renunciation, though not the nature of it, and several questions brought it forth—the old pioneer-dream of land-spaciousness, of cattle on a hundred hills, of one hundred and sixty acres of land the smallest thinkable division.

"But you don't need all that land, dear lad," Edmund said softly. "I see you understand intensive farming. Have you thought about intensive horse raising?"

Billy's jaw dropped at the smashing newness of the idea. He considered it, but could see no similarity in the two processes.

"You gotta show me!" he cried.

The elder man smiled gently.

"Let us see. In the first place, you don't need those twenty acres except for beauty. There are five acres in the meadow. You don't need more than two of them to make your living at selling vegetables. In fact, you and your wife, working from daylight to dark, cannot properly farm those two acres. Remains three acres. You have plenty of water for it from the springs. Don't be satisfied with one crop a year, like the rest of the old-fashioned farmers in this valley. Farm it like your vegetable plot, intensively, all the year, in crops that make horse-feed, irrigating, fertilizing, rotating

your crops. Those three acres will feed as
many horses as heaven knows how huge an
area of unseeded, uncared-for, wasted pasture would feed. Think it over. I'll lend
you books on the subject. I don't know
how large your crops will be, or do I know
how much a horse eats; that's your business.
But I am certain, with a hired man to take
your place helping your wife on her two
acres of vegetables, that by the time you
own all the horses your three acres will feed,
you will have all you can attend to. Then
it will be time to get more land for more
horses, for more riches, if that way happiness lies."

Billy understood. In his enthusiasm he
dashed out, "You're some farmer."

Edmund smiled and glanced toward his
wife.

"Give him your opinion of that, Annette."

Her blue eyes twinkled as she complied.
"Why, the dear, he never farms. He has
never farmed. But he *knows*." She waved
her hand about at the book-lined walls.
"He is a student of good. He studies all
good things done by good men under the
sun. His pleasure is in books and wood-
working."

"Don't forget Dulcie," Edmund gently
protested.

"Yes, and Dulcie," Annette laughed.
"Dulcie is our cow. It is a great question
whether Edmund dotes more on Dulcie, or
Dulcie dotes more on Edmund. When he
goes to San Francisco, Dulcie is miserable.
So is Edmund, until he hastens back. Oh,
Dulcie has given me no few jealous pangs.
But I have to confess he understands her as
no one else does."

"That is the one practical subject I know
by experience," Edmund confirmed. "I
am an authority on Jersey cows."

He stood up and went toward his book-
shelves; and they saw how magnificently
large a man he was. He paused, a book in
his hand, to answer a question from Saxon.
No; there were no mosquitoes, though, one
summer when the south wind blew for ten
days—an unprecedented thing—a few mosquitoes had been carried up from San Pablo
Bay. As for fog, it was the making of the
valley. And where they were situated, sheltered behind Sonoma Mountain, the fogs
were almost invariably high fogs. Sweeping in from the ocean forty miles away, they
were deflected by Sonoma Mountain and

shunted high into the air. Another thing:
Trilium Covert and Madroño Ranch were
happily situated in a narrow thermal belt,
so that in the frosty mornings of winter the
temperature was always several degrees
higher than in the rest of the valley.

Edmund continued reading titles and selecting books until he had drawn out quite a
number. Saxon received them from Edmund, and she heaped them in Billy's arms.

"Come for more any time you want
them," Edmund invited. "I have hundreds of volumes on farming, and all the
Agricultural Bulletins. And you must
come and get acquainted with Dulcie your
first spare time," he called after them out
the door.

XLV

MRS. MORTIMER arrived with seed-cata-
logues and farm-books, to find Saxon im-
mersed in the farm-books borrowed from
Edmund. Saxon showed her around, and
she was delighted with everything, includ-
ing the terms of the lease and its option
to buy.

"And now," she said. "What is to be
done? Sit down, both of you. This is a
council of war, and I am the one person in
the world to tell you what to do. I ought
to be. Anybody who has reorganized and
recatalogued a great city library should be
able to start you young people off in short
order. Now, where shall we begin?"

She paused for breath of consideration.

"First, Madroño Ranch is a bargain. I
know soil; I know beauty; I know climate.
Madroño Ranch is a gold mine. There is a
fortune in that meadow. First, here's the
land; secondly, what are you going to do
with it? Make a living? Yes. Vegetables?
Of course. What are you going to do with
them after you have grown them? Sell.
Where?—Now listen. You must do as I
did. Cut out the middleman. Sell directly to the consumer. Drum up your
own market. Do you know what I saw
from the car windows, coming up the valley,
only several miles from here? Hotels,
springs, summer resorts, winter resorts—
population, mouths, markets. How is that
market supplied? I looked in vain for
truck-gardens. Billy, harness up your
horses and be ready directly after dinner to
take Saxon and me driving. Never mind
everything else. Let things stand. What's

the use of starting for a place of which you haven't the address? We'll look for the address this afternoon. Then we'll know where we are—at." The last syllable a smiling concession to Billy.

But Saxon did not accompany them. There was too much to be done in cleaning the long-abandoned house and in preparing an arrangement for Mrs. Mortimer to sleep. And it was long after supper-time when Mrs. Mortimer and Billy returned.

"You lucky, lucky children," she began immediately. "This valley is just waking up. Here's your market. There isn't a competitor in the valley. I thought those resorts looked new—Caliente, Boyes Hot Springs, El Verano, and all along the line. Then there are three little hotels in Glen Ellen, right next door. Oh, I've talked with all the owners and managers."

"She's a wooz," Billy admired. "She'd brace up to God on a business proposition. You oughta seen her."

Mrs. Mortimer acknowledged the compliment and dashed on.

"And where do all the vegetables come from? Wagons drive down twelve to fifteen miles from Santa Rosa, and up from Sonoma. Those are the nearest truck-farms, and when they fail, as they often do, I am told, to supply the increasing needs, the managers have to express vegetables all the way from San Francisco. I've introduced Billy. They've agreed to patronize home industry. Besides, it is better for them. You'll deliver just as good vegetables, just as cheap; you will make it a point to deliver better, fresher vegetables, and don't forget that delivery for you will be cheaper by virtue of the shorter haul.

"No day-old egg-stunt here. No jams or jellies. But you've got lots of space up on the bench here on which you can't grow vegetables. To-morrow morning I'll help you lay out the chicken-runs and houses. Besides, there is the matter of capons for the San Francisco market. You'll start small. It will be a side line at first. I'll tell you all about that, too, and send you the literature. You must use your head. Let others do the work. You must understand that thoroughly. The wages of superintendence are always larger than the wages of the laborers. You must keep books. You must know where you stand. You must know what pays and what doesn't, and what pays best.

Your books will tell that. I'll show you all in good time."

"An' think of it—all that on two acres!" Billy murmured.

Mrs. Mortimer looked at him sharply.

"Two acres your granny," she said, with asperity. "Five acres. And then you won't be able to supply your market. And you, my boy, as soon as the first rains come, will have your hands full and your horses weary draining that meadow. We'll work those plans out to-morrow. Also, there is the matter of berries on the bench here—and trellised table-grapes, the choicest. They bring the fancy prices. There will be blackberries—Burbank's; he lives at Santa Rosa—Logan berries, mammoth berries. But don't fool with strawberries. That's a whole occupation in itself. They're not vines, you know. I've examined the orchard. It's a good foundation. We'll settle the pruning and grafts later."

"But Billy wanted three acres of the meadow," Saxon explained at the first chance.

"What for?"

"To grow hay and other kinds of food for the horses he's going to raise."

"Buy it out of a portion of the profits from those three acres," Mrs. Mortimer decided on the instant.

Billy swallowed, and again achieved renunciation.

"All right," he said, with a brave show of cheerfulness. "Let her go. Us for the greens."

During the several days of Mrs. Mortimer's visit, Billy let the two women settle things for themselves. "I'm not done with you children," had been Mrs. Mortimer's parting words; and several times that winter she ran up to advise, and to teach Saxon how to calculate her crops for the small immediate market, for the increasing spring market, and for the height of summer, at which time she would be able to sell all she could possibly grow and then not supply the demand. In the mean time Hazel and Hattie were used every odd moment in hauling manure from Glen Ellen, whose barnyards had never known such a thorough cleaning. Also there were loads of commercial fertilizer from the railroad station, bought under Mrs. Mortimer's instructions.

It was on a bright morning the following June that Billy told Saxon to put on her riding-clothes to try out a saddle-horse.

"Not until after ten o'clock," she said. "By that time I'll have the wagon off on the second trip."

Despite the extent of the business she had developed, her executive ability and system gave her much spare time. She could call on the Hales, which was ever a delight. In this congenial atmosphere Saxon burgeoned. She had begun to read—to read with understanding; and she had time for her books, for work on her pretties, and for Billy.

Billy was even busier than she, his work being more scattered and diverse. And, as well, he kept his eye on the home barn and horses which Saxon used. In truth he had become a man of affairs, though Mrs. Mortimer had gone over his accounts, with an eagle eye on the expense column, discovered several minor leaks, and finally, aided by Saxon, bullied him into keeping books. Each night, after supper, he and Saxon posted their books. Afterward, in the big Morris chair he had insisted on buying early, Saxon would creep into his arms and strum on the ukulélé, or they would talk long about what they were doing and planing to do.

They cantered out the gate, thundered across the bridge, and passed Trilium Covert before they pulled in on the grade of Wild Water Canyon. Saxon had chosen *her* field as she called an opening on the big spur of Sonoma Mountain as the objective of their ride.

They reached Saxon's field, and then came to the rim of Wild Water canyon. Leaning far back in their saddles, they slid the horses down a steep declivity, through big spruce woods, to an ancient and all but obliterated trail.

"They cut this trail 'way back in the Fifties," Billy explained. "I only found it by accident."

Lying low against their horses' necks, they scrambled up a steep cattle trail out of the canyon, and began to work across rough country toward the knolls.

"Say, Saxon, you're always lookin' for something pretty. I'll show you what'll make your hair stand up—soon as we get through this manzanita."

Never, in all their travels, had Saxon seen so lovely a vista as the one that greeted them when they emerged. The dim trail lay like a rambling red shadow cast on the soft forest floor by the great redwoods and overarching oaks. It seemed as if all local varieties of trees and vines had conspired to weave the leafy roof—maples, big madroños, and laurels, and lofty tan-bark oaks, scaled and wrapped and interwound with wild grape and flaming poison oak.

At last, after another quarter of an hour, they tied their horses on the rim of the narrow canyon that penetrated the wilderness of the knolls. Through a rift in the trees Billy pointed to the top of the leaning spruce.

"It's right under that," he said. "We'll have to follow up the bed of the creek. They ain't no trail, though you'll see plenty of deer-paths crossin' the creek. You'll get your feet wet."

Saxon laughed her joy and held on close to his heels, splashing through pools, crawling hand and foot up the slippery faces of water-worn rocks, and worming under trunks of old fallen trees.

The climbing grew more difficult, and they were finally halted, in a narrow cleft, by a drift-jam.

"You wait here," Billy directed, and, lying flat, squirmed through the brush.

Saxon waited till all sound had died away. She waited ten minutes longer, then followed by the way Billy had broken. Where the bed of the canyon became impossible, she came upon what she was sure was a deer-path that skirted the steep side and was a tunnel through the close greenery. She caught a glimpse of the overhanging spruce, almost above her head on the opposite side, and emerged on a pool of clear water in a claylike basin. Across the pool arose an almost sheer wall of white. She looked about for Billy. She heard him whistle and looked up. Two hundred feet above, at the perilous top of the white wall, he was holding on to a tree trunk. The overhanging spruce was near by.

"I can see the little pasture back of your field," he called down. "No wonder nobody ever piped this off. The only place they could see it from is that speck of pasture. An' you saw it first. Wait till I come down and tell you all about it. I didn't dast before."

It required no shrewdness to guess the truth. Saxon knew this was precious clay required for brick making. Billy circled wide of the slide and came down the canyon wall, from tree to tree, as descending a ladder.

"Ain't it a peach?" he exulted, as he dropped beside her. "Just look at it—

With downcast demurest eyes and hesitating speech, Saxon said, "I did something yesterday without asking
your advice, Billy." He waited. "I wrote to Tom," she added, with an air of timid
confession. Still he waited—for he knew not what

hidden away under four feet of soil where nobody could see it, an' just waitin' for us to hit the Valley of the Moon. Then it up an' slides a piece of the skin off so as we can see it."

"Is it the real clay?" Saxon asked anxiously.

"You bet your sweet life. I've handled too much of it not to know it in the dark. Just rub a piece between your fingers—like that. Why, I could tell by the taste of it. I've eaten enough of the dust of the teams. Here's where our fun begins. Say, you know we've ben workin' our heads off since we hit this valley. Now we're on Easy Street."

They sat hand in hand beside Wild Water and talked over the details.

"Say, Saxon," Billy said, after a pause had fallen, "sing 'Harvest Days,' won't you?"

And, when she had complied, "The first time you sung that song for me was comin' home from the picnic on the train—"

"The very first day we met each other," she broke in. "What did you think about me that day?"

"Why, what I've thought ever since— that you was made for me. I thought that right at the jump, in the first waltz. An' what'd you think of me?"

"Oh, I wondered, and before the first waltz, too, when we were introduced and shook hands—I wondered if you were the man. Those were the very words that flashed into my mind: *Is he the man?*"

"An' I kinda looked a little some good to you?" he queried.

"*I* thought so, and my eyesight has always been good."

"Say!" Billy went off at a tangent. "By next winter, with everything hummin' an' shipshape, what's the matter with us makin'

a visit to Carmel? It'll be slack time for you with the vegetables, an' I'll be able to afford a foreman."

Saxon's lack of enthusiasm surprised him. "What's wrong?" he demanded quickly.

With downcast demurest eyes and hesitating speech, Saxon said,

"I did something yesterday without asking your advice, Billy."

He waited.

"I wrote to Tom," she added, with an air of timid confession.

Still he waited—for he knew not what.

"I asked him to ship up the old chest of drawers—my mother's, you remember— that we stored with him."

"Huh! I don't see anything outa the way about that," Billy said with relief. "We need the chest, don't we? An' we can afford to pay the freight on it, can't we?"

"You are a dear stupid man, that's what you are. Don't you know what is in the chest?"

He shook his head, and what she added was so soft that it was almost a whisper.

"The baby clothes."

"No!" he exclaimed.

"True."

"Sure."

She nodded her head, her cheeks flooding with quick color.

"It's what I wanted, Saxon, more'n anything else in the world. I've ben thinkin' a whole lot about it lately, ever since we hit the valley," he went on, brokenly, and for the first time she saw tears unmistakable in his eyes. "But after all I'd done, an' the hell I'd raised, an' everything, I—I never urged you, or said a word about it. But I wanted it—oh, I wanted it like—like I want you now!"

His open arms received her, and the pool in the heart of Wild Water Canyon knew a long, tender silence.

THE END